W9-CEJ-968

Also by Evelyn Skye
The Crown's Game
The Crown's Fate
Circle of Shadows

EVELYN SKYE

An Imprint of HarperCollinsPublishers

Balzer + Bray is an imprint of HarperCollins Publishers.

Cloak of Night

Copyright © 2020 by Evelyn Skye

All rights reserved. Printed in the United States of America.

No part of this book may be used or reproduced in any manner whatsoever without written permission except in the case of brief quotations embodied in critical articles and reviews. For information address HarperCollins Children's Books, a division of HarperCollins Publishers, 195 Broadway, New York, NY 10007.

www.epicreads.com

Library of Congress Control Number: 2019953343

ISBN 978-0-06-264375-9

Typography by Jenna Stempel

19 20 21 22 23   PC/LSCH   10 9 8 7 6 5 4 3 2 1

❖

First Edition

To Renee, my college roommate and dearest friend—
for taking my hand that first night of freshman year to make me
run across campus with the infamous Stanford Band,
and for never letting go of me since

and

To Tom and Reese—
this book and every book

CHAPTER ONE

Empress Aki woke up completely disoriented and with a skull-hammering headache.

She opened her eyes slowly, because even that movement hurt her head. There was dirt beneath her, and the air here was sharp and sour, as if a crate of cleaning solution had been left open and undiluted. Her throat ached from breathing it.

What is this place? Aki certainly wasn't in the Imperial City anymore.

The last thing she remembered was her brother, Gin, taking control of her mind and forcing her to abdicate the throne in his favor and then one of his ryuu turning everything in the world green and knocking her unconscious.

Carefully, the former empress rose, bracing herself against a wall. She was still in the taiga uniform she'd donned before the battle with Gin, and now her sleeves caught on the jagged rock walls.

Aki was in a grotto of some sort. A waterfall crashed

twenty yards away from her, and a pool of churning water spanned the short distance between the grotto floor and the base of the falls.

She crept along the narrow ledge of rock around the edge of the pool. Surely this was more than a mere grotto. Gin wouldn't leave her alone if she could simply swim her way out.

She approached the underside of the waterfall and stretched her hand toward it.

The droplets burned her fingers, and Aki jerked her arm away. "Nines!" she cursed, falling backward onto the ground. Wisps of smoke rose from her fingertips.

Acid.

Instinctively, she began to plunge her hand into the pool to cool it down, but she caught herself at the last moment. The pool might be filled with the same thing.

Aki cradled her hand and gaped at the torrent of acid raining down in front of her. Was this a fabricated prison that the ryuu had created? Or was this a real waterfall, and they'd somehow transformed the water into something deadly? In either case, it was terrifying.

A girl laughed from the other side of the grotto. Aki startled but didn't see anyone there. She scurried back to the opposite part of the cave.

Out of thin air, the girl materialized.

Virtuoso. Aki gritted her teeth from both the pain of the acid burn and seeing the ryuu who had knocked her out during the battle at Rose Palace.

The girl didn't even bother with a greeting before she stalked over, kneed Aki in the stomach, and shoved her onto the slick ground.

Tears stung Aki's eyes. "Please. You have to let me go," she said.

"No," Virtuoso said curtly.

"I demand it."

Virtuoso shrugged.

Aki had nothing. She was a prisoner. She couldn't cast spells like her brother and the ryuu and taigas could. No one knew where she was, or even that she was still alive. She might as well be dead.

She slouched against the wall, no longer bothering to hide the fingers burned by the acid.

Virtuoso smirked at Aki's blistering skin. "I see you've discovered that these are no ordinary waterfalls."

"You did this?"

"It was my idea. Another ryuu executed it for me. Want to go for a swim?" she sneered.

"I thought my brother wanted me alive. You know, so I could suffer in exile as he had to. Isn't that what he said before he had me thrown in here?"

Virtuoso glared daggers at her.

Aki set her jaw. She refused to give away the fear chewing at her bones.

The acid in front of Virtuoso began to boil. What in Sola's name was this? Aki pressed herself even harder against the wall to get as far away from it as possible.

An enormous emerald bubble—seven or eight feet in diameter—rose from the depths of the acid. The orb bobbed to shore and opened as if it were yawning. It was empty, except for a large armchair.

Virtuoso glowered. "There's a small cell behind this rock wall, sheltered from the acid. Squeeze through the crevice over there"—she pointed to a person-sized crack in the grotto wall, obscured by the falls' shadows—"and you'll find a mattress, water, and food. Enough to survive. Barely."

Then she stepped into her green bubble, sat in it like the captain of a small ship, and sank into the water, leaving Aki behind.

Alone.

Possibly for the rest of her life, because Gin wanted her to rot here as punishment.

She hugged her knees to her chest and looked at the curtain of acid locking her into this prison.

But there was still one hope, even if it was a small one.

"League of Rogues," Aki whispered. "If you're out there, please don't give up on me."

CHAPTER TWO

Hana clenched her fists as she rode away in her bubble. As Virtuoso, Emperor Gin's second-in-command, she was supposed to want to snap the former empress's neck in the grotto. But there was a part of Hana that was relieved she wasn't allowed to kill Princess Aki. Prisoner or not, she was still royalty.

Unfortunately, it was that kind of wishy-washy commitment that had made Hana weak before. She'd fallen for her sister's attempt to reconcile, letting Sora go instead of turning her in. *If I had revealed Sora as a mole in our ranks, the Society of Taigas wouldn't have been warned of the impending attack, and the ryuu could have taken the Imperial City without as much ryuu bloodshed.* They also could have avoided killing some taigas who would have been valuable once they were brainwashed and turned into ryuu.

That had all been because Hana had wavered in her allegiance.

I won't make that mistake again, she thought. From now

on, whatever Emperor Gin wanted, she would be single-mindedly dedicated to him and his pursuit of the Evermore.

"Nothing will sway me," Hana said aloud, as if doing so would further bind her to the pledge. "Nothing."

CHAPTER THREE

It's a strange thing, Sora thought, *when a boy you've known your entire life is suddenly an enormous electric wolf.* It was stranger still to ride on his back as he flew through the night, sparks flickering off his blue fur. She, Fairy, and Broomstick clung to Daemon, bracing themselves against the biting chill.

They'd fled Kichona, beaten and terrified, after Prince Gin—the Dragon Prince—seized the throne. But now, just hours later, the decision nipped at the edges of Sora's mind.

They were supposed to be the protectors of the kingdom. Was it irresponsible to abandon their people?

But the rest of the Society of Taigas had been beaten, and if Sora and her friends had stayed, Prince Gin might have captured and hypnotized them, too. And then Kichona would have no one left to save them.

Still, it felt wrong to run away.

"Turn around," she said to Daemon.

"What?"

"Turn around. We need to go back."

"Are you out of your mind?" Daemon said, his voice half growl. "Prince Gin just took over the minds of every warrior we know, and we only barely escaped."

"Which means that the prince won't expect us yet," Sora said. "He probably thinks we'll disappear for a while to lick our wounds. No one would guess we'd turn around after losing a battle and fly straight back."

With a reluctant sigh, Daemon changed directions and headed back to Kichona.

Eventually, a crescent-shaped island came into view. Isle of the Moon had been the retreat of the Society of Taigas' council, before the ryuu destroyed it. Even from this height, Sora could see the red bridges smashed into ponds and the toppled Constellation Temple.

But its devastation also made Isle of the Moon the perfect place to regroup before they returned across the channel to Kichona's main island. No one would expect them to choose this as a hideout.

"Try touching down on that strip," Sora said, pointing to a narrow clearing.

"I hardly know how to fly, let alone land," Daemon said. "I might dash us all to pieces."

"You can do it," she said, even though they'd only discovered his magic hours ago. She tapped into the mental bond she shared with Daemon and sent him a ribbon of reassurance. It coursed through their connection like the scent of salt water and sunshine on a summer day, and she could immediately feel the muscles in his shoulders release some of their tension.

She looked down again at the island. The destruction was even more stark as they got closer. Gardens were flooded.

Beams from broken buildings littered the ground. Rainbow koi swam in puddles on top of broken rooftops instead of in the carefully tended ponds they'd once called home.

"I'm going to aim for that meadow at the edge of the woods," Daemon said. "There's slightly more space there. Everyone, hold on."

Sora leaned into the fur on the back of his neck and hugged him, feeling his lupine strength beneath her, and for just a moment, she let the wonder of Daemon's transformation sweep over her. Even though he was a wolf, he smelled like cypress trees and sky, like a boy born of the forest and the stars. Every nerve in her body tingled, awake in a way she'd never before experienced.

Fairy tightened her grip around Sora's waist, bringing Sora out of her thoughts. Broomstick stretched from behind Fairy and wrapped his arms around both of them, his reach long enough to secure them all together. Daemon began his descent.

The wind stung Sora's face, and her ears felt tight from the pressure of flying downward at such speed. A flock of birds squawked and broke formation to allow Daemon through. The open air quickly gave way to treetops, and then—

"Jump!" Daemon shouted as he careened, out of control, toward the grass below.

Sora leaped off his back, tucked her body into a ball, and somersaulted as she hit the ground. She rolled once, then sprang to her feet, as agile as if she'd intended such a landing all along. Beside her, Fairy also landed lightly, as did Broomstick, his massive body graceful from years of taiga training. It didn't matter that he was the size of a small rhinoceros;

he moved like an acrobat—strong and fluid and effortless.

Daemon was not as lucky. He crashed into the meadow, bouncing several times, and stopped only when he'd skidded several hundred feet into the wet, sandy remnants of a meditation garden. His groan rumbled like an unhappy thunderbolt.

They rushed to him.

"Wolf!" Fairy cried. Sora was the only one who called Daemon by his birth name. Likewise, he was the only one who called her Sora.

He rose on wobbly legs, his paws crossing awkwardly as he stumbled.

Broomstick reached him first and braced Daemon against his own frame. "Steady there."

Daemon grinned sheepishly, which was quite an accomplishment for a wolf. "I told you I might crash."

"But you're all right?" Sora asked.

"Ego bruised, but that's the worst of it."

She nodded. "Let's find a place to settle down. It's been quite a day."

That was, of course, a massive understatement, but so much had happened since the sun rose that morning, Sora could only process parts of it at a time. Prince Gin had hypnotized the entire Society of Taigas except Sora, Daemon, Fairy, and Broomstick. He had also destroyed Rose Palace, sacrificed two hundred innocent people in a bloody ceremony, and possibly murdered his sister, the empress. It was almost too much to bear.

"Hey-o," Daemon said, "that house over there looks intact."

Sora and Fairy followed him and Broomstick. Upon closer

inspection, the building wasn't a house but a large hall, possibly a meeting space for when the Councilmembers had their annual retreat. Also, it wasn't so much "intact" as not falling down. The front door barely hung on its hinges, the rice paper on the windows was torn open, and the glass ceiling was completely shattered. But it was the best they had.

"Let's see if there's any food," Sora said, "and figure out a plan."

"Can we sleep a little before we have to think again?" Daemon asked. His shoulders slouched from the effort of flying for hours with three people on his back.

Sora paused. Time was of the essence. If Empress Aki was still alive, they'd have to find her quickly before Prince Gin had a chance to move her out of the Imperial City.

But when Sora looked at Daemon, she knew what the answer had to be. His muscles trembled beneath his fur, and the gales outside had almost blown them out of the sky several times as he tired.

"Yes, of course," Sora said. "We should definitely sleep. I'm sorry I didn't think of it before."

They walked through the creaky front door. It was indeed a meeting space, which apparently doubled as a dining hall, too. Smashed plates and teacups and the moldy remnants of a meal lay in the mess of broken tables and chairs.

Broomstick eyed the room warily, as if the ryuu who had done this might still be lurking, just waiting for them to let down their guard before they sprang again. "We can take turns on watch."

Sora waved him away. "I'm having trouble shutting off my brain. You guys go ahead and get some sleep."

Fairy hesitated.

"I swear I'll wake you if I need someone to take over," Sora said.

Daemon stumbled into the far corner of the hall and collapsed on a pile of tablecloths. Within seconds, he was snoring wolfishly.

Broomstick and Fairy went off to find their own nooks to sleep in.

Or at least Broomstick went to find his own space. Fairy went straight to Daemon's corner of the room and settled against his blue fur.

Sora's chest knotted; she'd almost forgotten about the two of them holding hands before the Citadel battle. It had been difficult to see, since Sora had only just realized her feelings for Daemon then, too.

But the Society of Taigas forbade romantic relationships between geminas. So if Daemon was going to be with anyone other than Sora, she was glad it was Fairy. There was something lovely about your favorite people in the world coming together.

Right?

Annoyed at herself, Sora distracted her mind by clearing the debris on the floor to make some space—none of the chairs were sturdy enough to sit in—and cast a simple spell to light a fire next to her. They were indoors, but with the shattered glass ceiling, they might as well be outside.

Then Sora finally had time to think about everything that had happened.

Empress Aki was missing—possibly dead. Prince Gin had sworn loyalty to Zomuri, god of glory, and dedicated the kingdom to the pursuit of the Evermore, a mythological paradise obtained through war and bloodshed. And every single one of the Society's leaders—no, *all* the taigas—were either dead or brainwashed and under the prince's control.

Sora curled up next to her fire. What was she going to do? There really was no one left except her, Daemon, Fairy, and Broomstick. Her earlier confidence faded.

Eventually, though, Sora's fatigue caught up to her, and she dozed off.

A while later, she startled awake. The fire next to her had burned out. She scrambled to her feet.

"Don't worry," Broomstick said from nearby. "I was awake about the time you fell asleep. It's been quiet."

"That makes me nervous," Sora said as she stretched.

"Makes me nervous, too." Broomstick rubbed his hands over his head. It was normally shaved, but now platinum fuzz was beginning to show.

Sora's own hair had seen better days as well. It was limp and greasy against her face, and the white-blond roots had started to grow out while the black dye faded on the rest. Her tunic and trousers were in similar shape, mud-spattered and wrinkled, no longer the formidable black uniform taigas were used to wearing. She was pretty sure she smelled a bit like old cheese, too. Ugh.

At least the nap had done her some good. She still didn't know how the four of them could save a kingdom, but she wasn't drowning in utter despair anymore. The wheels in her brain creaked, eager to turn and come up with a plan.

But there was also something else. Sora finally understood Empress Aki's imperial crest, the one with the crowned tiger and the words "Dignity. Benevolence. Loyalty."

It was about giving yourself to something bigger.

Sora took a deep breath. What lay ahead of them was going to be the most difficult task they had ever faced. She had to be prepared.

"We should start brainstorming our next steps," Sora said.

"I'll wake Fairy and Wolf." Broomstick rose and headed to the back of the hall.

A few seconds later, he yelped.

Fear rose like an alarm in Sora's chest as she sprinted to help him. Were they being attacked?

When she reached Broomstick, though, it was apparent he didn't need help. At least, not in the way Sora had imagined.

Fairy was still next to Daemon, but he wasn't a furry, electric-blue wolf anymore. He was six feet two inches of stark-naked, tautly muscled boy on a bed of tablecloths. The only hint of his wolfishness was his hair, which had lost its black taiga dye in his transformation and was now its natural midnight blue.

Sora's jaw dropped, her pulse beating traitorously at double time.

"Good gods, you two!" Broomstick said. "I don't normally care what you do on your own time, but here? When Spirit and I were twenty yards away?"

Both Fairy and Daemon seemed just as shocked as Broomstick and Sora, though. Daemon curled up into a ball and desperately heaped tablecloths on himself to cover up. Fairy had sprung to her feet and leaped away from him, her eyes wide.

"It's n-not . . . ," she said. "We didn't . . ."

"When did I turn back into a human?" Daemon asked,

curling more tightly into himself.

The four of them stood frozen for another moment, brains trying to catch up with the scene before them.

Suddenly, Broomstick snorted. "You had no idea he was naked, did you?" he said to Fairy.

"None." She shook her head to emphasize the point.

The real evidence, though, was the hot rush of Daemon's embarrassment through his and Sora's gemina bond. He was absolutely mortified.

"Oh, Daemon." Sora summoned her cloak from the other side of the room. It flew swiftly to him, and he yanked it to his body. Her poor gemina. He was possibly a demigod, but he was also still the boy she knew, self-conscious and uncertain in his magic. They didn't know the extent of his powers or how to control them, and this surprise was an unfortunate result.

"We'll find an extra set of clothes for you in the council-members' rooms," Sora said. "You can join us when you're, uh, ready."

"Thanks," Daemon said, his embarrassment still burning through their bond.

Sora began to walk away, with Fairy and Broomstick right behind her. She almost expected a joke from one of them, Broomstick especially, about how teasing Fairy and Daemon was part of his sacred duty as a best friend.

But there wasn't a single word. Their usual lighthearted banter was gone, as if the weight of Prince Gin's fledgling reign was already taking its toll.

Everything had changed.

CHAPTER FOUR

Sora sat cross-legged on the floor and nibbled on a piece of fish jerky. Broomstick restrained himself and ate only half a package of rice crackers, saving some for the others. It was all they could find in the pantry, since most of the food left behind after the ryuu's attack had already spoiled. Fairy scrunched her nose as she took a piece of jerky. "I miss sweet red beans and pancakes from the mess hall."

Broomstick nodded. "And pork sausages and fried eggs and steamed rice with breakfast pickles."

"Rose-apple jam and buttery rolls," Fairy said.

"Forest mushroom tarts and seaweed scrambles," Broomstick added.

Sora's stomach rumbled. Of the four of them, she was the one who usually waxed poetic about food.

Daemon walked toward them, fully dressed now, and dropped beside Sora with a heavy sigh. He folded his long legs beneath him.

Everyone shifted awkwardly, as if the noise of their

shuffling would spare them from having to talk about the earlier incident.

Broomstick was the first to speak. "Stale cracker?" He held out the package.

Daemon shook his head and sighed again. The sensation dribbled through Sora's gemina bond, a mixture of frustration and resignation, like soggy autumn leaves being trampled in the mud.

"I didn't mind being an electric wolf in the middle of battle," he said, "but gods dammit. I'd really like to get a handle on what these powers are and how to control them so I can avoid . . . well, you know."

Sora reached over and patted his knee. "We'll figure it out. I promise."

"Yeah," Daemon said without much conviction.

"You should really eat something," she said, taking the rice crackers from Broomstick and pressing them into Daemon's hand. "Everything seems worse when you're hungry. At least that's true for me. But don't worry, the four of us will work this out." She managed to dig up a smile for his sake.

"And I'm sure Spirit has already thought of a plan," Fairy piped up. "She's always got something up her sleeve. Right?"

Sora worried her lip. "Well, sort of. We obviously need to destroy Prince Gin. If we can kill him, we cut the head off the dragon, and the body can't function without him. No one else can control minds like he can. Without a leader, maybe the ryuu will fall apart. Plus, that will free the taigas from his hypnosis.

"We also need to figure out if Empress Aki is still alive.

17

If she is, we'll have to rescue her."

Daemon let out a scoff of a laugh.

"What?" Sora said.

"That's too much to expect of us." He sat hunched over, looking smaller than usual. "We can't do it."

"I admit I've thought that, too," Fairy said. "But we don't have a choice. We have to save Kichona."

"Are you listening to yourselves?" Daemon asked. "There are only four of us. Prince Gin has an entire army with superior magic. He hypnotized two hundred people—*civilians*—to murder themselves. And he captured the empress. Don't you see? We've already lost."

"And what should we do instead?" Broomstick asked, crossing his arms across his chest. "Flee from Kichona to save ourselves? Those are our friends back there. We grew up with them in the tenderfoot nursery, sparred with them since we were old enough to hold weapons and cast spells, and stayed up way too late playing cards and drinking cheap rice wine. You really want to abandon them all?"

"You're making me sound like an asshole," Daemon said.

"That's not what he means," Sora said. "Trust me, we're all beaten down, too. You say we've already lost. You're right. If the four of us don't step up, then every single one of our friends *is* lost. Right now, Prince Gin has control of their minds. He's brainwashed them to love him, to want to charge into battle and die for him.

"Maybe we'll fail. But if we don't try, then it's all over for everyone we know and love. We owe it to them—and to Kichona—to take down the Dragon Prince and restore our kingdom to how it's supposed to be."

They were quiet for a minute. Then Daemon let out a

long breath. "I feel sorry for our kingdom that all they get is our ragtag crew." But there was a slight lift in the corner of his mouth, and she knew he was in, even if reluctantly.

"We don't look *that* bad," Fairy said.

"Actually, we do," Sora said. "But no one said heroes had to be pretty."

"Wait a minute," Broomstick said. "You want to rescue Empress Aki. How do we even know she's alive? She might be dead."

"If she is, then the Dragon Prince is the true ruler of Kichona," Daemon said, "and even without being compelled, the people would be obligated to carry out every one of his deluded, twisted wishes."

Reality killed the momentary high Sora had felt from rousing her friends. She frowned. "We don't know that the empress is alive. But until we're certain she's dead, I think we should assume the opposite and that she needs our help. The last time I saw her, she had a knife at her throat, but they didn't kill her. If Prince Gin wanted his sister dead, wouldn't he have done it then? It would have had greater effect at the Ceremony of Two Hundred Hearts, in front of a crowd."

Broomstick nodded slowly. "Good point. But how do we find her?"

"The Imperial City seems like a good bet," Sora said. "Not much time has passed—she could still be there."

"Return to the dragon's den so soon after we escaped?" Daemon asked. "That's suicide."

"We could save a lot of lives if we go back," Sora argued, waving a piece of fish jerky for emphasis. "Not only the empress's, because we'll also kill Prince Gin if we can. He's bringing war to Kichona. If we thought the Ceremony of Two Hundred Hearts was bad, just wait until he antagonizes all seven of the kingdoms on the mainland. Their armies and navies will fight back by coming here and slaughtering millions of innocent Kichonans. We have to stop Prince Gin."

"I say we blow up that mind-stealing bastard." Broomstick's fingers moved as if already imagining the explosives he'd rig for the purpose.

Daemon groaned. "Couldn't we find somewhere quiet and let me work on my magic first? We don't stand a fighting chance if we face the Dragon Prince right now."

Sora shook her head. "What if it takes us months to figure out how to change you from wolf to human? For you to hone your electricity into a weapon? How much damage will Prince Gin have done by then?"

Daemon sagged as if deflated. Dammit. Sora should have known better. He'd never been great with magic, and now she'd basically said as much, demigod power or not. It was like hitting an exposed nerve with a sledgehammer.

"I'm sorry," Sora said. "I didn't mean—"

"It's fine." He huddled over his knees.

"No, it's not." She moved over to him and held him by the shoulders, forcing him to look her in the eyes. "You're more powerful than ever before, and you've already saved us, twice, in the short time since you discovered your abilities. You're invaluable. I'm sorry that what I said came out the wrong way. I only meant that we don't understand what your magic is yet, and it's going to take time to figure it out. Together. But we can't lose the element of surprise while the ryuu are regrouping—it's all we have right now."

He held her gaze for a moment, in a way that made Sora

tingle, as if the sparks from his wolf form were still some-how inside the human version of him and traveling through their gemina bond. He was strong in ways that she wasn't and vulnerable in other ways that she could complement. If he was the sky at night, she was the earth in the day, and together, they were one.

But then Fairy said, "She's right, Wolfie. You're incredible."

Daemon blinked. He looked over at Fairy and actually smiled.

He may be mine in some ways, but he's not in others, Sora reminded herself. *And I'm happy that he has Fairy. She's brave and bold and beautiful—everything he deserves.*

However, it took more effort than Sora wanted to convince herself of that. But what could she do? She couldn't have Daemon. It was against Society Code. And he didn't want her; he was with Fairy. If Sora was a good friend, she'd stop whining to herself and be happy for them.

Sora swallowed the truth, but it went down like bitter tonic.

Broomstick chewed on his nails, studying all three of them. He made a small noise under his breath.

"What?" Sora said.

"Nothing."

She frowned.

But he just moved on. "Really, it's not important. Tell us the plan. *That's* what matters right now."

Sora sighed. He was right.

"We'll go back to the Imperial City," she said, "and cross the Field of Illusions together. Once we're all across, I think we should split up into pairs. Fairy and Broomstick know every room, corridor, and hidden passageway in the Citadel, so they'll search for Empress Aki there. Daemon and I will look for her in Prince Gin's castle."

"How long until we regroup?" Broomstick said. "We should set a rendezvous time."

"Good idea. Is four hours enough?"

"Too long," Daemon said. "We don't know what we're walking into. Although it's probably a death trap."

"Come on. I know it's daunting, but we can do this," Sora said. "Besides, they've just taken over the Imperial City. They're probably still cleaning up after a massive battle, shepherding newly converted taigas into training, and settling into a new castle. The ryuu can't possibly be organized yet."

Fairy leaned in. "How about three hours? It's enough time to cover the most likely places the empress could be kept prisoner. And if anything seems even a little suspicious, we abort."

"I like it," Sora said. "Three hours from when we split up, we'll meet in the chestnut grove in Jade Forest. Remember, the number one priority is rescuing Empress Aki."

"And if we have a shot at killing the Dragon Prince?" Daemon asked.

Sora swallowed. "If we have a chance to kill Prince Gin, we take it."

CHAPTER FIVE

Daemon's clothes were only a little damp by the time they reached the Imperial City. They'd wanted to come back right away, but because he couldn't yet summon his wolf powers at will, he couldn't fly them there, which meant they needed to budget enough time to swim across the channel from Isle of the Moon to Kichona's main island, then make their way on foot from the coast to the Imperial City before infiltrating the Dragon Prince's castle. Even with sailfish and cheetah spells, the journey would take a couple hours. Plus, there was the time required to actually search for Empress Aki and, hopefully, kill Prince Gin. Besides, this wasn't the sort of mission one rushed through. So they'd decided to wait until sunset to break into the city.

Honestly, Daemon still doubted their ability to save the kingdom on their own, but if the rest of them were in, he was, too, and he would do everything he could to keep them safe.

Now, as the cloak of night settled over the kingdom,

he, Sora, Fairy, and Broomstick stood on the edge of the Field of Illusions. Its black-and-white sands shifted incessantly in dizzying optical illusions. Sometimes there were whirlpool-like spirals that seemed to suck the sand into the ground. Other times, diamond fractals kept changing color, making them hard to keep track of. And then there were the constantly moving black-and-white waves that rocked the brain into a kind of psychological seasickness. Only taigas could traverse the Field of Illusions successfully; any non-taigas who wanted to enter the Imperial City needed a warrior to escort them across. Otherwise, they'd lose their way.

"How do you want to do this?" Sora asked. There were many ways to approach crossing the obstacle; the only common thread was not to look at the changing patterns, because they were meant to cause confusion.

"Broomstick and I are going to use mole spells," Fairy said.

"I don't really feel like digging tonight," Sora said. "But you two go ahead."

Daemon knew that wasn't why she objected, though. She did it for him. Mole spells allowed taigas to burrow beneath the illusions and travel quickly, but for a boy who constantly craved the openness of the sky, being buried under several feet of sand was more than a little anxiety inducing for Daemon. Sora had spoken up so he didn't have to admit yet another weakness. Gratefulness overflowed in Daemon's chest, like a mug of beer filled to the brim, foam spilling out of the glass.

He looked at the Citadel, several hundred yards away. With the onset of night, the ryuu had lit torches on the tops of the fortress walls. "We can use hydra spells," Daemon said to Sora. "We'll be blind to the shifting sand but drawn by the torchlight."

"Sounds good to me."

They pinched their fingers into their respective mudras and chanted the spells. Sora's, Fairy's, and Broomstick's took immediately, but Daemon's spell didn't. *I really wish I could just turn on some wolf magic whenever I wanted it,* he thought. Finally, after the fourth attempt, he got the mudra right.

His vision darkened, as if he was looking into an endless cave. But in the distance, flickers of light glowed, and Daemon was drawn to them as if by magnetic pull.

"We'll meet you at the Citadel wall," Broomstick said.

He and Fairy dove into the Field of Illusions, spraying sand on Daemon.

"Ready?" Sora asked.

"Ready. Focus on the torchlight."

It took them thirty minutes to cross, although it felt twice as long. When they finally reached the base of the Citadel gates, Daemon and Sora hurried to where Fairy and Broomstick were pressed against the fortress walls to avoid being seen by guard patrols.

"We have a problem," Fairy said when Sora joined them. "How do we get in?"

The looming gates were meant to admit only those who were supposed to enter. Which, at the moment, did not include the four apprentices trying to take down everyone behind said ten-story gates.

Daemon looked up, and up. Even with the stone staircase the ryuu had built in their attempt to breach the Citadel during the battle here, there was too much distance left to the top of the fortress. The walls were as slick as if they'd been greased with oil. They couldn't just cast gecko spells to scale them.

It'd be awfully helpful if he could fly. He squeezed his eyes shut and tried to remember what it was like the moment he'd turned into a wolf, how the magic had coursed through him like rivers of electricity and how he'd hurled himself into the air on instinct and managed to stay there. But try as he might, Daemon couldn't recall the exact moment of transformation. In fact, he hadn't even realized he'd changed from human to something else until *after* he'd rescued Sora from plunging to her death. So it was impossible for him to re-create the feeling now.

At the sound of Sora's voice, Daemon's eyes fluttered open.

"Don't worry, I've already thought of how we get in," she was saying. "With ryuu magic, I can jump the distance from the highest stair to the top of the fortress wall."

Oh. Right. She didn't need his help for a mere four-story leap.

"And the rest of us?" Fairy asked.

"I'll float you over," Sora said. "I couldn't risk doing something that conspicuous to get us across the Field of Illusions, but this will be quick. I'll go first and make sure we're clear of any ryuu guards, and then I'll bring you up, one by one. Okay?"

Fairy and Broomstick nodded. Daemon lagged, but then he kicked himself in the proverbial ass and got himself together. So what if he'd been a magical wolf for one brief, glorious night? Sora had always been better at this stuff than

26

he was. Things were no different now. He could handle this.

Daemon, Fairy, and Broomstick kept watch from the base of the Citadel walls while Sora ran silently up the stone steps. When she was near the top of the staircase, they triple-checked that there weren't any ryuu in sight.

She took the last steps at a full sprint and jumped.

Sora landed on the parapet, disappearing from view behind the crenellations of the wall. Daemon's heart stopped. There could have been ryuu hidden there, waiting to ambush her.

But a moment later, Sora popped up.

"Thank the gods," Daemon whispered.

She pointed to Fairy.

"Here I go," Fairy said as Sora began to float her up, just as she'd done with the piece of Rose Palace. Hopefully, though, she wouldn't drop any of them. Like the piece of Rose Palace.

Daemon remembered then that Rose Palace was now a pile of rubble. What stood in its place was the Dragon Prince's bloodstone castle. His stomach turned.

Sora deposited Fairy successfully beside her and began to work on Broomstick. It was a more wobbly effort, since he was twice Fairy's size, but a minute later he, too, was safely posted on watch at the top of the Citadel's entrance.

Daemon stepped forward. He thought he might feel something at the touch of ryuu magic, but other than levitating off the ground, nothing was different at all. Ryuu magic was even subtler than taiga magic, at least as far as he could tell. Or maybe it didn't affect him because he was essentially a parcel being transported from one place to the next, like the citrus crate Sora had hidden in when they were on Prince Gin's ship.

She set him down carefully on the battlement. "Everyone all right?" Sora asked.

"Yes and no," Broomstick said.

Daemon crept up to where his friend was peering through the crenellations at the Citadel below.

"Daggers," Daemon cursed. The ryuu weren't up at the castle anymore, as they had been after the battle. They were swarming here at the Society's headquarters, at least a thousand of them taking it over as though the Citadel was theirs. Sharpening swords in the armory courtyard. Training in the sparring arena. Meeting in the outdoor amphitheater. They just hadn't been guarding the entrance because there was no one—other than Daemon, Sora, Fairy, and Broomstick—to attack.

And the ryuu seemed more organized than Sora had accounted for.

"We need to split up now," Sora said. "Rendezvous in Jade Forest in three hours. But whoever finds Empress Aki first, don't wait. Grab her and get out. All right?"

"All right," Fairy said.

"And remember, if you can kill Prince Gin, do it. His death ends everything."

They huddled for a moment, each knowing—but not saying—that this could be the last time they were together. The grimness was like a knife at Daemon's throat.

"We've got this." Sora stacked her fists over her heart. "Work hard. Mischief harder."

Daemon took a deep breath. Then he pumped his fists to his chest, too. He was here. He was a part of this, whether he liked it or not. And hells if he was going to let his friends down.

"Good luck, League of Rogues," Daemon said. "We'll see you on the other side."

CHAPTER SIX

As Spirit and Wolf took off to make their way up the mountain to the castle, Broomstick and Fairy surveyed what had once been their home. The Citadel had always been a dark place—black was the color of the Society of Taigas, so all the buildings were black—but there was something else now that seemed like an eclipse over the headquarters, a bleakness that swallowed everything the Society stood for. All Broomstick's nerves stood on end, and he had to steady himself against the battlement wall.

"I suppose it's time we split up, too," he said to Fairy, nervously tapping his fingers on the nearest crenellation. Spirit had suggested it because Broomstick knew the warrior side of the fortress better. He had worked in the administration offices in Warrior Meeting Hall, and he and Wolf spent lots of time after hours in the nearby sparring arena doing extra drills.

Fairy would search the student part of campus. She knew all the best places for hiding. Plus, she could fit in passageways that Broomstick couldn't.

"I don't want to split up either," Fairy said. "But Spirit's right that it's smarter for us to divide and conquer."

He pinched his lips but agreed. "Keep our gemina bond open. I suppose we should get going. Time's ticking."

"Yeah," she said, although she didn't move. Their connection vibrated with an anticipation that was half hope they would succeed in finding Empress Aki and ending this nightmare now and half fear that they'd discover something even worse than what they already knew.

Fairy went first, giving Broomstick a short nod before disappearing over the fortress wall, climbing down the handholds placed on the interior of the wall to allow taigas to defend the Citadel from invaders. He watched until she melted into the darkness like a shadow. Then he made his way down and headed to his first destination—the Society's training arena.

Broomstick crouched in the stands and stared wide eyed at the sparring below, full of new recruits freshly hypnotized by the Dragon Prince. A short distance away, Blade, a girl who had lived down the hall from Fairy and Spirit, summoned gravel from the arena floor and formed it into giant axes and battering rams. Her hold on ryuu magic faltered every now and then, and the weapons would disintegrate into gravel again, but she kept at it, sweat dripping in rivulets down her face.

Near her, eleven-year-old Quicksand was enhancing typical taiga spells to make them better.

"Gods, no," Broomstick whispered. He was Quicksand's mentor in the school's Exemplar Program, which paired young students with older ones they could look up to. Broomstick had known Quicksand when he was a tenderfoot still called Wyato, because he was too young for a taiga name.

Now Quicksand was learning to be one of Prince Gin's foot soldiers, sprinting back and forth from one side of the arena to the other like a cheetah spell sped up by a factor of ten. Broomstick barely managed to keep himself concealed because he wanted to jump out and grab the boy, to try to shake the mind control out of his head and save him from the ryuu.

Then Broomstick saw Philosopher, his lab partner from physics class, working on digging tunnels in the ground without the use of mudras or chants. And Summer, the girl who worked at the desk next to Broomstick's in the Society's administrative offices, held her hands out in front of her as two small tornados appeared in her palms.

Outrage rose in Broomstick's belly. These were their friends, students Broomstick had spent his entire life with, who had played with blocks with him when they were tenderfoots, who'd tried to ski down the Citadel rooftops in winter when they were Level 7s, and who stayed up late helping each other study every spring for final exams. They had lived and breathed the Society of Taigas' centuries-old commitment to defend all that was good about Kichona, just like Broomstick did. Yet here they were, practicing a magic that would destroy the very kingdom they'd sworn to protect.

How dare Prince Gin steal their friends like this? And he was going to send them to war, to die for a cause they didn't believe in and weren't even aware they were a part of.

Broomstick sank against the bleachers.

The boy, Quicksand, tripped and skidded several yards in the gravel. Philosopher stopped the tunnel she was working on and ran over to help him up. "Are you all right?" she asked as she extended her hand.

Embarrassed, he nodded but didn't look at her.

Philosopher brushed the gravel off his uniform. "Don't worry," she said. "Magic takes practice, and all of us have fallen face-first in this arena many, many times. Just remember that we're training to make Kichona great, that Emperor Gin expects us to do the best we can. That means we have to make mistakes, but it'll be worth it."

Broomstick wrinkled his forehead as he listened to the conversation. He'd expected the hypnotized taigas to be mindless pawns. But Philosopher seemed to be the same sweet girl he knew, an actual person rather than a witless weapon. The main difference was her devotion to the Dragon Prince and his pursuit of the Evermore. It was a confusing mix of traits that Broomstick tried to wrap his head around.

In a twisted way, though, it gave him hope. The real taigas were still in those minds and bodies. They'd had part of their brains hijacked, but there was something worth saving.

There was nothing more to see here, though. Before watching his friends, Broomstick had searched the sparring arena's storage spaces and back rooms, and there was no sign of Empress Aki. However, this new understanding of how the taigas operated could come in handy. Maybe he'd be able to get some information out of them just like he had in the past, by chatting up his coworkers in Warrior Meeting

Hall. He'd have to pretend he was a ryuu, though.

I hope they were too caught up in the battle to notice that I escaped the Dragon Prince's claws and I'm part of Spirit's rebellion. Broomstick crossed his fingers and hurried to Warrior Meeting Hall.

The nearest room was a large conference space. He glanced inside, but it was just a bunch of ryuu—not new recruits but Prince Gin's original warriors from the Blood Rift—sharing several bottles of something and singing drunkenly. It was as if this once sacrosanct building where the Society governed was nothing more than a tavern, the long conference table converted into a sloshy bar.

Broomstick couldn't bear to listen. He headed farther down the corridor.

Most of the meeting rooms were empty, but the lights in the administrative office were on. Broomstick took a deep breath, put on his most gregarious expression, and strode in as if he belonged there.

"Hey-o," he said to the half dozen taigas—no, ryuu recruits—who were busy going through stacks of files. "What'd I miss?"

Crossbow, a taiga in his thirties, looked up through his glasses. "Broomstick, where've you been? Your shift was supposed to start two hours ago. We've been buried in paper here."

But Moss, a Level 11 apprentice who worked part-time in Warrior Meeting Hall like Broomstick did, set down the files in his hand. "It's not just two hours. I haven't seen you at all in the dormitory. Suspicious, don't you think? That you've been missing ever since Spirit and Wolf disappeared?"

Broomstick's heart seized for a second. But then he let loose an easy smile and shrugged. "You caught me. I ran off with my traitor ex-friends but then decided the smartest thing to do was walk right back into the Citadel and return to my job helping you losers sort through paperwork."

Crossbow and the others laughed.

Moss kept his eye on Broomstick a moment longer. But a reluctant laugh escaped his lips. "Sorry. It sounded better in my head, but once I said it out loud . . . I guess it's pretty ridiculous."

Broomstick's heart resumed beating. "I really do apologize for being late. The Council has been questioning me since the battle to see if I knew anything of Spirit's plans." He scowled for good measure, as if he was disgusted that he'd once considered her a friend. "Between that and practicing this new magic, I haven't even been back to my room. So if I don't totally make sense, it's because I'm severely sleep deprived."

"This ryuu magic *is* incredible," Crossbow said. "I'm dying to finish sorting through all these reports so I can get back to the sparring arena again."

Everyone nodded. Thank the gods they'd swallowed Broomstick's excuses. It was something Fairy had taught him—if you're caught in an untruth (for her it was usually gossip), either get angry while you defend it as truth or confess to it as if the deception was the most obvious mistake in the world. Either way, people ended up believing your initial lie. Psychology was a strange beast but a helpful one.

Broomstick picked up a pile of loose papers. "So what are these, and what are we doing with them?"

"Initial responses to the emperor's decrees," Moss said. "We have to organize them by subject and geographical location for Virtuoso to review."

Holy heavens. Virtuoso was Spirit's sister, who Broomstick knew as Hana. She was also the Dragon Prince's right-hand ryuu. Sadness for Spirit prickled at Broomstick, along with a sharp stab of fear—Hana wasn't someone to trifle with.

"The red folders are for tax reports," Moss said, continuing on from before. "Orange for confiscation of tiger pearls, yellow for updates on weapons manufacturing, and green for the collection of all fish, meat, fruit, vegetables, and grains for the army."

Dread mounted inside Broomstick. Kichona was being transformed into a war machine, and at a horrifying pace. Spirit had been very wrong that the ryuu would still be picking up the pieces from their battle. Instead, the Dragon Prince had already issued decrees seizing everything that defined the kingdom—the tiger pearls; the happy, colorful tunics and dresses worn by the people; the bountiful orchards full of yuzu; and the nets full of shrimp and fish. And that wasn't even touching upon what he could eventually do to the minds of the citizens themselves. He would probably conscript them for the army, to support the ryuu.

"The speed that we're getting ready for war is, uh, exciting," Broomstick said through gritted teeth. "How long is this war supposed to take? And how do we know when we do enough to bring paradise on earth?"

Because that was the point of it all. The Evermore—a promise of transforming Kichona into a utopia and giving all Kichonans eternal life to enjoy there. The only problem was that hundreds of thousands—probably more—would have to die before Kichona achieved the goal.

"We'll be granted the Evermore when Emperor Gin delivers the hearts of all seven monarchs to Zomuri," Crossbow said matter-of-factly.

Broomstick paled as he ran through the countries and their rulers.

High King Erickson of Shinowana

Ria Kayla of Brin

Emperor Geoffrey Stafford of Caldan

Queen Meredith of Fale Po Tair

Tsarina Austine of Thoma

Empress Viviana of Xerlinis

Queen Everleigh of Vyratta

How long would it take to win against all of them? To conquer their kingdoms, capture the monarchs, and murder each one? It would be decades of bloodshed.

On top of that, the start of war against the mainland meant the other kingdoms would band together to fight back against Kichona. Like Sora had said, they wouldn't stay overseas either. They would come here, and everything Broomstick had ever known would be destroyed. Cities and villages torched. Innocent people—like his parents, brothers, and sisters at home—would be taken prisoner, beaten, and killed. Kichona's beautiful, peaceful way of life trampled in the mud and rotted by death.

Moss reached over to grab a report on increased output goals for mining iron ore. His actions were, again, that horribly bizarre mind control where Broomstick's old friends seemed completely normal except for their unflinching lack of morality and their dedication to the Dragon Prince's war. Broomstick, on the other hand, could hardly breathe, let alone read the papers in his hands.

If he, Fairy, Spirit, and Wolf couldn't assassinate Prince Gin, Kichona would cease to be Kichona.

CHAPTER SEVEN

Fairy darted through the Citadel's grounds, keeping away from the paths and staying along the back sides of the buildings whenever possible. Her first stop was the mess hall. There was a boiler room beneath the main dining room that no one ever went to except the maintenance staff, and it was both out of the way and uncomfortable enough to be used as a prison cell.

She tiptoed to the back door of the mess hall and pressed her ear against it. It was relatively quiet on the other side. Thank the gods it wasn't mealtime.

But Fairy didn't go inside. If the boiler room was being used as a jail for the empress, the main access door from the inside would be locked and heavily guarded. Luckily, Fairy knew a secret way in. (She'd brought a boy down there once, but it had been way too steamy—and not in the good way.)

She knelt in the garden behind the mess hall and brushed the ground with her hands, searching. Mud caked in her fingernails, and a couple rocks scraped her.

She kept digging. It had to be around here somewhere.

The footsteps were nearly upon her before Fairy noticed. Her pulse flitted like a caged hummingbird.

Nines, she swore as she dove into the bushes. Hopefully it was dark enough that they wouldn't see her, or if they did, she'd pass as the silhouette of one of the boulders scattered around the garden.

"It's better than we could have imagined," a woman was saying. "Who knew that when he swore loyalty to Zomuri, it would impact the people?"

"Still not as strong as direct mind control," a man said as they approached where Fairy hid.

"No, but it's achieved with zero effort. And I'm sure Emperor Gin will find a way to magnify Zomuri's influence."

They passed Fairy without noticing her, but panic spiked in her chest nevertheless. Something was happening to the people of Kichona because Zomuri was the official god now? What was it? She hadn't felt it herself, or noticed it in Broomstick, Wolf, or Spirit. Maybe they were protected because Luna, as goddess of the taigas, was still their patron god.

Even so, she worried for everyone else.

Broomstick's concern pulsed through their gemina bond. He'd sensed her worry, and now undulations like sound waves drummed through their connection, a continual question about whether he needed to come to her aid.

She sent back an arrow of reassurance. He'd understand that she was dismayed but not in danger.

Fairy had to get back to digging. Finding Empress Aki was more important than ever. They had to stop whatever it was that Prince Gin and Zomuri were doing to the kingdom, put the empress back on the throne, and make Sola, goddess of the sun, the people's patron god once more.

With a renewed sense of urgency, Fairy started scraping through the mud again. This time, she found the wooden trapdoor she was looking for, the planks softened from years of being forgotten and buried in the earth. She pried it open.

A blast of dank air greeted her. Fairy cast an owl spell, the skin around her eyes tightening as night vision took hold, and she slipped into the darkness and cobwebs of the abandoned staircase.

Soon, the humidity was so heavy, it was hard to breathe. The steps ended in what appeared to be a wall. It was actually the back of a massive boiler, though, installed at some point in the past for additional heat but with the side effect of rendering the emergency exit stairwell virtually unusable. That is, except for someone as tiny as Fairy.

She paused here and listened for any sign of guards or a prisoner. The room was filled with the labored pumps of steam through the pipes that crisscrossed the walls and ceiling. Fairy released her owl spell—she couldn't see anyway, with the heavy mist clouding the air—and cast a new one to allow her to hear better.

As her ears tingled, she began to discern the sounds layered beneath the churning of the boiler. There were kitchen workers' footsteps in the mess hall above. Rats skittering inside the walls. Moths clustered in the warm corners of the ceiling.

But no soldierlike sounds. No methodical pacing inside or outside the boiler room. No idle conversation between bored guards.

And there weren't any prisoner noises either.

Fairy crept out from behind the boiler, stiletto knives in each hand. "Your Majesty, are you here?" she whispered.

The only answer was the rhythmic bursts of steam in the pipes. Dammit. Fairy lowered her knives. The chances had been slim of her guessing correctly on the first try where Empress Aki was hidden, but the failure was still disappointing.

If the empress wasn't here, then it meant the main boiler room door wouldn't be locked or guarded. Fairy might as well exit the mess hall that way. Fewer cobwebs.

She took one last pass around the boiler room, then headed up the stairs. She listened to make sure there was no one outside the door before she snuck out.

As soon as she was on the other side, the rich aroma of braised beef stew embraced her. Fairy's stomach rumbled. She'd only had a few crackers and picked at a piece of fish jerky earlier. Now she realized she was ravenous.

I'll just sneak into the kitchen and steal a bite, she thought. And maybe, if it was busy enough that the staff wouldn't notice another body in their midst, she could get some provisions for Broomstick, Wolf, and Spirit. They'd be hungry when they reconvened.

Someone was coming down the hall. No, *several* someones. Fairy tucked herself into a corner.

Three women hurried by. They were dressed in plain brown tunics and trousers, white aprons around their waists, hair pulled back in neat buns. The Society employed an entire staff of non-taigas like these kitchen girls to help the Citadel run. Fairy recognized one of them as Mariko, who was friends with Broomstick and often would give him extra cookies when the baker made too many.

"Psst, Mariko!" Fairy whispered. Hells, she knew it was risky, but maybe they could help her. Or if they tried to fight, Fairy could easily take out three untrained girls in two seconds. Four seconds, at most.

No, definitely two.

The girls passed her, though, chattering excitedly about cooking for Emperor Gin.

Had they been hypnotized?

If so, maybe Fairy shouldn't call out to Mariko. She did follow them down the long corridor, though. After all, it looked like they were heading to the kitchen, which was exactly where Fairy's stomach wanted her to be.

The kitchen was bustling, preparing for dinner in a couple hours. It smelled not only of stewed beef but also dumplings, fried noodles, and roasted vegetables. Fairy's stomach threatened to stage a revolt if she didn't eat something soon.

She stepped into a nook with shelves lined with folded uniforms. Fairy grabbed one of the starchy white tops and buttoned it over her black tunic and pulled a matching white apron over it. Now she looked just like Mariko and the other girls.

Fairy emerged into the main part of the kitchen, next to a counter lined with baskets of rolls ready to be set on the long rows of tables in the mess hall. The rolls were shaped like triplicate whorls, the symbol the goddess Luna used to mark those she blessed as taigas. Fairy clenched her jaw. How dare the ryuu use the taigas' symbol! She had half a mind to poison their meal, and she began to reach for the satchel on her belt.

But then she stopped. If she poisoned the food, she'd kill not only Prince Gin's ryuu but also the innocent taigas who'd been hypnotized.

Gods dammit.

She left her satchel alone but grabbed a roll and crammed it into her mouth. The buttery dough seemed to melt on her tongue, and she almost moaned aloud, catching herself at the last moment. She gobbled up three more rolls to silence herself. Then she found an empty rice sack next to the counter and upended a couple baskets of bread into the bag to bring to her friends.

"Hello, servants," a gruff voice said from the entryway to the kitchen.

Fairy looked up to see three ryuu—a man and two women. She didn't recognize them.

"Master Ram," the head chef said, bowing and fawning. "And Masters Quill and Edgewood. How can we be of service?"

They stormed into the kitchen and began snatching dumplings out of pans and sticking their fingers in bowls of sauce to taste them. "We want snacks in the sparring arena in five minutes," Quill barked.

Fairy seethed. When the taigas had been in charge here, they were always respectful and grateful to the staff.

Mariko and a handful of girls hurried over to the stove to transfer the dumplings from the pans to platters.

"Those are disgusting," Ram said, spitting out the chewed-up remnants of a dumpling he'd pilfered. "There are consequences for serving garbage to the Dragon Prince and the most powerful army in the world.."

He glanced at a handful of knives on the counter next to

him. One leaped into the air, as if of its own accord, and flew across the room.

It hit Mariko directly in the forehead.

"No!" Fairy shouted.

Blood dribbled around the blade. Mariko's body and the platter of dumplings she'd been holding toppled to the floor.

But strangely, the kitchen didn't erupt into chaos. None of the servants ran shrieking for cover.

Ram stared at Fairy.

Oh, gods help me, she thought as she realized why she'd been the only one to shout—everyone in here was hypnotized. Like with the people who sacrificed themselves during the Ceremony of Two Hundred Hearts, there would never be any panic, just continual devotion to whatever the Dragon Prince needed and wanted done. But Fairy had screamed and, therefore, stood out. . . .

"The dumplings!" she cried, throwing her arms up as if she were concerned solely for the food that had spilled when Ram killed Mariko, rather than being upset over the girl herself. Fairy threw herself on the ground near Mariko and began frantically collecting pot stickers off the kitchen floor.

She felt the eyes of the three ryuu still on her.

But then finally, Quill shouted, "You heard Ram. Snacks in the sparring arena in five minutes—actually, three minutes now." Then they turned and left.

The kitchen servants sprang back into action, as if one of their own hadn't just been killed. Fairy fought back tears as she dragged Mariko to the side of the kitchen, out of the way of the commotion. The bread Fairy had eaten threatened to come up.

She couldn't collapse here, though, not right now. She had to continue on her mission in order to save all of Kichona, including the Citadel's staff.

Fairy looked around the room at the frenzied kitchen girls. She forced herself to memorize their faces, as well as Mariko's lifeless body on the floor.

I am Fairy. I'm a taiga, and I still believe in the Society oath: Cloak of night. Heart of light.

Goodness could still prevail.

She would fight for everyone here who couldn't fight for themselves, and she would make sure the rest of the kingdom didn't succumb to their fate.

It was a promise.

CHAPTER EIGHT

Sora looked up at Prince Gin's castle. It was a long way up the steep, winding road, and she wanted to make both her and Daemon invisible. But casting a spell on herself was one thing; doing it to someone else was another.

"What if I lose hold of the magic?" she asked. "Then they'll see you."

"Would it be easier if we moved as a single unit?" he asked.

"I don't understand how that would help."

"When I was a wolf and you were riding on my back, my magic was able to envelop all of us. What if that's because we were all essentially one unit?"

The corner of Sora's mouth quirked. "So you're saying that if I rode piggyback on you, it would be easier to include you in my invisibility, instead of casting an entirely different spell for each of us. But it's a lot of work for you."

"Well, *you* could carry *me*, I suppose . . . ," he said.

Sora sputtered.

Daemon laughed. "I'm just teasing. You need to focus all your energy on keeping us invisible, not hauling my dead-weight up the mountain. Get on."

She hit him for the joke, but as soon as she was on his back, all was forgiven. She wrapped herself around him and felt the strength of his muscles against her own. His hair brushed against her cheek, and she wanted to reach out and run her fingers through it. Sora swallowed a sigh that would give her away.

"Tell me when we're invisible," Daemon said.

She nodded into his shoulder.

Then Sora called to the ryuu magic. It was always there, everywhere, but it remained quietly in the background unless summoned. Now, at her beckoning, it appeared like emerald dust glimmering in the air, eagerly awaiting instructions.

Make us invisible.

The ryuu particles streamed into Sora's body, the heat seeping through to her core, like a sponge greedily soaking in perfumed bathwater. She gave herself a second to revel in the feeling, despite the underlying guilt that the ryuu magic was a "gift" from her enemy.

But it was a gift she would use against him.

She looked down at Daemon. He was saturated with ryuu particles, too. "It worked," she whispered into his ear. "You're invisible, too."

He didn't move.

Gods, had something gone wrong with her spell? Sora tapped her hand on his chest. "Daemon? Are you all right? Answer me."

His body trembled, and he shook his head as if waking.

"I'm fine. That was just unexpected."

"Did you feel it, too?"

"It's like drinking a warm dose of joy. I didn't feel it when you floated me over the Citadel walls earlier, but becoming invisible is . . . different."

Sora smiled a little. There were plenty of reasons to hate ryuu magic, but the warmth that came with it wasn't one of them.

They made their way up the winding mountain path. Daemon cast a cheetah spell on himself so they could cover the distance faster. Sora managed to keep them invisible, even after she got down from Daemon's back. He just had to stay close by and be vigilant in case her magic dropped.

They pressed themselves against the outer walls and caught their breaths. There was a surprising lack of patrols— it seemed most of the ryuu were down at the Citadel. Was the Dragon Prince so secure in his position that he didn't feel the need to have more warriors guarding him?

But why would he? He was controlling the minds of the entire Society of Taigas, minus the four of them. He had powerful magic at his fingertips, and he was holed up in a bastion protected by an army of ryuu in a fortress. There was little reason to be threatened, especially by four kids, who he probably thought were off feeling sorry for themselves somewhere.

Surprise, Sora thought. *Here we are. And I'm going to stick a throwing star in your eye. Maybe two.*

She and Daemon snuck around the perimeter of the castle.

And almost ran right into a group of ryuu pouring out of one of the side doors.

Sora jerked Daemon back. Despite their invisibility,

they needed to be careful, because the ryuu knew there was a rogue ryuu running around who could make herself invisible. If they felt something touch them that they couldn't see, the conclusion would be easy to draw.

"That was close," Daemon said.

But she didn't respond, because a familiar caustic voice carried in the wind, giving orders to the ryuu. Sora didn't need to look around the corner to know who the voice belonged to.

Hana.

Sora cringed as she remembered the scathing hatred on her sister's face when they'd fought on the Citadel walls. And the taunt as Hana held Empress Aki's unconscious body atop the bloodstone castle, a knife pressed to the empress's throat. Sora had lost track of them during the Ceremony of Two Hundred Hearts, when Prince Gin had compelled innocent men, children, and women to cut out their own hearts as sacrificial gifts to Zomuri. Whatever progress Sora had made in reconciling with Hana while they were both ryuu, it was destroyed now.

Maybe I didn't try hard enough to save her. Sora touched the necklace at her throat. It was the gold memorial pearl her mother had given her during Autumn Festival, in remembrance of Hana. Sora still wore it, even though she now knew that Hana was alive.

"Hey-o, are you okay?" Daemon asked. Sora's distress had curdled their gemina bond like sour milk.

"Hana is just around the corner," Sora whispered. She wasn't prepared—physically *or* emotionally—to face her sister again. To see her fury seething beneath the surface, waiting to be unleashed.

Daemon's eyes widened in alarm. "We need to get inside the castle, now. Hana can see us even if we're invisible because you have the same ryuu talent, right? She'll kill us."

Sora bit her lip so hard it split open. "Wh-what if we could convince her to abandon Prince Gin?"

"And fight on what might be the losing side, just because it's right?" Daemon asked. "Sora, you already tried that, and Hana rejected you. I know you're hurting, but we can't save her right now. If you confront Hana, it's the end of both you and our hopes of saving Kichona."

"I don't want that to be true."

"But it is. I'm sorry. We need to move." He pointed up to the third floor of the tower near them. "I think we can get in through that open window. We have to climb, fast, before the ryuu head this way."

Sora glanced with longing at the bend in the castle perimeter, as if she could just will Hana to shift allegiances from around the corner. But Daemon was right. Sora had already attempted that, and it had backfired.

Daemon was already halfway up the wall with a gecko spell when he looked back down at her. "Sora! Come on!" He shot a sharp arrow of alarm through their bond, and it pierced through the fog of her regret, jolting her to action.

She followed him up the wall and swung herself in through the window frame, landing on the floor without a sound. Just in time, too, because the ryuu turned the corner where she had just been. Sora let out a long exhale.

Daemon looked around the room, perplexed. "It's completely empty in here."

"The castle is only a few days old," Sora said. It was probably too much to ask that it already be furnished.

With Hana left behind, Sora forced herself to get back to her job. She tiptoed to the door and pressed her ear against it. It was quiet on the other side, so she pushed it open a crack and slipped through.

Here, there were torches. The tower was narrow, and the center was mostly a spiral staircase with only a room or two on each level. The walls were made of black stone streaked with crimson, and the flickering of the torch flames made the red look like pulsing veins full of blood.

She and Daemon poked into the room opposite. Again, no one there.

"If you were the Dragon Prince, where would you stash a usurped empress?" Sora asked.

"Nowhere as obvious as a tower," Daemon said.

"My thinking as well."

They trod carefully down the stairs. The ground floor connected the tower with the rest of the castle. Sora and Daemon hurried along the corridor.

They examined every room they passed for Empress Aki, listening for hollow spaces in the walls and floors where she could be imprisoned. They went up and down the other towers, too. But other than a locked room—which was totally silent—and a few ryuu here and there, the blood-stone castle seemed abandoned.

It was too quiet. The little hairs on Sora's arms stood on end.

And too much time had passed already. "We need to get out of here soon," Daemon said.

"One more passageway," Sora said. There was a corridor up ahead that branched off from the others.

As they turned the corner, she took in a sharp breath.

If the rest of the castle was already eerie with its red-streaked, black stone walls, this dark hallway was the crown jewel. There were no windows, torches, or lanterns; the only light came from the sinister glow of what looked like giant dragon's teeth, each taller than Sora and composed entirely of crimson crystals seemingly lit from within. It was like walking straight into a dragon's jaws.

The corridor led to a heavy set of wooden doors. The handles were carved with dragons, their eyes inset with red rubies, their claws outstretched as if ready to tear into prey.

"I have a feeling one of the two people we're looking for is behind those doors," Daemon whispered. "And it's not Empress Aki."

Their gemina bond tightened, the taiga equivalent to holding hands to give each other strength. Sora nodded at Daemon. There was no time like the present for regicide.

Knives and throwing stars at the ready, they snuck up to the twin keyholes and peered inside.

Gods almighty.

The throne room was a massive receiving hall, with walls made of the same red-streaked black stone as the castle. There was a huge mural painted on the ceiling—although Sora couldn't quite make out its subject from the angle of the keyhole—and also a throne, a menacing opus of crimson stone and black velvet, with fiery flames made of orange sapphires to frame Prince Gin's head.

He wasn't sitting on the throne, though. The Dragon Prince knelt before the fireplace in front of real flames, chanting over and over in what sounded like Kichonan but older. Like an ancient version of their modern language.

"What is he doing?" Sora whispered.

Daemon didn't get to answer, though, because the fire in the throne room suddenly extinguished itself, and a giant appeared in the air in its place, his long dark beard fluttering like a flag, his ten-fingered hands stained red with a millennium's worth of blood.

Zomuri.

CHAPTER NINE

Sora staggered back a step. Gods rarely deigned to inter-act with humans. Sola, goddess of the sun, would visit the emperor or empress only if summoned with imperial blood and a sacrifice of a year of his or her life. Non-royals like Sora never got to see deities. She would light incense and pray, hoping that the smoke would carry her wishes to Celestae, the island paradise in the sky where the gods lived. But people didn't expect to ever see a god during their lifetimes, let alone twice. Yet Zomuri had appeared for the Ceremony of Two Hundred Hearts, and here he was again.

Why?

It had to be bad. Zomuri may have been more willing to appear to humans than the other gods, but still, he came only if there was something worthwhile to him. Hearts to eat. Emperors' promises of glory in Zomuri's name. Or pos-sibly worse.

Sora pulled herself together and mashed her ear against the keyhole to catch what she could of their conversation.

"I do not like being summoned like a dog," Zomuri said. "What is the meaning of this?"

Prince Gin bowed to the ground. "My lord, you know I am your most humble servant. I am working toward creating a vast empire to worship you and to achieve the Evermore for my people. However, I've been reviewing my research on the emperors of the past who marched this path before me, and always, they fail before conquering all seven of the mainland kingdoms because the Kichonan forces are outnumbered. I want to ensure that I'm not susceptible to this same human frailty, and so I have a request to make of you."

Zomuri's voice rumbled ominously in the back of his throat. "Why should I give you anything more? By declaring your kingdom's loyalty to me, rather than the sun goddess, you have already gained an advantage."

"What?" Daemon whispered, confused.

Sora shook her head. She didn't understand either.

Prince Gin dipped his head in acknowledgment. He clearly knew what Zomuri was talking about. Then again, he'd been a devotee of Evermore legends since childhood. "I understand the effect your reign will have on the people of this kingdom. But what I'm proposing is a deal that will benefit both of us even more—a *guarantee* of glory and empire for you and a clear path to the Evermore for me, my ryuu, and all of Kichona."

Zomuri floated above the throne. "I'm listening."

The Dragon Prince rose to his feet and took his time walking to his throne. He sat in it casually, with a surprising lack of deference, given the fact that he was in the presence of a god. Maybe being emperor allowed him that.

Or maybe he's just an arrogant snake, Sora thought.

"Make me immune to death—invincible," Prince Gin said.

Sora's jaw dropped. Was that possible?

"You already have magic superior to that of anyone else you will face," Zomuri said.

"True, but I can still die, and my enemies are clever and savage. Give me the power over death, my lord. You and I both know that I'm your best chance at achieving what you've craved for centuries—the entire mainland united under your name. The people of the world will worship you and offer all their riches for your blessings. There will be no god as loved as you're loved. No god as wealthy and glorified as you. If you grant me invincibility, I can all but guarantee this to you."

"Invincibility . . ." The god pulled on his beard as he contemplated Prince Gin's offer. "Perhaps I could do that. But it would cost you."

"What do you want?" Prince Gin said.

Sora held her breath as she waited for Zomuri to reply to the prince. Anyone who knew anything about the Kichonan gods knew that Zomuri loved only three things: blood, glory, and treasure.

"I want your soul," the god said.

Prince Gin crossed his arms. "Choose something else. If I give you my soul, then it won't get to rest in the afterlife if I die before reaching the Evermore."

Zomuri chuckled, and it shook the room. Sora and Daemon had to let go of the doors or the handles would jiggle too much and give them away.

"You speak of your research," the god said, "but for a man who prides himself as a scholar of Kichonan legend, you are woefully undereducated. You must not have read the legend *Dassu and the Warrior*."

Daemon whispered to Sora, "I've heard that one before. . . ."

Zomuri, in the meantime, continued speaking to Prince Gin. "If you had, you would know that you are condemned to the same fate. Ten years ago, when you were on the cusp of death and your soul traveled down the final tunnel of light, you caught a glimpse of the glittering emerald magic that awaited you there. But instead of crossing the threshold to the afterlife, you reached in, stole the ability to see the magic, and brought it back to this life, where it is not supposed to be used in so powerful a manifestation. Do you really think the gods will let your soul rest in peace after that?"

Daemon threaded his hands through his hair and tugged on the blue locks. "That's how he got ryuu magic?"

Sora just stared through the keyhole. She didn't know it was possible to go to the brink of death like that and return, let alone steal an ability like Sight from the afterlife.

Prince Gin seemed equally stunned by what Zomuri had said but for a different reason. "If I die without agreeing to your terms, my soul is condemned to the hells?"

Zomuri laughed, as if dealing with a less than diligent student. "Go back and study your books, Gin, and you will find the answer."

The Dragon Prince took a moment to pull himself together. But then he shook away his shock and asked, "What happens if I give you my soul instead?"

"I haven't decided yet. But that's a risk you're going to have to take." Zomuri rubbed his hands together in malicious glee. "There is, however, a third option—you achieve the Evermore and you never die. If you do this, your body will live freely and forever in paradise, while your soul merely looks pretty in my treasure vault. This gives you even more incentive to make sure you achieve what you've set out to do. But I am finished with this discussion. Do you accept my offer or not?"

"No," Sora whispered, sick to her stomach. If Zomuri made him invincible, Prince Gin couldn't be killed. There was no way Sora would be able to save Kichona, even if they did find Empress Aki. Everyone would become a puppet of the prince. Pawns on the front lines of his wars. Marching toward their deaths without even realizing they were at the ends of their lives.

Daemon stood motionless, as horrified as Sora was.

Prince Gin took a long moment to consider Zomuri's offer. On the one hand, there was invincibility. On the other hand, there was the risk of a cruel god's whim.

But in the end, Prince Gin must have either thought it was worth the gamble or had immense confidence in his own abilities if he were both a ryuu and invincible because he said, "You are a shrewd negotiator, my lord. I accept. I offer you my soul."

Zomuri grinned, baring his gold teeth and the dried blood on his lips, likely from the Ceremony of Two Hundred Hearts.

"We have to get to Prince Gin now," Daemon said to Sora. Their gemina bond burned violet with fear. "We have to stop this before it begins." He grabbed the door handles.

Sora threw her arms around Daemon to pull him back, to keep him quiet. "That's the Dragon Prince and the most vicious god in the realm in there! If we charge in like this, we're dead. And then Empress Aki and all the brainwashed taigas might as well be dead, too, because we're the only ones left to save them."

Zomuri plunged his hand down the prince's throat, so far that his arm seemed to disappear. Prince Gin's eyes bugged, and his body convulsed.

Sora stood frozen as the improbable unfolded before her.

A few seconds later, Zomuri yanked his arm from the prince's throat. He held what looked like a small gold pearl.

"To safety, in my vault," he said to the soul pearl. In a puff of smoke, it disappeared, magicked away.

Prince Gin straightened his robes, as if what had just happened to him was no big deal. Then he unsheathed a sword and rammed it straight through his own middle.

Sora gasped.

He twisted the blade through his organs, then withdrew it. The sword dripped with blood.

But Prince Gin was still standing. He pushed aside the fabric at his stomach. The gaping wound healed before his eyes, the blood and flesh reabsorbed into his body, the skin smoothing without a scar.

"Excellent," he said before sitting back on his throne. He cast his sword to the floor and smiled smugly.

Sora's knees nearly buckled beneath her. There went her hope of assassinating the Dragon Prince tonight and putting a quick end to this. As long as Zomuri had the soul, they wouldn't be able to kill Prince Gin or stop him from turning all of Kichona into a mindless game of war.

"There must be a way to fight back," she whispered.

"He's invincible," Daemon said. "It's over."

CHAPTER TEN

Sora and Daemon stepped into the chestnut grove in Jade Forest.

Cold, sharp steel immediately pressed to their throats. "Don't move."

Nines, Sora swore to herself as she stilled. The ryuu had found them.

"We don't have anything valuable on us," Sora said, in case the knife at her throat belonged to a thief.

"Oh, thank the gods, it's you," Fairy said. She dropped the blade.

Sora exhaled. Thank the gods indeed.

"Sorry it took us so long," Daemon said as he rubbed his neck where Broomstick's knife had pressed.

"Yeah," Sora said. "Daemon had to carry me on his back both ways so I could keep us invisible. I slowed him down."

"You can make other people invisible?" Broomstick asked. "Why didn't you do that to us while we were crossing the Field of Illusions or when Fairy and I were in the Citadel?"

"It takes a lot of concentration for me to cast that kind of magic on someone else," Sora said. "I needed my wits to cross the shifting sand, and I couldn't think that hard while also making all four of us invisible. Maybe with more practice, I'll be able to."

They settled beneath the dense canopy of the chestnut trees. Fairy handed out thick, woolen cloaks—she and Broomstick had had the foresight to grab fresh clothes, sleeping mats, weapons, and food for everyone—and they huddled together around a campfire.

"I assume, since we're all here and the mood isn't celebratory, that none of us managed to find the empress or kill Prince Gin?" Broomstick asked.

Everyone shook their heads.

"Damn," Fairy mumbled. She proceeded to tell them about Mariko's murder.

Everyone was silent as that sank in.

"Mariko was always so nice to us," Daemon said. "She shouldn't have been at risk. She wasn't a soldier, just an ordinary person trying to do her job."

"Yeah . . . ," Fairy said.

Sora wrapped her arms around her knees, as if that would help settle her. She'd been so focused on the Evermore as the ultimate evil that she hadn't really thought about *why* it was atrocious.

It wasn't the striving for paradise on earth that was inherently bad. It was every ruthless thing that would be done in order to get it. This war wasn't just about conquering the mainland. It was a war on Kichona itself. Prince Gin and the ryuu were the invading horde, and the people were their targets. The terrible irony was, if the prince murdered and brainwashed enough and Zomuri made the Evermore a reality, there would be no Kichonans left to enjoy it.

But this was why Sora had to fight back. She took a deep breath to compose herself, then turned to Broomstick. "Please tell me you have a better report."

He shook his head. "What I saw was just as horrible, in a different way." He looked a little green as he reported watching Blade, Quicksand, Philosopher, and other apprentices they knew training with ryuu magic.

"Stars, even the kids like Quicksand?" Daemon asked. "Did you see any of our mentees?"

Broomstick nodded sadly. "Yours. I didn't see Fairy's or Spirit's, but that doesn't mean they're not being trained. Anyone who was a taiga apprentice is learning ryuu magic. That means kids as young as seven. Who knows? Maybe even the little tenderfoots in the nursery."

Daemon punched the tree nearest him.

"I also spent some time in Warrior Meeting Hall." Broomstick recounted what he'd seen there.

Sora curled into herself even more. And yet she couldn't stay like that for long, because then it was her turn to tell Fairy and Broomstick what she and Daemon had discovered in the castle.

"Do you want to give them the bad news, or should I?" Sora asked Daemon.

Fairy let out an involuntary cry. "How can it get worse?"

"The Dragon Prince gave up his soul," Daemon said, cutting quickly to the point.

"What do you mean?" Broomstick said, his deep voice cracking.

"He struck a deal with Zomuri," Sora said. "He gave up his soul in exchange for being invincible."

Fairy opened her mouth to say something, but nothing came out. Broomstick was equally speechless.

"Don't resign yourself," Sora said. "This isn't over until we say it is."

"I'm not so sure about that," Daemon said. He picked up a twig from the ground and speared it through a hapless mushroom.

"It isn't over yet." Sora glared at him and sent a stab of displeasure through their gemina bond.

He cringed but didn't retract his dismay.

She needed to do whatever it took to get her head in order. Those who'd lost their lives in the Ceremony of Two Hundred Hearts should not have died in vain. And Sora had to stop this war before it began, or her fellow taigas and too many citizens of Kichona would die under Prince Gin's command. Her kingdom needed her.

If stashing the soul pearl in Zomuri's treasure vault kept the Dragon Prince safe, Sora would have to change that.

"Listen," Sora said gently, trying to change tack to persuade Daemon, Fairy, and Broomstick that they still had a fighting chance. "We're going to find Zomuri's vault to retrieve the soul pearl. If we can reunite it with Prince Gin's body, he won't be invincible anymore, and we can kill him. It's the only way to stop this madness."

"I'm sorry," Daemon said. "Did you just say we're going to steal from a god?"

Sora flushed. "Um, yeah."

He jabbed his twig at more mushrooms near his feet. "Tell me, assuming we could pull off a theft like that, how do we even find the soul pearl? Where does a god stash his treasure?"

"I . . . don't know." Sora deflated. She hadn't gotten that far yet in her plans.

"This is not a good idea, Sora," Daemon said.

Fairy perked up. "Is there anything you remember from your mother's books?" Mina Teira was one of Kichona's most famous authors, known especially for her volumes on the kingdom's myths and legends.

Sora shook her head. "I thought about it the whole trek here from the castle. But nothing jumps out at me."

Broomstick picked up some chestnuts that had fallen from the tree. He started throwing them one by one in frustration.

Daemon growled. "That's not helping."

"Oh, because the sound of a few nuts is distracting you from a brilliant revelation?" He chucked one at Daemon's head.

"Guys—" Sora began.

"What the hells," Daemon said. He grabbed a chestnut from the ground and hurled it. But Broomstick rolled out of the way, and it smacked into Fairy instead.

"Stop it, both of you!" She scowled at Daemon and whacked Broomstick on the back of his head. "If this is what the last hope for Kichona looks like, I might as well start writing my tombstone now."

"Sorry," the boys mumbled under their breaths.

"I didn't hear that," she said.

"We're sorry, Fairy," Daemon and Broomstick both said.

"Damn right you are. Now sit with your hands folded in your laps and do something useful."

In other circumstances, Sora would have laughed at the two boys sitting with legs crossed beneath them and heads bowed like chastised tenderfoots.

But instead she groaned as she thought of something that could spell the end of their plans.

"What is it?" Fairy asked.

"Zomuri's treasure . . . What if it's not here on earth but up in Celestae?" Sora looked fearfully at the sky. "I'm an idiot for assuming the vault was somewhere we could find. But if it's up there, we can't get to it."

"Maybe Wolf could fly," Broomstick suggested earnestly.

Daemon shot him a black look. "How? By flapping my arms?"

"Calm down; he wasn't trying to insult you." Fairy physically inserted herself between them before they started throwing chestnuts again. Or actually fighting.

"But what if . . ." Fairy's brow furrowed as she thought. "What if we could help you fly? Then you really would be able to take us to Celestae."

"You're saying we should work on Daemon's powers?" Sora asked. She still had the same concern as before—they weren't even sure what it was Daemon could do, let alone how to summon or control it. Figuring it out could take weeks or months. "We don't have the time to do that."

"Oh. Right." Fairy's shoulders drooped.

But Sora's mind raced as if finishing the last pieces of the puzzle. Prince Gin had given his soul pearl to a god. It might be hidden in Celestae, the home of the gods. Or it might be here on earth, in a hiding spot chosen by a god. The common denominator in all of this was . . . a god.

She bolted upright. "I've got it."

Broomstick and Fairy both looked at her expectantly. Daemon continued beating up the mushrooms.

"Who would know best where a god might hide his treasure?" Sora asked.

"Um, the god who hid it in the first place?" Broomstick said.

"Besides him."

Fairy scrunched her nose as she thought. "Someone who knows how gods think."

"Another god," Broomstick said.

"Exactly," Sora said. "And we might have a connection to another god if Daemon is the demigod constellation we think he is."

"What are you suggesting?" Fairy asked.

Sora looked up at the sky. "We should try to summon Vespre, Daemon's dad."

CHAPTER ELEVEN

Daemon thought he might keel over. All his life, he'd wondered where he came from and who his parents were. *Will Vespre answer our summons? Will he be happy to see me? Can he tell me who my mother is?*

But then he thought of another question. Why hadn't Vespre reached out to him sometime in the past eighteen years? If he really was Daemon's father . . .

Their imagined reunion suddenly didn't seem so sweet.

"Maybe I'm not his son," Daemon whispered.

"What?" Sora said.

He felt so cold. "Maybe we're wrong and I'm not a demigod, just a freak of nature or a fluke. Maybe I'm not as special as you think."

She seized their gemina bond and shook it hard. "You turned into a flying wolf that protected us from the Dragon Prince's mind control. You're special. Face it."

Daemon just crossed his arms.

"Hey," Sora said softly. She reached out and actually touched him.

Goose bumps immediately rose on every inch of his skin. Daemon slammed his mental ramparts up so that Sora didn't feel his reaction through their gemina bond, and he jerked away.

He was with Fairy now. Shouldn't that have cured him of his feelings for Sora?

Unfortunately, emotions didn't vanish just because another one showed up and tried to take its place.

Sora didn't know why Daemon had pulled away, though, and hurt made little spots of red blossom on her cheeks. He wanted to brush his fingers over her face and soothe the blotches away.

Instead, he scooted farther back.

"I'm sorry," Daemon said. "I'm going through . . . a lot." He didn't elaborate. It was better for everyone if Sora thought it was solely about all this demigod business. Besides, he really liked Fairy, who was brilliant and brave and gorgeous, just in different ways from Sora. And that was all right. It didn't make him a bad person to fall out of love and into another love at the same time. He was only human.

Maybe.

"I know all this wolf stuff is overwhelming," Sora said. "And you've been working so hard; you need a break. We'll start turning this site into a mini temple to pray to Vespre. Why don't you go for a walk in the woods? Or climb a tree? You always feel better when you're up high."

Daemon sighed. *Why did she have to be so amazing?* He'd

been petulant and cynical these past couple days, but she was still there for him.

But he only said, "I don't want to leave you guys to do everything."

"We don't mind, I promise," Sora said. "Go."

He nodded slowly and got to his feet. "All right. Thanks." It actually would be helpful to have a break. He needed to get his head on straight.

Daemon hiked a ways into the woods, closed his eyes, and listened to the forest. There was the soft rustle of leaves in the breeze, like silk fans in late-autumn heat. The murmur of the river, slowing down as it prepared for winter to take it. The silence in distant parts of the woods, where tigers and other predators hunted.

What he didn't hear, however, was the call of the sky. He didn't feel the tug that he used to, the insistent need to climb as high as he could go. Nothing made sense anymore.

"Are you all right?"

Daemon opened his eyes. Fairy had followed him.

"Oh. Hi." He forced himself to smile.

"Do you want company? Or did you want to be alone?" There was no flirtation in her voice, just genuine concern.

"Um, I was trying to clear my head."

"I'll give you space, then." Fairy began to turn to go back to the chestnut grove.

But the moonlight illuminated her, and she looked almost angelic.

"Wait," he said. "Come with me. I'm going to climb up closer to the sky."

"I'm right behind you," Fairy said without asking why.

He found a tall cypress nearby, with a thick trunk and long branches spread out like open arms. The majestic tree must have been a couple thousand years old. Daemon scaled the tree easily, climbing the trunk and then leaping from branch to branch. He checked to see if Fairy needed any help, but she'd cast a squirrel spell and was almost as nimble as he was. He stopped at one of the sturdier branches, not quite at the top but high enough, and a few seconds later, she landed without a sound next to him.

"What are we——?"

"Shh," he said.

He waited for the familiar feeling to come—the sensation like a part of him had been missing but now, so far from the ground, the sky could pour into him, fill the emptiness, and make him whole. But there was nothing. He closed his eyes and puffed out his chest, as if inviting the sky in.

Nothing.

"It's not working," he muttered.

"What's not?" Fairy asked.

"I don't feel a thing."

She moved closer to him. His eyes were still closed, but he sensed the slight shift in weight on the branch beneath his feet.

"Tell me if this helps you feel," she whispered.

Then her mouth was on him, soft but insistent, for the first time since he'd kissed her in the Citadel infirmary. She smelled of plums—how did she do that, after being on the road for days?—and her lips told him that the incident in the dining hall on Isle of the Moon when she'd jumped away from him hadn't been rejection, that she still wanted him.

71

Another surge of heat flooded his body, and while it wasn't the same as the sky pouring into him, he couldn't care less right now.

Her lips parted his, and their tongues found each other. Daemon circled Fairy's waist and lifted her. She threw her arms around his neck and wrapped her legs around him. He moved closer to the center of the tree and pushed her back against the trunk.

She kissed his neck and toyed with his collar. His hand slid under the hem of her tunic, to bare skin like satin.

"The things I want to do to you," she purred.

Oh gods. It was as if he were on fire, inside and out. His temperature spiked. Sparks flew.

"Wolf," Fairy said, and hearing her call out his taiga name with her voice husky from desire made him burn even more.

But then she shoved away from him. "Wolf!"

"Did I do something wrong?" Daemon said, flustered.

Fairy's mouth, which only a second ago had been expertly working against his, now hung open, useless. She blinked rapidly and pointed at him. "Y-you. Wolf."

Daemon shook his head. But then he followed her finger and looked down at himself.

He was a wolf again, covered in blue fur, and the sparks he'd felt between them were literal sparks, like blue lightning buzzing and zapping all around him. His cloak and other clothes had fallen onto the branches.

"Gods dammit," he said. "Really? Right now?"

Meanwhile, Fairy was pinching at her tongue, pulling out strands of fur.

If Daemon could possibly feel any hotter, the embarrassment did it. "I'm so sorry. I didn't mean to—"

She held up a hand. He stopped talking.

She spat out one last piece of fur and started laughing.

"What?" Daemon asked. He failed to see what was funny about this situation.

"Look on the bright side," Fairy said.

"I can give you a ride to Celestae now?" Daemon grimaced.

"Yep," she said.

"Other than that, are you completely repulsed that I'm a wolf?" Part of him didn't want to know the answer.

Fairy shrugged. "I'm only going to kiss the boy version of you. And besides, it's not like you're actually an animal. You're a demigod. And that, like I said before, is very sexy."

He smiled a little. But it vanished quickly, because he remembered that they only *thought* he was the missing wolf constellation from the sky. They didn't know for sure. "What if it turns out I'm not a demigod?"

With that self-doubt, there was a blinding burst of blue light. When Daemon looked down, he was a boy once more. And naked. Again.

"You've got to be kidding me." He grabbed at the cloak and wrapped it around his waist. "Nines, I hate my life."

"I don't hate mine," Fairy said, openly ogling his shirtless torso. "And hey, think of it like this. Now you definitely know that what happened to you during the battle at the Citadel wasn't a fluke. Turning into an electric wolf *twice* is no accident."

Daemon sighed. He made Fairy turn around as he put his clothes back on.

She had a point, though. Transforming into an enormous flying wolf once was like a dream he could be woken from. But twice was the beginning of something real.

"All right, fine, you win," he said when he was fully dressed. "Maybe I'm a *little* special. Let's go summon Vespre. He can settle this once and for all."

CHAPTER TWELVE

Sora had only ever prayed to the gods inside proper temples, like the black pagoda in the Citadel. Here in Jade Forest, though, they didn't even have incense sticks to make smoke for carrying their words up to Celestae. She had no idea if this would work.

There was also the question of whether these summons would cost them anything. Emperors and empresses had to give up a year of their life every time they called upon Sola. Would Vespre demand something like that, too? It was impossible to know, since gods didn't usually appear to humans outside of the imperial family.

But if the god of night does require something, it will be worth it, Sora thought. Because if they couldn't reach Vespre, there was no hope for the four of them and Kichona anway.

Sora and Broomstick did what they could to prepare a templelike space, clearing the ground in the chestnut grove and setting up a makeshift temple, with rolled-up sleeping mats as kneeling cushions and twigs to light in place of incense.

When Daemon and Fairy returned, Sora didn't need to look at them to know something had happened up there in the trees. Daemon had shut his mental ramparts, and Broomstick said Fairy had, too.

It's a good thing, Sora thought, although as before, it took work to convince herself. Fairy had been able to help Daemon when Sora couldn't. *I shouldn't be upset about that.*

And really, Sora wasn't mad at Fairy at all. She just wished she was in Fairy's place.

But since she wasn't, Sora forced a smile as they approached.

"Welcome back," she said, holding out a handful of twigs. "Here."

"What are these?" Daemon asked.

"Incense sticks. Sort of. When one twig burns down, light another, and keep the entreaties constant," Sora said.

He and Fairy each took a bundle.

"This is already kind of a gamble," Sora said, "so I think we should all focus on our strengths to maximize the chance that Vespre will not only hear us but actually respond."

"What do you mean?" Fairy asked.

Sora pointed at Broomstick, who was finishing up stacking a huge pile of sticks. "Broomstick is Mr. Charisma, so he's going to pray with the equivalent of his blinding smile. Instead of boring entreaties, he should appeal to Vespre's fascination with humans, like inviting him to hang out on earth."

Daemon twisted his mouth. "We're trying to be drinking buddies with my father?"

"If he brings me the alcohol of the gods," Broomstick hollered from the other side of the chestnut grove, "I'll not only be his drinking buddy, I'll be his best friend."

"I thought the myths only mention Vespre's interest in earth's *female* population," Daemon said.

"That's it!" Fairy's eyes lit up. "I'm good with guys. I'll try to tempt Vespre to visit us."

"Absolutely not!" Daemon said.

"Ew, not like that!" Fairy waved him off. "I just meant that I'm good at getting boys to do things for me, like grabbing the best knives when a new weapons shipment comes in or saving me a good seat in class."

Daemon crossed his arms.

"Present company excepted," Fairy said. "I promise I don't manipulate you at all."

Broomstick jogged over, snickering. "You manipulate everyone at least a little. You can't help it. You're just so little and cute, and they can't resist you." He pinched her cheek.

"Shut up." She swatted him away and made a face, the two of them as usual teasing each other.

Meanwhile, Sora had been contemplating Fairy's suggestion. "Tempting a god sounds like trouble," Sora said.

"I know what I'm doing," Fairy said. "You just have to trust that I can take care of myself. You do, don't you?" She looked at Daemon.

He grumbled but gave in. "I trust you."

Fairy hugged him and, at the same time, gave him her best puppy-eyed look.

"All right," Sora said. "That leaves me and Daemon. I'll try the earnest approach with Vespre, laying out what's at stake and why we need him. And Daemon——"

"I know," he said. "Tap into the fact that he's my dad. Well, *might* be."

"Only if you're comfortable with it," Sora said. "If you need to sit out——"

"I'm fine. But what if this doesn't work?"

"Then we'll try again tomorrow night," Sora said. "Getting Vespre to help us is our best hope right now."

They were quiet as they set up their prayer stations, because they knew what she'd said wasn't entirely true. The god of night was not just their best hope; he was their *only* one. They couldn't find the soul pearl without Vespre's knowledge; if Zomuri's vault was in Celestae, they would even need to ask Vespre to get it for them or take them there. And without the soul pearl, they had no path forward. There was no way a novice ryuu, a sometime-wolf/sometime-boy, and two taiga apprentices could defeat the Dragon Prince and an entire army of ryuu.

This had to work.

Sora lit a twig and put it in the small pile of sand in front of her. It burned more quickly than an actual incense stick, and she rushed to kneel on the sleeping mat so she could get a prayer off before the twig incinerated completely.

Vespre, my lord, please hear us, Sora thought. *I'm here with a boy who I believe is your son, the constellation wolf, and we need your help. Our beloved kingdom is under siege. Gin Ora has usurped the throne and pledged himself to Zomuri. Prince Gin has already murdered innocents in the Ceremony of Two Hundred Hearts, taken over the entire Society of Taigas, and is on the brink of beginning a world war. We need to know where Zomuri's vault is because there is something in there that could prevent the destruction of Kichona.*

Please, please help. Our kingdom needs you. Your son needs you.

The twig fell over, engulfed in flames, just as she finished her plea. This was going to be harder than she thought. The sticks were really nothing like incense.

But Sora lit another twig, planted it in the sand, and repeated her prayer. Over and over and over again. Nearby, Daemon, Fairy, and Broomstick whispered to Vespre as well.

Five hours later, their knees ached and their stomachs gnawed at them. The smoke of so many sticks clouded the air in the chestnut grove, as if the path to Celestae was blocked and the smoke had nowhere to go. Sora's eyes watered from it, and she was beginning to feel dizzy. Broomstick coughed in the polluted air.

"We need to rest," Fairy said.

"No," Daemon said, suddenly the most fervent of the group, when earlier he'd had only enough enthusiasm to poke at mushrooms. "We have to keep going."

"Our prayers are stuck under the canopy," she said, waving at the smoke. It was thick enough that seeing through it was a bit difficult. "We can at least wait until this clears out before we send more pleas."

"No!" Daemon said, clutching a fresh twig to his chest.

A swirl of bitter and sweet, like chicory steeped in cloying syrup, flooded through Sora's bond with him. It was so powerful, she could almost taste Daemon's longing, his wish that Vespre would not only be able to help with the pearl but also confirm his parentage.

Sora picked up another stick. What Daemon needed was equally important to her as stopping Prince Gin. And that was urgent. Every hour that ticked by was another hour that Empress Aki could be killed. Another hour closer to

Prince Gin launching a war against one of the mainland kingdoms, and their hypnotized friends dying in the fight. Sora shuddered at the possibility.

Vespre, my lord, please hear us. . . .

The night eventually shifted to early morning, and the dark gave way to dawn. Nothing changed in their makeshift temple except that all their eyes were rimmed in red from the smoke, and their backs hurt from kneeling in one position for so long.

As the sun rose, they did, too. There was no point in reaching out to the god of night during the day.

Sora had known it would be difficult—maybe impossible—to get Vespre's attention. And yet disappointment swamped her gemina connection like the stifling mugginess of a bog, making it hard to keep their chins up.

"We tried our best," Sora said as they unrolled their mats and got ready for bed. She had to stay upbeat, for everyone's sake. "But it was only our first attempt. Get some sleep. Tonight, we'll try our best again."

CHAPTER THIRTEEN

By the time everyone else woke up in the afternoon, Fairy was nearly bouncing out of her skin. "I have an idea," she announced as she darted from sleep mat to sleep mat.

Broomstick rubbed his eyes, still half asleep. "You're making me dizzy by flitting around like that."

"Yeah, stay still," Wolf said. "But if your idea is to magically find us coffee, I'd be all right with it."

Fairy laughed, but only for a moment. She'd been waiting forever for them to wake up so she could share her epiphany. "I think we need to change the sticks we use with our prayers."

"To what?" Spirit asked as she yawned and stretched.

"The twigs we used last night were just chestnut branches," Fairy said. "But I think we'd have a better chance of Vespre paying attention to us if we made smoke from night-blooming flowers."

"Why would that work?" Broomstick said.

"You don't remember the story from Spirit's mother's

books? Mortal women who want Vespre's attention set out night bloomers like wisteria, moonflowers, and certain types of jasmine to summon him to their beds." It was one of Fairy's favorite myths because it had to do with plants. And she wouldn't admit it, but it had also been her earliest primer on how to attract boys.

Wolf sat up on his mat, though, eyes alert with horror all over again.

"Stars, no!" Fairy said. "I promised you I wasn't trying to flirt with your dad, and I won't! That's disgusting. Besides, we're *all* going to use these flowers to contact him."

"It's a good plan," Spirit said. "But where do we find the flowers? It's daytime now, and you're the only one who would recognize them in their unopened state."

"Oh, you don't have to worry about that." Fairy grinned and pointed to the base of one of the chestnut trees, where a mound of flowers was piled several yards wide and almost as tall as she was. "I didn't sleep because I was too excited about the idea, so I went foraging for us."

Broomstick, Wolf, and Spirit blinked.

"Wow," Wolf said. "You did all that while we were asleep?"

"Yup! And I also gathered some lolaro berries. They're actually five times as caffeinated as coffee beans!"

"You don't say," Broomstick said. "How many have you had?"

Fairy stopped bouncing in place—only for a second—to stick her tongue out at him.

"Anyway," she said, "as soon as it's dark again, we can start burning flowers, and the perfume will carry our prayers up to Celestae. In the meantime, who wants some lolaro? They taste like cherries mixed with apricots and a dash of sunshine!" She skipped from Wolf to Broomstick to Spirit, offering the purple berries. No one extended their hands.

She couldn't understand why.

CHAPTER FOURTEEN

A couple hours later, Daemon carefully placed a stem of night jasmine in front of him. Without water, it had wilted a bit, but it still seemed to wake beneath the moonlight, delicate petals opening and releasing their powerful perfume.

Please work, he thought as he knelt on his rolled-up mat.

Daemon took a deep breath and began to recite a plea, but it was very different from yesterday's.

Hey-o, he began. *I'm going out on an arrogant limb and hoping that, because I might be your son, you'll hear me. Kichona has fallen into the hands of a delusional maniac who worships Zomuri, who, you probably know, is also insane. The only ones who can stop him are me and my friends, but as you can see, we could use your help. Me, in particular. I switch from wolf to pathetically naked boy at random, which pretty much sums up our position. So will you do it? I could really use some fatherly guidance here. I mean, even if it's not you, just someone up there, please help.*

Was it too up front? Possibly. Requests to the gods were

supposed to be laden with deference and ceremony. But so far, the stiff approach hadn't worked; maybe normal entreaties were just background noise in Celestae. Daemon hoped his informality would make his plea stand out.

As with yesterday, they kept praying steadily through the night, but they took breaks when the smoke got too thick, since it was compounded with the heady perfume of the flowers tonight.

As night gave way to early morning, Daemon began to sag on his mat. The brashness of his pleas shifted to dispirited resignation. At one point, he caught himself staring blankly at nothing in front of him, the flowers just a smoldering pile of ash.

But at the moment Daemon was about to give up, some of the stars directly above him seemed to wink out, as if a giant cloud had blown in to cover that portion of the sky.

He didn't move.

Did I imagine that?

Daemon looked again at the spot in the sky. Where a constellation had twinkled earlier, now there was a distinct splotch of black sky.

"I think something's happening . . . ," he said.

Someone in the thicket of trees cleared his throat.

Daemon, Sora, Fairy, and Broomstick were supposed to be the only ones in the chestnut grove.

They turned toward the noise, half-hopeful their pleas had been answered but half-afraid they'd find a squadron of ryuu standing there. Everyone drew their weapons.

A young man stood in the shadows on the other side of the grove. He was so still he could have been mistaken for a tree. He stepped forward into the moonlight, revealing that he wore nothing but a loincloth made of alligator hide.

It wasn't the ryuu. But it wasn't Vespre either.

"Greetings," said the boy in an oddly formal way. He looked only a little older than Daemon. "I apologize for my appearance. Is this what a proper human looks like?" He gestured over the length of his body.

"Hi there. . . ." Sora's jaw dropped.

Jealousy made Daemon clench his. But why was he feeling that way at all? Daemon was together with Fairy, and Sora was free to ogle whoever she wanted. Still, he couldn't shake the tightness in his chest, even though he wanted to.

"What do you mean, a 'proper human'?" Broomstick asked.

"I have never set foot outside Celestae," the boy said as if that explained everything.

"You're a god?" Daemon asked. The boy didn't look like any of the major ones, at least not from the descriptions they'd read all their lives.

"I'm Liga," he said. "I heard your prayers about an oncoming war, and I smelled the night bloomers, two things that don't usually go together. I was curious, so I came."

Sora frowned. "That doesn't explain much."

"It doesn't?" Liga scratched his head, as if confused why this, too, wasn't a sufficient answer.

It was then that Daemon noticed Liga's reptilian claws—at least three inches each and not "proper human" by a long shot—tucking his long hair behind his ear.

Dark blue hair, just like Daemon's. Faint sparks off his skin lit Liga like a distant halo.

Daemon swallowed and took a couple deep breaths. "Is Liga short for 'al*liga*tor'?" he asked in a whisper, because the idea seemed both inane and full of hope all at once.

Liga nodded.

"I don't understand," Sora said.

But Daemon did. "You're the alligator constellation from the night sky."

Liga smiled. "Yes, brother. I am."

CHAPTER FIFTEEN

That means Daemon really *is* the wolf constellation," Sora said. "But . . . how?"

Liga wrinkled his forehead. "What do you mean?"

Now it was her turn to be perplexed. She tried to think through what he might be confused about. The best way, she decided, was to explain specifically what she was asking. "How did Daemon go from being a demigod in Celestae, like you, to being a taiga apprentice on earth?"

"Aha." A smile spread across Liga's face. "I understand now. You would like to hear a story, correct? Because telling stories is how humans process a world that is otherwise too vast for you to comprehend." It sounded like an insult, but he said it matter-of-factly.

Sora knew that he was probably right. Liga didn't seem mean; he simply didn't know how to interact with humans, which made his speech a bit awkward and, sometimes, too blunt. So she pushed away the indignation that had flared at Liga's condescension and said, "Yes. We'd like to hear the story of what happened to Daemon."

"As you wish." Liga looked up toward the sky, and the air above their chestnut grove turned hazy, as if a purple cloud had descended. As he began to speak, moving images appeared in the violet fog, like a vivid, realistic miniature of everything that had transpired.

Celestae was a paradise, an island in the heavens that looked as if it were made of honey, translucently golden and crystalline. Sweet peaches and plums bowed the tree branches, and the air smelled of their nectar. There were lakes of such stunning turquoise, no color on earth could compete, and mountains topped with thick snow as fine as powdered sugar. Each god lived in a grand palace of their own making, with every luxury they could ever desire, and they entertained themselves with contests of strength and speed, celebrations full of music and dancing, and bountiful feasts with endless fountains of rice wine.

But there was one denizen of the heavens who grew tired of his idle life. The constellation wolf did not know how long he had lived here—time did not exist in Celestae, and so a day could be years, or a millennium could be a minute—but he did know he was bored. He craved, for better or for worse, hardship and challenge.

So he went to his father, Vespre, the god of night, who stood on the balcony of his palace, watching the sky below as it turned to the purplish-gray of gloaming. Vespre was seven feet tall with skin the color of midnight, broad shoulders, and muscles bulging across his chest. His eyes flickered like nebulas, bright and dark and multicolored at the same time, and his cheekbones and jawline were sharp and edged in white light, like the lines of a constellation. A trail of orange fire like a comet's tail followed his feet.

"Father," the wolf said, "I want to leave the heavens."

"Are you unhappy?" Vespre asked. "Is Celestae not enough?"

"On the contrary, Celestae is too much."

The god of night's eyes swirled in confusion. "Too much? You would desire less?"

The wolf tried to explain. Perhaps it was the humanity in him—his mother had been mortal—that needed a purpose in order to be happy. But Vespre did not understand.

"You are one of my favorite children," Vespre said. "I know I promised my human lovers that I would never deny their offspring's requests to visit earth, but that was to be temporary, if they wanted to see their mothers. But your mother is gone. She died in childbirth. There is nothing for you among the mortals."

"You would keep me prisoner here against my will?" the wolf said.

Vespre grew angry then, the color in his eyes suddenly gone and replaced with darkness, like black holes. "You are half god, and you belong in Celestae. I will not discuss this further." With that, the god vanished, leaving the wolf standing alone on the cusp of twilight.

But another god had overheard their argument, and she landed on the balcony beside the wolf. It was Luna, goddess of the moon and the constellation wolf's grandmother.

"If you wish to leave the sky, I can help you," Luna said. "But you must be sure, for if you do, there is no return. Once your father finds out, he will banish you forever from Celestae."

The blue wolf nodded. "I am sure."

"Then come with me on the next full moon."

When Luna again brightened the night sky with her glorious light, the wolf slipped away from his brothers and sisters and *followed Luna's downward climb. They touched down on the soft Kichonan dirt just outside a cave in Takish Gorge.*

"You would not like being a mere mortal," Luna said to him. "After a lifetime with magic, being an ordinary human would be torture. But I can make you a taiga. And you can, in turn, serve me in return for the favor of releasing you from the sky."

The wolf bowed his blue-furred head to the ground.

Above, the clouds cracked open, pouring forth rain and lightning. The god of night had awoken to find his son gone.

The wolf's mane shone like the stars one last time. Then Luna cast a spell, and he was a constellation no more. His spirit, however, curled into the form of an infant and, reincarnated, began a life anew.

"I name you Daemon," she whispered, because the bellowing storm sounded like demons marching from the hells. "It will take you some time to find your way, but when you're ready, you shall be a light when others attempt to bring darkness." Luna marked her triplicate whorls on the baby's back.

A pack of wolves emerged from the cave. The alpha and his mate bowed low to the goddess.

"Care for this child as if he were your own," Luna said. "And one day, his people will come for him."

Sora tried to catch Daemon as his legs gave way beneath him, but she wasn't fast enough, and they both fell to the ground. The earth smacked against their knees, but he seemed to hardly feel it. Their gemina bond was a daze, Daemon completely bewildered by Liga's story.

"I—I don't remember any of that," he said.

"Because Father was angry after you left," Liga said as

he waved away the purple haze hanging over them. "He did, in fact, banish you from ever entering Celestae again, and he buried your memories of it where you could not find them. If you didn't want to be there, he didn't think you deserved to remember it either."

"That's horrible," Fairy said.

"Our father is passionate," Liga said. "For better or for worse."

"I suppose that means he's not coming tonight," Sora said.

Liga sighed. "Or any other night. I'm sorry."

Daemon wasn't listening to their conversation, though. He had huddled into himself on the ground. "I was foolish to leave Celestae," he said.

Even with their gemina bond still frazzled from his shock, Sora knew what he meant. For eighteen years, he'd felt inadequate. Daemon had wished for a better command of magic. He'd prayed for something that would make him stand out from the other taiga apprentices. And to think he'd already had all that when he was a demigod. Now he was thinking it was his fault, that he'd gone and *chosen* an inferior life.

"You weren't foolish," Sora said, crouching and putting her arm around him. "You wanted something different, and you were brave enough to chase it, even though it cost you everything."

"You can be brave and stupid at the same time," Daemon muttered.

"Maybe so," Sora said. "But regardless, you're *our* brave and stupid." She sent him a wave of pride and loyalty, hoping he'd understand how much she meant it.

It seemed to at least wash away some of his bewilderment over what Liga had told him.

Daemon let out a long exhale. Then he looked up to face his half brother. "I'm sorry for the offense I caused our father—and you and all my siblings—by leaving Celestae. But I'm a different person now than the wolf you knew before. It sounds like I was spoiled and naive and ungrateful then."

"And now?" Liga asked.

"I'd like to think I'm a better version of myself."

Liga nodded thoughtfully.

With the break in their conversation, Broomstick rose and approached Liga. "I have a question. How were you able to leave Celestae if Wolf needed Luna's help years ago? Do some demigods have permission to come and go, but others don't?"

"I could come because Wolf invited me just now in his prayers," Liga said. "Eighteen years ago when he wanted to leave, he had no such invitation from someone on earth."

"Oh," Broomstick said. "That's it?"

"Indeed," Liga said.

Fairy joined them. "I have a question, too. You said you came because you heard our pleas and you were curious?"

He arched a brow. "Yes?"

"We need to know where Zomuri's treasure vault is."

"Why?"

Fairy looked to Sora.

Sora tried to sound persuasive. "Because Prince Gin gave his soul to Zomuri as part of a bargain, and we have to steal it, reunite the soul with the Dragon Prince, murder him, and save Kichona."

The corners of Liga's eyes crinkled in amusement. "You

want to steal from a god?" He turned to Daemon. "Brother, I see you're keeping similar company to your friends in Celestae. You always were attracted to mischief."

Sora's cheeks reddened. Luckily, no one else seemed to notice. They were all focused on Liga.

"Unfortunately, I cannot help you to the vault," he said. "Zomuri has fortified it with protections that repel gods, because he is paranoid that we want to steal from him, as if we care about human trinkets. No offense, of course."

"None taken," Fairy said. "But let me understand—are you saying that the vault is in Celestae?"

"Goodness, no," Liga said. "Zomuri wants to keep his precious treasure as far away from all of us as possible. Just like he chose to live on earth, he also buried his vault here, although in an even more remote location than the sulfur caverns that he calls home. The vault is beneath what he calls the Lake of Nightmares."

Sora shivered. That did not sound good.

"Where is this lake?" she asked.

Liga shrugged. "I do not know for sure. Somewhere very cold, I imagine. Gods loathe the cold, so none of us would bother to go there, no matter how glorious the treasure was."

"Naimo Ice Caves." Sora gasped. They were glacial underground labyrinths in the southernmost part of Kichona. Both remote *and* bone-chillingly frigid. "I'm willing to bet that the lake is there."

The others thought it over, listing other chilly places in Kichona. But after a few minutes, they agreed that Naimo Ice Caves was the most daunting—and the coldest—of the possibilities.

"Assuming that's where the Lake of Nightmares is," Broomstick said, "we still have a problem. If the vault is protected against gods and demigods, then how do *we* have a chance?"

The lines around Liga's eyes creased again, as if he were barely restraining his laughter.

"What?" Broomstick said.

"We're not important enough for the gods to worry about," Fairy said. She turned to Liga for confirmation, although she was surprisingly unperturbed. "Isn't that right? It's kind of like what you were saying, that you don't care about human trinkets."

"It isn't that we don't care about humans," Liga said. "It's more that we don't notice you all that often. For example, how closely have you been paying attention to those ants?" He pointed to a tree on the far side of the grove. Sora couldn't even see the ants without a hawkeye spell, let alone expend any thought to what they were doing.

"And how worried are you about them stealing your things or ruining your plans?" Liga asked.

Daemon grumbled, but it came out more like an offended growl. "Humans aren't ants."

"It's an imperfect analogy—" Liga began to explain.

"I understand," Sora said. "There's a lot going on in the world, as well as in Celestae, I imagine. Our human affairs are small in the grand scheme of it all. But ironically, it helps us if Zomuri didn't put much thought into protecting his vault from humans. We should head to the ice caves as soon as possible."

"I can't go," Daemon said.

Right. Because he was a demigod, and Zomuri *had*

protected the vault against them.

"You could wait outside the ice caves," Broomstick said.

Daemon shook his head. "And be completely useless while you all have to face whatever's in there? No way."

They stood around for several moments, trying to come up with a better idea.

"I could stay with Wolf outside the caves," Broomstick said. "We could be your guards."

"Or maybe we could try to rescue Empress Aki first," Fairy said. "She might know a weakness—or something like that—about her brother that can help us get close enough to him so that we can reunite him with his soul and kill him."

Sora chewed on her nails. "I think you're both right," she said.

"How?" Fairy asked. "Our suggestions are mutually exclusive."

"No, they're not. We'll divide up again," Sora said. "We have three things we need to get done right now: retrieve the soul pearl, find and rescue Empress Aki, and do everything in our power to stop—or at least slow down—Prince Gin's progress toward attacking the mainland kingdoms. So Broomstick and I will go to the ice caves to take care of the first part, and Fairy will stay with Wolf here to work on the other two. With our gemina pairs divided, we'll be able to use our bonds to check in with each other."

"And each pair will also have some brawn," Broomstick said.

Fairy rolled her eyes. "We don't need boys to protect us." She glanced at Daemon, though, and seemed to realize something. "But still, I can stay with Wolf. I feel like we could use that time productively."

Jealousy reared its ugly head at Sora, but she shoved it away. *I'm happy for them*, she reminded herself.

It helped to keep focused on the gargantuan tasks before them. "Maybe Liga can also teach you how to use your powers," Sora said to Daemon, "and you can train for our inevitable showdown against Prince Gin."

"Oh no." Liga raised both hands in the air. "I only came to sate my curiosity about your prayers and to see how my brother was doing."

"What?" Sora shook her head. "We're up against an army with more magic than we've ever encountered before. You have to help us."

"I can't risk being seen involved in a plot against Zomuri and his Evermore army."

Sora huffed. "You're a coward!"

"I beg your pardon?" Liga looked as if she'd slapped him.

"You're scared to pit yourself against Zomuri?" She shook her head in disbelief.

"Yes, I am," Liga said. "Have you noticed that he eats hearts for pleasure? I'm half human. If he wanted to punish me, I could die, just like you. I can only live forever while under my father's protection in Celestae. But if I wrong another god, my life is fair game."

He's not immortal. It began to sink in why Liga would be afraid. But still, they needed him.

"Please." Sora lay herself in a bow before him. Maybe she should have done this all along. Maybe she needed to show him more respect and offer him something, like how Sola took a year of life. It wasn't an easy thing to give up, but what else could Sora do?

"My lord," she said, "the citizens of Kichona have

worshipped the gods for millennia. They pray to you every night, throw festivals in honor of you every season, and put all their faith in you that you'll protect them and their children. Don't you owe it to them to do something more than just bless their harvests? Teach Daemon how to serve them. Teach him how to use his powers so we can save the kingdom. And in return, I offer you a year of my life or whatever you wish to take."

Liga started laughing.

Sora rose from the ground. "Why is that funny?"

He couldn't stop. "Because . . . you . . ." He pointed at her, still on her knees. "I . . ." He gestured at the piles of flowers and the sleeping-mat prayer stations. "I'm only a demigod. No one prays to *me*."

Daemon offered his hand to Sora and pulled her up. Then he stepped forward. "All the more reason to help us, brother. Your mother was mortal, just like mine."

"And the alligator constellation is still relatively young," Fairy said. "I know you don't mark the passing of time in Celestae, but it's possible your mother is alive."

The laughter left Liga's face. "She might be here on earth?"

Sora nodded. "If I remember correctly, your constellation has only existed for twenty-some years. If you help us fight for Kichona, you might be helping your mother, too. And Zomuri wouldn't be mad. You're not doing anything related to Prince Gin's soul or actually fighting him. That's our job."

Liga considered it.

"What do you say?" Sora asked.

"Well, even if I assented, I could not stay long. If our

father notices I'm missing and why, I might be exiled from the sky, too. I'm happy to have reconnected with you, Wolf, but I don't wish to leave Celestae as you did."

"I understand completely," Daemon said.

Liga looked around at Sora, Fairy, and Broomstick. "You've picked a scrappy crew, brother. Clever, too."

Daemon nodded. "It's what makes us good."

Sora glowed with pride.

Liga thought about it for a moment more. "I can stay for a short while before Vespre notices I'm gone. I will teach Wolf about his powers." He grinned. "Things were getting dull in Celestae anyway."

CHAPTER SIXTEEN

The acid pool in the grotto boiled, and Aki's stomach clenched—another ryuu visitor was coming again.

Instead of one orb this time, though, two enormous emerald bubbles surfaced from the depths. The first one opened, and Virtuoso hopped onto shore with a smirk on her face. "Hello again, princess."

Then the second bubble yawned open. Gin stepped out, wearing a crown of gold claws and opulent, embroidered silk robes with dragons slithering up both his arms.

Aki let out an unintentional gasp.

"Hello, sister." He hopped out of the orb as lightly as if this were a social call.

She stood as regally as she could, even though she didn't feel the least bit royal. "What are you doing here?"

"Aren't you happy to see me?"

"When you stole my throne and locked me in some sort of acidic waterfall prison? Not particularly. Why haven't you killed me yet?"

Gin frowned. "Have you already forgotten? Because you made me suffer for the past ten years. Now you'll endure the same fate."

Aki shook her head sadly. "I didn't want to fight you during the Blood Rift. I didn't want you to be hurt or exiled. That was your own doing."

Gin strode across the grotto and grabbed her arms, pinning them to her sides. Aki tried to wriggle away, but his grip was firm.

His nostrils flared as he shook her. "My own doing? After all these years, why can't you see that the Evermore is good for our kingdom and our people?"

Aki closed her eyes for a brief moment. Her brother had always been obsessed with the Evermore.

"It's not worth the cost," Aki said, wrenching herself free from Gin's grip. "It never has been and never will be. Too many lives will be lost. Not only Kichonans but all the people in the mainland kingdoms you have to slaughter in the names of war and glory. What happened to your compassion? You didn't used to be this cruel."

The scarred ridges on Gin's face seemed to harden as his expression did.

Virtuoso took a step forward. Aki had almost forgotten the girl was there.

"There's always a price," Virtuoso said. "But leaders who are truly great aren't afraid of paying it."

"Besides," Gin said to Aki, "whatever qualms I may have harbored disappeared when I gave my soul to Zomuri."

"You gave up your soul?" Dizziness hit Aki, and she had to prop herself up against the grotto wall.

Her brother laughed. "In exchange for being invincible."

"This is wrong," Aki said.

Gin leaned down so he was eye level with her. "I'm going to get what I want. You tried it your way, and you lost. Now it's my turn, and I'm going to succeed in achieving what no other has done before: uniting all the heathen kingdoms on the mainland under our gods and living forever as their immortal emperor. It is what is best for Kichona, and if you'd admit I was right, I might show some leniency. Or you can continue being stubborn."

She looked straight back at him without flinching. "We're twins. We were both cursed with the same obstinacy."

"That's too bad for you." Gin rose. He moved with a sense of cruel purpose.

Fear lodged in Aki's throat.

CHAPTER SEVENTEEN

Hana watched as Emperor Gin stood over his sister and gestured at his orb.

"What are you doing, Your Majesty?" Hana asked.

A coil of thin tubing floated over to him. "Showing my sister something I learned about while in exile. I'll get it started, and you'll finish it."

Hana nodded obediently as the heat of anticipation washed through her body, the magic at her fingertips eager to serve the Dragon Emperor.

A bucket floated out of Gin's orb and dunked itself into the pool of acid.

Empress—no, *Princess* Aki pressed herself into the wall, as if an extra millimeter would keep her safe.

"Dear sister," Gin said. "I'd like to introduce you to Shinowanan acid torture. It's a slow drip, terribly painful but effective." He cast a spell to bind Princess Aki's arms behind her and her ankles together.

"Hey!" She struggled but couldn't break free of the bonds.

The ryuu magic lifted her several feet off the ground and rotated her as if she were a rabbit on a spit.

Something inside Hana trembled. But why? She believed in Emperor Gin and his pursuit of the Evermore, and this was part of what it took to achieve it.

There was a tiny spigot at the bottom of the bucket. Gin attached one end of the tube to it, then floated the bucket above Princess Aki's head. The acid dribbled down into the tube. Gravity would do the rest.

Hana gasped. "Your Majesty, you don't mean to . . . ?"

"She's my twin," Gin said. "My suffering began not with exile after the Blood Rift. It started long before that, when I was made hideous with these scars. My sister is about to learn how it feels to be so ugly."

A drop began to form. It would fall on Princess Aki's cheek any second.

Oh gods. Hana had to look away. She had killed her fair share of people, but this was a member of the imperial family, someone anointed by the gods. . . .

"Gin, please!" the princess cried.

"It's your choice how long this goes," he said. "You always have the ability to make it stop. Just say I'm right. Just say you, too, want the Evermore for Kichona."

"I won't."

Hana dared to look back.

The drop of acid swelled.

And then it fell.

Princess Aki screamed as the acid seared the apple of

her cheek. Her flesh bubbled and popped where the acid had hit.

A wave of nausea surged in Hana's gut.

Another drop was already forming.

The princess tried to twist away from its path, but there would be no way to escape it.

Gin just shook his head, as if he thought his sister ought to take her punishment with more dignity. "Virtuoso, take it from here. I'm going back to the castle."

Hana stared wide eyed at the bucket of acid. "But she's a member of the imperial family."

"And I'm the emperor, giving you a direct order." He shook his head. "You're usually a tornado of violence when presented with opportunities like this. You had no issue with the command to assassinate my sister in Dassu Desert, but you can't do this?"

Hana twisted the hem of her tunic. "Spirit carried out your orders in Dassu Desert."

Princess Aki stared at Hana, as if just realizing that she was Spirit's younger sister. Two siblings on opposite sides of a war, just like the princess and Gin.

The second drop of acid splattered on Princess Aki's cheek then, searing into her skin, and she screamed.

Hana cringed.

"Virtuoso," Emperor Gin said, "whatever your lingering issues about the imperial family, get over them. Aki is a prisoner of war, and you will treat her as such."

Hana's heart pounded as if attempting to stage a rebellion.

I am a good solider, she told herself. *The most loyal of all ryuu.* If the emperor said this was how it had to be, then he was right. The gods *wanted* him to do this; they let him come back from the brink of death with new magic because pursuing the Evermore was his destiny. And serving him was Hana's.

Emperor Gin stepped into his green orb.

"Brother—" Aki strained at her bindings.

"I wish it had turned out differently," he said. "Maybe if you'd just let me rule from the start, we wouldn't be here like this. But . . ." He shrugged as though there were nothing he could do to change the course he was taking. The emerald sphere closed around him. It sank into the grotto pool, whisking Gin away.

Another drop of acid hung like a threat above Aki.

"Please," she said to Hana. "I can tell you still don't want to carry out his orders. Just like Spirit, you're better than this."

Hana's eyes flashed. "Don't you dare compare me to Spirit. As far as I'm concerned, I have no sister."

And yet, after another scathing glare, Hana floated the bucket of acid away and lowered Princess Aki to the ground.

What am I doing? Hana asked herself. *I need to follow orders. I won't be weak like I was before.*

"Thank you." Princess Aki exhaled.

Her gratitude—as if they were on the same side—snapped Hana back to her senses.

"Don't be so hasty in your thanks," she said. "Emperor Gin is right. You're a prisoner of war, and I need to treat you like it. I may not burn you with acid, but I'll still carry out the intent of what he wants." Hana raised her fist.

The princess cowered.

"This is for defying the emperor." Hana smashed an uppercut into Princess Aki's face.

"This is for refusing to support his pursuit of the Evermore." Hana kneed her in the gut, and the princess doubled over.

"Please . . . ," Princess Aki gasped. "Please stop."

Hana scoffed, but she turned as if she were going to walk away.

Then she paused. *There's one more thing that deserves punishment.*

"And this, Your Highness, is for bringing up my sister." Hana whirled, leg extended, then hooked it with vicious flare.

The princess crumpled, unconscious, onto the grotto floor.

A chill of guilt rippled through Hana.

But her anger and sense of righteousness were stronger, and they quickly burned away the cold pang of conscience. She had been too soft in the past, too easy on Sora and Princess Aki, and the mess of that battle in the Imperial City had been the result. Hana needed to make up for it.

She climbed into the emerald orb and sailed away, without bothering to look back.

CHAPTER EIGHTEEN

After Sora and Broomstick left the next morning, Daemon turned his attention to learning how to use his new magic. It was what he'd wanted from the start, when Sora had decided to return to Kichona. If Daemon could turn into a wolf and use his speed and electricity at will, the balance of power would change between their side and Prince Gin's. Daemon would be able to fly, and Sora could make them invisible; they might be able to reunite the soul pearl with the Dragon Prince before he even realized they were upon him.

And then Daemon and Sora could kill him.

"Shifting forms is easy," Liga said. He changed himself from human to giant blue alligator and back again.

"You can't just do it and not explain it," Daemon said, frowning.

"Ah, right. The way to transform is . . ." Liga leaned against one of the chestnut trees as he thought through the process.

Fairy busied herself nearby on a set of boulders, which she'd converted into a temporary botanicals lab. Since waking up, she'd already distilled five new potions and was in the process of sun-drying several types of wild herbs.

Liga didn't move a muscle for a good five minutes. Daemon kept watching him, expecting some explanation on how to manage the shift. But it apparently wasn't forthcoming.

"You know," Fairy finally said as she poured black liquid into a vial of red powder, "when humans start sentences, they usually finish them. Within a few seconds."

Liga looked at her and smiled as if this were fascinating. "Really?"

"Um, yes?" She sneaked a look over at Daemon and mouthed, *Are we sure about him?*

Daemon smirked. Still, he liked Liga. His brother was a little . . . different, but what did they expect? Unlike Sola, Luna, Vespre, and Zomuri, Liga had never been on earth before. All he knew of mortals were stories he'd been told in Celestae. It also explained why his speech was so odd— deities didn't speak human languages in the heavens, so talking to Daemon and Fairy like this was a completely new experience for Liga.

"So about the shift?" Daemon prompted.

"You need more conviction," Liga said.

"Which means?"

"Embrace your identity, and show us who you really are."

Daemon sighed. Typical Liga, trying to be helpful but coming out nonsensically cryptic instead.

"Wolf, you did it the other day," Fairy said.

"By accident. I'm terrible at magic—taiga *and* demigod."

"I have faith in you," Fairy said.

"That's it precisely," Liga said. "Wolf, you haven't been able to shift forms at will because you haven't believed in yourself."

Daemon grumbled. "To be fair, I haven't known I was a demigod for that long."

"A valid point," Liga said, pacing like one of the Society teachers would in front of a classroom. "But from what I've gathered, you've not believed in yourself for much longer than that. It's time you accepted who you are and everything you can do."

"Maybe that's the problem. I don't *know* what I can do."

Liga nodded thoughtfully. "Let me show you." He leaped into the air and hovered there, as if a current kept him buoyed. "All demigods can fly, as well as conjure small things." He snapped his fingers, and the sound of lutes filled the chestnut grove.

"We are stronger, faster, and more agile than taigas and ryuu could ever dream of." Liga zipped through the trees in a blur, so quickly that Daemon swore he could still see the silhouette of an alligator between the branches even after Liga had already returned to where he started. "We're not immortal, but we can heal ourselves if given the chance." He sliced his skin with a talon. Fairy gasped, but his flesh melded itself together before their eyes.

"On top of that," Liga continued, landing on the forest floor, "all of Vespre's children have powers related to the stars or night sky. Some, like me, can dim light." He looked up at the sky, and it shifted from bright morning sun to the purpled gray of dusk and back again to daylight. "Others can ride electricity like comets. And you—when you were still a constellation in Celestae—were able to manipulate gravitational pull, as stars and black holes do."

"I could do what?" Daemon's eyes widened in disbelief.

"You could play with gravity."

Daemon's jaw dropped. "I can't believe I had all of that once, and I gave it up."

Liga smiled. "You can still have it. You just have to try. Starting with the basics."

Just try. Daemon took a deep breath, shook out his limbs, and prepared to shift.

"I am an electric wolf," he said.

Nope. He was a boy.

"I am an electric wolf."

Still a boy.

"Say it with more feeling," Liga said.

"I am an electric wolf!" Daemon shouted.

Nothing, gods dammit!

Fairy wrinkled her nose.

"What?" Daemon said, a little more harshly than he meant to.

"Nothing."

"Sorry, I'm frustrated." He took a deep breath. "Do you have a suggestion?" he asked slowly so that he didn't snarl the question.

"It's just that . . ." She waved a fern frond in the air as she figured out the best way to say it. "I don't think yelling equates with believing in yourself. It might actually be the opposite."

Daemon kicked a tree, and chestnuts rained down on him. "Ugh! I'll never be able to do this."

"Do you want to take a break from practicing?" she asked. "We need to go into the Imperial City anyway."

Before Sora and Broomstick had left, they'd agreed that Daemon and Fairy would return to the Citadel and bloodstone palace every day to keep looking for clues to Empress Aki's whereabouts and to try to put a wrench into whatever the Dragon Prince's plans were. Sora had created several dozen dragonflies made from ryuu particles and enchanted them to be able to find her. That way, Daemon and Fairy would be able to send daily messages to her and Broomstick and vice versa, on top of communicating emotions through their gemina bonds.

"I don't think we should go into the Imperial City until it's dark," Daemon said, wiping sweat from his brow.

"That's probably wise," Fairy said. "Keep practicing, then."

Liga had been studying Daemon. He snapped his fingers, and blue sparks appeared, hovering in the air and forming themselves into a three-dimensional wolf made of stardust. "Perhaps if you envisioned the end state," Liga said.

Daemon looked at the illusion dubiously. It wasn't the easiest advice to follow, since being a constellation was so new. Or rather, he supposed, it was old knowledge, but Vespre had hidden it from Daemon when he left the sky and was reincarnated as a newborn baby. The memories were still inside Daemon, but buried deep, as his other powers had been.

"Wait, I have an idea," Fairy said. She set down the plant she was dissecting and bounded over to Daemon. "This worked last time to give you some confidence."

Before he knew what she was doing, she stood on the tips of her toes and kissed his neck softly. Then another, her lips like warm silk. He turned to putty.

"Liga, go for a walk, please," Daemon said, his voice gruff.

His brother chuckled. "I'll give you ten minutes, but then we have to get back to work." He turned away and disappeared into the woods.

Daemon's mouth was on Fairy's in an instant, his days'-old stubble against her smooth skin. Their bodies smashed together, too, and the force sent them tumbling to the ground, scattering dried leaves and chestnuts everywhere.

Holy heavens, he'd been stupid to wait so many years for something like this.

Fairy lay on top of Daemon and turned her attention to his neck again. He moaned and wove his hands through her hair.

"You're going to leave a mark," he said.

"No, I'm not. It'll disappear as soon as you change into a wolf."

"What if I can't shift?"

"Then your neck will be marred forever." Fairy flashed a wicked grin.

"You're going to pay for that."

"Oh, really? How?"

"Like this." Daemon wrapped his arms around her back and rolled so he was on top. She shrieked in surprise.

He wanted her perfect little mouth again. Their lips parted, and their tongues danced slowly with each other. Daemon pressed his body against Fairy's, and she arched her back and hips to meet him. The only thing between them was a few layers of clothing. Damn the late-autumn chill for all these clothes!

Fairy reached up to unfasten his cloak but only made it through one button.

"Why are you stopping?" Daemon asked.

"The sky is darkening like a storm's coming."

"It didn't look like rain earlier."

She smiled regretfully and refastened his cloak. "I don't think it's a real storm. I think it's Liga giving us a warning that our ten minutes are up."

Daemon sighed heavily. "And here I always thought I'd love having a sibling." He rolled off Fairy.

She kissed him one last time, then climbed to her feet and offered him a hand up. "Do you feel a little better about yourself now?"

He couldn't help but laugh. "It'd be impossible not to. The way you want me . . . it makes me feel like a god. Well, a demigod."

"Good. I'm here for reassurance whenever you need it." Fairy winked. "Although eventually, it would probably be good if you could shift forms without me having to kiss you. Not that I don't want to, but it might be difficult if, say, we were in the middle of a battle."

"Are you two decent?" Liga called from nearby. The sky cleared back to its normal morning brightness.

"You didn't give us enough time to be otherwise," Daemon said.

Liga emerged from the woods. "My apologies, brother. But I need to return to Celestae soon, so I must teach you what I can quickly."

Daemon bit his lip, but he crossed his arms over his chest and stood tall. "I'm ready."

"Remember," Liga said. "You are not merely a boy. You are a son of Vespre and grandson of Luna. You are the wolf of the stars and a master of gravity. Embrace who you truly are."

Daemon closed his eyes for a moment and imagined himself as all those things.

Not just a boy.

Wolf of the stars.

Descended from gods.

Daemon's skin buzzed, lightly at first, then strong enough that his skin vibrated. Heat prickled in his veins, and when he opened his eyes, he saw the tiny sparks bursting around him creating a faint blue aura.

"He's doing it," Fairy said, but her voice was almost lost in the noise of the electricity.

It felt different this time. In the past, he hadn't noticed the subtle changes that happened before he turned into a wolf. Maybe he did now, though, because he was asking for the shift, coaxing the magic to transform him.

Daemon could tell when the shift really began to take hold, because the power of the sky filled his lungs, his heart, and his entire being to their limits. He was suddenly bigger than he'd ever been, not just physically but intangibly, too, as if his existence had expanded. Every sound was sharper, every color more saturated. He thought if he tried he'd be able to see around to the other side of the worl

Liga's clapping brought him back from awe. "Well done, brother."

Daemon looked at his thick blue fur, his paws, at the tail behind him. He was solid, an understood that this was what it meant to be a stars connected the way humans thought of it, n of the stars and a master of gravity. Embrace who you truly are."

Daemon closed his eyes for a moment and imagined himself as all those things.

Not just a boy.

Wolf of the stars.

Descended from gods.

Daemon's skin buzzed, lightly at first, then strong enough that his skin vibrated. Heat prickled in his veins, and when he opened his eyes, he saw the tiny sparks bursting around him creating a faint blue aura.

"He's doing it," Fairy said, but her voice was almost lost in the noise of the electricity.

It felt different this time. In the past, he hadn't noticed the subtle changes that happened before he turned into a wolf. Maybe he did now, though, because he was asking for the shift, coaxing the magic to transform him.

Daemon could tell when the shift really began to take hold, because the power of the sky filled his lungs, his heart, and his entire being to their limits. He was suddenly bigger than he'd ever been, not just physically but intangibly, too, as if his existence had expanded. Every sound was sharper, every color more saturated. He thought if he tried, he'd be able to see around to the other side of the world.

Liga's clapping brought him back from his awe. "Well done, brother."

Daemon looked at his thick blue fur, at his paws, at the tail behind him. He was solid, and yet he understood that this was what it meant to be a constellation—just not the way humans thought of it, not mere stars connected by empty space and drawn-in lines. Sparks danced around Daemon like stardust, and he could feel the pull of earth's gravity at his mind, almost inviting him to play.

He started to reach for it.

The chestnut trees creaked, as if whimpering, and began to bow toward him.

"Halt!" Liga said.

Fairy was crouched on the ground, arms over her head to protect her from falling trees.

Liga wagged a taloned finger. "First you need to practice transitioning back and forth from wolf to human and back again. It'll give you a better feel for your magic. Then you'll be able to reacquaint yourself with your gravitational power without inadvertently damaging anything."

"Spoilsport," Daemon grumbled.

The trees eased gratefully back into their normal positions. *Sorry*, he thought to them.

"How do I turn back into a boy?" he asked.

"The same way you shifted into a wolf," Liga said.

Daemon nodded. It had really been as simple as knowing he could do it and then thinking about the end state. He began to concentrate on his human form again. Until he remembered that he'd be naked when he shifted. His clothes were jumbled in a pile nearby, but that wasn't the same as covering him the moment he turned into a boy.

"Uh, do you two mind turning away?"

Fairy let out a fake indignant huff. But then she winked and spun around.

Despite currently being a wolf, Daemon flushed.

Liga pointed at him with an alligator claw. "Focus, brother. Once you have better control of your magic, you'll be able to conjure clothes to cover yourself simultaneously with your shift." Then Liga also averted his gaze.

Daemon glanced down at his furry paws. He flicked his tail in the air. And then he imagined those gone, replaced instead by the version of himself he'd known for eighteen years.

The buzzing and blue light came faster this time, as did the transformation.

He'd hardly taken a breath, and he was a boy again.

CHAPTER NINETEEN

Two days after they'd left Jade Forest, Sora and Broomstick arrived in Samara Village at the base of the mountain where her parents lived. It was on the way south toward Naimo Ice Caves, and Sora wanted to look through her mother's research to see if there was anything in there about the Lake of Nightmares. What Liga said didn't seem right—that Zomuri wouldn't bother protecting his vault from mortals. They might not have god magic, but there was still treasure in there, and greed was a well-known human flaw. Retrieving the Dragon Prince's soul was too important for Sora to skip a quick detour for whatever information she could find.

Sora smiled, though, as she led Broomstick into the village. Shops with colorful wooden doors lined the streets, the smell of morning frost filled the air, and birds chirped from the rooftops. Broomstick had never been here before—he always went home to his own family during school holidays—and Sora could hardly wait to show him around her cheerful little village and take him up to her house on the cliffs.

"Come this way," she said, leading him toward the main square. "There's always a rainbow of lanterns strung up this time of year. And musicians take turns playing in the plaza at all hours. Oh, and you have to see the huge fountain where Daemon, Hana, and I used to play during Autumn Festival breaks. . . ."

Sora caught herself at the casual mention of Hana. It poked like a splinter beneath her skin.

But she didn't want to feel sad or worried right now, not when Samara Village was home to so many *good* memories. Sora squeezed her eyes shut to wring out the disquieting thoughts and focused back on the heartwarming ones.

"You know what else you'll love?" she said to Broomstick, slapping a smile back on her face. "There's a dumpling shop that makes all their wrappers by hand for the perfect texture. They're usually not open this early, but I know the owner, so we might be able to pop in the back door to see what he's cooking up today and steal a bite—"

Sora stopped short as they entered the square. Instead of brightly painted shop doors and rainbows of flags and kites flying from the eaves, the plaza was gray with smoke. Sparks from at least two dozen anvils and the steady pounding of metal—swords being forged—filled the air with an ominous rhythm.

"Wh-where's my fountain?" Sora said.

Broomstick's mouth set in a grim line. "Replaced by a weapons forge for the Dragon Prince."

She spun around. The doors to the stores, once painted with lively pictures of what was sold inside, were all covered in soot and ash. Sora ran to the back entrance of the dumpling shop and pounded on it.

"Mr. Zaki! Are you there? It's Sora Teira. Please open up!"

The door opened a crack. Kind Mr. Zaki peered out, his wrinkles like a shar-pei's, his hands covered in flour. He must have been in the middle of making dumpling wrappers.

"What do you want?" he spat.

Stunned at his meanness, Sora stuttered as she tried to speak. "I-it's me. Um, Mina and Jiro Teira's daughter."

"Do you think my memory's gone just because I'm old? I don't have time for this." He began to slam the door shut.

Sora stuck her foot in the small opening just in time, wincing at the impact.

What had happened to him, though? She'd never heard Mr. Zaki utter an unkind word before. He always had a smile ready for every customer, and at the end of each night, he put out leftover dumplings in a dish behind his store so the stray cats would have something to eat.

"Mr. Zaki," she said carefully, "are you all right? Is something going on?" Sora lowered her voice to a whisper. "Has Prince Gin made things difficult for you with this weapons forge in the square?"

"How dare you speak about our sovereign with such disrespect!" Mr. Zaki's eyes went wide with outrage. "Get out before I report you for being disloyal to the crown!" He grabbed a metal spatula and lunged toward Sora.

She gasped and jumped back.

He slammed the door shut.

Tears welled and threatened to spill over. Broomstick,

who had witnessed everything, wrapped his arm around her.

"I don't understand," he said. "Prince Gin couldn't have already made it here to hypnotize everyone. He and the ryuu have been busy in the Imperial City." They hurried out of the main square and to the outskirts of town, toward the mountain. "There's something bigger than us going on here."

"You can say that again," Sora said weakly.

Broomstick steered Sora out of the village. "Come on, let's get you to your parents. I'm sure you'll feel better once you're home."

Sora didn't say anything as they started up the winding switchbacks. It hadn't sunk in before that Prince Gin's war machine could already have reached Samara Village, even though she knew what his goals were.

Then something else dawned on Sora. If this inexplicable wretchedness could affect the people in Samara Village, then it could reach up the mountain, too.

"Mama! Papa!" She started sprinting.

"Spirit, pace yourself," Broomstick yelled from behind her. "Or at least let me get us some horses to help!" There was still a long way to go up the steep mountainside.

He had a point. But Sora couldn't slow down. "I'm sorry, I have to go ahead. Meet me there!" She commanded the ryuu particles to lift her, and they whisked her up the switchbacks, leaving Broomstick behind in the dust.

CHAPTER TWENTY

Her parents' home perched on the cliffs above the glistening sea, serene and so removed from the smoke and noise of the village below it seemed possible that everything would be all right. The air was scented with damp cypress boughs, just as Sora remembered, and the steps leading up to the front door were swept clean. She made her way into the small courtyard, with its wooden path and well-tended garden of ferns and baby maple trees and river-polished pebbles, and paused outside the room to the right, Papa's pottery studio.

He sat at his wheel, pumping the pedal steadily to keep the platform turning, oblivious to the fact that anyone was watching. He had clay on his mustache and a smear of paint across his cheek, and those details combined with the soothing rhythm of the pedal filled Sora's chest with relief. All was well here. She'd been afraid for nothing.

"Hello, Papa," Sora said softly.

His hands faltered at the sound of her voice, and the clay

he'd been carefully working wobbled on the wheel, growing lopsided. He snapped up his head and glared at her.

Sora took a step back. Papa had never looked at her that way before. Both her parents doted on her but Papa more so. He was the one who always insisted on giving her the best bed when she came to visit. Who couldn't stop smiling proudly at his taiga daughter when she and Daemon did their exercises in the mornings, keeping in shape on school breaks by sparring on the deck and jumping in the trees that clung to the cliffside. Scowling was so unfamiliar it seemed uncomfortable on his face.

"Look what you've done," Papa said, grabbing the lopsided clay from the wheel and hurling it at the wall. It hit with a loud splat, and Sora jumped. "I suppose you expect that you can just drop in unannounced because you're a taiga and that your mother will have food on the stove for you and a bath drawn to welcome Your Honor's return? All hail Luna's chosen one."

Sora cringed at the acidic sarcasm with which he said the moon goddess's name and the title "Your Honor." It was the standard honorific for taigas, but she'd always insisted that her parents call her Sora. It had been their choice over the years to address her and Daemon as "Your Honor." Papa had claimed it was a privilege to be able to do so, because not everyone got to have a child blessed by Luna with taiga magic.

"I—I'm sorry," she said. "I happened to be passing through the area, and I wanted to check on you."

Papa frowned. He stared at his pottery wheel as if he were deep in thought, then shook his head sharply. "Your Honor," he said, with reverence this time. "I apologize. I don't know what came over me. Of course you are welcome home anytime." He rose, took off his apron, and approached Sora with arms outstretched to give her a hug.

She let him, but she was tense, not sure if this was real remorse or if he would lash out again.

It was a genuine embrace, though, and when he released her, Papa smiled in his familiar way, eyes glistening and crinkled at the corners.

What in the hells is going on? Sora thought.

He led her through the interior courtyard, into the main house. It was a small structure, but he hollered nevertheless. "Mina! Guess who surprised us with a visit!"

Mama burst out of her study, pencil still in hand. "Your Honor!" Her eyes brightened, and she bowed deeply.

Their joy made everything feel normal and right, if only for a moment. But then Sora remembered that she hadn't seen them since she found out that Hana was still alive, and that she hadn't been killed as a child during the Blood Rift.

Should I tell them?

They had a right to know. And yet, this didn't seem the proper time. It would mean explaining not only that their younger daughter was alive but also that she was fighting for the wrong side. That Sora had tried to show her the error of following Prince Gin, but that Hana had turned her back and chosen the pursuits of blood and glory and the Evermore instead.

And then there was Prince Gin's promise—that the next time Sora and Hana met, one of them would end up dead.

It was definitely better not to tell Mama and Papa about Hana now.

A second later, Mama whacked Papa with her pencil.

124

"What kind of host are you? Have you offered our daughter something to drink? A place to sit? She must be exhausted."

"How is this my fault?" he said. "You're the rude one, holed up in your office and not greeting her properly."

"I didn't even know she was here!"

"Maybe if you paid better attention—"

"Whoa whoa whoa," Sora said, horrified. "I'm fine. Don't worry. Everything's fine."

Except it wasn't. There was something wrong with her parents, just like something had been wrong with Mr. Zaki in the village. As if the sunlight that usually shone on their lives had been replaced with putrid green rot.

Sora gasped. *Or like Sola's brightness on our kingdom has been overshadowed by Zomuri's selfish pettiness.*

Could this be what that conversation Fairy overheard in the Citadel was about? Something about how Zomuri being the kingdom's new patron god was influencing people? It certainly seemed as if his cruelty were dripping into Kichona, like a sickness falling over the people and the land.

Sora looked at Mama and Papa casting daggers of blame over an imagined problem. Their fury sliced into Sora, too, but in a different way—it pained her to see them like this.

This has to be stopped. Sora couldn't let Mama and Papa stay this way forever.

For now, though, she needed to distract them from their argument. "Papa, I want to bring a gift back to my teachers," she lied. "Would you be able to pick a sake set from your collection for me? They are always so impressed with your artistry. And Mama," she said, "I have a mythology project for my literature class that involves the Lake of Nightmares. But I have no idea where to start. Have you come across this lake in your work, maybe in your research for the Kichonan Tales?"

They both blinked.

Papa nodded happily. "I would be honored to give a sake set to your teachers. I'll look for something right away." He hurried out of the house toward his studio, almost skipping as he went.

Mama, however, frowned. "You said your project was on the Lake of Nightmares? What an esoteric legend. There really isn't much about it."

"But you've heard of it?" Sora asked.

"Oh yes, of course I've come across it. Legend has it that Zomuri buried his treasure deep inside ice caverns, at the bottom of a lake enchanted to give anyone who touched its waters horrible nightmares. Those greedy enough to try to break into the god's vault will see visions of the worst versions of themselves. The hallucinations are so vivid, people either drown as they get lost in them or drown themselves out of despair for who they think they'll become in the future."

A chill ran down Sora's spine. So Liga *had* been wrong about the vault not being protected against mortals.

"Do you think those stories are true?" Sora asked.

"Perhaps." Mama shrugged as they walked into her study. "I believe that mythology stems from a combination of truth and fantasy. Most storytellers are not so creative that they can invent tales from whole cloth. They begin with reality, then embellish it."

Sora chewed on her lip as she thought about that.

Mama climbed a short ladder so she could reach her top bookshelf. She coughed as she retrieved a dusty box.

"There might be something in here," she said, setting the box on her desk. Mama began to flip through the notebooks and papers inside.

Sora gave her space to work. Soon enough, Mama pulled out a small journal the size of her palm. "This is what I was looking for. I used to carry it in my pocket when I was a university student. That was the only time I did any research around the topic of the Lake of Nightmares." She handed the journal to Sora.

Inside, Mama's neat cursive filled the pages. There were notes on all sorts of random things, like a snapshot of her young mind and its many interests before she found her calling in retelling Kichonan legends. There were a few pages on imperial coronation fashion through the ages, a section with doodles of griffins and an idea for a short story, and a page with her monthly budget as a student. Sora smiled at this insight into Mama's life.

Then Sora found what she was looking for. On a tea-stained page, Mama had jotted some notes about a single historical account from a man who had purportedly found the Lake of Nightmares and returned to tell about it.

- *Party of 10 went in; all died but 1.*
- *Magnetic fields in the ice tunnels. Party split up, and half got lost, never heard from again.*
- *Ghost faces and snow monster.*
- *Lake will keep you if you step foot in it.*

Sora flipped to the next page. There were a bit of poetry and another griffin doodle but nothing more about Naimo Ice Caves or the Lake of Nightmares.

"Is this all you have?" Sora asked.

"Yes," Mama said. "That's why I never bothered to write a story about the lake. There's not enough information out there."

Papa barreled into the study then, carrying a tray of small blue cups and a sake carafe in his right hand and a box with orange cups and matching carafe in his left. "Do you think your teachers would like blue or orange better?" he asked.

"You stupid man!" Mama said, snatching both the tray and box away from him. "The Society is too important and busy to care about your pottery. Can't you see that our daughter was just trying to give you something to do so you'd feel important while she took care of the real reason for her visit—discussing her school project with *me*?"

"Your arrogance is out of control!" Papa shouted. "Ever since you were awarded that prize for literature, you think you're the greatest living mind in the kingdom!"

"You're lucky I deigned to marry a pea brain like you!"

"I seem to recall *you* admired *me* when we first met. My family have been master potters for centuries—"

Sora watched sadly. "I'm sorry I can't help you right now," she said, even though they couldn't hear her over their own yelling. "But I'm going to stop this madness as soon as I can. Everything will be better then. I promise."

Her parents didn't even notice when she ducked out the door and left the house.

Half a mile down the road, she met Broomstick, who had somehow procured horses for them and just turned the final bend in the switchback. He was covered in dust and sweat, and he looked like he could have used a good meal and bath at her parents' house.

But one look at the way Sora's shoulders drooped and he offered her a horse and turned them around, heading away from food and rest, going back down the mountain.

"Were they like the dumpling maker?" Broomstick asked.

Sora nodded, lips pressed tightly together. She'd held her emotions together in front of her parents, but now that she'd left them, it began to sink in how bad the situation was. How her parents' goodness was being eaten away, like a worm nibbling through an apple. If the worm got to the core, would Mama and Papa rot for good? Sora stifled a sob.

"With Kichona dedicated to Zomuri," Sora said, "I think the kingdom will only get darker. We have to get that soul and kill Prince Gin before it's too late. Kichona needs Empress Aki and Sola."

Sora wiped away the tears threatening to overflow. She wouldn't cry. Not yet. She was a fighter. A warrior. The last of the protectors of Kichona. She would not let her parents succumb to Zomuri and the Dragon Prince's rule.

She pulled her shoulders back. "No more stops," she said. Partly because she couldn't bear to see other people influenced like Mama, Papa, and Mr. Zaki and partly because she wanted to get to Naimo Ice Caves as quickly as possible.

"We're going to find Prince Gin's soul," Sora said. "And we're going to destroy him, no matter what the cost."

CHAPTER TWENTY-ONE

Fairy held tightly to one of the ridges on Liga's back as they flew through the moon-shadowed sky. She'd thought sitting on an alligator would be a lot less comfortable, but because Liga was in constellation form—albeit with his sparks dimmed to keep them concealed—his hide was strangely ethereal, buttery smooth yet light as stardust. Combined with the fact that Wolf was pressed warmly behind her, Fairy was quite content as they glided toward their nightly mission to keep tabs on Prince Gin and look for any clues about Empress Aki's whereabouts.

"How do we engage in subversion?" Liga asked in his typical awkward way as they approached the Citadel. He'd offered to come not only because it would be easier for Fairy and Wolf if he flew them but also because he was fascinated by the human conflict unfolding before him.

Wolf spoke up to answer Liga's question. "We sneak very quietly, make sure we don't get caught, and throw wrenches in the ryuu's gears."

"I didn't bring any wrenches," Liga said.

"Not literal wrenches," Fairy said. "It's just a saying—"

But Liga wasn't listening, because at the same time he said, "Ah, but I can conjure them when you need them!"

She just let that one go.

They landed in the Citadel in the middle of the outdoor amphitheater with its broad black stage and rows of benches set into the grass, where the apprentices had watched many years of graduation ceremonies before them. After a quick pass, they confirmed there was nothing suspicious there.

Next was the sparring arena, where they'd spent countless hours with the taiga weapons master throwing knives, dueling with swords, and fighting with bare hands. Like when Broomstick had last been here, there were a few ryuu practicing their skills, even this late at night. Fairy refused to look into the center of the arena; she didn't want to see if any of the girls from her dormitory or other classmates were there. And it seemed like business as usual—at least, business of the ryuu variety—so she, Wolf, and Liga quickly moved on.

They snuck through the warrior enclave, a neighborhood of black wood-framed homes for Councilmembers, teachers, and other taiga warriors who lived at the Citadel. Then the apprentice portion of the campus, with its dorms and the tall building where they had classes. Fairy could almost smell the chalk and hear their teachers' voices. Seeing all this at once—and knowing what was going on inside these fortress walls—was even harder than the last time she'd spied here.

"Perhaps we should take to the air again," Liga said after they'd almost been caught several times.

"Agreed," Fairy said. "It'll be good to get a bird's-eye view to see if there's any unusual activity."

"You mean an alligator's-eye view," Liga said.

Fairy groaned.

"I understand that is what mortals call a joke."

Wolf chuckled under his breath, although Fairy was pretty sure he was mostly laughing *at* his brother, not with him.

They climbed onto Liga's back again, and he soared upward, doing an aerial pass over the Citadel.

Near the far edge of the fortress, Liga made a guttural noise in his throat. "I may not know much about humans, but I'd wager *that* qualifies as 'unusual activity'?" He pointed his snout toward what were usually fields for sports and other games.

They weren't empty lawns anymore.

Fairy leaned forward. "Are those *ships*?"

Wolf pressed against her to get a better look. "Good gods. They've turned our athletic fields into a shipyard."

Indeed, there were dozens of war vessels in various stages of construction. Fairy shook her head in disbelief. "How did they build that many so quickly?"

"If I may posit a theory," Liga said, "perhaps it is the doing of their so-called ryuu magic. If they possess the ability to work with wood, metal, and other such elements, it is possible to draw the conclusion that they could construct entire naval fleets much more rapidly than ordinary humans."

"Translating for my brother," Wolf said, "the ryuu are evil, magical shipbuilders."

"And from the looks of it, it won't be long until they're

ready to attack one of the mainland kingdoms," Fairy said.

"They'll probably hit Thoma first," Wolf said, shaking his head sadly.

Fairy cursed. Thoma was a small island just off the coast of the continent. It wasn't technically part of the mainland, but it used to be part of Xerlinis until an earthquake broke it off a couple centuries ago. That's why, to this day, whenever anyone talked about the "mainland kingdoms," those still included Thoma.

"You're right," Fairy said. "With these ships and that ryuu who controls the water, they could overwhelm Thoma before their forces had a chance to fight back."

"We need to stop their progress," Wolf said. "I think this calls for some sabotage, don't you?"

"I do love a bit of intrigue," Liga said. "Just tell me what to do."

Fairy turned to consult with Wolf. "Ideas?"

He took in the shipyard below. "Setting it all on fire would probably be too obvious."

"Agreed. We want to hurt them without letting them know we're around. Otherwise we won't be able to come back, and we have to be able to do that so we can keep searching for Empress Aki."

Wolf rubbed at the stubble along his jaw. "We could punch holes in the bottoms of the ships."

Fairy smiled. "And if we made the holes small enough, they wouldn't notice until they were ready to launch."

"Too bad we don't have any tools on us."

"What sort of tools do you need?" Liga asked. "What about these?" A leather sheath full of needle-tipped awls appeared from thin air.

"Wow." Fairy gawked as she reached for one. It weighed nothing, yet it was solid in her hand. The tip of the awl gleamed almost wickedly, seeming to be made of something much sharper and stronger than metal.

Wolf took an awl out of the leather sheath, too, and whistled appreciatively.

"Shall we engage in some sabotage, then?" Liga asked. His flying grew bouncier with his excitement. "It appears the ryuu have ceased their shipbuilding operations for the night. I surmise this would be the perfect opportunity."

Wolf and Fairy shared a smile.

"Take us down, Liga," she said. "I feel like causing some trouble."

CHAPTER TWENTY-TWO

A day after fleeing from Samara Mountain, Sora finally slowed down.

Broomstick pulled on the reins of his horse. He hadn't complained at all, knowing that Sora needed to put some physical space between herself and what she'd seen of her parents.

However, during their ride, a dragonfly messenger from Daemon and Fairy had caught up with them.

"An entire shipyard? Crow's eye," she'd sworn, horrified, as she passed the tiny scroll to Broomstick. Daemon, Fairy, and Liga had also flown over the nearby towns as dawn broke, and they'd observed formations of men and women marching in unison; it appeared that the Dragon Prince had begun hypnotizing ordinary people to conscript them into his army. The ryuu were fierce warriors, but any army also needed foot soldiers as the first line of defense—or, if you thought of it more cynically, sacrifices.

Broomstick skimmed the scroll and cursed, too. "They're

really moving quickly on their plans to launch a war."

"And Daemon and Fairy still haven't found any signs of the empress."

Sora and Broomstick had been stunned into silence and rode the rest of the afternoon without much conversation.

Now, though, it was time to let the horses rest and to send a message back to Daemon and Fairy.

Broomstick took the horses off to find a place to drink, and Sora tucked herself between a mossy rock and a scraggly tree growing sideways to protect itself from the wind. She began to call on her ryuu particles to form a tiny dragonfly, then she stopped.

Her messengers didn't have to be dragonflies. This was *her* magic. She could make the messenger anything she wanted. Sora smiled a little. When life seemed impossible, holding on to small joys helped her get through to the possible.

Sora closed her eyes and rested her head against the moss. She wanted to create something beautiful, because there was enough that was ugly in the world right now.

She remembered her Level 10 year. The apprentices had learned to dive like the pearl divers did. Sora still recalled one of their lessons when their teacher had led them to the bottom of a sandy canyon and motioned for them to be still.

He'd pointed a stick into the distance.

Sora squinted for a moment, not seeing anything in the sandy water.

Suddenly, though, something emerged from the haze. A fever of eagle rays—eight in all—flapping their wings majestically and in perfect formation like elegant raptors flying in the sky, except they were massive beasts in the bottom of the Kichona Sea. Sora had let out a gasp and forgotten for a moment that she was underwater, that she needed to conserve her breath. Daemon had been there to quickly nudge her chin to close her mouth.

Sora envisioned that dive now as she called on the ryuu particles around her. They coalesced into a shimmering, emerald eagle ray, although much smaller than the ones she had seen. Sora also made it visible, not just ryuu particles that she could see, because otherwise Daemon and Fairy wouldn't know it was there.

Broomstick returned with the horses. He gawked appreciatively at her work.

But whatever joy Sora had felt at creating the eagle ray vanished as she wrote the note to go with it.

> *Dear Daemon and Fairy,*
> *We got your report about Prince Gin's shipyard and how quickly he's going to be ready to declare war. We have to stop him as soon as we can. Keep searching for Empress Aki and hurting Prince Gin in whatever way possible.*
> *Broomstick and I just passed the Striped Coves, and we're about two days away from Naimo Ice Caves. Along the way, though, we've learned a few things—*
> *1. With Zomuri as Kichona's patron god now, Zomuri's viciousness is leeching into the people. They're more irritable than usual and, sometimes, flat-out mean.*
> *2. Mama didn't have much on the Lake of Nightmares other than a few notes, including one that the Lake of Nightmares is made of water that causes hallucinations, making anyone who tries to swim in it believe the worst version of themselves.*

Still, we have to try to get to Zomuri's vault to retrieve the soul pearl. I hope his defenses were made with ordinary humans in mind, not taigas. Broomstick and I will need your help through our gemina bonds. The Lake of Night-mares will try to make us lose faith in ourselves, and you'll have to remind us that we're better than the hallucinations want us to believe.

Broomstick read the note over Sora's shoulder. "I hope your mother's research is wrong about the lake."

Sora nodded. "But I suspect it's not."

She rolled up the paper, attached it to the eagle ray's tail, and sent it off toward Jade Forest.

CHAPTER TWENTY-THREE

Seeing Liga's demigod powers in action and sabotaging the ryuu's shipyard energized Daemon. Anxiety for Sora and Broomstick, on the other hand, sapped him. The only thing he could do to balance the two—and to keep himself from going insane with worry—was throw himself into his magic.

The next day, he practiced shifting from boy to wolf form again and again until he could do it seamlessly, including conjuring clothes for himself at the switch. He and Liga flew figure eights and barrel rolls and nosedives while Daemon learned to suppress the blue sparks that leaped off his fur.

After a particularly impressive set of aerial tricks, he thought of Sora. It seemed wrong that she wasn't here as he finally came into the magic he'd been waiting for. He wanted to watch the smile bloom on her face as he performed a loop-de-loop in the air, her eyes crinkling with joy. Then Daemon would land and charge straight at her, toss Sora on his back, and feel her body pressed against his. . . .

Fairy cheered for him from the ground below. Daemon shook himself from the daydream.

What is wrong with me? he scolded himself. His subconscious needed to let go of its old fantasies.

When it was time for a break from flying practice, he sat on the ground in the chestnut grove with Fairy and played with his other demigod powers, like conjuring something better to eat than the berries Fairy had scavenged. His rose-apple jam and flaky biscuits weren't as good as the ones from the Citadel dining hall, but they pleased her so much, Daemon swore to himself he'd keep on trying to perfect them. Plus, Liga really liked tasting human food.

When evening fell, though, a storm broke out over Jade Forest. Lightning slashed through the sky, and thunder shook the trees. All the remaining chestnuts pelted Daemon, Liga, and Fairy. They were soaked from the rain within seconds.

"It seems our dear father has noticed my absence," Liga said.

Fairy looked up at the gray clouds. "You mean this isn't a normal storm?"

"I recognize the pattern of the lightning," Liga said. "What you see is actually the flash of Vespre's sword as the blade slashes through the sky."

Daemon felt the thunder's vibrations as if they were in his bones. They were an echo of a memory from his past life in Celestae, when he'd witnessed his father's fury firsthand. "You'd better go," he said to Liga. "I'm sorry I kept you for so long."

"But we still need him," Fairy said, rushing forward and

grabbing Liga's wrist, as if that would keep a demigod from leaving if he wanted to. "Wolf, you don't know how to use all your powers yet. What about gravitational magic?"

Liga rested his hand on hers where she gripped him. "I believe my brother can figure it out on his own from here, now that he's reconnected with his true identity. Besides, you have a mission to fulfill—sabotage and spying and an empress to find. That is still important, is it not?"

"But—"

"Fairy," Daemon said gently, "we have to let him go."

Reluctantly, she uncurled her fingers from Liga's wrist. "I know you gods don't like to get involved in human affairs, but don't forget us when you go back to Celestae, okay? Our invitation to you is always open."

Liga smiled. "I promise I will not forget you. And I will return as soon as I can. It turns out I find earth rather fascinating. I cannot let my brother monopolize it all for himself."

Lightning flashed again, brighter and angrier this time. "Go," Daemon said.

"Until next time." Liga gave Fairy a courtly bow, tipped his head at Daemon, then vanished as if he'd never been there.

Daemon blinked at where his brother had just stood. Even though he knew Liga was a demigod, the magnitude of his magic still surprised Daemon.

"I'm going to miss him," he said. Ever since Daemon was taken from the wolves in Takish Gorge, he'd wished for a family. Now he had one, even if it was far away. He looked up. It was too stormy to see the sky, but Daemon smiled anyway, knowing that every constellation up there was a brother or sister. He'd never have to feel alone again.

"I'll miss him, too," Fairy said, "even though he was a little weird."

Daemon laughed. "Well, it's probably good that he's gone, or I would've been tempted to keep practicing with him. But it's night; we need to head back to the Imperial City." They had to keep searching for the empress. Every day that passed increased the risk that the Dragon Prince would do something awful to her or kill her. And it was also of the utmost importance that Daemon and Fairy keep trying to slow his plans in any way they could.

The little space between Fairy's eyebrows crinkled. "It's probably too risky to go back to the Citadel so soon. I hope they didn't discover what we did in the shipyards, but just in case, maybe we should try the castle tonight."

"There's that locked room near the top that Sora and I couldn't get into last time," Daemon said. "Now that I can fly, maybe we can access it from the outside. Do you have your potion that dissolves glass?"

Fairy patted the satchel on her belt, smiling. "I never leave home without my best ones."

Daemon shifted into wolf form and flew to the Imperial City with Fairy on his back. Technically, he could fly at the speed of light, but it would make Fairy ill if he went that fast, so he tried to go at a less sickening pace. And he knew now how to dim his sparks, so even if he flew slower than the speed of light, Daemon would be able to approach the bloodstone castle unseen.

Unfortunately, Prince Gin's lair was more populated than the last time Daemon was here. Many of the rooms flickered with candlelight, and the one in particular that he wanted to break into glowed through its two-story windows, a large fire in the hearth. The flames silhouetted eight people inside, sitting formally in a circle.

"That seems like it could be an important meeting!" Fairy shouted into Daemon's ear over the wind and rain.

"What should we do?"

"Take a closer look, I guess."

"But how?" Daemon hovered in the air. It was uncomfortable, not having a plan. If Sora were here, she would have mapped out what to do ahead of time. Fairy, on the other hand, had no problem with winging it.

"Fly in," she said. "We can cling to the walls and eavesdrop."

It was as good an idea as any. He swooped in toward the castle.

Fairy began to whisper a gecko spell to stick to the wall.

"Wait," Daemon said. "You don't need to do that."

He concentrated on the ledge right beneath the tall windows and imagined it extending itself.

"What are you doing?" Fairy asked.

The stone glowed blue at the ends. Then the ledge began to grow sideways, until it was five feet longer on one side of the windows.

"Making you a foothold." He smiled and flew over to deposit Fairy on it.

"Wow." She tested its sturdiness with one foot, then, judging it strong enough, hopped on with her other. "Much better than clinging with a gecko spell."

Daemon landed on the ledge a bit precariously—it was hard to fit the width of his wolf body and all his paws in a narrow line—and shifted into human form. He was happily covered in a proper uniform and cloak, too. All his practice had paid off.

It wasn't a moment too soon either, because a patrol rounded the corner of the castle below. "Guards," he whispered.

They pressed themselves against the wall and remained still.

When the guards had marched out of view, Daemon and Fairy cast moth spells, which not only allowed them to communicate ultrasonically, but also gave them exceptional hearing. They leaned harder against the wall to try to listen to the conversation inside.

Even with their best eavesdropping spell, though, the voices were muffled. The bloodstone was too thick to conduct sound well.

Daemon began to miss Sora again. She would have thought through all this beforehand, and they wouldn't have gotten stuck like this, perched uselessly on a narrow ledge in the rain.

"I'm going to peek in the windows so we at least know who's in there," Fairy said.

"Don't! You might be seen."

"I'll be quick, and I'll stay low. I'm small. No one will notice me." She lowered herself to all fours and slithered forward on the ledge on her belly. When she was beneath the windowpane, she lifted her head just enough to spy through the glass.

"It looks like a study or library," Fairy said. "Prince Gin's in there. And a grizzly-looking old ryuu, a couple of younger men, and three women." She ducked.

"That's only seven." Daemon paced along his short

stretch of the ledge. "I saw eight silhouettes when we flew in. I'm sure of it."

Fairy raised her head and peered in again, scanning the room a little too long for Daemon's comfort.

"Get down," he said. "What if the eighth person was Sora's sister, but she went invisible when she saw us?"

"Then she'd pounce on us any moment now," Fairy said.

Daemon prepared himself for an attack. Fairy crawled back from the window and readied her knives.

But there was nothing, not even a gust of wind, and after a few minutes, Daemon relaxed.

"It must have been shadows playing with my eyes," he said.

Fairy nodded. "There were definitely only seven people in there. One of the women was talking and using a pointer on a map on the wall."

"We have to get inside and see it for ourselves," Daemon said.

"We'll go as soon as the meeting ends."

Time seemed to slow as they waited, as if the hourglass had been turned sideways and the sand forgot to fall. Eventually, though, the glow from the windows dimmed as the fire inside died down. Daemon snuck a peek through the windows.

"The room's finally empty," he said. "Can you break us in?"

Fairy nodded. "I'll need to remove a pane of glass big enough for us to fit through." Although the wall was floor-to-ceiling windows, most were too small. "The ones at the top will work," she said, pointing.

Daemon squinted at them, looking from the narrow

window frames to his own body. "It's going to be a tight squeeze."

"I guess you'll have to stay out here while I go inside and have all the fun," Fairy teased.

"How did I get stuck with such a cruel girlfriend?"

She smiled and pecked him on the cheek. It warmed away the chill of the rain.

"I'll cut the glass as close to the frame as I can to give you space," she said. "Just hold me steady."

They cast gecko spells this time and climbed. At the top of the windows, Daemon stuck one of his hands firmly to the wall and made sure his feet were also well attached. Then he looped his free arm around Fairy's waist; this freed her up to work with both her hands.

She pulled a slim vial from her botanicals pouch and what looked like a thin paintbrush. She dipped the brush into the viscous pink liquid and began painting the edge of the closest windowpane. The glass sizzled, then dissolved. Daemon kept their bodies close yet carefully away from Fairy's concoction. One errant drop and their flesh would be burned straight through to the bone.

As she finished the final edge of the window, Fairy adhered one of her sticky feet to the glass so it wouldn't fall and shatter. Her potion completed its work, and the windowpane released itself from the frame. It clung to her foot as if held tightly by a suction cup.

"And now for the acrobatics portion of tonight's entertainment," Fairy said.

She slipped the foot holding the glass inside the study, latched both hands onto the top of the window frame, and swung herself through. Her body arced upward one hundred eighty degrees so she was upside down. She stuck one foot to the wall above her and kept the other one—with the glass pane—far enough away so she didn't break it.

"Bravo," Daemon whispered.

Now it was his turn. With Fairy out of the way, he could get through the window frame.

He didn't move immediately, though. Something creeped along the back of his neck, like an army of baby spiders. He slapped at them, but there were no spiders, just little hairs standing on end.

Was someone watching them? He was still a little worried about that eighth person he swore had been in the study earlier. But he darted a glance back at the ground and the wall beneath him, and there was no one there. If it were Hana, surely she would have attacked them by now.

You're getting paranoid, he chastised himself. Daemon faced the window frame once more.

As predicted, it was a tight squeeze. The fighting arts teacher at the Citadel had always told him there was no such thing as too much muscle, but as Daemon contorted his body to fit through the space, he started to doubt the wisdom of his extra weight-lifting sessions.

With a gasp and some raw skin, though, he made it through.

"Maybe I should rub you with oil before you try that again," Fairy said.

Oh gods. Daemon fumbled for words, but all that came out was incoherent noise. It also felt very hot in the room all of a sudden. Had the fireplace been stoked again?

Fairy moved quickly on to business, though, and flipped herself down, landing her free foot on Daemon's shoulder while holding the one with the glass out in front of her. She released her hands from the window frame and balanced like a circus performer as he climbed down the wall.

When they reached the floor, he took the glass pane away from her and set both Fairy and the window down gently. They would replace it again on their way out, welding it back into place with Daemon's sparks.

Now he could really take in the soaring room, two and a half stories tall. The walls were the same red-streaked black stone as the rest of the castle, and one wall was a towering bookcase, each shelf packed full of hardback tomes. Across from the Dragon Prince's desk was the wall of floor-to-ceiling windows with views of the ocean. Beyond that sea lay the mainland and the seven kingdoms he aimed to conquer. It was like a target set out before him so he would never lose sight of the bull's-eye. Daemon's stomach turned.

Ahead of him, there was nothing to see but the closed door to the hallway, decorated on either side by the long yellow-and-green, fork-tongued banners of the Dragon Prince. But on the fourth wall was the map the group of ryuu had been looking at. It was of Kichona and the mainland. There were ships and little soldiers, too—Prince Gin's navy and army—with dotted lines marking possible routes of attack.

"Looks like we were spying on a war council," Daemon said. "We were right to sabotage the shipyard last night."

"I'm going to copy that map so we can study it in more detail later," Fairy said.

"I'll search the rest of the room," Daemon said.

He started with Prince Gin's desk. The bronze chair was severe yet luxurious, the metal like dragon's scales but the seat a thick cushion upholstered in gray silk. It reeked of violent power, and even sitting on its edge made Daemon cringe. The desk was decorated with similar bronze scales.

There was only one long shallow drawer, where Fairy had gotten the paper to copy the map. He slid it open, but inside there was nothing more than parchment, pens, and wax for sealing documents. No wonder it hadn't been locked. Still, considering what had been in the captain's quarters of Prince Gin's ship—detailed warrior profiles and a list of the ryuu's targets—Daemon had expected something less mundane than stationery here.

The truly important things were probably concealed. But after checking the drawer for a false bottom—there wasn't one—Daemon abandoned the desk to search the rest of the study.

He turned his attention to the bookcase, because Prince Gin had mentioned research when he spoke to Zomuri. This could take a while, and that was time Daemon didn't have. He would have to flip through the books quickly, checking for hidden compartments inside them, as well as in the bookcase itself. He began on the lowest shelf.

The first book felt heavy in his hands, and he eagerly opened it, thinking there might be something inside. But it turned out to be rather ordinary, albeit with very thick pages, which accounted for its weight.

He moved on to the next one, which also proved to be nothing special. As did the next and the next and the next.

Three shelves later, Daemon rubbed at a cramp in his neck. He glanced over at Fairy, who was halfway through her sketch. They'd need to leave as soon as she finished. Taiga training had taught them to get in and out as fast as possible, because every minute increased the risk of being caught. Daemon and Fairy had already been in the study for half an hour. They were courting disaster.

He needed to go about the books in a different way. Daemon shifted into wolf form and drifted upward, peering at each level of shelves, scanning the spines for titles that sounded significant or books that looked particularly worn, and poking at the back wall of the bookshelf in case there were hidden panels. But he found none.

The last shelf at the top of the bookcase was just the size of a cubbyhole, dark because of its size. Daemon flew a little closer.

Aha! Inside, flush against the wall, was a stack of three books. He hauled them into his paws and flew to the ground with them.

Once in boy form, Daemon inspected them, and his stomach flipped. These were books about old legends; Zomuri had taunted Prince Gin about needing to read them. One of the books was *The Book of Sorrow*, the third volume from the Kichonan Tales by Sora's mother. The spine was creased to breaking, and the book fell open to the oft-read fable of the Evermore.

Daemon studied the cramped notes written in the margins of the story. They'd clearly been added to over the years, beginning with Prince Gin's childish block printing then graduating to a more mature, impassioned script. Were there any clues here that could help them stop the pursuit of the Evermore?

The fable was about Emperor Mareo, the first to swear his loyalty to Zomuri in an attempt to win paradise on earth. It included the Ceremony of Two Hundred Hearts, which Prince Gin had already conducted. After that, though, the story concluded with Mareo setting off to attempt to conquer the kingdoms on the mainland. It was the same part of the tale that Prince Gin was currently in—nothing that would help them now. Besides, Mareo, like all the emperors who followed in his footsteps, had failed to come even close to achieving the Evermore.

"How's it going?" Fairy asked.

"I've found nothing. No clues about Empress Aki or much else either."

Fairy rolled up her scroll, her sketched copy of the map complete, and came over to his side. "Maybe there's nothing else here to find."

"Maybe," Daemon said, "but Zomuri told Prince Gin to read up on old legends, so I feel like there might be something here." He set *The Book of Sorrow* on the desk while Fairy began investigating the walls of the study, tapping to listen for hollow compartments and checking for disguised buttons.

He picked up one of the other books. Its burgundy leather cover and the gold flames on the spine looked familiar. The title on the cover was *Obscure Folklore*.

This is the one, Daemon remembered. He'd seen another copy of this book before, when he was at the Society outpost in Tiger's Belly, after Sora had been hypnotized on the Dragon Prince's ship and Daemon had been left behind. This book contained the legend of Dassu, about a taiga who combined his magic with devilfire and burned down the middle of Kichona. When Daemon last read it, he'd been preoccupied with finding an explanation for why he was immune to Prince Gin's mind control. But now, because of Zomuri, Daemon knew there was something else important in this book.

A few of the pages were dog eared. He opened to the first one: "Dassu and the Warrior."

Daemon's heart beat faster—this was the story he was looking for.

It was almost as he remembered. A taiga wanted more power, so he made a deal with a demon, Dassu, allowing Dassu to blend the taiga's magic with his own. But when the gods found out what he'd done, Luna sent the demon back to the hells, and she smothered the taiga to death.

However, there was a part of the story that Daemon hadn't paid attention to the last time he read it, because it hadn't been relevant to his immunity from Prince Gin. He saw it now, though, because it had been underlined.

> *The warrior's small daughter rode in the saddle in front of him, and as he lit the ground aflame with his newfound magic, she whispered, "Papa, I want fire, too."*
>
> *Kitari was his only child—her mother had died shortly after the girl's birth—and the warrior spoiled her because she was the only thing connecting him to his wife. He could not deny Kitari any request, especially when she looked at him with her mother's eyes. And so he held his daughter close and breathed some of the devilfire into her cupped hands.*

Daemon frowned as he read to the end of the legend, where Luna killed the warrior and sent his soul to the hells as punishment for distorting the magic she'd given the taigas. That part Daemon had inferred from what Zomuri had told Prince Gin.

But the part that bothered Daemon was that there was no mention of what happened to Kitari, other than the warrior asking Luna to spare her. Had the girl survived? Or maybe the author hadn't wanted to include the grisly death of a child in the story.

But then why mention her at all?

Maybe there's something else about her in this book.

He flipped farther into the book, and sure enough, one of the other dog-eared pages marked a tale titled "Kitari and the Curse."

Fairy returned to the desk. "Nothing in the walls," she said. "What are you reading?"

Daemon explained the legend of Dassu, then shifted the position of the open book so Fairy could read Kitari's story at the same time he did.

Magic did not belong to humans. Only the Society of Tai-gas was permitted its use, and even then, solely in the limited capacity granted by Luna. Kitari was well aware of this, for she had watched her father die for his transgressions, his soul sent to the hells to be tortured for all eternity. Because of this, she hid the devilfire he'd given her, hoping to avoid the same wrath of the gods.

The years passed uneventfully. Kitari grew from a child to a woman, making a quiet living as a laundress in a town by the sea. She married a shrimp fisherman and bore him three children. Their hut was filled with the contentment of a small but safe existence, and as the years passed, Kitari let down her guard and began to use devilfire here and there, but only innocuously, to light a fire in the hearth when they were out of wood or to put on shadow puppet shows for her children. After a long life, Kitari passed away peacefully in her sleep.

But her spirit did not walk through the tunnel of light to the afterlife. Instead, the path led her down, down, down, until it ended at an archway made entirely of flames.

"What is this place?" she cried as her skin began to crisp and blacken, like fish too close to the charcoal.

A figure emerged from the archway, holding out his hand. His face was partly ash, flakes falling off as he approached, and yet she knew him from his first step.

"Father."

"Kitari," he said as he ran to her. "I am so sorry. I gave you devilfire, and thus you are condemned to the hells."

She looked wildly around her, all while frantically slapping at her arms to stop the relentless burning. "But I tried to be good!"

"It doesn't matter. You possessed illegal magic, and thus you are here."

Kitari sobbed, but it made no difference. Her skin began to turn to ash like his. When she was completely burnt, her skin healed itself, and the fire began the process of frying her all over again.

"I hate you," she said to her father.

"I know."

But he took her hand, and they walked through the archway of the hells, to suffer through eternity together.

"Stars," Fairy said when she finished. "That was one of the darkest things I've ever read."

Daemon stared at the book. He pointed at the Dragon Prince's handwriting in the margin, which said, *Must achieve the Evermore.* "D-does that mean what I think it means?"

Fairy cocked her head at Daemon. "I don't follow. I must have missed something."

"If Prince Gin brings the Evermore to Kichona, he and all his warriors will be immortal. But if he doesn't, I think this means that anyone with ryuu magic will be damned to the hells for eternity after they die."

"Oh gods," Fairy said as understanding settled in. "Because Prince Gin stole Sight from the afterlife, and he's gifted it to the ryuu, just like the warrior gave devilfire to Kitari."

"Which affects every single one of our friends and teachers that Prince Gin hypnotized. And . . ." Daemon couldn't finish the sentence.

He leaned heavily against the desk.

"Including Spirit," Fairy said. All the color in her face drained away. "We have to send a message to them right away!"

"No," Daemon said quickly. "You can't tell someone via dragonfly messenger that she's damned for eternity. I . . . I want to break the news in person." He sagged against the desk.

Fairy looked at the floor. "That makes sense. But I can't just do nothing. Maybe we could find a way for Spirit to be forgiven?"

"You saw Kitari's legend. She possessed illegal magic, and that was that."

"But who decides which souls go to the peaceful afterlife and which go to the hells?" Fairy asked. "It's the gods. We could appeal to them to pardon Spirit. It wasn't her fault she got ryuu magic, and she's using it for good. That has to count for something."

Daemon shrugged listlessly. "Maybe it does. Maybe it doesn't. Kitari used devilfire peacefully, and she was still condemned."

"Liga promised he wouldn't forget us. I'm going to try summoning him again and ask if he can help." Fairy took Daemon's hand. "Hope isn't lost yet, all right? The League of Rogues has always considered rules negotiable, and I'm not about to stop now. So come on. We'll get to the bottom of this and find a way out."

He sighed but nodded. "You're right. We can't give up without a fight."

CHAPTER TWENTY-FOUR

Invisible, Hana slithered to the floor of the study. She'd been watching Wolf and Fairy the whole time, amused by their complete obliviousness to her presence. She had intended to spring on them when the moment felt deliciously dramatic enough.

But then they'd found that story and the possibility that the ryuu were eternally damned. . . .

Was it true? The implications were so overwhelming, Hana felt suddenly paralyzed, and she'd let Wolf and Fairy escape.

"Why would Emperor Gin do this to us?" Hana asked the empty room.

But maybe he hadn't known. Yes, that must be what had happened. Emperor Gin had discovered ryuu magic a decade ago. Back then, he was about the same age Hana was now. He couldn't have known the repercussions of taking Sight from the afterlife. Maybe he only read that story later, and that's when he wrote the note in it.

Or maybe Wolf and Fairy were wrong, and their theory was just plain stupid.

The only way to find out was to ask.

Hana pulled herself off the floor, smoothed her tunic, and exited the study. Emperor Gin had told his war council he'd be in the throne room if anyone needed him, so that's where she headed.

She slowed as she entered the hall that looked like a dragon's mouth. Hana smiled at the toothlike crimson crystals that lit the corridor; they reminded her of the emperor's uncompromising determination. The ryuu had been refugees in the Shinowana mountains for a decade, but he'd led them through that adversity, never wavering in his belief that they would one day prevail. And look at them now.

Hana rapped on the door.

"Enter," the emperor said from within.

She pulled on the carved dragon handles and strode into the throne room. Emperor Gin sat relaxed on the crimson stone of his throne, the orange sapphire flames at the top crowning his head like an opulent threat. Hana bowed.

"Ah, Virtuoso, I was wondering what was taking you so long. What do you have to report?"

Hana was confused only momentarily before she remembered that she'd made herself invisible in the middle of the war council meeting because she'd seen Wolf and Fairy hovering outside. She hadn't said anything about it then, but the emperor knew that she would only vanish like that if it were important.

"I wanted to ask you a question, Your Majesty—"

"And I want your report first." His gaze was steely and stern.

"Um, right, of course," she said, years of military obedience kicking in, even though she desperately wanted to discuss Wolf's theory. So she spilled her report as quickly as possible. "Your Majesty, I went invisible because two of Spirit's friends were hovering outside the study. I'm certain they couldn't hear through the castle walls, which is why I didn't sound the alarm right away. Instead I waited to see what they'd do. They broke in after your meeting dispersed."

Emperor Gin sat taller in his throne and looked down at Hana. "You let them break into my study?"

"I—I thought I might be able to learn something from eavesdropping. We haven't known what they were up to since we defeated them and took over the capital."

He frowned, and Hana felt it overtake her like a shadow. She'd always been his star student, and she hated feeling like she'd failed him.

Finally, he motioned with his hand for her to continue.

"It turns out, Your Majesty, that my sister's team has been actively trying to sabotage us. They did something in our shipyard that will delay our plans to attack Thoma. As soon as I'm done here, I'll give the order for the ryuu to investigate and fix the warships."

The emperor huffed. "Those taigas are like an infestation I just can't get rid of."

"There's more, Your Majesty. They copied down the map on the wall."

Emperor Gin's nostrils flared as he sat at full attention. "They can't have a copy of our plans; you shouldn't have let them escape."

"But I—"

"Take Firebrand and Menagerie and find them. Destroy the map; kill the taigas."

"Your Majesty—"

"That's an order."

"Y-yes, sir."

"If there's nothing else, you're dismissed." He tilted his head back and looked at the mural painted on the ceiling. It was a scene of his near death after the Blood Rift Rebellion, when he'd crossed almost to the afterlife and took its magic to bring back to the living. Emperor Gin had believed his ability to do so was a gift from the gods. Now, Hana wasn't so sure.

"Actually, Your Majesty, I still have a question. While Wolf and Fairy were in the study, they read a story about a girl named Kitari, and they said they thought . . . Well, this is probably a stupid leap to conclusions, but Wolf thought you'd dog-eared those pages because they were an analogy to our situation."

Emperor Gin raised a brow, but he didn't comment. Hana stumbled on awkwardly. "Um, they thought you were like the warrior in the legend of Dassu, and by gifting us with ryuu magic, it was like the father gifting his daughter with devilfire, and that meant we were all damned." Hana laughed nervously. "But that's nonsense, right? Gods, I'm sorry I even brought it up."

The emperor's face softened. "Come here, Virtuoso." He beckoned with a wave of his hand. "You're so competent as a soldier, sometimes I forget that you are still a child."

Hana hurried to the throne and knelt at Emperor Gin's feet.

"All I want," he said gently, "is the best for Kichona.

That means uniting all seven of the mainland kingdoms under our gods, with Zomuri as our patron, rather than continuing to let those pagan kingdoms worship their own heathen deities.

"When we have done this, we will achieve the Evermore and bring paradise to earth. You and I and all Kichonans, including our new subjects on the mainland, will live forever.

"But in order to do so, I needed a drastic change. Just being taigas wasn't enough; you saw how we were defeated by my sister ten years ago. And so, when I had the opportunity to take the knowledge of more powerful magic from the afterlife, I did it. And I shared the new powers with all my warriors, even if it costs us, because it was the means to the Evermore. Do you understand?"

Hana's mouth hung open. The emperor had done the opposite of what she'd expected—he'd confirmed Wolf's reading of Kitari's story. "B-but . . . you damned us to the hells. Why would you do that to someone? To me, when I was just a child?"

"I didn't know," he faltered. "I found out about the consequences later. But don't you see that it's still worth it?" Emperor Gin stroked her cheek like she really was still a child. "I love you and all my ryuu. I want the Evermore for you, and when we achieve that goal, it won't matter that we were marked for the hells, because we'll never die. We will be immortal in paradise."

She wanted to pull away, but she was in too much shock. "What about the ryuu who died in the last battle, though? They don't get to live in the Evermore, and they don't get to rest in the afterlife either."

Emperor Gin merely shrugged. "There's always a price to pay. Weren't you the one who told Aki that? You said that leaders who were truly great weren't afraid of paying it. And that is what I did. I know you understand."

Hana looked up at him and the jeweled flames above his head. They no longer seemed beautiful. They were only a promise of her future in the hells if she died while fighting these wars against the mainland.

And yet she'd always known that fighting for a cause came with sacrifices. The Evermore was worth it, right?

"Now it's time to get back to work," the emperor said, patting her cheek affectionately, like a proud father. "But let's keep this Kitari story between you and me, all right? The other warriors are not as wise as you, Virtuoso, and may not take to it as well. I'd prefer not to have to hypnotize my original ryuu if possible. I like having a loyal, passionate contingent of visionary warriors who understand, of their own accord, the need for the Evermore. But I will take their minds if necessary. Understood?"

Hana, schooled to be obedient, bowed her head as if in complete agreement, even though she was rattled by what was clearly a threat to control her mind if she didn't do what he wanted. The emperor only ever used his powers on people he considered his enemies, or on unreliable, ordinary people, like when he'd hypnotized the subjects in Paro Village during the ryuu's initial campaign into Kichona.

But now he considers me a potential enemy? She was his second-in-command, the most loyal of the loyal. Was it that easy for him to turn on the ones who were ready to give their lives for him and his pursuit of the Evermore?

"Get a team to inspect and fix my new warships,"

Emperor Gin said, his voice no longer kind but back to business now. "And take Firebrand and Menagerie to smoke out those taigas."

Hana rose slowly. She wasn't sure how she felt or what she was going to do, but she needed time to sort through all this new information. At least if she had an excuse to go after Wolf and Fairy, she could interrogate them to see if they'd gotten in touch with this Liga person, whoever he was, and learned anything more about the damnation or a way out of it.

"Yes, Your Majesty," Hana said, saluting despite the confusing swirl of feelings in her head. "You can count on me to find them."

CHAPTER TWENTY-FIVE

Pain jerked Aki awake. After Virtuoso had left, Aki had squeezed through the crooked, narrow opening into her tiny cell. She'd collapsed on the bed, a wooden pallet and lumpy sack of straw, and smeared a thick layer of seaweed salve on her burns. After that, everything was a haze as she tumbled in and out of consciousness.

It had probably been a few days since Gin had held a bucket of acid over her head and Virtuoso had beaten her. Aki's hands flew instinctively to her tender cheek. The touch sent a searing firebrand of agony through her skin, and she cried out.

Was this how she would die? Was this the price—the years—she'd paid summoning Sola before?

Aki tried to sit up, and the room spun around her. Only her right eye would open, her left swollen shut from Virtuoso's attack.

Of course, Virtuoso had done that on her brother's orders, and as bad as the beating was, it had been a lot less than what he'd wanted her to do.

Gin . . . What have you become?

Where was the boy who used to go fishing with Aki in the palace moat? Who used to make sure he'd be the first to wish her happy birthday at the exact moment of her birth and then laugh when his turn came nine minutes later? How had he turned into a man who could inflict acid torture on his sister's face?

Sobs shook Aki's body.

She cried over the loss of her brother. Over her pain and imprisonment. Over the darkness of Kichona's future.

When the tears ran out, she stared at the rock walls.

"What am I doing, just waiting for the League of Rogues to save me?" Aki didn't know what had become of them. She only hoped they were still out there, putting up a fight against Gin. But even if that were true, they probably had more urgent things to deal with than rescuing her.

"Is this really how Father raised me? To be a helpless princess?"

She stood up, brushed off the dust from the taiga uniform she was still wearing—there was no change of clothing in her cell—and tugged on the fabric to pull out the wrinkles as best she could. It didn't do much, but smoothing the uniform made her feel a little better about herself. A little more like a warrior.

Now, how to get out of this prison? Obviously not through the acid falls.

She explored every nook and cranny in her small cave, the grotto, and the crevice that connected the two. There was no way out.

But then Aki smiled for the first time since she'd

regained consciousness: when she'd fallen near the water, the ground hadn't been solid stone. It was hard-packed clay.

I could make my own way out.

She found a sharp rock, shoved her pallet aside, and began scraping at the floor. It came off in sticky globs.

It might take a long time, but time was all Aki had. She would work on digging a hole, and then a tunnel, hiding the hole beneath her bed. And if no one came to liberate her, she'd burrow her own way out, one clay scraping after another.

"I am empress of Kichona," she said as she dragged her rock over the ground again. "And I don't plan on quitting until the day I die."

CHAPTER TWENTY-SIX

At first glance, Naimo Ice Caves was a wonderland of pale ice deep in the pits of the southernmost island of the Kichona archipelago. Glaciers had carved majestic caves underground, like frosty, high-ceilinged ballrooms lit through natural skylights of translucent ice. A labyrinth of sparkling tunnels connected each cave to the next, the wind singing a gentle melody through its halls, the winter berries that grew in the icy crevices perfuming the chilly air with their honey sweetness.

But this beauty also guarded Zomuri's most valuable possessions. Although the gods generally didn't interact with people, Sora wasn't sure that applied to those who stole something from under a god's nose. Every step would have to be taken with care.

"I wish we actually knew what we were about to face," Broomstick said.

"Me, too. But no matter what happens, we have to get

that soul pearl. We have to reunite it with Prince Gin and kill him."

Sora's muscles seized up for a moment, a panic attack threatening to take over. But she gritted her teeth and kicked the anxiety away, shoving it into a box in her mind, where she'd also stashed the fear of what would happen if she failed today. There wasn't time for contemplating defeat.

Instead, she and Broomstick peered into the maze of tunnels winding underground, and they gathered their supplies—compasses, flares, weapons, and explosives. Then they tied their horses and left them behind.

As if for luck, Sora touched the necklace at her throat. She would unfasten the pearl pendant and leave it as a decoy when she found and stole the Dragon Prince's soul.

But that was later. Now, she called upon the ryuu particles to show her the path to follow to get to the Lake of Nightmares.

A faint trail lit up, descending into the caverns. Broomstick couldn't see it, though, so she went first, and he followed with his compass.

"Mark each turn in the ice," Sora said.

"Why?" Broomstick carved Luna's triplicate whorls into the tunnel wall at their first bend.

"In case . . ."

"In case what?"

Sora pursed her lips. "In case something happens to me and you don't have my ryuu particles to help guide you out on the journey back." She turned away so she wouldn't have to see his reaction. They knew they were risking their lives. But it was still sobering to think about actually dying.

As they traveled deeper, the natural skylights vanished,

leaving them in the dark. Sora commanded her magic to light the way, and the emerald dust glowed, casting an eerie luminescence around her and Broomstick's shadows on the walls of ice.

An hour into the tunnels, Broomstick swore.

"What is it?" Sora asked.

He showed her his compass. The needle had begun to spin in lazy circles, as if unable to find north but not caring.

"We must have run into the magnetic fields mentioned in Mama's research," Sora said.

"Yeah, which also means that at least one of her notes is true. And maybe the others are, too."

Sora stopped for a moment as this sank in. First, magnetic fields to confuse those who tried to find Zomuri's vault. If the notes were correct, next would be "ghost faces," whatever that meant. Then a snow monster. And a lake filled with water that gave you hallucinations of the worst version of yourself.

She ran through the details of her plan.

When the "ghost faces" appeared, she'd make herself and Broomstick invisible, in hopes that the ghost guards wouldn't be able to see them.

Broomstick's bombs were for blowing up the snow monster.

When that hurdle was cleared, they'd reach through their gemina bonds to Daemon and Fairy. The idea was they'd tether Sora and Broomstick to reality, like when Sora had been shot with genka and Daemon had coaxed her back to reason through their bond. Of course, this situation could be totally different, but it was the best analogy she had. She and Daemon, and Broomstick and Fairy, had spent over a decade bonded to each other, finely honed to every spike or nuance in their gemina connection. If there was any chance of Sora and Broomstick keeping their wits about them as they swam through the Lake of Nightmares to get to Zomuri's vault, their gemina bond was it.

Admittedly, it was a sketchy plan. But it was what Sora could do with the very limited information she had. She just had to trust herself to adapt to the rest.

They followed the path of ryuu particles deeper into the tunnels. As the hours passed, the sweet perfume of winter berries faded, replaced instead by the strangely dead, hollow smell of cold, stale air. The hairs on Sora's arms stood up. Everything about these barren ice caves felt like a cemetery.

Broomstick pointed at a part of the glacier wall that was recessed, with six long icicles like spears stabbing the labyrinth floor. "Is it me, or does that seem ominous?"

A sprinkle of ice fell on them from above.

Sora and Broomstick jumped. But in the same second, they had knives and throwing stars in hand.

Silence.

Was it the ghost faces? Or the snow monster? Or another threat they didn't know about?

"Get some of your bombs out," Sora whispered to Broomstick. He palmed a few of the smaller ones from his bag.

They waited.

No more ice falling.

No monstrous footsteps.

Nothing.

Sora exhaled.

And then they heard it. A steady pounding—no, a

beating from the tunnels above them, growing louder as it approached.

"What in Luna's name is that?" A chill as cold as the ice caves themselves ran up Sora's back.

"It sounds like a monster," Broomstick said, eyes wide with fear. "I say we run."

They sprinted down the tunnel. The noise behind them grew.

"It's gaining on us," Sora said, putting on more speed. She took a corner too quickly and slammed into a wall of ice. Broomstick crashed into her, and they tumbled to the icy ground.

"Dead end," she said, scrambling to her feet. They had to backtrack.

She ran the way they'd come. There had been a fork in the tunnels not too far up—

As soon as they reached the intersection, over fifty owls with pale, white faces met them. The owls shrieked in unison, wielding talons like blades on their feet.

Oh stars, it wasn't a single enemy. Ghost *faces*, plural.

The synchronized beating of their wings echoed through Naimo Ice Caves like the rhythm of a death march.

Holy heavens, what have I signed up for?

"Show me where to go!" Sora shouted.

"What? I don't know!" Broomstick said.

But she wasn't talking to him. She was yelling at the ryuu magic around her. Sora focused her thoughts on an icy lake, hoping that would be enough for the ryuu particles to go on.

The owls shrieked again and dove. Several reached Sora,

stabbing with their razor-sharp beaks and slicing with their claws.

Broomstick swung his sword, and they swooped off.

The emerald dust coalesced into a glittering path down the ice tunnel to Sora's right.

"This way!" She made the sharp turn and began to run. Broomstick was on her heels, but so were the owls.

"We need to get rid of them," he said as he tried to keep up. Because Broomstick couldn't see the green trail the ryuu particles were showing her, he was a fraction of a second behind on each sudden turn as they sprinted deeper into the tunnels. Sora tried to shout the turns to him ahead of time, but sometimes the path zagged so suddenly, she hardly had enough notice to adjust herself. The small lag helped the owls stay on their trail.

"I don't want to hurt them," Sora yelled over their shrieks, which had reached a bloodcurdling pitch.

"Yeah, but they don't feel the same way about us. I think they're trying to murder us."

But what if the owls were just regular animals, albeit ones enlisted by Zomuri to discourage anyone from going farther into the caves? That would explain why the tunnels were so confusing; they were built to look natural but also to make people lose their way. After encountering the labyrinth and the owls, most people wouldn't venture deeper.

Most *regular* people. Not taigas or ryuu.

Sora remembered then that she'd had a plan for these ghost faces.

The emerald path veered to the left up ahead. She purposefully ran the wrong way, to the right.

A hundred yards later, she skidded to a halt. "Broomstick,

stay close. I'm making us invisible."

She dropped to the ground and curled into a ball. Broomstick ducked right next to her. Sora commanded the ryuu particles to infuse them both.

The rush of magic flooded their cells at the same instant the owls swooped into that part of the tunnel. She checked on Broomstick. He stared at her intently, as if afraid that losing sight of Sora would loosen her magic on him.

The owls flew past them.

Sora exhaled.

Broomstick stood, looking a bit intoxicated from the feel of ryuu magic on his skin.

"You need to blow up this tunnel to block it," Sora said. "Then we'll go the way we came and take the other turn."

He looked at her but with a goofy smile on his face, as if he wasn't quite seeing her.

She slapped him on the cheek. Nicely. Or as nicely as possible in this situation.

"I know ryuu magic is a bit of a shock the first time you feel it, but I need you to get ahold of yourself and set off your bombs."

"Oof, sorry." Broomstick rubbed his cheek but held out his hand. There were three small explosives shaped like eggs.

The owls' screeches and beating wings were getting louder again.

"They're coming back this way!" Sora said. "Throw them now!"

He flicked a match on the bottom of his boot and lit the fuses.

As the first ghostly faces reappeared in the tunnel,

Broomstick hurled his bombs one after the other at the ice above them. The bombs burst on impact, and the tunnel ceiling crashed down in a fury of icicles and smoke, trapping the owls on the other side. The ground quaked, and Sora fell.

Broomstick grabbed her hand, pulled her up, and they sprinted.

After a minute, though, the rumble of the cave-in stopped, and Sora and Broomstick did, too. She leaned against the wall. Her throat was raw, and her side ached from running.

"Let go of the invisibility spell on me," Broomstick said. "You need to conserve your energy."

She did as he said, but she was also distracted by something else. The shimmering emerald path now branched off in three different directions.

"What the hells does that mean?" Sora said aloud.

"I can't see what you see," Broomstick reminded her.

"Right, sorry. I don't know which way to go. There are three paths."

"Then I think we just choose one, before the owls find an alternate path to us or something else decides to chase us."

She gave herself another moment to catch her breath, then chose the third route, since three was her lucky number.

The tunnel wound down endlessly. Just when Sora was convinced that it would never end and that the Lake of Nightmares didn't exist, the tunnel stopped abruptly and spit them out into a colossal cave.

"Good gods," Sora murmured.

The ceiling was hundreds of feet high, and the other side of the cave was so far away it was almost out of sight.

But there were definitely two other tunnel openings over there. That must be why there'd been three emerald paths, because there were three different ways to get here.

And most important: in the center of the cave was a vast pool of glacial water clear as glass.

"Wow," Sora murmured. "Let that be a lesson in perseverance."

"It's not all good news, though," Broomstick said, pointing.

They could see straight down to an iron trap door at the bottom, likely where Zomuri's treasure was buried. But the door wasn't the only thing in the water. There were corpses, about a hundred of them suspended in the water, frozen at various depths and none decomposed. They were mostly men; some must have been centuries old, judging by the ancient robes they wore and their plaited hair, and others drowned perhaps only decades ago. The one unifying feature, however, was their gape-mouthed horror. Sora's stomach turned.

"Do you think they froze to death?" Broomstick asked.

Sora was staring at the water. "Or they were tortured by the lake," she said, remembering that those who dared to step foot in the water would be met with visions of horrible imagined futures.

The hallucinations are so vivid, people either drown as they get lost in them or drown themselves out of despair for who they think they'll become in the future, Mama had said.

And their suffering was preserved for eternity in their underwater grave.

"This is a bad idea," Broomstick said.

"I know," Sora said. "But we still have to do it. If we

don't retrieve the Dragon Prince's soul, we don't stand a chance. Maybe we'll die today trying to do this, but if we don't, then we'll die for sure."

"That's not much of a pep talk," Broomstick said.

"It's the truth, and at this point, it's the best motivator we have. We have a chance at surviving the lake. Remember, I have magic more powerful than what those who came before us had."

"And what about the snow monster?" He set his bag down on the ice. "We haven't seen it yet."

Sora frowned as she picked up some of his waterproof bombs. "You're right."

"What should we do?"

She fastened the explosives to her belt with metal clips. "I'll go in the water. You stay onshore."

"No way! That's not what I meant."

Sora held out her hand to stop his protest. "Hear me out. Suppose the monster doesn't show up until after we enter the water. What if it's a trap and that's how people end up drowning there?"

"Because the snow monster won't let them onto shore . . . ," Broomstick said.

"Exactly. And maybe it's smarter to have you act as the sentry on the shore while I swim to the vault. That way, if the lake is as bad as the legend says it is, only *I* lose my mind. You'll be our backup plan to find another way to get into that vault."

"No. I should be the one to swim," Broomstick said.

But Sora shook her head. "My ryuu magic is stronger than your taiga magic, though. And Daemon and I have connected before in a similar situation."

"That was genka related."

"I know, but still. It has to be me."

Broomstick sighed. "I don't like it."

"I'm not arguing," Sora said. "You know this is the way it has to be done. One of us has to keep watch onshore for that monster, if it's real. And if I fail, you *have* to be here to give the kingdom a second chance."

He clenched his teeth. But she was right and Broomstick knew it. He sighed and gave in. "I'll keep watch over you from here; the water is clear, and I'll be able to see you the whole way down. And I'll make sure nothing disturbs you."

"Thank you." Sora tried to look fearless as she stood on the shore. But there was no way it was going to be as simple as reminding herself that the lake was enchanted. If it were that easy, more people would have survived to tell about it. That's why she needed Daemon to keep her tied to reality.

She reached out to him through their gemina bond, and her fear filled their connection. It was like falling off a rock face without a belay.

It took only the space of half a heartbeat for Daemon to catch her.

His presence washed through Sora like an embrace encased in gold. She closed her eyes, and she could practically feel his arms around her, strong and unyielding, and his whisper in her ear that he was there, that he would never leave her. Sora sank into the feeling, letting him hold her from afar, just for a moment.

Just in case this was the last time.

Then she opened her eyes, cast a whale spell on herself, and dove into the lake.

CHAPTER TWENTY-SEVEN

It was the middle of the night, but Daemon and Fairy sat wide awake. Sora's message had told them to be ready to help her and Broomstick, and now Daemon knew she'd jumped into the Lake of Nightmares, because her shock chilled their gemina bond like a blizzard.

His entire body rattled, both her fear and his own engulfing him. Did Sora know what she was doing? She hardly had any information to go on. And while she was risking her life to swim through cursed waters, Daemon was hundreds of miles away, helpless to do anything for her.

What if he lost her?

And if he did, it would mean she was damned to the hells, because she had ryuu magic.

The thought was like swallowing a hundred swords all at once, and Daemon gasped.

Fairy reached for him and held his hand, even though she was focusing on her connection with Broomstick. "We have to be strong for them."

It was as if Daemon didn't hear her, though. He hardly felt Fairy's fingers against his. The only thing that mattered was the throbbing cold of his gemina bond with Sora. And how to make it warmer.

He wrapped his cloak more tightly around himself, as if the heat would travel through their connection.

The first time he tried to protect her with their bond, Sora had been under the effects of genka, and Daemon had taken the hallucinations from her through their connection. But now he understood that he didn't actually have to go so far in order to help her. What Sora needed most as she entered the lake was to remember the real world. Daemon was her tether to it. Instead of taking on the nightmares like he had the genka hallucinations, his job was to manipulate their gemina bond to keep a constant flow of reminders to Sora that the enchanted water wasn't everything. His actual thoughts wouldn't transfer through their connection, but the emotions associated with them would.

So Daemon began to think of the happiest memories he had of their lives together.

When he was first brought, snarling and biting, to the Citadel by the hunter who'd found him in the woods, and Sora had pushed her way through the crowd of scared tenderfoots, the only one of them who approached him and smiled.

The apprentice initiation ceremony when they were seven, when Luna's moonbeams lit up the Citadel's amphitheater and the silver swirls on Daemon's and Sora's backs glowed at the same time, pairing them as geminas.

The first time he, Sora, Fairy, and Broomstick had been caught during one of their pranks, and how they'd all happily served detention together peeling potatoes for a week in the mess hall.

Daemon pumped the feelings of these memories and more, one after another, through their connection. The recollections felt like curling up against his wolf cub brothers and sisters—toasty comfort and safety and the knowledge that you were right where you belonged.

Gods dammit, he missed her. There was something about the way Sora made him feel—how thinking of their shared past made Daemon smile so broadly, it could illuminate the forest—that he didn't have with anyone else.

He turned his head and looked at Fairy. She was focused on her own gemina bond with Broomstick, her nose scrunched as she concentrated. Her intensity and courage put an additional glow on her beauty.

And yet Daemon's attraction to her didn't feel nearly as strong as his connection with Sora; it was like a string compared to a thick nautical rope. Would it always be this way?

Our relationship will deepen, Daemon thought. He couldn't compare it to his and Sora's, because they were geminas and knew each other inside and out. He and Fairy hadn't had the chance yet to develop the depth that he and Sora had. But it was nothing to worry over. He and Fairy just needed time.

Foggy confusion—not his own—spilled through Daemon's gemina bond.

Sora.

He tossed his other thoughts aside and sent her the feel of another memory—of when they were twelve and he couldn't sleep, and she broke curfew to join him on the roof of the boys' dormitory so he could be closer to the night sky. Daemon could still feel how she'd lain next to him to keep warm, how her head fit right into the crook of his neck like Luna had always known they were a matching pair, and how Sora had nuzzled closer to him when the sky filled with shooting stars.

"You can do this, Sora," Daemon said, even though she couldn't hear him. "If anyone can steal from a god and get away with it, it's you."

CHAPTER TWENTY-EIGHT

The water was unnaturally frigid, frosting against Sora's skin as soon as she plunged into the lake. She opened her mouth in shock and almost gasped out the precious air she needed to conserve for the dive down; her whale spell would help only if there was oxygen in her lungs.

Daemon launched a dose of calm through their bond, and not a moment too soon. Like when she'd gone diving with the eagle rays, Daemon's presence helped Sora come to her senses, and she clamped her mouth shut, swallowing the air back where it belonged. She'd swum herself upside down in the pain of the freezing water, but now she settled back into position to swim toward the trap door.

Sora kicked downward. She would need to blow open the door, find the golden soul pearl, replace it with a decoy, and get out of there, all before her air ran out.

But as she pushed deeper into the lake, her vision began to turn milky white at the edges. *Am I low on air already?* The whale spell was supposed to give her about twenty minutes underwater, though, and it had only been two, maybe three. Panic rose in the back of her throat.

The milkiness in her vision persisted, oozing in like a spilled bottle of cream until she could see nothing else. Sora rubbed at her eyes with the heels of her palms. It didn't change a thing.

A sharp tang, like vinegar, suddenly filled her nose, which made no sense, since she wasn't breathing in. And the water seemed to thicken like jelly. The muscles in her arms and legs strained as she tried to keep swimming.

Oh gods . . . I'm really going to die in here.

Then, all of a sudden, the milkiness in her vision and the vinegary smell cleared. The thick gel of the lake was gone, too, replaced with solid ground.

What in all hells?

Sora looked down. She stood on top of a pile of dead soldiers wearing uniforms that belonged neither to the taigas nor the ryuu but to a foreign army. All around her, a battlefield was littered with corpses, and the air was tinged with the smells of steel and blood.

But instead of fear or horror, pride inexplicably swelled in Sora's chest.

She took in the scene around her, and the drunken heat of victory began to course through every vein in her body, filling her with delight. *All this death was* my *work,* my *power!* A flagstaff suddenly appeared in her right hand, and she impaled its sharpened end through the bodies at her feet. Another wave of satisfaction surged through her as the pole pierced through lifeless flesh.

"Well done, sister," a voice said from behind her. Sora turned to face Hana.

"Is this the future?" Sora asked, part of her still conscious that the battlefield wasn't reality, that her body was somewhere else . . . although she couldn't remember where.

"Yes," Hana said. "This is us, destroying the Faleese army."

"So this is Fale Po Tair." Sora looked past the battlefield to get a glimpse of the kingdom, but it was just a flat expanse with a mountain in the distance and seagulls hovering over the ocean.

Hana laughed, and it was like iron nails on crystal. Sora cringed.

"Fale Po Tair? No, sister. This is Kichona. Look more closely at the mountain. I think you'll recognize it."

Sora squinted at the distance, and this being a prophecy not governed by the ordinary rules of the world, the mountain came into sharp focus. It was purplish-blue against the sea, its scraggly trees clinging to the steep cliff faces, a tiny building halfway up the switchback passes. Sora gasped. "Is that Mama and Papa's house?"

"It was," Hana said without emotion. "They've been dead since the first attack on Kichona by the Southern Alliance."

Sora's giddiness from standing on a pile of vanquished enemies petered out. "The Southern Alliance?" She was afraid to ask, but she had to.

"The united armies and navies of Fale Po Tair, Xerlinis, and Vyratta. But don't worry. You've slaughtered thousands. Including that ex-gemina of yours."

Oh gods. Daemon?

Horror shuddered through Sora's body. Her consciousness was fighting back now, reminding her that she was actually swimming in an underground lake in Naimo Ice Caves, not here on a battlefield in the future. But that also meant she was beginning to process what this all meant— that she would become part of the Dragon Prince's bloody pursuit of the Evermore. That Kichona would be razed by the Southern Alliance. That Sora would kill Daemon.

"This can't be true," she said.

"But it is," Hana said with a smile. "Aren't you happy we've been successful together?"

"Yes. I mean, no!" Sora shook her head to try to get her thoughts straight.

Something shot through the back of her mind like a spear and hurtled to the forefront. It pierced Sora's consciousness, and a sensation of unbreakable connection washed over her, as if she were tethered by the rope on a harpoon.

Daemon!

He sent surges of confidence to her, and she held fast to their bond, feeling him tugging to extricate her from this so-called prophecy.

She remembered clearly now that she was swimming in the Lake of Nightmares.

Sora grabbed hold of their gemina bond and hauled herself out of the vision, hand over hand as if climbing a rope. Future Hana scowled at her. But Hana was already blurring, and milky white poured out from the center of the scene until it filled all of Sora's vision again.

She blinked, hard, and the cloudiness dissipated. The vision of the battlefield disappeared, and Sora saw the water again. She was twenty feet down from the surface, still another thirty or so to go to the trap door at the bottom.

Sora clung fiercely to her gemina bond as if it were a

lifeline so she didn't lose her mind.

Daemon Daemon Daemon.

He must have been concentrating intensely, because his emotion soaked her as if she were caught in a rainstorm. It reminded her of ryuu magic, but while that was intoxicating, this was something more, like drinking lightning and the night sky, their brightness and darkness filling her at the same time. These were Daemon's rawest feelings, unfiltered, and even though Sora didn't know the thoughts that lay behind them, this was still the closest she'd ever been to anyone, even him. She wanted to keep drinking in this feeling of being one with somebody else, where it wasn't just about him or her but about *them*, together.

I'll find my way back to you, she thought.

But that would happen only after she finished this mission. So with Daemon holding on to her through their gemina bond, Sora refocused on one thing alone—getting to the trap door.

Instead of swimming through the thick water and using precious energy, she tucked her legs into her chest, released a little bit of air from her lungs, and let herself sink slowly like a rock. She swallowed to clear her ears as she descended deeper into the lake. Only when she stopped sinking did Sora jackknife herself and start swimming to the door.

She grabbed on to the heavy iron ring on the front and planted her feet against the lake bottom, which was as frozen as the ice caves above. She allowed herself a couple seconds of rest. *I made it. I defied the Lake of Nightmares. I'm still alive.*

But that was only half the plan—there was still important work to do.

Broomstick had invented a super adhesive that was

waterproof, and Sora smeared it onto one of the bombs. She glued it right next to the trap door's top hinge, then stuck another one on the bottom hinge. There were four bombs left on her belt.

Matches wouldn't light underwater, but thankfully she didn't need to rely on traditional fuses. Sora swam a safe distance away and commanded the ryuu particles to ignite the bombs on the door.

There was a pause, then dual hisses as the magical flame traveled down the length of the fuses.

One of them sputtered.

Light it again, Sora ordered. The emerald particles obeyed swiftly.

The first fuse was nearly at its end. Sora braced herself. The bomb exploded, and the shock waves threw her backward along the glacial bottom of the lake. For a second, she lost her hold on her gemina bond, and the vision of her power-hungry smirk leeched into her brain.

But then the second bomb went off, and the vibrations from its explosion shook her back into focus.

The top hinge was blasted apart completely. The bottom hinge was only mangled, though, and the trap door itself remained stubbornly in place. Also, the impact of both explosions had knocked most of the air out of Sora's lungs.

Nines! Panic burned at the back of her throat again.

She commanded the emerald particles to her aid, using one of the very first spells she'd learned as a ryuu. The magic formed an enormous hand and seized the ring on the door.

Now pull.

The sparkling hand tugged. The ring strained against the door.

Harder!

The intact bottom hinge groaned.

Sora's lungs screamed at her. She was nearly out of oxygen, and part of her was tempted to flee back to the surface.

But she was so close to success. . . . If Sora could at least get through the trap door to look at what was inside, she could go back to the surface, swallow another lungful of air, and return again.

One more pull!

The hand jerked hard, and the trap door flew out of its frame completely.

There was a dim room with bare dirt floors on the other side. It could be another trap, but she didn't have time to hesitate.

With her lungs aching, Sora grabbed the door frame and propelled herself into what she hoped was Zomuri's secret vault.

CHAPTER TWENTY-NINE

Broomstick watched Spirit dive into the lake. She swam slowly, as if movement were harder underwater, but she didn't freeze up or seem bothered by the corpses suspended around her. He cheered her on from shore: "You've got this!" Maybe they'd finally caught a lucky break.

Suddenly, Spirit stopped swimming. She floated in the middle of the lake, nowhere near the bottom, and planted her feet as if she were standing on the ground. Broomstick ran to the edge of the water. "Spirit, no! Whatever you're seeing in your head, it's not real! You have to fight it off and keep going."

She didn't move. At the same time, the cave around Broomstick shuddered. The icicles hanging off the rock walls rattled, like a million chandeliers about to break. The walls of the cavern groaned.

Was it the monster? Or something else?

He unsheathed a sword and took several steps back from the water's edge. Whatever was coming, he couldn't afford to get knocked off his feet and into the lake.

The cave shook again. This time, the walls couldn't hold on to the icicles. But the icy spears didn't fall straight down either. Instead, they flew across the colossal cavern and began to come together just a hundred feet from where Broomstick stood. The icicles hovered in the air, assembling themselves into something.

First an icy heart.

Then a barreled chest around it, the icicles still loosely linked together like chain mail so Broomstick could see through the holes between them.

Arms. Legs. And last of all, a head with icelike swords as its teeth. The monster roared, letting out a breath as rank as thawing corpses, while its components jangled against one another, sounding much more dangerous now than collapsing chandeliers.

Broomstick recoiled. But then he saw the lake out of the corner of his eye, and he remembered his promise to Spirit that he would stay alive, in case they needed a second chance at the vault.

He brandished his sword and looked straight into the monster's crystalline eyes. "Hello, Snowy. What brings you to these parts this fine day?"

The icicle creature roared again, then charged.

"So much for pleasantries." Broomstick sprinted straight for the monster.

As soon as it got close enough, he leaped. Broomstick landed on the creature's knee and scrambled up to find purchase. The monster swiped at him with icicle claws and tried to shake him off.

Broomstick raised his sword and plunged it into the creature's thigh.

It didn't react.

"For Luna's sake," Broomstick muttered.

He started hacking at the knee. Icicles broke off, and the monster took in a raspy inhale as his leg sagged for a moment. It didn't give out, but it was a revelation for Broomstick—each shard of ice seemed to contribute to the creature's power.

Broomstick hit the butt of his sword against more icicles. A few broke off, and the monster's leg twitched. But now it was really angry, and it clawed at Broomstick with both hands.

An icicle stabbed his shoulder. He let out a cry and grabbed the wound.

The claws came again. Broomstick, bleeding steadily, still managed to avoid the blow by slipping around to the back of the monster's knee.

What he needed was an ax to hack off the leg. But all he had was a sword. Broomstick wrapped his own legs tightly around the creature's, held his left side with his arm, and started to saw at the ice with his sword hand.

The ice monster bellowed. It kicked out its leg and sent Broomstick flying off. He landed with a thud, and he skidded on the slick ground toward the lake.

No!

Broomstick dug his sword into the frozen ground to stop his momentum. He slid right into the blade, just inches from the water. The sword cut into his flesh, and even more blood dribbled out of him, two streams of red trickling into the lake.

Small waves began to form on the surface, and the water lapped farther up the shore, as if it were hungry for another body and mind to consume.

He clambered backward and yanked his sword from the ground.

Behind him, the heavy footsteps of the ice monster advanced, bouncing the cave floor with each stomp. It wouldn't take much this time for the creature to knock Broomstick into the water. Just a flick of its gargantuan finger, and Broomstick would be done for.

He scrambled to where his and Sora's bags were. The monster blew its rotten breath, and frost coalesced around Broomstick, beginning to surround him in a fence of ice. If he didn't figure out something fast, he'd be set adrift on an iceberg into the lake and left to die.

What can I do, though? Owls he could handle, but this? It wasn't as simple as setting up a bomb in the ceiling to block off a single tunnel.

But while Sora hadn't wanted to hurt the owls, Broomstick had no such reservations about this icicle abomination.

Instead of blowing up a tunnel, he could try to blow up the monster itself.

The fence around him was now up to his chest. If he was going to have a chance, he had to take it fast. Broomstick riffled through the bags for bombs. Sora had taken a bunch of them and he'd used a handful earlier, but surely those weren't all they had? He thought he'd packed a lot more.

The first bag was full of fish jerky and canteens of water. He ransacked a second one and found his small chest made of reinforced steel. He unlatched and opened it carefully.

Inside, cradled neatly inside padded compartments,

were dozens of bombs of various shapes, sizes, and potency. "Hello, you beautiful things." He weighed a few in his hands and picked one with a good amount of heft.

The monster ripped an icicle the size of a stalactite off the roof of the cavern and hurled it at Broomstick. It landed with a sharp rasp and embedded itself just six inches to his left. A second later, another giant icicle flew toward him. This one landed right next to the first.

"I know you're trying to kill me," Broomstick said, "but this is actually helpful. Thank you." He grabbed hold of the ice post and hauled himself up, gritting his teeth as the wound in his shoulder and arm throbbed. The blood hadn't stopped; the snow beneath him was splattered with crimson. But he kept going through the excruciating pain until he pulled himself up to the top of the ice barrier.

Then Broomstick tossed the bomb in the air and hit it with his sword as if they were a ball and bat.

The bomb collided with the monster's chest and exploded on impact, ripping the ice heart apart like glacial shrapnel.

Unfortunately, the force of the blast also blew Broomstick backward.

Nines!

He splashed into the shallow part of the water near shore. The sharp ice that formed the lake bottom scraped his knees as Broomstick tried to crawl out.

But the frigid water already had a taste of his blood, and the lake pulled at him greedily, lapping against him and rocking him away from its shore. Broomstick took a last breath before the milky white clouded his vision, and then he gave in to the water's embrace.

CHAPTER THIRTY

Sora tumbled through the trap door. She'd meant to swim, but the water stopped abruptly at the threshold, as if held back by an invisible barrier. She scraped her hands and knees on the gravel floor, and she filled her lungs with warm, humid air almost too thick to breathe.

When her lungs had stopped aching from being so close to oxygenless, Sora took in her new surroundings. The tiny room was made of solid mud walls that led nowhere. A dead end.

Sora chewed on her lip. Had Liga been wrong? What if this wasn't where Zomuri kept his treasure?

But it had to be. The Lake of Nightmares hadn't been created for no reason.

Maybe this was another defense? It could be another ruse. After the lake, Sora should've known better than to believe the first thing she saw.

She walked up to the mud wall opposite the trap door

and pushed. It was solid and left a reddish-brown smear on her palms.

"I refuse to believe it," she said to the room. "You're just showing me my worst fear, that I've come all this way for nothing."

The walls throbbed, just barely, under her touch.

Aha. This really was more than it first appeared.

She took a few steps back, ran toward the wall, jumped, and kicked.

Her leg smashed through the mud. The facade of the cramped, empty room shriveled away as suddenly as a popped balloon.

Instead, Sora found herself in a vast space where every inch of the walls and ceiling was studded with rubies, sapphires, and diamonds. The ground was over four feet deep in gold coins and other trinkets, like small statues carved of flawless marble, crowns of filigreed platinum, and necklaces spilling out of suede satchels, all of it tossed haphazardly among the gold as if it were inconsequential. Which it probably was to Zomuri. He had enough treasure here to buy the world a million times over, and what did he even need it for? He was a god. He was hoarding for hoarding's sake.

"How am I supposed to find a single gold pearl in here?" She couldn't dig through all the treasure in the vault. It would take forever, not to mention the fact that she didn't have anywhere to put what she'd already sorted through. There were so many riches in here, as soon as she dug a hole, more gold and jewels would cave in to fill the empty space. She wouldn't be able to separate it to keep it straight.

But surely Zomuri wouldn't just toss something as

important as a soul into the pile, would he?

Sora perked up. "Or if he did, it would be on top." After all, the golden pearl of Prince Gin's soul was a very recent addition.

She began crawling on hands and knees over the surface of the treasure, moving slowly so she could examine every inch around her. It was better than trying to search all the treasure, but progress was still almost sloth-like.

Methodically check a three-foot radius around herself.

Shift forward.

Repeat.

Soon, Sora's neck began to ache, and her eyes were crossing from focusing too hard. She couldn't keep this up.

What Sora needed was better vision. She had an arsenal of taiga eyesight spells that she could cast in her sleep, but ryuu magic was more powerful. Perhaps she could combine the two, but which spell to choose?

Not a hawkeye spell. Nor a jaguar or lemur. Sora needed something that would be good for identifying things that were ordinarily underwater, like pearls.

"Octopus spell!" she said, surprising even herself. Octopodes had some of the most impressive vision in the sea. They could see colors and textures where other animals couldn't; that's how they were able to camouflage themselves so well.

Instead of linking her thumbs together in the taiga mudra and undulating her eight other fingers as if they were tentacles, she conveyed the intent of the spell to the ryuu particles. *Sight like an octopus*, she thought over and over until the magic understood what she wanted and her vision opened wider and sharpened at the same time.

"Yes," she gasped.

The room wasn't just shiny with gold and jewel tones anymore. It was now a kaleidoscope, variations of light and all manner of colors that Sora had never seen before. Each piece of treasure stood out as unique, with different smoothnesses, brighter or darker reflections of the gems next to it, varying degrees of smudges and dust.

That's how Sora saw what she was looking for. On top of a pile of gold to her right, there was a small ivory jewelry box that was free of any dust at all, as if the lid had recently been opened.

She crawled over and carefully opened the box.

A single gold pearl rested inside, on a pillow of deep green satin. It rolled right off the satin and into Sora's fingers, as if it had been waiting for her all along.

"Got you," she whispered.

Sora reached behind her neck and unfastened her necklace, the one Mama had given her during Autumn Festival break when they'd been at Hana's shrine. It was a traditional Kichonan memory pendant, with a single golden pearl representative of the deceased's soul. The pearl on Sora's necklace was only a little smaller than Prince Gin's actual soul that had been on the satin pillow before her.

She could slip the pendant off the chain and leave it as a decoy.

Could a god be tricked that easily?

Either he's going to notice the soul pearl is gone or he isn't, she realized. Maybe it wasn't worth leaving this behind. A different pearl in the soul's place probably wouldn't make a difference. And irrational as it was, Sora had been a little sad about leaving her pendant here. The necklace had been a tribute to Hana, and it had also been a family jewel for a decade.

If only her sister could see that she was fighting on the wrong side. If only Sora could have another chance to convince her that the Dragon Prince was misguided.

But if she didn't, she wanted to have something to remember Hana by, to hold on to that memory of when she still looked up to Sora and wanted to be on the same team.

So Sora clasped the necklace back on. She just had to hope Zomuri wouldn't realize the soul pearl was missing before she could reunite it with Prince Gin.

But when Zomuri did notice, how would he punish her?

She curled into herself for a second, thinking about how gruesome Zomuri's retribution would be.

I'll face whatever consequences there are, Sora thought. Taigas were trained to sacrifice everything, if they had to, for their country. She could do this.

Sora took a deep breath. Then she tucked the soul pearl into a secure pocket deep inside her tunic, clung tightly to her gemina bond, and jumped up through the vault door, swimming back into the Lake of Nightmares.

CHAPTER THIRTY-ONE

Sora kicked upward through the water. Daemon's presence in their gemina bond was as solid as a mountain, so she knew she'd be able to get to shore without losing herself in the nightmares again.

But there was also something else in their connection. A slight hint of sour, like lemon juice in the back of her throat.

Sour was the taste of fear.

She tried to swallow it, but the fear wouldn't go away. It didn't feel like Daemon was worried about his hold on her, so what was it? Were he and Fairy okay?

Then Sora saw it. A short distance away, Broomstick floated aimlessly, his eyes staring straight forward, frozen but terrified. *Nines!* He was stuck in a vision. Fairy would be able to feel it through her gemina bond with Broomstick; Daemon, who was with Fairy, would know something had gone wrong—hence the sour in Sora's own bond.

She kicked with everything she had to get to Broomstick's side.

Sora grabbed his wrist. His pulse was slower than it should have been.

Alive, yet caught in the grip of the Lake of Nightmares.

She shook Broomstick hard, but his gaze remained fixed on whatever heinous vision the water was showing him. She slapped him across the face. It did nothing to bring him back either.

Her lungs burned, reminding her that her time down here was finite. She hooked her arm through one of Broomstick's and began to swim upward. He was more than twice her size, and the water had again taken on the thickened quality of jelly. Sora swam as hard as she could.

She lost her hold on Broomstick. His arm flopped uselessly, bleeding. Sora's chest tightened painfully, desperate for oxygen, furious that she'd subjected it to deprivation again so soon.

She took both of Broomstick's arms and draped them over her shoulder, hauling him piggyback. She kept kicking, lungs burning air faster because she was using so much strength in carrying him through the gelatinous water.

Her chest constricted just as she burst through the surface of the lake. Sora gasped while jerking Broomstick's head above water, too. She didn't know if he'd had time to cast a whale or sailfish spell. He wasn't supposed to go into the lake. He must have fallen in.

Onshore, Sora straddled him and pressed the heels of her hands against his chest. She had to not only revive him but also get the water out of his lungs. Who knew what damage the lake could do if its effects were allowed to linger inside his body?

She pumped on his chest. Then she pinched his nose,

sealed her mouth over his, and forced breaths into him.

Broomstick lay still.

She did it again. *Pump pump pump. Breathe, breathe.*

"I don't know what you had to fight while I was underwater," Sora said, taking in the shoreline and the remnants of what had obviously been an explosion. "But whatever it was, you beat it. And you won't die now. You're too good to lose to a bad dream."

Sora forced a couple more breaths into him.

"Do you hear me, Broomstick? You will *not* die now." She pumped harder on his chest.

Pump pump pump. Breathe, breathe. Again and again and again.

On the last one, he convulsed and started coughing up water.

"Thank the gods." Sora gripped his tunic for a moment, then sat back to give him space.

Broomstick coughed as he pushed himself onto his elbow.

"How did you end up in the lake? Are you hurt? What happened?" Sora knew she should give him a bit longer to recover, but she couldn't help it. She had to know.

"Monster . . . made of icicles," Broomstick rasped.

Sora's eyes widened. "Is it still here?"

"I killed it . . . I think." Broomstick sat up all the way, but he immediately grabbed his head and sank back to the ground.

"Broomstick!"

"I'm fine. Just . . . head hurts."

"Rest," Sora said. "You can fill me in later."

He closed his eyes but insisted on talking, although his speech was slurred and slow, like he had to piece the sentence together word by word. "Aqueous bombs . . . explode . . . when they touch . . . water . . . but . . . they *really* explode . . . when they hit . . . ice."

Oh. So that's how he'd gotten blown into the lake. No wonder his head hurt. Sora was amazed Broomstick had gotten away with only that.

Well, other than almost drowning. She let out a long exhale, relieved she hadn't lost him.

"Tell me . . . the vault?" Broomstick asked.

Sora reached into the hidden pocket just inside her collar, pulled out the gold soul pearl, and held it out to him. "I got Prince Gin's soul."

Broomstick's face contorted, and he jerked away from the pearl as if it were a plague.

Sora frowned. "It won't hurt you."

"N-no," Broomstick said, shaking his head vigorously. "Get it away from me. You can't trust me with it. I'm a bad person."

"What are you talking about?"

Suddenly, the words spilled out in a nearly delirious flood. "I'm going to kill a lot of people in the coming war, Spirit. The Dragon Prince is going to use me as a weapon on the mainland to slaughter city after city, country after country. I'll pretend to be friendly and plan big parties for them, and entire towns will show up, excited to be invited. Because, you know, people trust me. I'm nice. I like talking to them and hearing about their families and their hobbies and their dreams. But once I've lured them in, I'll blow them up. All their loved ones they just introduced me to. All their hopes and wishes blasted into ashes. I'm an evil person. Keep that soul pearl safe from me."

Maybe he still has water in his lungs. Broomstick was out of the water, but the lake's effects lingered, refusing to relinquish its hold on him.

Sora tucked the golden pearl away, not because she didn't trust Broomstick but to calm him down. "You're a good person," she said. "One of the best I know. The visions you saw weren't real—"

"But they could be!" He jumped up.

Her heart ached for him. Broomstick was the kind of person who threw surprise parties for his dormmates and sent birthday gifts to his coworkers' children. All he wanted was to bring joy into others' lives. The idea that his charisma could be used to cause harm was an assault on his very being.

If there's water in his lungs, can you get it out? Sora thought to the emerald dust that now floated lazily in the air.

But the magic just eddied for a few seconds around Broomstick before returning to doing nothing.

Did that mean it couldn't help? Or that Sora was wrong and there was no water in Broomstick's lungs?

Gods, no. If it was the latter, that meant the lake's enchantment had infiltrated something deeper inside him. Maybe Daemon had been able to protect Sora through their gemina bond because he was a demigod, like how he'd kept her tethered and therefore shielded from the Dragon Prince's powers of hypnosis. But Fairy had only taiga magic for Broomstick to latch on to, plus he'd been unprepared for falling into the lake.

"We need to get out of here," Sora said. "Maybe Liga will be able to help."

Broomstick broke into a cold sweat. "You should leave me here. Then I can't hurt anyone."

"No! Don't you see? The fact that you're worried about hurting others proves that you're good. The evil is only in your head. It's not real. You have to fight it."

"I can't." Broomstick let out a sob. "I saw what I'm going to do to those people. I can't let it happen. I can't make all those people love me, watch them get dressed up for the best night of their lives, and then murder them. I can't. I won't." He sprinted for the water, determined to throw himself in.

Sora threw a net of ryuu particles at him. It tangled Broomstick's feet, tripping him. She pounced and hit him in the back of the head with a chunk of ice.

Broomstick slumped to the ground.

"I'm sorry." Sora looked at him. "I said you wouldn't die today, and I meant it."

She packed up their bags, then asked the ryuu magic to find her a path out of the caverns. It took a few moments, but soon enough, an emerald trail glittered against the ice.

Her gemina bond sparked as if Daemon were reaching out, asking if she needed help.

"Yes," she said softly.

She wrote a message to Daemon and Fairy explaining what had happened. She could get Broomstick out of here, probably as far as Paro Village, the nearest town in this southern part of the kingdom. If Daemon could fly, they could come to meet them. Sora created another miniature eagle ray and sent the letter off to Jade Forest.

Then she placed the soul pearl in a small silk pouch, tightened the drawstring, and secured it in the interior pocket of her tunic.

Levitate Broomstick, she said to the ryuu particles. It would cost Sora a great deal of energy to float him all the way to Paro Village. But she would do what she had to do to get them out of here.

She slung their bags over her shoulders and motioned for the emerald dust to carry Broomstick out of the tunnels.

"Let's get out of these caves," she said, "and never, ever come back."

CHAPTER THIRTY-TWO

Zomuri looked into the saucer of blood in front of him and chuckled.

The girl had managed to get past his guards and break into his vault. She had absconded with Gin's soul and now carried her lug of a friend in tow like a giant sack of taro roots. Zomuri laughed again. He had to admit, it was quite a show; he was almost tempted to applaud.

Even better, she believed the boy had water from the lake in his lungs. But he didn't. Humans needed only a hint of self-doubt planted in their minds before insecurity ran rampant, overtaking everything like weeds. It was the beauty of the Lake of Nightmares—one swim and most mortals were done for.

The girl, however, had escaped that fate, and so she would need to be punished for her theft.

But Zomuri could do that at any time.

He switched the vision in his dish of blood to show the young emperor.

The ryuu had fixed the holes in the warships and were now transporting them to the coast. Gin supervised their swift progress. They would be in Toredo by day's end, and from there, they'd be able to launch an attack on their first target: the island of Thoma. Gin certainly was zealous about conquering those seven kingdoms.

No doubt the girl and her friends would try to stop the emperor. Zomuri contemplated what to do, if anything. He could crush the girl now. But she was feisty, and her antics were interesting in their unpredictability. And even though she had gotten hold of the soul pearl, the emperor would remain invincible as long as the soul remained outside his body. Gin had plenty of fight in him and didn't need a god to intervene.

Zomuri decided he could be angry at the girl later for stealing from him, but at the moment, he wanted to be entertained. And so the god conjured a chair lined with lion's fur and settled in. It was going to be amusing to watch how this mortal theater played out.

CHAPTER THIRTY-THREE

Fairy was a mess of tears as she paced around the chestnut grove. "Something's wrong. It felt like Broomstick was losing his mind—our gemina connection was all chaos and black smoke and then it suddenly went blank. Where did he go? What happened? Do you think . . . . ? Oh gods."

Wolf tried to catch her, to put his arms around her and comfort her, but she shook away from him and continued her frenetic pace around the clearing. It was as if standing still would allow all the fear to catch up to her. She had to keep moving.

"Something definitely happened," he said. "My connection with Sora is taut, like a fishing line. She's worried—I can feel it in the tension of the bond—but at the same time, I can tell it's not despair."

"Why can't I feel Broomstick, then?"

"I don't know," Wolf said gently. "I do know, though, that I lost track of Sora before and she ended up all right. Broomstick lost track of you, too, remember?"

Fairy gave Daemon a flat stare. "Yes, because I was drugged to a deathlike state of unconsciousness."

"You weren't dead, though."

"I could have been!" Fairy threw her arms in the air.

"He's . . ." Wolf shook his head. "He's got to be alive. I'd know it if he weren't. Sora would send me some hint of it through our bond."

Fairy paced some more. She understood the logic of what Wolf was saying, but it didn't make being here—away from her gemina—any easier. What was she supposed to do? Just sit around and wait until Sora sent them another messenger? Or until there was complete emptiness in her connection? Warriors who had lost their geminas described the feeling as a boulder slamming their bond shut, a heavy finality when there was no longer someone else on the other end. That's not what she sensed now, but it was eerily silent, as if she was walking through an abandoned corridor that might lead to that boulder.

"We have to go to them." She marched toward their meager camp.

"What?" Wolf trailed behind her. "We're supposed to stay here and keep searching the Imperial City for Empress Aki. And we're still waiting to get a response from my brother." They'd been trying to reach Liga ever since they returned from the Dragon Prince's study but to no avail.

Fairy whirled on him. "The empress isn't here, all right? We've spent days crawling through the castle and the Citadel and haven't found a trace of her. For all we know, Prince Gin already killed her. But my gemina—our *friend*—isn't dead yet, and we need to help him!"

Wolf stopped short. He looked guiltily at his feet. "You're

right. We're supposed to be there for each other."

He closed the distance between himself and Fairy and held open his arms. This time, she let him hold her. She buried her face in his chest and allowed the fear to hit her fully, tears streaming down her cheeks. "What if Broomstick isn't all right? What if he dies and I wasn't there for him?" she said.

"Shh." Wolf stroked her hair. "He's not going to die. And we'll fly to Naimo Ice Caves as soon as we're packed."

Fairy pulled away and wiped her eyes and nose on her sleeve. "I don't want to waste another minute. He needs me." She hurried over to fold her sleeping mat and gather her weapons. She packed up the wild persimmons she'd found on a tree that morning during foraging, then grabbed her copy of the map from the Dragon Prince's study and rolled it into a scroll, placing it safely inside her bag.

Beside her, Wolf also packed his bags, but instead of stashing knives and other weapons into his sleeves and hidden pockets, he unloaded all of them into a satchel.

"Aren't you going to need those?" Fairy asked.

"Can't use them when I'm a wolf."

Oh, right. How else were they going to fly down to the other side of the kingdom? Worrying about Broomstick was clouding her head. But the thought of Wolf in his demigod form lifted her spirits a little.

He began to lay out a system of straps he'd been working on while they were stationed here in the forest. It was a harness to allow him to carry their supplies.

When they were ready, Wolf shifted in a glow of soft blue light. His transitions were smooth now, after all the practice Liga had put him through. "You know how the harness works?"

Fairy nodded. She threw the straps over his back, then lay on the ground, scooting to slide under him and secure the harness around his belly. Another set of straps looped around his front legs. Then she tied each of their bags onto his sides, making sure to evenly distribute the weight.

"Does it feel all right?" she asked.

Wolf walked around the chestnut grove, testing out the harness as he moved. He wiggled his shoulders, shifting where the straps dug in.

"All good. Hop on."

Fairy jumped up and lay a strap across her hips, pulling to tighten it. That had been another of Wolf's ideas, to create belts like makeshift saddles, so his passengers wouldn't plummet to their deaths. She leaned forward and hugged his neck, allowing herself the comfort of nestling into his fur.

He took off at a run and leaped into the air. They sailed up easily, as if he'd been doing this his entire life.

She supposed he had, at least in his previous one. Fairy wondered if he still regretted giving up his right to live in Celestae.

As Jade Forest and the Imperial City grew smaller below them, sadness ached in Fairy's chest. This might be the last time she saw the place that had been her home for eighteen years. Even in the best of circumstances—where they succeeded in killing Prince Gin and stopped the impending war—she wouldn't get to come back here for a while.

Then something dive-bombed at them, and Fairy shrieked.

Wolf dodged, but barely. "What in all hells was that?"

Fairy scanned the air. A massive buzzard flapped its wings, pivoting to come back at her and Wolf again. She cursed under her breath.

Wolf let loose a shock of electricity, throwing bolts of lightning toward the buzzard. It dove out of the way.

Something moved in the periphery of Fairy's vision, below on the forest floor. She whipped her head around to look at it.

"Wolf, watch out! Someone's down there!"

The ryuu shot flames at them. Wolf tried to dodge, but they grazed his fur. He howled in pain.

"Stars!" Fairy smothered the fire out with her cloak and poured some water from a canteen to cool the singed skin. Wolf sucked in air through his teeth.

More flames barreled toward them. But Wolf flew higher, and the fire arced back down to the ground.

"We're out of range," Fairy said in relief.

She spoke too soon. A figure materialized out of nothing and stood next to the fire ryuu. Fairy didn't need to be close to know who it was.

"Spirit's sister . . ."

Wolf growled. "I just saw Hana, too. How did she find us?"

"I don't know," Fairy said as they flew farther. "But it looks like we got out of there just in time. They were laying an ambush."

"And they'll send reinforcements soon," Wolf said.

"Or now." Fairy pointed at a flurry of black flying at them from Jade Forest.

Wolf put on speed. Unfortunately, the burst of power

also set off brilliant sparks, and he streaked light through the sky like a comet.

"You're too bright," Fairy said, clinging to his fur as the frigid wind gusted in her face. "Douse your sparks, or we'll never be able to lose them if they can see you like this."

Them were hundreds of bats, flying in formation like a single enormous creature with sword-long fangs. Menagerie, the ryuu who controlled animals, must be commanding them.

Wolf quelled his sparks. But it probably wouldn't matter anyway. The bats would use their sonar to track him, as long as they stayed close enough.

He accelerated to the right.

They followed.

He careened down, back into a different part of Jade Forest.

They didn't lose his trail, even weaving in and out of the trees.

Wolf pulled back up into open air, breathing hard. "What do I do?"

"Speed of light," Fairy said. "Get us out of here."

"It'll make you sick if I fly any faster than this."

"Just do it!"

Too late. The buzzard swooped near them. Menagerie crouched on its back, a smug smile on his face.

"Watch out!" Fairy cried.

Menagerie pounced onto Wolf's back. "Impressive magic you've got here," he said. "Sure you don't want to join the ryuu?"

Wolf snarled. "Never."

Fairy twisted to fight Menagerie, but she was partially

trapped by the harness that was ironically meant to keep her alive. She pulled out a stiletto blade with one hand and fumbled to undo the belt across her lap with the other.

"Do not unbuckle," Wolf said. He jerked sideways mid-air to dump Menagerie off his back.

The ryuu let out a yell as he tumbled off. But he fell only about ten feet.

"How?" Fairy gawked at him, dangling beneath them but trailing everywhere they went.

"I'm holding on to a rope of ryuu magic that you can't see," Menagerie taunted. "It's also a noose around your pack mule's neck." He yanked on it, and Wolf gasped.

"He can't strangle you from there," Fairy said. "He doesn't have enough force to pull the rope tight enough."

Wolf growled. Fairy knew it wasn't much in the way of reassurance. It hardly comforted herself.

She looked down again. Menagerie wouldn't stay there for long. He was already climbing up the invisible rope. And where were Firebrand and Hana in all this?

Meanwhile, the bats attacked again. Fairy ducked as they came in screeching. Their talons and fangs grazed her neck and arms and Wolf's back. "You'd better not have rabies!" she shouted as they retreated, regrouping for their next assault.

"They don't have tails," Wolf said.

"That's a Liga-like non sequitur that makes no sense. Do tailless bats not have rabies?" Fairy held tightly to Wolf's fur as they swerved again. Menagerie was making progress climbing up his rope of ryuu particles.

"I don't know. But most fruit bats don't have tails. Sora saw them before, after I'd left Prince Gin's ship. Another ryuu battled Menagerie in a duel by drawing the bats away with fruit."

"My persimmons!" Fairy said.

"Exactly what I was thinking."

Wolf swooped, swinging Menagerie beneath him. The ryuu cursed as his grip slipped farther down the rope.

Fairy stretched over Wolf's side for one of their supply packs. She flipped open the top, grabbed the first persimmon she could, and threw.

At first, the bats in that part of the formation scattered. But then one of them realized what had been fired at them, and it broke off to chase the falling fruit. Several others, catching on, also dove off to pursue.

She pumped her fist. "Taigas: one; flying rats: zero."

"Don't get too cocky," Wolf said.

"No such thing," Fairy said.

She threw another persimmon. More bats peeled off to chase the food.

Fairy began a full-on assault, igniting a feeding frenzy. The bats' neat formation fell apart as more of them got distracted by the prospect of dinner.

Meanwhile, Wolf flew faster and swerved from side to side to slow Menagerie's progress. He was halfway up the rope, only five or so feet away now. But Wolf's erratic flying made the ryuu pause his ascent just to hold on.

"Fly south to the pear orchards outside Tanoshi," Fairy said, leaning closer to his ear. "We can lose the last of the bats there."

Wolf veered southwest.

Menagerie flung a dagger into his belly.

"Agh!" Wolf lost altitude just as they reached the

outskirts of the orchards, and Fairy screamed at the sudden dip.

Menagerie launched another knife at him.

"You bastard!" Fairy unstrapped herself from the harness.

"What are you doing?" Wolf shouted. But there was a quiver in his voice, and his words were almost carried away with the wind.

"I'm taking care of him," she said. "You just get us into those orchards." Half the bats were still on their tail.

She looped her arms around Wolf's neck, then swung to the underside. She looked straight down at Menagerie, and dropped.

"What in the hells—" Menagerie shouted as Fairy smacked into him.

Fairy latched on to Menagerie, holding on for dear life. Wolf dove into the trees. The branches were laden with fruit, and their perfume filled the air.

The bats chirped in surprised delight. Within seconds, they dispersed every which way, each finding their own pear tree on which to gorge.

"Lower!" Fairy said. From here, she could see the knife handles protruding from Wolf's belly and the blood flowing out like sadistic ribbons.

He obeyed and flew nearer to the ground. She and Menagerie crashed into it, and Fairy wrestled him from the invisible rope. They tumbled away together as Wolf flew on, carried forward by momentum.

Menagerie stabbed her in the side.

Fairy gasped but held on to him tightly.

The buzzard swooped down, this time carrying Hana. She leaped off.

"Retreat to Firebrand," she ordered Menagerie. "I'll finish these two."

Menagerie freed himself from Fairy's weakening grip and scrambled to his feet. "I didn't get the map yet, Virtuoso," he said.

"Don't worry about it," Hana said. "I'll find it."

"I can stay—"

"I want a private word with Fairy." Hana said her name with disgust. "Now go!"

Menagerie remained for a second but then jogged over to the buzzard. "Enjoy your slow and painful death," Menagerie said to Fairy. Then the buzzard lifted off with a wicked cry, taking Menagerie away.

Fairy shuddered but pulled a long, slender stiletto blade from her sleeve as Hana stalked closer.

"Stay back," Fairy said.

Hana frowned but stopped.

She called on her ryuu magic and had it tear the knife loose from Fairy's grip. The blade flew into Hana's hand instead.

Fairy gasped at her own empty palm.

"You're a fool if you think you can defeat a ryuu with a knife like this," Hana said.

"We're not trying to defeat you, you idiot," Fairy said, exasperated. "We're trying to save you. That Dragon Prince of yours might have damned you."

Hana shot her a nasty glare. "I know."

"Wait, what? You know, and you're still serving him?"

Fairy winced as more blood poured from the knife wound Menagerie had inflicted.

"I was in the study when you and Wolf read 'Kitari and the Curse,'" Hana said, closing the distance between them. "Emperor Gin confirmed that it's true the ryuu are damned. But you and Wolf said there might be a way that the gods can forgive us. I need to know more."

"Then why are you here instead of in a library, researching?" Fairy tried to inch farther from Hana, but it was hard to move with a knife in her side. She didn't want to pull it out, though, because then she'd bleed so much she might pass out. Fairy very much needed to be conscious right now.

Hana's breath seemed to speed up, as if she was working hard to keep her composure. Or maybe she was just getting madder. "I'm here because I thought you and Wolf might have more information than I have."

"And you thought that attacking us was a good way to get us to share what we know? Prince Gin really did a poor job of teaching you social skills."

"I'm getting impatient." Hana twirled Fairy's stiletto blade between her fingers.

"You know," Fairy said, still scooting slowly away on the dirt, "Spirit still wants you to join us."

Hana's entire body visibly tensed. "I already told her no."

"So you're still loyal to the Dragon Prince?"

Hana hesitated. It was only half a breath, but Fairy caught it.

"I am a ryuu warrior," Hana said, her face growing hard again. She took a stride forward and erased all the progress Fairy had made in inching away. "Tell me what you know about undoing the damnation."

Fairy laughed without humor. "Why, so you can destroy Kichona but redeem your soul right before you die? No, thank you, I'll pass."

Hana darted around Fairy and pushed the tip of the blade against the nape of her neck. "Tell me, or I'll kill you."

"Lucky for me, then, I don't have anything to tell," Fairy said. She'd been close to death so many times in the recent past it was surprisingly easy to remain calm. "Wolf and I don't know anything yet, but we're going to figure it out, somehow. And when we do . . . we'll tell you."

"You will?" Hana let the knife point slip.

"Of course," Fairy said. "If you join us."

"You're just as infuriating as my sister!" Hana slashed the back of Fairy's neck.

Fairy inhaled sharply. She didn't dare to slap her free hand over it with Hana right there behind her, but Fairy could feel the blood beginning to trickle down her neck and onto her collar.

"Hana—"

"My name is Virtuoso!"

"No, you're always going to be that tenderfoot I knew before you were ever given a taiga name. You're Hana, who loved her sister and loved the Society. I know who you are deep inside, and Spirit does, too."

Hana was silent behind Fairy. Was she going to strike her again? Or was she considering it?

"Tell me we have a deal," Fairy said, trying again. At the same time, she tucked herself into a ball and somersaulted between two pear trees, getting away from Hana.

But when Fairy rolled and sprang to her feet, there was no one there with her.

"Where did you—?"

The wind rustled through the orchard. A few seconds later, the giant buzzard from earlier swooped down, paused as if picking up a passenger, then flew away.

Hana was gone. Fairy wasn't sure what that meant, but what she did know was that Hana could very easily have killed her, but she hadn't. That was . . . something.

For now, though, Fairy needed to tend to these wounds. She had a powder made of dried thistledoon leaves that acted as a coagulant. But it wasn't in the little satchel she kept on her belt; it was in one of the bags on Wolf's harness. If she could find him, maybe she could stop both their bleeding.

Fairy held on to her side and the back of her neck and slowly rose to her knees.

"Wolf!" she shouted. "Where are you?" The effort sent searing pain through her rib cage.

He didn't answer. But how far could he have gone? He'd probably crashed soon after she and Menagerie hit the ground.

"Wolf!"

Please be all right. Gods dammit, everyone was going down. Maybe they *were* fools for thinking they could fight the ryuu, for believing they had a chance against the Dragon Prince.

"Wolf!" Fairy sucked in a sob as the knife shifted inside her. The slice in the back of her neck didn't seem too bad, but her side was in bad shape. She could pull out the knife, but then there'd be nothing to stop the bleeding. Her tunic and the left side of her trousers were already soaked as it was.

A short distance away in the orchard, in the opposite direction from where the buzzard had retrieved Hana, there was a weak howl.

"He's alive," Fairy whispered, barely holding it together as she started to run. She pressed her side, wincing as the blade stabbed her insides with every bouncing stride, but she didn't slow down. Not until she reached Wolf, collapsed at the base of a pear tree in a puddle of blood.

"I'm here," she said, forgetting her own wound for the moment and scrambling to the bag that held the vial of powdered thistledoon.

Wolf looked at her but didn't seem to really see her. He just whimpered "Sora?" and then his eyes rolled to the back of his head.

CHAPTER THIRTY-FOUR

Fairy knelt next to Wolf, frozen.

"What did you say?"

Of course there was no response. He was unconscious, and "Sora" hung in the air like the last, off-key note of a song.

The throb of the knife flared in Fairy's side, and at the same time, Wolf's entire body shuddered.

Get yourself together, Fairy thought.

Besides, there must be an explanation. Maybe he could feel Spirit through their gemina bond and that was why he called her name. Regardless, Fairy was made of stuff too strong to be taken down by boyfriend problems. She could deal with it later. Right now, she had lives to save, his and her own.

Fairy pressed a hand to Wolf's belly and grasped one of the knives with her other. "This is going to hurt," she said. "But it has to come out. I'm sorry."

She took a deep breath, then pulled the blade out, feeling

the flesh try to hold on to it for a moment before letting go. Blood started to gush immediately, and she smashed her palm against the wound while she discarded the knife and reached for her vial of thistledoon.

To apply the powder to the wound, Fairy had to let go of Wolf for a second so she could pour the thistledoon into her hand. She moved away from his stomach and tilted the vial.

When she looked back, though, his blood had already congealed. "How . . . ?"

Liga had shown them that demigods could heal faster than humans. Could that be what was happening?

Fairy funneled the thistledoon powder back into the vial and moved her hands to the other knife in Wolf's belly. *I hope I'm right about this.* She extracted the blade, and the same stomach-turning sensation of metal sliding from bloody flesh reverberated through her fingers.

This time, though, she didn't look away. And as she watched, Wolf's bleeding slowed. His skin melded together, smooth like molten rock, where there had, only seconds ago, been a vicious cut. It still looked angrily red and raw, but it was no longer an open wound.

"Holy heavens," Fairy said.

Her own wound stung then, and she remembered that Menagerie had also left her a sharp souvenir.

Fairy didn't want to pull it out. What if she fainted? Or died? Then there would be no one to take care of Wolf. But if she left it in, it would only make the damage worse, and she might faint anyway from the shock of the foreign object jammed into her ribs and the inevitable infection for leaving a wound exposed like this.

She poured the powdered thistledoon into her hand

again, then clenched her teeth and slid the knife out of her side, gasping. Stars blinded her vision.

"Fairy?" Wolf asked, his voice like sandpaper.

It was enough to remind her where she was, what she had to do. She smacked her palm against her side and smeared thistledoon into the wound, painting her skin with blood in the process. She bit her knuckle as the thistledoon did its work, stinging like salt against her raw flesh. The pain was almost enough to push her over the brink to unconsciousness.

She held her side and curled into Wolf, tucking herself into the space against his chest, away from his healing belly. "Wolf," she whispered, answering him. "We're okay. We're going to be okay. Just . . . rest." Her eyes fluttered, tempted to close.

Something shimmery darted through the trees. Fairy sat up, as excruciating as the movement was. At first, she thought it was a beetle, but then it landed right in front of them.

"One of Spirit's messenger rays," she said.

Wolf stirred beside her, but he didn't say anything. She didn't know if he was still awake.

Fairy's hands shook. Would the message explain why her gemina bond had gone dark? What if it was a distress call? She fumbled with the tiny paper and only managed to get it open after four tries.

Fairy read aloud, in case Wolf was listening. "'We have Prince Gin's soul. But Broomstick fell in the Lake of Nightmares, and he's not quite himself.'"

It was suddenly hard to breathe, and she didn't know if it was this news about Broomstick or the knife wound in her side. Or both.

She forced herself to keep reading Sora's message. "'We're going to Paro Village to recover. If you can fly, please meet us there, and bring Liga. Maybe he'll know how to help.'"

Fairy collapsed against Wolf's chest. The swell of relief and distress, combined with the pain of her wounds, was too much. Broomstick was alive, thank the gods. But what had happened to him in the Lake of Nightmares? No wonder Fairy's gemina bond had gone blank.

Wolf shifted and stretched his leg to wrap around her. "We'll go . . . soon," he said.

She wanted to believe it. But she also knew things could end badly if they tried to travel while hurt like this. "We're no good to them, no good to Kichona, if we're dead."

"Sleep, then," he said. "When we wake up, we'll . . ."

Wolf didn't finish what he was going to say. And it didn't matter anyway because Fairy could barely hold on to consciousness either. The pain of her wound and her anxiety over Broomstick conspired against her, and like weighted curtains, her eyelids fell closed.

At first Fairy thought it was a dream, because the space around her was a vacuum. No colors or sounds. Neither hot nor cold. Just a black abyss, sucking Fairy deeper and deeper into its depths.

Until suddenly, her bare feet touched sand. Or what seemed like sand, soft and cool between her toes. Everything remained black, but Fairy reached her arms around her. Her fingertips landed on smooth walls.

A moment later, beautiful emerald light appeared a short distance away, sparkling to reveal the tunnel she stood in.

"Where am I?"

A whisper beckoned from the end of the tunnel. *Come, young apprentice. You did not get to be a warrior in life, but as a reward for your service to Luna, you can play with more powerful magic in death.*

"Oh gods." Panic fluttered in Fairy's throat. This wasn't a dream. "I'm dead."

Except . . . wait.

The Dragon Prince had said he stole Sight from the afterlife without actually dying. So Fairy wasn't dead yet, not until she stepped across to the light.

The green glitter was mesmerizing, sparkling like millions of shards of emeralds. Warmth blossomed from the end of the tunnel, and the magic smelled of all of Fairy's favorite things—crushed lavender and rose water and rock sugar—like the most perfect bubble bath ever to be drawn.

Fairy walked slowly toward it, stopping on the threshold.

The promise of otherworldly joy sang to her, and she leaned hungrily toward it. Maybe this was why Prince Gin was so obsessed with bringing the Evermore to Kichona. He knew there were things much greater than ordinary life, and he wanted them. Just like Fairy wanted to luxuriate in that green light now.

Do not be afraid, the afterlife whispered. *Those you loved in life will follow you in death when their time comes.*

But another voice in the back of her head called to her. "Fairy, it's not your time yet. . . ."

The sensation of a pair of arms latched on to her as if in an embrace. Was it Wolf from the other side, his demigodness somehow allowing his voice to follow her here? Fairy's heart pounded so fiercely it echoed into the afterlife.

She remembered that she was still needed in the world of the living.

An idea flickered in Fairy's head. She could steal the knowledge of Sight and return as a ryuu. Then both she and Spirit would have these powers, plus Wolf with his demigod ones. It would help the odds in their fight to save Kichona.

But Fairy quickly killed the notion, because she remembered that taking the ability to see the magic like that would doom her, just like it had Prince Gin. She closed her eyes and purged her memory of how the emerald particles looked. *I leave that knowledge here, where it belongs.*

Then Fairy stepped back, away from the end of the tunnel. "I'm not going to die," she said to the afterlife. "Not yet."

The tunnel sighed, almost as though disappointed. But Fairy's will was strong, and after another whine, the green and the tunnel imploded, as if sucked into a single point. A shock of bright white blinded her vision.

Fairy jolted where she lay on the ground in the orchard, but she couldn't move. Her eyes flew open, and she saw not green dust but everything else as she'd known it. The blue of the sky above. The gnarled brown of the tree branches.

And the very real, muscled arms that held her tightly.

"You're back." Wolf exhaled but didn't loosen his grip.

"I'm back."

"I thought I lost you."

Fairy leaned back against him and smiled weakly. "I'm not that easy to kill."

CHAPTER THIRTY-FIVE

Hana returned to the Citadel, feeling as if a few chinks were missing from her armor. Fairy's mention of Sora had caught her off guard. She'd thought she was over her sister wanting to recruit her. Hells, they had literally been at each other's throats during the last battle. Why did hearing about Sora get to her now?

Maybe because Hana had never before questioned her own loyalty to Emperor Gin. His beliefs and his promises had been the moral guideposts for most of her life. But now . . .

"We should report our failure to His Majesty," Firebrand said as they passed through the fortress gates. Hana had told them that Wolf showed up and used his strange magic to help him and Fairy escape.

"Go away," Hana grumbled at Firebrand.

"But the mission—"

"I'll take care of it later," she said with more force this time.

"Virtuoso," Menagerie chimed in, "with all due respect, we're supposed to report mission outcomes immediately."

"Fine! Tell him whatever you want!" Hana's magic hurled Firebrand and Menagerie across the courtyard, slamming them into the walls of the nearest building.

The ryuu gaped at her, but they didn't try to approach her again.

Hana glared once more, then marched away.

What to do? How to feel?

Fairy had promised to share how to undo the damning of souls if they discovered it. But that was dependent on them not only finding it but also surviving long enough to get the information to Hana. And what if Hana did join them? Emperor Gin would crush them. Why did her sister and her friends find it so appealing to die for the losing side of history?

If Hana stayed with the ryuu, however, there was a chance she would live long enough to see the Evermore. Then the damnation would be moot.

Of course, there was the possibility that in the many forthcoming years of war with the mainland, Hana would be killed. And in death, she'd be trapped in the hells forever.

She tore at her hair as she stomped through the Citadel. The other ryuu who saw the storm clouds in her expression darted out of her way.

What to do?

The best way to handle this, Hana thought, *is to lie low for now*. Continue fighting for Emperor Gin, because maybe he was right and this would all be worth it. But she'd keep an eye on Sora and her friends, in case they figured out how to undo the ryuu's damnation.

And what about how to feel?

"The best thing to feel right now," Hana said quietly to herself, "is nothing."

CHAPTER THIRTY-SIX

Sora had used ryuu magic to carry Broomstick out of Naimo Ice Caves, but as soon as they emerged from the caverns, he'd woken up, and she didn't have the heart to knock him out again. Plus, she realized she couldn't keep up the effort of using magic to carry him all the way to Paro Village.

Unfortunately, he was still convinced it would be better for Kichona—and all the kingdoms on the mainland—if he remained buried deep inside the Lake of Nightmares. So Sora had tied him up with invisible rope and laid him across his horse's saddle, carried like a prisoner. Undignified but necessary. And maybe the bouncing of the horse would jolt the rest of the water out of his lungs, if that was, in fact, what was ailing him. That wouldn't be a bad thing. Sora's most immediate priority was fixing Broomstick. But she also had to get them back to the Imperial City soon. The soul pearl in her pocket needed to be reunited with Prince Gin.

Late the next day, they reached Paro Village. Even

though she'd been here before, it still struck her as such an oddity. The little hamlet was so deeply buried in dense forest that Sora wondered how sunlight managed to reach it. Thick curtains of flowering vines draped heavily everywhere—around the perimeter of town, in between the shops and homes, even in the middle of its main street. The thick perfume and dampness of foliage weighted the air, and it took a little more effort than normal to breathe.

She released the rope that bound Broomstick. It was too far for him to run back to the ice caves now.

Sora really didn't want to go into the village, though. After seeing her parents, she and Broomstick had avoided people. If she'd had her choice, they would have headed straight to Jade Forest. But Broomstick needed a place to recover, and hopefully her messenger had gotten to Daemon and Fairy, and they'd be on their way with Liga soon.

"Let's skip the village and go around to the Society of Taigas outpost," she said. "There will be beds there and maybe food, if those feral little kids didn't eat it all."

"Feral kids?" Broomstick asked. He hated and feared himself, but otherwise he still functioned normally. The key, Sora thought, was to keep conversations away from Prince Gin and Zomuri.

Not an easy task, given the circumstances.

Still, she took what she could get in the moment. "When Daemon and I were here last time, a bunch of children had overtaken the outpost, playing at being taigas. They pelted us with acorns and rocks. I'm kind of looking forward to seeing the Little Ferals again."

Broomstick's smile vanished.

She understood immediately. He was worried what he

might do to the kids, how he might accidentally charm them, then hurt them.

Sora had another worry, though: the possibility that the kids had been tainted by Zomuri, too.

They pushed through the final curtain of flowers and emerged into a clearing.

"Where's the Society outpost?" Broomstick asked, confused that there was nothing but trampled undergrowth and mossy boulders in front of them.

"Look up," Sora said.

He craned his neck upward. "Daggers," he said. The Society post was a sprawling black structure with black thatched roofs that spanned across half a dozen trees, camouflaged into the shadows of the thick canopy of leaves. Octagonal platforms were interspersed through branches around the tree house, places where taiga warriors could hide and launch weapons in case of attack. And then there were the non-fighting elements of the post, like the hammocks swinging between boughs and the sundeck overlooking a small lake behind the treehouse. Paro Village may have been one of the most remote outposts in the kingdom, but it would not be a bad place to serve the Society.

Twenty or so tiny smudged faces popped up around the tree house, in windows, doorways, and even from the thatched roof.

"Hey-o, fierce taigas of Kichona!" Sora shouted. "We are weary warriors from the north, come to see the great fort of Paro Village. Will you allow us to enter your fortress?" Her phrasing was a bit stilted, but from her prior experience with the children here, they liked playacting. Sora thought the theatrical formality might predispose them to liking her better, instead of pelting her like they had before. Broomstick hung back and watched, keeping himself out of the way.

A girl, about ten years old, stepped forward. Her hair stood in every direction, and it was tangled with branches. Little Feral, indeed.

"Why should we let you in?" she said.

"Are you the commander?" Sora asked, continuing to play their game.

"Yes. I'm Rilyko— I mean, I'm Whiplash." The girl put her hands on her hips and stood taller. It was cute.

But Sora pretended to take her very seriously. "Commander Whiplash, we are on our way to a secret mission for Emperor Gin. And we need your help."

"A secret mission?" Her eyes lit up. Kichonans looked up to taigas but the children especially. Sora's life was their fantasy.

"Yes," she said solemnly. "I can't tell you what it is exactly, but it involves spying and blowing up our enemies."

"Sharp Ax!" Whiplash called to a boy, probably five or six years old, who must have given himself the adorable, if awkward, taiga name. "Let them in."

The boy hurried to unroll a rope ladder. After tugging to make sure it was securely tied above, Sora climbed up.

"Well?" Sharp Ax asked, tapping his little foot as he scowled at Broomstick. "Are you coming up? Or are you chicken?"

Broomstick flushed. But he couldn't resist the boy, who looked a lot like the tenderfoots in the Citadel mentoring program. Broomstick climbed up the rope ladder. Still, when he reached the top, he kept his distance from everyone.

In the meantime, the soul pearl seemed to stir in the hidden pocket in Sora's collar, and she flinched. It was as if the pearl had been asleep but had now awakened, if that were possible. It strained against the thick cloth of the tunic, like an iron pellet attracted to a magnet. The movement was faint enough that it wasn't visible, but it *was* alarming, and Sora pressed her hand against her chest in an attempt to stop it.

Why was it moving now, when it had been dormant before?

The little commander strode up to Sora and Broomstick, brandishing a switchblade. "Both of you, lift the backs of your tunics."

"Excuse me?" Sora, surprised at the child's brashness, momentarily forgot about the pearl.

"If you're really a taiga," the girl said, "the mark of the silver triplicate whorls will be there on the small of your back. If not, I'll slice your throat from ear to ear."

Sora didn't know what to say. First off, there was a child threatening her with a knife, which was both amusing and alarming, because some of the most dangerous people were the ones who thought they knew how to use weapons but didn't. And second of all, Sora couldn't let the kids undress her just because they wanted proof of who she and Broomstick were. That was not how this power dynamic was supposed to work, even if Sora was playing along that Whiplash was in charge.

"How about this instead?" Sora pulled a throwing star off the leather strap on her chest, twirled it in her fingers a few times, then sent it flying into a nearby tree.

Whiplash screwed up her face. "Any normal person could do that."

But Sora wasn't dissuaded. "Do normal people walk around with cases full of explosives?" She gestured at Broomstick.

He hesitated, but eventually he opened one of his bags and slid out a slim metal box. He flipped the lid open to reveal almost a dozen small bombs nestled in individually cushioned pockets.

"Whoooa," Whiplash said, suddenly an awestruck child. "Okay, you're good." She put away her switchblade. "We're excited to have you here. We can show you all the progress we're making, and when you go back north, you can report on our work to His Majesty."

Broomstick's forehead wrinkled at the mention of the Dragon Prince. "Your progress?"

Whiplash marched ahead as if she really were a commander. "When the emperor was here, he asked everyone in Paro Village to begin preparations not only for his coronation but also for pursuing the Evermore." She checked to make sure Sora and Broomstick were following, then continued down the hall.

The pearl in Sora's collar strained in the same direction. *Is it attracted to Whiplash for some reason?*

Meanwhile, the little commander kept talking. "The grown-ups are busy chopping down the forest for wood so Emperor Gin can build ships to cross the ocean. Obviously, we kids aren't big enough to do that, so we've been working nonstop on other things, like stitching together sails." They arrived at a large room, probably the taiga warriors' main gathering hall. There were two dozen children spread across the floor, huddled over large swaths of canvas, needles and thread in hand, sewing edges of fabric together.

The soul pearl started rolling in the small space of Sora's collar pocket, pulling to the right, then switching to the left, then forward, as if it wanted to go in all directions and couldn't decide.

It's the kids, Sora realized. Not just Whiplash in particular—she'd just happened to be the closest at first. But what was it about the Little Ferals that the pearl was attracted to?

Sora watched them for only a few seconds before she noticed something besides how diligently they worked. She leaned over to Broomstick. "They're scrawny. And filthy."

"It's like they're literally working nonstop, without breaks for food or baths," he said. "Why would they do that?"

Sora looked around the room again, but before she could answer, Whiplash ushered them out to a deck that overlooked a lake.

"What's going on here?" Broomstick asked. There was another dozen children out there, some wading in the brackish water, some sitting on the pier with fishing poles. Despite the late autumn chill, some of the boys had their shirts off. Sora could see their ribs beneath their mud-crusted skin.

At the presence of more children, the pearl began pushing against her collar pocket again, this time as if trying to get into the lake.

"We're catching frogs and fish to help feed the emperor's navy," Whiplash said. "And only a handful of us have drowned so far," she added proudly, pointing to four lifeless bodies on the far shore.

"What?" Sora rushed to the edge of the deck in alarm. "Kids have died? You have to stop. How are the adults letting this happen? You're just children!"

"We are *not* just children!" the little commander shouted. "We have sworn our lives to His Majesty, and we won't rest until he has what he wants!"

All the blood drained from Broomstick's face. "Um . . . Commander Whiplash, do you mind if I have a moment in private with my colleague?"

The girl eyed him suspiciously.

"To explain to her why what you're doing is important," he lied, turning on his easy smile so Whiplash would feel like they were on the same side.

She scrutinized him, as if she could see whether he was telling the truth.

"Permission granted," she said. "But only for a minute."

When she'd gone inside, Broomstick stepped up to the deck's edge next to Sora. "When you and Wolf were in Paro Village before, Prince Gin had already been here, hadn't he?"

She nodded, still staring in shock at the corpses of the Little Ferals who'd drowned. "This was the first place he came to gather Hearts."

"So these villagers—the grown-ups *and* the kids—were hypnotized?"

"Yes."

"I think that's why they're so devoted to sewing sails and catching fish," Broomstick said. "Prince Gin brainwashed them into absolute loyalty. It's different from how Zomuri's influence made your parents and the dumpling maker irritable. This is actual hypnosis, like what Prince Gin did to the taigas, which means the citizens of Paro Village will do whatever he needs. But unlike adults, the kids don't know how to balance that with taking care of themselves."

Sora tore her gaze away from the lake. She couldn't look anymore. "Stars. The kids would rather starve or die than stop working because of the Dragon Prince's magic."

That's when it hit her. The pearl moved toward the Little Ferals not because they were children but because Prince Gin's magic had touched them. His soul was attracted to his magic, to traces of him. Which made sense—a body and soul were meant to be together while on earth, and the soul was trying to get back to the Dragon Prince. Right now, these kids, with his magic in them, were the closest thing to the man himself.

But Sora had also been touched by Prince Gin's powers—she had Sight and the use of ryuu particles. Why hadn't the pearl reacted to her?

Maybe it had. She thought back to when she'd opened the jewelry box in Zomuri's vault. The pearl had rolled off the green satin pillow right into Sora's hands. And come to think of it, her chest felt a little tender where the soul pearl's pocket was, as if it had been burrowing against the collar to get as close to her as possible. Only now, surrounded by other traces of the Dragon Prince's magic, had it started moving toward them.

She pressed her hand to her collar again. The pearl was still moving, but her pocket was secure; the soul shouldn't be able to escape unless Sora let it out.

But this could serve as an excellent warning system if any ryuu came near.

Broomstick was still staring at the Little Ferals. "We need to convince them to take care of themselves."

Sora shook her head sadly. "If it were that simple, we could have talked sense into the other taigas after Prince Gin took their minds. We wouldn't be the only ones left fighting him."

"What about your ryuu magic?" Broomstick said, pacing the deck. He waved his arms in the directions of the kids at the lake and inside the tree house. "You can't cast some kind of counterspell? They're all going to work themselves to death soon."

"There's nothing I can do to alter Prince Gin's magic," Sora said, "other than kill him to release all those under his spell. That was our ultimate goal. It still *is* our goal. I'm just waiting for Daemon and Fairy and Liga to show up. They'll help you feel one hundred percent like yourself again, and then we'll go put an end to Prince Gin and find Empress Aki."

Broomstick glanced at the lake where, with a maniacal fervor, the children gutted frogs and strung fish up to dry. He looked inside the outpost, where Whiplash yelled at another child over a mistake in the sails.

"What if you're wrong? What if there's no turning back from this?"

"I refuse to accept that," Sora said. "For their sake, for my parents', and for yours."

CHAPTER THIRTY-SEVEN

"How's your wound?" Daemon asked as he knelt next to Fairy. The pear trees shielded them from the direct sun, but even so, he tried to provide her with more shade as he brought his fingers gingerly to the blood-soaked fabric on her side.

Even at so light a touch, Fairy winced. "You were worse off than me," she said.

Daemon's fingers went instinctively to his stomach. He lifted his tunic. There were only scars now where he'd been stabbed. "Holy heavens."

"It's unfair that you can heal so fast. But my wound is worth it," she said, still weak from just coming back from the brink of death but already with a lilt of humor in her voice. "Hana came, and I got to talk to her."

"She found us and didn't kill us?"

"Unexpected, isn't it?" Fairy said, closing her eyes because the sun was too bright.

Daemon conjured an umbrella to shade them with.

Surprised, she let out a small laugh, then told him about her conversation with Sora's sister.

"Do you think Hana might be considering joining us?" he asked.

"At the very least, I think she has doubts about Prince Gin," Fairy said. "I'm not sure how strong her misgivings are, so we shouldn't get our hopes up. But like you said, Hana didn't kill us when she easily could have. That's got to count for something."

"Sora will be glad to hear about this," Daemon said.

"Oh stars, I forgot about Spirit and Broomstick!" Fairy said. She tried to roll over to reach something, but she cried out and grabbed her ribs.

"Don't move." Daemon gently eased her back onto the sleeping mat. "What are you suddenly so worried about?"

"I'm a terrible person. How could I have forgotten? A messenger came from Spirit. Broomstick got hurt in the ice caves. I read the note to you, but I'm not sure how lucid you were."

Daemon only vaguely remembered it, but he tried to keep calm, for Fairy's sake. "Where's the message?"

"Near my bag."

He retrieved the tiny scroll and read Sora's brief account of what had happened at Naimo Ice Caves.

"You have to get to Paro Village." Fairy had closed her eyes. "I don't think I can travel yet. . . . You have to go alone."

"What? No." He put Sora's message down. "I'm not leaving you here. I'll stay."

"You'll go. We need to remember that there are bigger things at risk than just one of us being in pain. Our entire

242

kingdom is at stake. And don't worry about me. I'll be fine.

"Bring Broomstick and Spirit here," Fairy said. "I'll rest and try to reach Liga. . . ." Her voice trailed away at the end of the sentence, and her breathing slowed. She'd fallen asleep.

Daemon hated to leave her. She looked so tiny and frail, like a doll that might break if touched the wrong way. And yet he knew he was wrong. This was the girl who was constantly underestimated *because* she was pretty and small. The girl who hadn't hesitated to disguise herself as the empress and walk knowingly into an assassination trap. She could take care of herself.

Still, he wouldn't leave Fairy out here in the orchard.

Daemon changed into a wolf, and at top speed, he was able to scout the area and find an abandoned mining shack outside of Gorudo Hills. He returned to Fairy and scooped up her and their bags.

When he'd settled her into the shack on an old hay mattress, he made himself human again. Her eyes fluttered open. "Where are we?"

"Far enough away from where the ryuu attacked us that you'll be safe."

"Are you going now?"

"I don't have to."

"I wasn't asking you to stay," she said hoarsely. He handed her a canteen, and she sipped, capping it and laying it beside her when she was done.

"Everything you need is within arm's reach," Daemon said. "There are some crackers here, and your bag full of the stuff you foraged in Jade Forest. If I go now, and Sora and Broomstick are still at Paro Village, we can be back late tonight. But if we're not—"

"They need you, too. Don't worry about me."

Daemon would worry anyway—a lot—but he bent down and kissed Fairy.

He almost missed his mark, and their lips met awkwardly. Closed and pressed a little too lightly.

Maybe this kiss was off because Fairy was weak.

Or maybe everything was fine between them, and Daemon was overanalyzing it. He did have a tendency to think too much.

"Bye, Wolfie," Fairy said, already drifting back to sleep.

He spread a blanket over her and conjured some drapes over the broken windows to dim the sunlight streaming in. Before he left, Daemon kissed her softly on the forehead, and that one felt all right.

"Now sleep. And when you wake up, I'll be back with Broomstick and Sora."

CHAPTER THIRTY-EIGHT

Watching Daemon descend as a wolf from the clouds was one of the most beautiful things Sora had ever seen. He looked like a blue streak of the aurora borealis in the dark sky, and she ran from where she stood on the tree house deck and scuttled down a rope ladder to meet him.

She wanted to throw herself at him as soon as he shifted into human form. But she managed to restrain herself and offered him a fist bump instead. "I'm so glad to see you again. I was beginning to worry."

Daemon's mouth pressed into a grim line. "Sorry I took so long."

Sora searched behind him. She'd been so focused on her own feelings about Daemon that she hadn't noticed he was alone. Alarm spiked in her chest. "Where's Fairy?"

"We were attacked and both wounded."

Sora gasped. "Tell me she's all right."

"She will be." He toed a rock on the ground. "I was able to heal myself, but she wasn't strong enough to make the trip."

"Crow's eye," Sora said. "Who attacked you?"

"Where's Broomstick?" Daemon asked, not so subtly changing the subject.

"What are you not telling me?"

Daemon let out a long breath. "A lot has happened."

"Start with the good news."

He nodded. "Hana was with the ryuu who attacked us. Fairy almost died."

"What? How is that good news!" Their gemina bond wilted, like an entire meadow of flowers dying all at once.

"Because Hana is having doubts about serving Prince Gin."

Sora's stomach flipped. "Really?" She had held on to a small hope that she could still convince her sister to switch sides, but to be honest, it had probably been more delusion than real belief. This, however . . .

"Yeah," Daemon said. "But there's more. Um, let's sit down."

"Just tell me," Sora said. "I can handle it."

Daemon took several long breaths. "Fairy and I broke into Prince Gin's study. While we were there, we found a book of legends, including the prince's handwritten notations. The stories were about another time in the past when magic was stolen from the gods, and we think . . ." Daemon winced and closed his eyes, as if what he was about to do was causing him physical pain.

Sora's heart climbed into her throat. "You think what?" she asked quietly.

He opened his eyes and looked straight into hers. "We think that anyone with ryuu powers is damned," he whispered. "The knowledge of that magic belonged to the afterlife, and Prince Gin stole it. Anyone who possesses the

246

illegal magic will be damned to the hells after they die."

"What?" Sora's whole body shook.

Daemon reached out and held her steady. "We're going to find a way out of this. Fairy is already reaching out to Liga. There must be a way to get the gods' forgiveness. You didn't steal Sight yourself, and you're using ryuu magic to fight the one who did. We'll save you. I'll do anything I can to make it happen."

But a knot formed in Sora's chest. It was difficult to breathe. The emerald particles around her reeled in a frenzy, stirred up in her panic.

"Get away from me!" She flung out her hand, pushing at the ryuu magic.

The dust blew a few feet away and remained there, as if cowed by her anger.

She could still feel the magic, though. It wasn't just the particles floating everywhere. It was the memory of the campfire warmth in her belly and the bliss rolling through her veins whenever she cast a ryuu spell. The feeling that the glittering dust had seeped not only into her skin but, apparently, also into her soul.

How could something so beautiful be so abominable?

"I can't . . ." She was breathing too fast. Her head began to spin.

"Deep breaths." Daemon wrapped his arms around her. Bolts of lightning shot through Sora's skin. Not literally, but it felt as if he had set his electricity on her, tingly and warm.

"Thank you, but I need . . . I don't know what I need. I have to think. I can't. . . . It's too much." She ran away from the Society post and into the dense woods that surrounded Paro Village.

Sora kept running. She shoved through vines and ducked under half-fallen trees. She zigzagged through rocks and pushed onward, even when thorns snagged the hem of her trousers and scratched the skin beneath bloody.

Finally, her legs turned to jelly from exhaustion, and she sagged against a boulder, shaded by a scraggly oak. She buried her face in her hands.

It was quiet here, not even a bird chirping, but still, she noticed when the breeze shifted ever so slightly above her.

"You followed me," she said, without looking up at the branches far overhead.

Daemon alighted from the tree and swooped to the forest floor. "I wanted to make sure you were all right." He sat beside her and put his arm around her again. "I'm so sorry, Sora."

She wanted to cry, but the tears wouldn't come. Instead, fury balled up her insides. "How could Prince Gin do this?" Sora pounded her fists against Daemon's broad chest. "What kind of monster can so cavalierly damn other people's souls for eternity just to get what he wants?"

Daemon let her keep hitting him. "The same kind of monster," he said, "who can sacrifice two hundred innocents and watch them cut out their own hearts."

"I hate him," Sora said, each blow landing on Daemon with a thump. "I hate him I hate him I hate him!"

It's all too much, she thought. Why bother fighting at all? Why not let Prince Gin do what he wanted instead? If he succeeded, he'd bring his dream of the Evermore to reality. Sora would be immortal. She wouldn't have to worry about her soul being condemned to the hells.

But as soon as Sora thought it, her conscience flared

up, so hot that she actually startled. How could she have believed—even for a second—that allowing the Dragon Prince to win was an option? Too many people would die on the quest to achieve the Evermore, and every ryuu who was killed would spend eternity being tortured in the hells. It was selfishness that drove Prince Gin, and that wasn't what Sora was made of.

She collapsed against Daemon. He held her as she shook in silent sobs, still no tears but sadness nonetheless.

"Distract me," Sora said. "Tell me about your training. How has it been going with Liga?"

Daemon laughed quietly. "It's been . . . interesting. Liga is still figuring out how to interact with humans, and it can be rather amusing. But he's a good and patient teacher, and I've learned a lot. I can shift easily now, and I can fly pretty well. He taught me some basic magic, too. I still have to work on my gravitational powers, though—"

Sora's mouth dropped open. "Your what?"

The grin on Daemon's face was bright enough to rival the moon. "All of Vespre's children have different powers related to the stars or the night. You saw how Liga made the sky dimmer when he first appeared. Well, I apparently used to be able to control gravity, one of the powers of the stars."

"Daemon, that's incredible."

"I can't believe I gave it up, but it's all right, because I'm going to relearn how to do it."

"I'm really happy for you." She rested her head on his chest, and she swore she could almost feel the intensity of his magic in each of his breaths. Gods, she had missed him. But being this close to Daemon was rejuvenating. Geminas were meant to be together. Maybe not romantically but at least physically and emotionally. She hadn't realized how much stronger she felt when she wasn't separated from him.

He told her some more about the smaller spells that he was using, like conjuring food (not great but edible), clothes (he no longer had to be naked when he shifted), and even a ledge outside the Dragon Prince's study. It was enough to distract Sora's mind for a while.

But eventually, he ran out of stories to tell, and silence settled into the forest again.

Sora sighed as she sat up, thoughts of her damnation rising again.

"Why does it have to be me?" she asked. "Why did I have to be the one to rebel, to be cursed with this magic?"

"Because you were the only one brave enough to lead us," Daemon said.

"I'm not that brave," Sora said in barely a whisper. "I'm only holding it together because I have to. If I fall apart, we lose everything."

"That's the hardest kind of courage of all."

She closed her eyes and burrowed into him again. Daemon tightened his arms around her.

A few minutes later, though, Sora bolted upright. "Oh gods."

"What is it?"

"It's not just me who's damned to the hells after I die. It's Hana, too . . . and all our hypnotized friends at the Citadel."

Daemon shuffled uncomfortably. "Yeah."

He'd already thought of that. Yet he hadn't brought it up, instead letting Sora process her own fate first.

The revelation that Hana and so many taigas were affected made everything worse. But in a bizarre way, it also made it possible for Sora to rise out of her despair.

No destiny is set in stone, she thought.

She looked at Daemon. "This isn't over until we say it is." That's what she'd told him, Broomstick, and Fairy back in Jade Forest. And it was still true. The stakes might be even higher, but that only made it more imperative that they fight.

"True," Daemon said. "We decide when the fight ends." He hugged her again.

The press of his broad chest on her face and his biceps around her made Sora feel safe, despite the odds. The woodsy, night-sky scent of his skin comforted her.

It also simultaneously stoked embers in the pit of her stomach.

Sora had to extract herself before she did anything rash. Like look up at how the wind tousled his wild, blue hair. Or stare at the sparks that danced in his eyes now that he'd awakened the demigod nature inside him. Or kiss him.

She ducked out from Daemon's arms and cleared her throat. "Let's find Broomstick and get out of here."

Sora could feel the weight of this new burden on her shoulders, but she could carry it. She had given herself to Kichona, to protect the kingdom and its people at all costs. And she meant to keep that promise, even if it meant her own death. Her own eternal damnation. "I'm not going to let my sister and all the other taigas be condemned to the hells. So let's go return the soul pearl to its owner and kill the Dragon Prince."

CHAPTER THIRTY-NINE

Early the next morning, Sora, Broomstick, and Daemon flew toward Gorudo Hills. Sora was looking forward to all four of them being reunited, but as soon as the old mining shack came into view, she let out a gasp.

Fairy lay in a limp heap next to the smoldering remnants of a campfire, and an arrow protruded from her chest.

"No!" Broomstick jumped off Daemon's back before they'd even landed. He was still haunted by the Lake of Nightmares, but seeing his gemina lifeless on the ground roused him to action. He sprinted to Fairy's side, skidding the last few feet before he threw himself over her body.

As soon as Daemon's paws hit the grass, he ran, too. Sora clung to his fur.

"Is she alive?" Daemon asked, panting.

Fairy moaned and rolled over, rubbing her eyes at the commotion. The arrow wasn't in her chest but embedded in the ground next to her. "You're back. Everyone's back."

"Oh, thank the gods," Broomstick said. "You're all right.

You're lucky." He plucked the arrow out of the grass and held it above his head. "It just missed her."

Sora began to scan their surroundings. "They could still be here."

"Who attacked you?" Daemon asked. "And what are you doing out here? I thought you were going to sleep inside the shack, where you wouldn't be seen."

"Attack?" Fairy pushed herself onto her elbows, pinching her lips at the pain. "I was alone the entire time you were gone. I took a nap and felt a little better, so I thought I'd try to contact Liga."

Broomstick was on his feet now, the arrow in one fist and a sword in his other hand. "You couldn't have been alone. This had to have come from somewhere."

"But why shoot only one arrow?" Fairy asked.

"It doesn't look right. Can I see it?" Daemon shifted into human form. Broomstick handed the arrow to him.

Daemon smirked. "That's what I thought. Fairy was right—she wasn't in any danger. This is from Liga. See the arrowhead? It's an alligator tooth."

Sora's breath caught with the hope that it held answers to help both Broomstick and herself.

Broomstick hurried to Fairy's side and helped her sit up properly. While he checked her knife wound, Daemon and Sora examined the arrow.

There was no obvious message on it, though. Sora untied the twine that held the tooth to the shaft. No paper rolled up around the arrow. No words written on the shaft itself.

"Are we supposed to do something to it?" she asked.

Daemon shook his head. "I have no clue."

Sora held the pieces of the arrow up to her ear, shaking

them to see if there was perhaps something stored inside.

Suddenly, Liga's voice filled the air, as if he'd been waiting for them to *hear* his message rather than see it. Of course. Liga didn't understand humans or the way they did things. An ordinary, written note probably hadn't occurred to him.

"My apologies that I cannot come to earth right now," he said, sounding as if he were standing right beside them. "I am working on a rather fascinating celestial project, and it is impossible to leave the sky."

"What could be more important than helping us prevent the destruction of Kichona?" Daemon grumbled.

Liga's message barreled onward. "To answer the question in Fairy's prayer, if Broomstick has god magic in him, it will take god magic to undo it. I doubt Wolf or I is powerful enough.

"However, I have better news for Spirit—there is a purification ritual to remove the taint on her soul, although I do not know the details. You would have to appeal to an actual god—not a demigod—for the answers on how to perform it."

They waited for more, but that was the abrupt end of the message, and the arrow's components disintegrated into dust.

Sora looked up at the sky, both relieved that there was a possibility to save the souls of all the taigas, including her sister's and her own, and disappointed that there were no instructions, nor a solution to Broomstick's predicament. "Your brother has yet to understand the finer points of human conversation."

Daemon grumbled. "And we're even worse off now than when we started. We still have no idea where Empress Aki is, and based on that war council meeting that Fairy and I saw, the Dragon Prince is about to begin his attacks. On top of that, you're contaminated by ryuu magic, and Broomstick is—"

"Evil," he finished miserably.

"You're *not* evil," Sora said.

"I don't believe you," Broomstick said.

Fairy leaned her head on his shoulder. "Do you believe *me*?" she asked softly. They were geminas in the way Luna truly meant for them to be—sister and brother warrior, bonded forever.

Broomstick hesitated, but then he rested his head on Fairy's. "Depends on what you say."

"I've been connected to you since we were seven years old, and I know you inside and out. There's not a mean cell in your entire body."

He shook his head. "I don't know."

"Why don't you rest for a bit?" Sora said. "We've been through a lot. Maybe you'll feel better after a nap."

"Doubt it," he said. "But it's worth a shot."

Fairy wanted a nap, too, so they went into the shack while Sora and Daemon stayed outside.

"What now?" Daemon asked.

Sora chewed on her lip. "I don't know. Liga's too hard to get answers from, and even when he does try to help, he's confusing. So I guess that means it's up to us to figure every-thing out—how to reunite this pearl with Prince Gin, how to kill him once he's no longer invincible, how to reach the gods to get them to fix Broomstick's confidence and purify me from the ryuu magic, how to find Empress Aki . . ." She slumped.

"It's too much to ask of us," Daemon said.

She scowled at him. "Don't start again with how impos-sible this is and that we need to give up. We're Kichona's last hope. We're *my* last hope. If we don't step in, no one will. So don't say that it's too much—" Sora caught the slight lift of his mouth, a smirk attempting to hide. "Oh. You're only pretending to be defeated in order to rile me up, aren't you?"

He feigned shock and pressed his hands to his chest. "Who, me?"

Sora punched him in the arm. But his ploy had worked.

"So," Daemon said, trying hard not to grin and show how pleased he was with himself, "I don't have answers to the things we need to accomplish, but I do have the map that Fairy copied down when we broke into Prince Gin's study. Maybe there's something on it that will help."

"Let me see it," Sora said. Having a task to focus on would be good.

She set up a table outside the shack, using two sawhorses and a wooden board, and Daemon retrieved the map. He unrolled it, setting a pair of wire cutters on one corner to keep the page from curling and weighting the other corners with a hammer, a lone glove, and a piece of broken brick he'd scavenged from the overgrown yard.

Sora bent over the map. It was of Kichona and the seven countries of the mainland, with the ocean between them. There were symbols like little men along the perimeter of Kichona, with a denser concentration near the Imperial City. "Ground troops," Sora said to herself. She traced her fingers along the ports of Kichona's eastern shore, which faced the mainland. Tiny black ship symbols clustered around the harbors. "And the navy."

"I think the Dragon Prince is planning to attack Thoma first," Daemon said, pointing at the dotted line that went from Toredo—a short distance from the shipyards in the

Citadel—to the small island kingdom just off the mainland.

"It wouldn't be hard," Sora said, nodding. "Tidepool—the ryuu who commands the sea—can easily get the ships to Thoma. In fact, she could probably launch a typhoon attack like she did to Isle of the Moon when all this began."

"Right," Daemon said. "But Fairy, Liga, and I slowed them down. We drilled holes in the bottoms of all the ships. Still, Thoma's a relatively easy target, so once those boats are back in commission, I'm pretty certain Prince Gin is going to serve up the Thomasian tsarina's heart as the first of the trophies he's required to give Zomuri."

Sora cringed.

"And once the ryuu seize Thoma," Daemon said, studying the map, "they'll be able to set up base there and be a lot closer to launch campaigns on Fale Po Tair, Xerlinis, and Vyratta."

At the mention of those kingdoms, Sora had to sit down. They were the "Southern Alliance" that had been in her vision in the Lake of Nightmares. They'd brutally retaliated against the Dragon Prince's advances, not only defending their own countries but traversing the ocean to demolish Kichona as well. Sora remembered the hill of dead she'd climbed over in victory, the ruined remains of Samara Mountain and her parents' home in the distance.

It wasn't real, Sora thought as she tried to shake the vision out of her head. She couldn't tell Broomstick not to believe in the lake's visions while succumbing to them herself. But the so-called prophecy had sunk long curled claws into her head, and it was difficult to jar them loose.

Daemon reached across their sawhorse table and touched Sora's arm.

Her skin lit up again like it had when Daemon touched her in Paro Village. The sensation helped her break free of the Lake of Nightmares vision. It also rekindled the desire to grab Daemon by the collar and bury her face into the crook of his neck, to have him not just as her gemina but as more.

"Sora?"

"Uh, sorry. I'm fine. Just . . . got distracted."

Did Daemon not feel the sparks between them, too?

Sora let her hair fall across her face so Daemon couldn't see her blush. "Hey, what's this?"

She pointed at a mass of troops on the northeastern archipelago. If Kichona were a tiger, this was the tip of its upper paw. All the other soldier and boat symbols on the map had dotted lines connecting them from Kichona to targets overseas. But this squadron didn't have a line going anywhere.

"Why would warriors be stationed there but not be involved in strikes on the mainland?" Daemon asked.

Sora chewed on her thumbnail as she thought it over.

"There's nothing out there on the tiny islands," Daemon said. "No people, just rocks, waterfalls, and animals."

"But we know from experience that Prince Gin likes to hide important things in remote places where no one will expect them."

Daemon's eyes brightened. "Like in Takish Gorge."

"Yeah." That was where Prince Gin had first hidden his ryuu before they were big enough to be considered an army. Sora tapped on the little island at the end of the tiger's-paw archipelago. "What if he's hiding something here, too? Something that requires guards. That would explain why these soldier symbols don't have attack routes drawn to the mainland."

"He can't be hiding his soul there," Daemon said. "You have it."

Sora patted the pocket in her collar, where the golden pearl lay pressed against her, now that they weren't near other traces of Prince Gin's magic. It was comforting, in a twisted way, because if the soul was still, that meant no other ryuu were near.

"But think," Sora said. "What else is too valuable to be found that we've been searching for?"

"Not *what* else," Daemon said, a smile growing on his face, the slash of scars on his cheek rising with it. "*Who* else. You think Empress Aki is still alive, don't you? And that the Dragon Prince is hiding her there."

"Yes. I'm willing to bet she's being held prisoner inside Dera Falls, and I think we should go save her."

"What about Prince Gin, though?" Daemon asked. "Isn't the priority to get the soul back inside him so we can kill him?"

"It is," Sora said, "but I also want to get it right because we might have only one chance, and I need more time to figure out how to get close enough to him to do it. I've been racking my brain since he first gave his soul to Zomuri, and I still haven't found an answer. Maybe Empress Aki can help us, though. She's his sister; she might know a weakness about him that we can exploit."

Daemon nodded. "Good point. So as soon as Fairy's well enough . . ."

Sora grinned. "We go on a rescue mission."

CHAPTER FORTY

Thoma was a sweet potato–shaped island across the ocean from Kichona. It was small but famed for its navy and had been an independent kingdom for two centuries.

Until today. Gin hopped off the rowboat that brought him to shore and surveyed his first conquered territory. The Thomasian navy had fought fiercely, but they were no match for his ryuu and their new ships. Without a pause, Gin's gaze swept over the palm trees and the crystalline blue waters of the lagoons that surrounded the island and landed swiftly on the prisoners lined up on the beach.

Tidepool, the ryuu who had led the attack, jogged over to Gin.

"What are our casualties?" Gin asked.

"Two, Your Majesty," she said. "Steeltoe and Morning Glory."

He frowned. Steeltoe, in particular, had been useful. She'd been working on a new kind of armor for the ryuu.

But Gin shrugged it off; giving up his soul made it easy to ignore any pangs of conscience at damning two of his soldiers to the hells. Besides, losses were expected in war, and since the ryuu were fighting ordinary soldiers—not taigas—they didn't have much use for traditional weapons and armor like Steeltoe had been working on. Gin's armies had simply overwhelmed Thoma's navy with magic.

He tilted his chin at the prisoners kneeling in the sand. "Are they ready to submit to a new ruler?"

"Unfortunately," Tidepool said, "they're true to the reputation of Thomasians—clever as dolphins, fierce as orcas, and obstinate as old barnacles. But their defiance is nothing you can't fix with your powers, Your Majesty."

Gin began to make his way over to them, sinking a little in the sand. Yes, he could brainwash the sailors. But there was also a prideful part of him that wanted to win them over on his own instead. The rulers of vast empires past hadn't needed to brainwash all the citizens in order to rule their lands. And the taigas who'd sided with him a decade ago during the Blood Rift—the warriors who became the original ryuu—had also believed in Gin willingly.

It might be amusing to try winning the Thomasian sailors over first.

"Prisoners!" Tidepool shouted. "Bow for your new emperor, His Majesty, Gin Ora!"

The Thomasian navy assembled on the beach refused to bow. They glared as Gin stopped in front of them, and the ryuu who guarded them began to kick them in the backs to force them to bend in respect.

Gin raised a hand and shook his head. "That won't be necessary. And let them stand."

His ryuu grumbled but obeyed.

When the prisoners were all on their feet, Gin put on a kind smile, one without a trace of arrogance or condescension.

"Honorable sailors of Thoma, you have fought valiantly, and I respect that. I visited your kingdom with my father when I was a child, and I remember the grand spectacle of your ships sailing in formation to welcome us and escort us to your beautiful island. From then on, I admired your navy and your people, and I always hoped to return some day."

The prisoners' expressions were still stiff. Gin had to soften them more.

"I understand that today may feel like a defeat," he said, pacing before them. "But I urge you to think of it differently. You are not familiar with our gods, but one of them has promised us the Evermore—a paradise on earth—if I can unite Kichona and the entire mainland. Therefore, I do not come here as a conqueror"—this part was a lie, of course—"but as an equal to your Tsarina Austine, seeking a partnership for our two kingdoms."

Most of the sailors' faces remained hard with skepticism, but some of the younger ones had begun to soften, their fists no longer clenched, eyes less narrow.

"To prove this to you, I have dispatched an invitation to Tsarina Austine for a summit, in which she and I—and our brightest advisers—will discuss our kingdoms' futures together."

One of the older sailors, whose skin was as rough as hide from a lifetime in the biting wind of the sea, said, "How do we know you won't kill her as soon as she agrees to meet you?"

Gin let his eyes and entire countenance droop, as if he were saddened by the accusation. "I suppose the cynical answer is that, if I wanted Tsarina Austine dead, it would have already happened. You've seen what my ryuu can do. It is no easy feat to win a battle against the world-famous Thomasian navy, and yet here we stand.

"But I reiterate: I want our kingdoms to work together. You'll have autonomy to keep running your crews as you are accustomed, and the people of Thoma will continue their lives as they've known them. The only difference is you will have the benefit of Kichona as a partner, and we will have the benefit of Thoma. What say you?"

"Are we allowed to discuss it?" a young sailor asked.

Gin smiled generously. He could feel his hook sinking in, the prize fish at the end weakening in its fight. "Of course," he said, motioning for his ryuu to back off and give the prisoners a facade of privacy. He, too, stepped farther down the beach.

Tidepool followed. "With all due respect, Your Majesty, you're not really going to negotiate with Tsarina Austine, are you?"

"How much of an imbecile are you?" Gin asked. "We'll bring the tsarina and her advisers onto my ship, and once we've returned to Kichona, we'll summon Zomuri to claim her heart."

"B-but then why bother with this pretense of good will in front of the prisoners? Won't they know soon enough that their tsarina is dead? And what about the other kingdoms? This will incense them before we're prepared to fight the entire mainland."

"We'll inform them that, during our negotiations with

Tsarina Austine, I proposed marriage, and she accepted my offer. She'll wish to stay in Kichona as the seat of our united empire, of course. But one day in the near future, she will die tragically of an illness while pregnant with our first child. The other kingdoms will not be suspicious for a while."

"That's pure genius," Tidepool said.

"I know."

The prisoners were engaged in a lively debate. Gin allowed it to continue. Tsarina Austine was being given ample time to prepare her things and her entourage for the summit (under careful watch of the ryuu, of course), so a few extra minutes on the beach meant nothing.

He walked down to the shore and finally took in the clear turquoise of the lagoons. The water was so clear he could see straight down to the corals on the sandy ocean floor, the sea teeming with colorfully striped fish. He could do worse than have this island as a gem in his crown.

Where the sky met the water, though, something white sped toward Gin. Was it a seagull skimming the surface?

"Tidepool," he said, "intercept that for me."

"Yes, Your Majesty."

A moment later, a wave leaped up and caught whatever it was in a fistful of water and rushed it to shore in a surge of foam. Tidepool grabbed it first to make sure it was safe.

"A seagull bearing a message," she said, releasing the bird and unfolding the paper carefully. It appeared to be enchanted with ryuu magic, but caution was advisable none-theless.

Tidepool undid the complicated folds. "It's fine, Your Majesty. A note from Menagerie."

Gin took the paper, which, having been opened, now flattened out its own creases.

Your Majesty,
We found where Virtuoso's sister and friends have been hiding, but they foiled our attack. We' ll redouble our efforts and make sure they won' t be a problem for us anymore.
Ever your servant,
Menagerie

Gin crumpled the note and hurled it into the ocean. Spirit and her friends had drilled holes into his ships and set back his timeline for this attack on Thoma. They also had a copy of the map from his study. Had they figured out where he was keeping Aki? Gods, they were pests.

"Send word to Skeleton and Skullcrusher to prepare their crews for immediate departure," he said to Tidepool. "I want reinforcements at Dera Falls to guard Aki's prison."

"Yes, Your Majesty." Tidepool jogged off to carry out his orders.

But how should he deal with Spirit? She was a fly to his bull, but even so, she could interfere again with Gin's progress toward the Evermore.

I could capture Spirit and her wolf gemina. Their powers could be harnessed for Gin's own purposes. In fact, he probably should have tried to do this earlier, but he'd been too busy with taking the throne and seizing control of the Society to bother with four rogue taigas. Now, however, if Gin guessed correctly, Spirit and her friends would attempt to rescue Aki.

And he could be there waiting for them. Dera Falls was on the way back to the Imperial City, and it was probably time that he paid his sister another visit anyway.

One of the ryuu who'd been guarding the Thomasian sailors ran down the shore. "Your Majesty, the prisoners have come to a decision."

Gin took a deep breath, put on a mask of benevolence, and walked calmly back to the sailors.

The older man with the sunburned skin stepped forward. "As men and women of honor, we respect the customs of war, and we accept that we are at your mercy. If we may make a request, it is that you will take care of our families. Then we pledge to be your humble servants on the seas in the bid to bring your Evermore to earth." He knelt in the sand and bowed his head. The rest of the sailors followed.

A smile bloomed on Gin's face. He hadn't needed to hypnotize these sailors to convince him of his cause. And they'd also given him an idea for making sure Spirit surrendered to him.

He thanked the prisoners and welcomed them into the Army of the Evermore, a fitting name for a force bigger than Kichona's alone.

Then he took control of their minds anyway. It had been fun, toying with them, but he wouldn't leave a chance for them to rebel.

Afterward, Gin retreated to his ship and called for Tidepool again.

She arrived at his captain's quarters a minute later. "You asked for me, Your Majesty?"

"I need something done on the other side of Kichona," he said from his desk.

"Not a problem," Tidepool said. "How soon?"

"Quickly." He relayed the details of what he wanted done.

A cruel smile twisted Tidepool's lips. "I'll send a pair of ryuu right away, Your Majesty." She bowed and left to dispatch the order.

Gin sat back in his chair, arms clasped behind his head, and exhaled.

Thoma was his, and Tsarina Austine's heart would soon belong to Zomuri.

CHAPTER FORTY-ONE

Sora hadn't been able to sleep, so she left the mining shack and went for a walk as the sun began to rise.

Back in Paro Village, she had sworn to herself that she'd do anything to save her sister, her friends, and Kichona, but at the moment, it seemed like her promise was just a lot of hot air. She had a plan to get to Dera Falls to rescue Empress Aki, but what if Sora was wrong and the empress wasn't there? And then there was the goal of reuniting the soul pearl with Prince Gin so they could kill him . . . but how in the world was Sora going to get close enough to him to get the pearl into his body?

Am I going to spoon-feed it to him and not expect any resistance?

Stars, these weren't feasible plans. They were just wishful fancies, the kind that tenderfoots made up when they daydreamed about saving the world.

She felt sorry for Kichona that the entire kingdom was relying on her brains.

Sora sighed. Of course, it was also possible that all her ideas seemed pathetic right now since she was so sleep deprived. Her emotions had been up and down ever since Daemon told her that her soul was damned, veering from fear-induced confidence to helpless despair.

At the moment, she was clearly wading in a pool of doubt.

Eventually, Sora headed back toward the mining shack and spotted Fairy outside doing some warm-up exercises in the dawn light. This made Sora smile a little—it was good to see her roommate up and about, feeling well enough to practice fighting stances.

"Hey." Fairy jogged over to her.

"Morning," Sora said. "You're moving pretty well."

"Thanks. The thistledoon is helping a lot. But that's not what I wanted to talk to you about."

Sora stopped to give her her full attention. "What's going on?"

"It's Broomstick." Fairy gestured toward the shack. "He won't get out of bed. He keeps telling me about what he saw in the lake, and I *know* he'd never do those things, but no matter what I say, he refuses to believe me."

"I don't know if there's anything we can do without the gods," Sora said.

"But we have to try. I mean, we don't even know for sure that there's lake water in him. It's like something in him broke, and as his gemina, I have to try to fix it. I just don't know how."

Sora bit her lip. She understood Broomstick's gloom, not only because she'd been in the lake, too, but also because she was swimming in her own insecurity. And yet, Fairy

269

was right, they had to try something.

"What's made him happy in the past?" Sora asked.

"Um . . . throwing parties. Play-fighting with tenderfoots. Blowing things up. But he can't really do any of those here."

"He could blow up the soul pearl and save me some trouble," Sora said sardonically.

"Oh!" Fairy's eyes glimmered. "That's worth a try."

Sora snorted, not because it was funny, but because she'd only said it as a joke, out of despair.

It would be convenient, though. She hadn't considered the possibility before, since she'd been more confident then, but now . . .

"I suppose he might as well try," Sora said. "Maybe if Broomstick can blow up the pearl, it would kill the Dragon Prince. We could end this all right now." She retrieved the soul pearl from the hidden pocket in her collar.

The tiny orb shone prettily in the sunlight.

Fairy wrinkled her nose. "I thought it would be more special."

Sora dropped it in Fairy's hand. "I hope it's not, and that it can be blown to bits like any other pearl. And I hope you and Broomstick succeed so that I never have to see it again."

CHAPTER FORTY-TWO

Fairy approached Broomstick with the idea.

"No," he said. "Absolutely not." He cowered under his blanket. Despite being twice Fairy's size, he looked so vulnerable, with his skin smudged with dirt and his eyes downcast. His anxiety about the Lake of Nightmares prophecy rattled again through their gemina bond.

"It'll be all right," Fairy said gently. "I'm here, remember? And the pearl doesn't pose any threat to you. It's the Dragon Prince who can hypnotize you, not his soul."

Broomstick shuddered.

"We can do this," she said.

He dared to look up from his blanket at the pearl in her hand. "You're assuming it's a real gem that can be blown up."

"No, I'm not. It could be anything. That doesn't mean we shouldn't try each new idea we think of. If none of them works, then we stick to our original plan of killing Prince Gin anyway. But it would be infinitely preferable to be able

271

to assassinate him without having to be near him."

Fairy grabbed Broomstick's arm and hauled him up from the sleeping mat. It was like wrestling with an enormous sack full of lead weights, but she prevailed through sheer determination.

"If we blow this up," she said, "you won't have to be afraid anymore. Prince Gin won't be able to hypnotize you, and that vision you saw in the lake will never come true."

Understanding seemed to soak into Broomstick.

"We have to kill the Dragon Prince," he said.

Fairy nodded. She held up the pearl in front of him. "And we might have a chance right now."

They ducked inside what had once been stables, a short distance from the shack. Broomstick wanted an enclosed space to catch the pearl if it flew off during an explosion, but the shack was where all their belongings were, and the toolshed next to it was too small to blow things up in.

The stables were long empty, the dividers rotten and caving in, but the space was still redolent of horse droppings and saddle soap. Broomstick would have walked straight back outside if Fairy hadn't stopped him.

"If I can stomach it, you can," she said.

He huffed, but he stayed and set his bag on the ground.

"Do you want the soul pearl?" Fairy asked, cupping it in her hand.

He chewed on the inside of his cheek.

Fairy chastised herself. Broomstick may have wanted to destroy Prince Gin's soul, but that didn't mean he'd get over his fear of the pearl immediately. She should have known that.

But she could help him salvage some of his pride by offering an alternative. "On second thought," Fairy said, "why don't we do this?" She found a bucket, turned it upside down, and set the pearl on top. "You can blow it up from there."

He stopped gnawing on his cheek and laughed instead.

"What?" Fairy said.

"How long have you known me?"

"Um, your whole life."

"And how long have I been blowing things up?"

"Since you singed off your eyebrows." Fairy remembered that day clearly. Broomstick had somehow gotten his hands on fireworks—who in their right mind gives a five-year-old an explosive?—and he'd set it off in the tenderfoot nursery. The rocket had shot through a window, burst on a nearby tree trunk, and set the leaves and grass around it on fire. Plus, the sparks from the takeoff had burned the ends of Broomstick's eyebrows, and they'd never grown back.

"Right," he said. "And since then, I've never blown anything up without a test chamber." He rifled through his bag and pulled out a metal box made of reinforced steel, several inches thick on each side.

"You've been lugging that around everywhere?" Fairy said. "No wonder your stuff is so damn heavy."

"I don't ever want to be in a situation where I could blow something up, but then the opportunity passes because I wasn't prepared." He smirked, and Fairy was glad to see this first small hint of the gemina she knew.

He opened the test chamber, and she set the soul pearl in the bottom. Then Broomstick opened the other cases he'd brought and spent some time inspecting the bombs, making little cooing noises as he came to his favorite ones. Fairy didn't laugh at him, because she was just as weird. Her potions and poisons were like babies to her, and she'd been known to talk or even sing to them.

Maybe this was why she and Broomstick were such a good gemina pair.

Finally, he chose a bomb. They lit the fuse and locked it inside the test chamber with the pearl.

Five, four, three, two, one . . .

A muffled explosion shook the test chamber.

Broomstick unlocked it. Black smoke poured out. Fairy coughed and waved an old horse blanket at it, trying to usher the smoke out of the stables.

"Did we do it?" she asked, once the smoke had cleared a bit. She peered inside the test chamber.

The walls were dark with soot, but the soul pearl sat, gold and unscathed, in the center.

"Stars," she cursed.

They tried half a dozen approaches, beating the smoke out of the stables each time before looking into the test chamber. After the sixth failure, Broomstick shook his head.

"I don't think we can do anything with this pearl. It's not just a gem from the ocean. It's like what Liga's arrow said—if there's god magic involved, it'll take god magic to undo."

Fairy sagged. "I suppose we should report back to Spirit and Wolf."

They walked out of the stable—wow, the air was so much fresher out here—and looked in the shack. There was no one in there, so they headed back outside.

Fairy spotted Wolf and Spirit among the crab apple trees. But when Broomstick lifted his hands to his mouth to holler at them, she put out her arm to stop him. "Wait."

Wolf and Spirit were standing next to each other, their backs to Fairy and Broomstick. They were probably just looking at something near the base of the tree in front of them, but Fairy suddenly remembered the sound of Wolf's voice after he'd been injured, when he was losing consciousness and called Spirit's name. There was something of longing now in the way they stood together, so familiar that they naturally leaned their heads toward each other, that where Spirit's hip jutted to the left, Wolf's body arced to allow a matching space, as if they were puzzle pieces that needed only a small nudge to nest into one another perfectly.

Fairy sighed.

"You know he's yours as long as you want him," Broomstick said. He understood Fairy well enough to know what worried her, even if she hadn't said a thing. "And Spirit would never interfere."

"I know . . . but you see it between them, don't you?"

"See what?" Broomstick asked.

"The inevitability."

He paused, as if considering what to say. But then he said, "I've seen it for a while. But I don't think they know it yet, and it doesn't mean you and Wolf can't work out for now."

"For now," Fairy echoed quietly.

"Maybe forever. Gemina relationships aren't allowed."

Except their world had capsized, and the rules had fallen overboard with it.

She watched Wolf and Spirit for another minute. He was using his gravitational powers to keep crab apples on the ground, and Spirit was trying to pry them up. He goaded her on, and she laughed as she lost her grip on the stubborn fruit.

Fairy's chest hurt. She had wanted to be the first to play with gravity with him.

Spirit tried again, and this time, Wolf released his hold on the crab apple at the same moment, so that Spirit used entirely too much force. The momentum threw her sideways into him, and she knocked him over with her, both of them falling to the ground in a tangle of limbs and hysteria. Their laughter filled the orchard.

It was then that Wolf saw Fairy and Broomstick.

"Um, we didn't know you two were back," he said, scrambling to his feet.

Fairy tried to give a nonchalant shrug. "We just got here."

Spirit, who hadn't yet caught on to the awkwardness, sprang to her feet with the crab apple in her hand. "Any luck with the soul pearl?"

"I'll fill you in," Broomstick said. He gave a meaningful look to Fairy; he was giving her space alone with Wolf, because he knew they needed to talk.

"Thank you," Fairy whispered as he led Spirit elsewhere.

Wolf approached Fairy slowly, like he knew something was wrong, but he wasn't sure what, so he was applying an abundance of caution. "Did I mess up?"

Fairy shook her head. She reached up and cupped his cheek. "You didn't mess anything up. But I realized you're not really mine."

"What do you mean?" Wolf's eyebrows knit together. "Of course I'm yours."

"You are, right now." She attempted a small smile so he'd know she wasn't accusing him of anything. "But there's something between you and Spirit that I can't compete with."

Wolf clasped Fairy's hand, pressing it harder into the scruff of his cheek. "I swear there's not. She's my gemina."

"You called out to her while you were unconscious," Fairy said softly.

The blood drained from his face, and he dropped his hand to his side. "Gods, I'm sorry. I promise I'm not leading you on. It's just that . . . Sora and me . . . I'm sorry." He brought his hands back up to his temples. "I like you so much."

"I know you do. But it's not enough," Fairy said. "I think there's always going to be a part of you that's in love with Spirit."

"That's not true—"

Fairy shook her head. "It is. Everything will be right, though."

And as soon as she told him that, she realized it really was true. She was sad, but not upset. Deep down inside, she'd probably already known that Wolf was supposed to end up with Spirit. "Everyone except Spirit knew you had a crush on her, and I should have known those feelings were too intense to just go away. We're so intertwined with our geminas. If I thought of Broomstick as more than a brother, I can imagine how complete that love would be."

"Fairy, we can work it out. I want to. I know I'm a terrible boyfriend—"

"You're not. But I don't want to be the consolation prize. I deserve better than that, and so do you."

"But—"

She stroked his cheek. "Let's end this while it's still good." But it wasn't easy to say, even though she knew it was the right decision. Her mouth puckered, as if she could actually taste the tang of bittersweet.

"That's it?" Wolf's head fell forward, like his neck was no longer up to the task of holding it upright.

"Please don't be sad, Wolfie. You're still one of my best friends."

"I wanted more than that."

"You'll have it, just not with me. You're supposed to be with Spirit, and you can be, because the old rules don't matter anymore. There's no one around to enforce them. Either we die before the Society is saved, or it will be rebuilt but completely different. There's no going back to the way things used to be."

Wolf closed his eyes.

"I'm sorry," Fairy said.

He exhaled and opened his eyes. "You have nothing to be sorry for. You're remarkable, you know that? Someone's going to be really lucky to have you one day."

"I know," Fairy said, and this time, the smile came more easily. "Do you want to walk back with me to the shack?"

He shook his head. "I'd like to be alone for a little bit."

"Of course." She pecked him on the cheek one last time.

Wolf began to walk away, shoulders hunched, but he stopped after a couple steps. "Um, let the others know we're still leaving for Dera Falls at dusk."

"All right."

Fairy watched as he left, going only a few yards before he shifted into his wolf form. Then he broke into a run and leaped into the air, disappearing into the clouds and leaving only the memory of blue electricity behind.

CHAPTER FORTY-THREE

Sora knew something had happened as soon as Daemon raised his mental ramparts, but she didn't know what it was. Their gemina bond had vibrated with sadness, but then the feeling had disappeared, replaced with a silent wall.

Broomstick was still telling her about the different ways he had tried to destroy the soul pearl, but Sora stopped listening and started to walk back toward the crab apple trees, where she'd left Daemon and Fairy.

"Where are you going?" Broomstick asked, jogging up beside her.

"I need to find Daemon," she said.

Broomstick reached out and put his hand on her arm. "No, you don't."

Sora frowned at his hold on her. "You know what's going on."

"Wolf probably needs space right now."

"Tell me what happened."

He let go of Sora and shook his head. "It's not mine to tell."

"Then that's why I need to find him." Sora set off toward the orchard again, and Broomstick let her go.

She ran through the trees, searching for Daemon. She didn't find him, but not far from where he'd been showing her his gravitational magic, she saw Fairy sitting in the dirt, back against a tree.

"Do you know where Daemon is?" Sora asked as she approached.

Fairy looked up. Her face was solemn, without a trace of her usual laughter. It was then that Sora noticed the ferns in Fairy's hands. The long leaves wove themselves into the shape of a dragon.

"Oh . . . are you all right?" Sora asked.

"Not really," Fairy said as she loosened the ferns. The leaf dragon fell apart. "I broke up with Daemon."

"What? Why? I thought it was going well for you two."

"It was."

"So . . . ?"

Fairy shrugged. "We're not right for each other."

Sora knelt in the dirt. "Why would you think that?"

"I probably would have been a bad girlfriend for him, in the long run. I'm not ready to settle down. I thrill in the chase of boys too much." Fairy set the fern leaves on the ground.

"You would never have hurt him," Sora said.

"I might have."

"Not like that."

Sora sat down beside her, looking straight ahead so Fairy wouldn't feel too put on the spot. They'd done this many times over the years as roommates, as a way to lend support. The one with the problem could speak or not. It was up to her, but regardless, she'd know her friend was there for her. "Do you want to tell me the real reason you broke up with him?"

Fairy sighed. "Not really."

"Then do you want to show me how to weave these fern leaves into a dragon instead? When we're done, we can light it on fire. Like an effigy of Prince Gin."

A surprised laugh escaped Fairy's lips. "I think I'd like that."

CHAPTER FORTY-FOUR

Aki crouched inside the tunnel, scraping at the clay with her rock. She had dug far enough that light could no longer travel down the passageway from her cell, so she groped at the earth and worked in pitch black. Her fingertips were raw, her nails filed down by the rocks and caked with mud. The burns on her face continued to hurt. And she was haunted by her brother's cruelty.

But ironically, the pain and sadness made her stronger. She was the empress, responsible to her people, in service to Sola. Aki would endure whatever Gin threw her way yet continue to fight for Kichona.

So she kept digging.

Of course, she still had doubts. There was no way to confirm she was going in the right direction. What if she was just digging deeper into these godsforsaken caves? Or what if she did make her way out—what would she do? Where would she go from there? It's not like she could outrun the ryuu once Gin discovered she was gone.

But then she heard it. The ocean through the rocks.

It was faint but unmistakable, the rhythmic slamming of the waves against stone. Aki cried out in relief and cast aside her worries about what she'd do once she escaped. Instead, she began digging anew toward the sound, albeit slightly upward. She didn't want to tunnel straight into the sea.

Now the pounding of the waves motivated her like the Society of Taigas' drums, big barreled things made of wine casks and pummeled with sticks as wide as a man's fists. With each beat, Aki heard Luna urging her on, as if she were one of the goddess's taiga warriors, unflinchingly brave and strong.

I'm a fighter, Aki told herself. She'd clashed with her brother before during the Blood Rift and prevailed. She could do it again, no matter how weak she was or how much Gin tortured her.

The ocean beat louder. Aki dug harder, scooping out chunks instead of just scraping.

When I get out of here, I'm not going to simply run away.

I will stand against Gin. I will save my people and my kingdom.

She couldn't do it alone, though. But who could she turn to? The League of Rogues hadn't come to rescue her. Perhaps they were already captured and part of the ryuu army. Or dead.

Aki let out a whimper. She stopped digging and leaned against the damp tunnel wall for support.

She remembered what Fairy had said about disguising herself as the empress to walk into a trap, that it would be an honor to do it, even if it meant Fairy's own death. But the taigas' pride and loyalty were inadequate consolation for Aki.

However, she also recalled something else Fairy had

said to her in that same conversation: "You *must* stay alive if Kichona is to survive."

Aki squeezed the rock in her hand. Fairy was right: no matter what happened, Aki had to survive and fight. She was the empress; only she had the legitimacy to retake the throne from Gin and restore Kichona to peace. The League of Rogues would have wanted her to carry on even if they were gone. She had to find other allies.

"The mainland kingdoms," she said out loud. The idea echoed through the tunnel and seemed to grow with each reverberation.

She would dig her way out of here and somehow find her way overseas. The kings and queens there knew her, and she had especially good relationships with the monarchs of Caldan, Brin, Fale Po Tair, and Thoma. If Aki could get messages there, they would help her. Together, they could save Kichona.

She pushed herself away from the tunnel wall. Her people needed her. When this was over and her kingdom was safe again, she would properly mourn all those lost. Until then, she would press on, as an empress should.

Aki dug for two more hours. The closer she got to the sound of the ocean, the softer the clay grew as more water permeated through. She burrowed with more vigor, hope rising like the sun in her chest.

And then she hit solid rock.

"No!" She was so close she could hear the sea just on the other side. Aki tried to dig slightly higher, and lower, and to the left and right, but to no avail. There was only solid rock between her and her escape.

She kicked it. She beat her fists against it. She backed

up and hurled her digging stone at it, only to have it break into pieces.

Aki withered onto the ground.

From the other side of the tunnel—in the direction of the grotto—glass shattered.

She jumped—that was the contraption she'd rigged to alert her when Gin or Virtuoso returned. It was part of a larger setup in the grotto, designed to buy her time.

Aki crawled as quickly as she could through the tunnel, using the slick of the clay to slide faster.

Within seconds, she was directly under her cell. She hoisted herself up through the hole in the ground, crawled out from under her mattress pallet, and hurried to the narrow passageway in the rock that led to grotto. It was such a tight fit that even she needed to scoot through it sideways.

She stepped out into the grotto just as her visitors untangled themselves from the net she'd made from knotting together strips of torn bedsheets. The trip wire—a thin rope she'd created from unraveling her cloak, then camouflaged by rubbing it in the clay—lay loose on the ground. Two glass jars—formerly full of dried apricots and biscuits—had shattered.

"Idiotic girl," the man closest to her spat. "As if your pathetic net would be any match for ryuu."

Aki tried to look as stupid as he thought she was, and scared. Of course she hadn't actually thought she could capture the ryuu. But if she'd put together something that was obviously an alarm, they would have suspected her. So Aki had purposely rigged a pathetic-looking trap because she knew they would think her dumb enough to try, and that would prevent them from realizing that she was smart enough to have something better, like a tunnel in which to hide. And the glass jars did double duty, serving not only as counterweights to hold the net up until her trip wire was triggered but also to alert her when she had company.

The man glowered at Aki. "I was planning to drop in and introduce you to your new guards before we went back outside," he said. "But now you've made me angry. So I think maybe we'll stay. Meet Bone One and Bone Two. There are hundreds more just like them outside the acid falls."

Aki's mouth hung open as two more men climbed out from the bedsheet net. She hadn't paid attention to them before, only saw their figures out of the corner of her eye. But now she saw that they weren't men at all.

They were skeletons.

Bone One pointed a sword at her. Bone Two circled to the other side of Aki, his movement as graceful as if he were still alive.

"How . . . ?"

"They don't call me Skeleton for no reason. I can control bones."

"A-and you dug up dead bodies as your minions?" She gaped at the moving corpses.

The ryuu smirked. "The Society of Taigas' cemetery, to be exact."

Bile rose in Aki's throat at the desecration of the taigas' hallowed burial ground. But she didn't say anything, because a third body emerged from beneath the net. This one, however, was fully fleshed out and still wore a taiga uniform. When she turned her head to reveal her face, Aki gasped.

It was Bayonet, one of her former Imperial Guards, but

slightly rotted. Maggots had taken residence in Bayonet's eye sockets, and the eyeballs themselves had sunken and shriveled like cherries left out for too long in the summer sun.

"She can't hear you," Skeleton said, his satisfaction dripping like grease off his voice. "She's just a sack of bones that moves at my command. A vicious sack, though."

The corpse stalked up to Aki until she was mere inches away.

"Bayonet," Aki said, "if there's any humanity left inside you—"

The former Imperial Guard opened her mouth to reveal a pit of worms.

Aki lurched backward. Then she fell to her hands and knees and threw up all over the grotto floor.

"Pitiful," Skeleton said. "I expected more from a former empress than a childish net and a weak stomach. You're not anything close to a threat."

"You're wrong," Aki said, even though she was currently heaped on the floor in a mess of mud and vomit. She might have been an acid-scarred prisoner in a grotto, guarded by an army of skeletons, but she was also a descendant of some of the greatest rulers in Kichona's history. There was gold in her hair, fire in her veins, and, most important, a fierce love for her people in her heart. No matter the obstacles she faced, she would fight to her last breath to save them from her brother's clutches.

"One day I'll be free of here, and then you'll see," Aki said. "You'll be sorry you ever crossed me."

CHAPTER FORTY-FIVE

The tiger's paw of Kichona was composed of four small islands. The one with Dera Falls was a sharp sliver, just the tip of a claw. That was where Sora thought Prince Gin might be hiding Empress Aki.

Sora lay on her stomach on another of the islands that formed the claw, crawling up to the edge of the white cliffs that dropped straight down five hundred feet into the sea.

The last few hours had been terribly awkward. Daemon had come back to the mining shack as dusk settled in, already in the form of a wolf.

"It's time," he'd said, but his growl lacked any bite, and even the sparks coming off his fur seemed dimmer than usual. They were a muted, dull blue, rather than the bright electric light that had previously illuminated him.

Sora walked up to Daemon and touched his shoulder softly. "Where did you go? Are you all right?"

"I'm fine."

"You don't seem fine. Fairy told me what happened.

Do you want to talk about it?"

Daemon's ears pricked, and the fur on his back stood alert. "What did she say?"

Sora tried to soothe the fur down. "Not much, just that she broke up with you."

"Did she say why?"

"Only that she wasn't the right girl for you. I tried to get more out of her, but she wouldn't—"

His ears relaxed, and he exhaled. "It's probably better that we don't know."

He seemed strangely relieved. Sora frowned. "But I don't get it. You guys seemed happy. Don't you want to know what went wrong? Maybe you can fix it."

Daemon shook her hand off his back and bared his teeth. "I can't. She doesn't want to be with me, all right? Now, do you want to go to Dera Falls tonight or not?"

Sora stopped talking after that. She'd only wanted to help, but she'd clearly pushed too hard.

And she had to be careful, too, because there was that whisper just beneath the surface of her skin that wanted him for herself. Which was not what anyone needed right now.

Probably the best thing was to bother Daemon as little as possible and let him heal.

Of course, he had to carry her, Fairy, and Broomstick while he flew to the islands of the tiger's paw, a trip filled with as much tension as one would expect. Broomstick tried to keep the mood light by rambling about inconsequential topics, like what kind of polish was best for keeping swords shiny, but his chatter backfired because every time Fairy said something, Daemon stiffened below them, and everyone could feel it against their legs. The conversation eventually died off, and they finished the flight in silence.

As soon as they landed on the white cliffs of one of the tiger's-paw islands, Fairy and Broomstick practically leaped off Daemon's back.

"We'll go scout down on the shore," Fairy said, heading away before Sora even had a chance to acknowledge her plan. Broomstick hurried off with his gemina.

Daemon didn't look as they left. "I'll do a few flyovers of Dera Falls." He snuffed out the sparks in his fur and jumped off the cliff into the air.

"I guess I'll stay here," Sora mumbled to herself. Which is how she ended up crawling on her stomach to the edge of the cliffs, where she could get a better look at the island that she suspected was Empress Aki's prison.

But what would they find when they got there? An empress, beaten down and tortured? Or one whose mind was stripped, who might look and act like the empress but was really the Dragon Prince's puppet?

Sora seethed. Not that long ago, Prince Gin had stolen her mind, too, filling her with a bloodcurdling greed for the Evermore and the will to do whatever was required to get there. She'd walked and talked like herself, but otherwise, she hadn't been Sora. She'd abandoned her friends because of Prince Gin, and almost killed Empress Aki. If it weren't for Daemon, Sora would already be well on her way to becoming the murderous general in her Lake of Nightmares vision.

I won't let anything like that happen to the empress, Sora thought, fingers tightening over the hilt of one of her swords.

But first, she had to *find* Empress Aki. Sora took a deep breath, then let go of the sword and instead pulled out a spyglass.

For a minute, she couldn't see much, because the moon was blocked by a thick blanket of clouds. There weren't any fires or signs of a soldier encampment over on the island, and her stomach knotted up. Maybe Sora had been wrong about the empress being here. Come to think of it, there were no ships either. Had she read the map wrong? Was Empress Aki elsewhere?

But the soul pearl stirred in Sora's collar. The Dragon Prince's magic was near.

She could use ryuu particles to fine-tune the focus on the spyglass. But Sora hesitated to touch that magic, the very thing that had damned her. Casting a ryuu spell would be like soaking her skin with pure evil.

But the magic itself isn't bad, she argued with herself. After all, it was the same magic used by taigas—the only difference was Sight, the ability to see the particles and use the magic in even more powerful ways. And Sight had come from the afterlife, where it was supposed to be a gift to taigas for a life well lived. It was only the act of stealing that had cast a wicked pall on the magic.

Besides, she would be using the ryuu particles to protect Kichona, the very thing taigas were supposed to do.

Sora made her decision and called to the emerald dust.

It infused the spyglass, sharpening its focus and allowing her to better scan the short coastline. The island was not much more than two miles long and a mile wide, like a chunk of the cliff Sora was lying on had fallen off sometime in the past, tumbled into the ocean, and decided not to sink but instead floated a short distance away. It was made of jagged outcroppings and scored with narrow fissures that were probably created by water wearing down the rock over the centuries.

Which means there might be caves inside, Sora thought. A perfect place to imprison a deposed empress.

Sora couldn't see Dera Falls itself, since it was on the eastern side of the island, but Daemon was taking care of that with his flyovers.

They needed to figure out a way to sneak in and out. Ideally, they'd get in, Daemon's magic would neutralize the Dragon Prince's spell—assuming he'd hypnotized the empress—and then they would smuggle her out without anyone knowing. Of course, that was unlikely, but so far, Sora hadn't seen much in the way of guards.

As she continued studying the island, the cloud cover shifted, and a little more light from the moon made it through the fog. The soul pearl strained against Sora's collar, and she moved her spyglass to follow its direction.

There! Movement at the top of one of the crags.

Crow's eye. A dozen guards on patrol, marching back and forth. But was she seeing correctly? Sora could make out their general outlines, yet the moonlight seemed to be shining through them. There must be some kind of reflection—maybe off the water's surface—playing tricks on her.

She squinted and adjusted the focus on her spyglass.

Sora let out a gasp. Her eyes hadn't been duped. Moonlight *was* shining through the soldiers, because they were made of bones.

"Skullcrusher and Skeleton," she murmured, remembering the brothers. The bone warriors were their doing.

How do you fight soldiers who can't die, because they're already dead?

The skeletons moved with confidence, their strides long and sure, their grips firm on the swords, spears, and other weapons they clutched. Most of the warriors were completely bone, but a couple still had flesh on them, including the one marching into Sora's view.

A sword protruded from his belly. But this soldier marched as if it didn't notice the blade. When it turned, the moon revealed that the sword actually went through the corpse's belly and out its back.

And then Sora saw its face.

Beetle.

A cry escaped her as she recognized the young ryuu who'd befriended her on Prince Gin's ship. His hair was matted, and his skin was veined and gray from necrosis, but it was still him. The full cheeks that held on stubbornly to his baby fat. The pockets of his uniform stretched from all the snacks he used to stash in them. His lighthearted gait, as if the world were full of wonders just waiting for him to discover them.

Except Beetle would never get to do that. His eyes were blank, seeing nothing.

The ryuu must have raised the dead from the last battle. And as for the skeletons—could it be that they raided the Society of Taigas' cemetery? It would explain why the skeletons moved with the grace and strength of warriors.

Sora looked at Beetle again. Her heart ached, but she couldn't make the mistake of thinking this was the same boy she'd known. He was only an empty shell, reanimated.

Still, she couldn't tear herself away from him. Sora

watched as he marched by, and she kept tabs on him as he disappeared along his path into the night, then circled back again. She lost track of time.

Fairy and Broomstick returned from the beach. "There are skeletons on a ship," they reported.

Sora shook herself out of her trance. "*More* skeletons?"

"You can't see them from up here because they're tucked into a shadowy alcove at the base of the island. But yes, there's a ship crewed by skeleton sailors."

"If this is what they have just to guard a single prisoner," Broomstick said, "I hate to imagine what kind of forces Prince Gin will send to attack Thoma."

"Oh gods." Fairy's face fell.

Sora could see her mentally tabulating all the different ryuu who could be unleashed. Ironside, whose hands were magnets that could steal away swords and other weapons. Ash, who filled the air with smoke so thick you couldn't see six inches in front of you. Carmine, who could make blood boil inside a person's body. Just to name a few.

"Don't think about Thoma," Sora said, because it would paralyze them and make it impossible to focus on the task at hand. "Let's face one horror at a time."

At that moment, Daemon landed on the cliffs and transformed into boy form. They forced themselves to set thoughts of Thoma aside and instead caught him up on what they'd seen.

"It's similar on the other side where Dera Falls is," Daemon said, "except it's even more fortified. An entire fleet of the skeleton navy, plus several troops around the waterfall."

There went the last of Sora's hope that they could sneak the empress out without being detected.

"There are only four of us," Broomstick pointed out, "and way too many of them. How is this even going to be possible?"

But then Sora thought of Beetle again—how he wasn't really himself anymore—and clarity hit her. "We defeat them by remembering they're not alive."

Daemon, Fairy, and Broomstick looked at Sora as if she'd lost her mind.

"How is that different from knowing that they're dead?" Fairy asked.

"I know it sounds the same," Sora said, "but what I mean is, if we think of them as actual creatures, we make the mistake of focusing on killing them. They aren't alive, though. They're just bones being controlled by two ryuu— Skullcrusher and Skeleton."

"So we should find those two," Daemon said, catching on.

"Right," Sora said. "If we eliminate Skullcrusher and Skeleton, the entire army and navy of dead will fall like marionettes who've lost their puppeteers."

Fairy scrunched up her nose as she thought about this. "Yeah, but what do we do about the marionettes *before* their strings are cut?"

Broomstick flexed his fingers and started to smile. "Even the undead can't fight if they don't have bodies."

"You're going to blow them up? Can I help?" Fairy's eyes brightened.

"Absolutely. Wolf can fly with Spirit to look for the two ryuu controlling everything. In the meantime, you blast apart the warriors on land, and I'll blow up the ships in the sea. If we can't stop Skullcrusher and Skeleton, we'll make sure they have nothing to use their magic on."

"Whoa," Daemon said. "I think that's a great plan, but Sora shouldn't be out there."

"What? Why not?" Sora asked.

"Because if you die, you're doomed," he said. "You should stay here and keep safe."

"I'm not going to hide while you all fight."

"The general of an army sends troops into battle," Daemon argued. "She doesn't dive into the fight herself."

Sora crossed her arms. "I don't know what generals you've been studying, but that's not the kind of leader I want to be. Besides, I'm a taiga. And that means I do what needs to be done to protect our kingdom, even if it means my own death and damnation. I think you all understand that."

There was silence for a moment, but she could read the thoughts on their faces. Fairy had disguised herself as the empress and walked straight into what she knew was an assassination attempt. Broomstick had barged into a god's lair to help steal his treasure. And Daemon had stood by Sora's side from the very beginning, risking everything to go undercover on the Dragon Prince's ship, to save Sora from the grips of genka, and train with his newfound powers to beat back the biggest threat Kichona had ever seen.

All three of them understood what it meant to be a taiga.

"We're agreed, then?" Sora asked.

They all nodded, even Daemon.

"Good." She stacked her fists over her heart. "Then I think the League of Rogues has a plan."

CHAPTER FORTY-SIX

L et's go," Sora said.

Daemon shifted into his wolf form. She climbed onto his back and held out her hand for Fairy.

He tensed when Fairy touched his fur, but it was a little less obvious than earlier. Maybe Daemon was starting to make peace with the way things had ended between them? Sora could only hope. She needed the League of Rogues as strong as possible.

When all three of them were on board, Daemon took a running start and hurtled into the sky. He kept his sparks muted so they could approach Dera Falls surreptitiously, but it didn't douse the thrill of soaring through the cold night air. Sora smiled as they picked up altitude, the wind gusting through her hair.

Her nerves came back, though, as they neared the eastern side of the island.

"I'll land just past the waterfall," Daemon said.

"No need," Broomstick said. "Dip down briefly, and Fairy and I can jump off."

"You sure?"

"Yes. Don't lose your momentum. Every second is going to count once we begin our attacks." They unfastened themselves from the harness.

"All right. Then here we go." Daemon veered around the waterfall, arcing out wide enough that the skeletons wouldn't notice him, then curved back inland. He slowed a little but not much as he flew close to the ground. "Jump in three, two, . . ."

Fairy and Broomstick leaped like acrobats and tucked themselves into their bodies. They hit the ground in somersaults, rolling rather than hitting the rock face hard.

"Beautiful," Sora said as she and Daemon rose back into the sky.

She watched as Fairy sprinted toward Dera Falls and Broomstick scaled the side of the rocky island to a vantage point where he could see the ships.

"They'll be in place soon," she said.

"Let me know when," Daemon said. "They'll need some light, and so will we, to find Skeleton and Skullcrusher."

They circled above for a few more minutes. Fairy found a cluster of bushes to hide behind at the top of the waterfall.

"Fairy's ready," Sora said.

"Broomstick?" Daemon asked.

"Not yet." Sora squinted at where she'd last seen him and caught movement along a rocky outcropping. Not long after, there was a flash. Broomstick had set off a very small explosion.

"Now!" Sora said.

A deep rumble resonated through Daemon's body, and adrenaline surged through their bond. Daemon stopped dimming his power, and bright blue electricity lit all around him and Sora as they tore through the air, leaving a streak behind them like lightning, the rumble in his chest bursting out and shaking the sky with his thunder.

The skeletons below froze at the light and the noise.

Fairy whipped into action, running through the nearest troop of warriors with her swords out, decapitating some and hacking at others at the ribs and knees. Another troop charged at her from farther out, and she launched a grenade at them. Bones flew everywhere, splashing into the water and careening over the edge of the falls.

Below, Broomstick set off an explosion in the helm of one of the ships. A few more blasts followed. The skeleton sailors on board scurried around in confusion.

"Now it's our turn," Sora said. "Let's find Skullcrusher and Skeleton."

Daemon swooped over the top of the island, his electric glow lighting the ground as if it were midday.

"There's one of them!" Sora shouted, leaning so far off Daemon's back she would have tumbled off but for the harness.

Skullcrusher was running from the other side of Dera Falls, yelling furiously at his warriors. Daemon charged down at him.

Sora commanded the ryuu particles around her to form stakes. She aimed them at Skullcrusher's eyes and threw.

He flung up a shield of his own particles. The stakes bounced off and disintegrated back into emerald dust.

Fairy blew up another group of skeletons. Meanwhile, a loud blast sounded in the ocean. Broomstick had managed to sink one of the ships, and the skeletons fell overboard.

Skullcrusher stood immobile, looking from the waterfall to the edge of the island.

Where is his brother? Sora wondered.

But the fact that he was alone benefitted her. Skullcrusher's indecisiveness allowed Fairy to destroy a few more warriors, and some of the skeletons in the water began to sink, since they weren't given commands to swim.

Suddenly, though, the corpses on land began to fight back. They coordinated themselves and came at Fairy all at once, rather than in haphazard attacks. As they closed in, they eliminated her ability to use Broomstick's bombs; if she threw a grenade, it would kill her as well as them.

Skullcrusher sneered up at Sora and Daemon. "Is that all you've got?"

"We have to try something new," Sora said. "He's onto our methods. Can you use your other powers while flying?"

"I'll try." Daemon growled. "I'd be a pretty pathetic demigod if I couldn't."

He hovered to a halt in the air. Sora held her breath, the adrenaline like wildfire in their bond now.

"Let's see how well you can fight when the rules of gravity no longer apply." Daemon let loose a howl that made the stars cringe. Then the earth beneath them shook, and the skeletons began to rise into the air.

Skullcrusher's mouth hung open. But he quickly gathered himself and tried to regain control of his army.

They flailed their limbs, though, unable to find purchase anywhere. Daemon lifted them higher.

Then he slammed them down onto the rocky face of the island. Most of the skeletons shattered. Their bones flew in shards and splinters everywhere.

Broomstick sank another ship.

"Gods-damn you!" Skullcrusher shouted. He retreated toward Dera Falls.

Making herself invisible, Sora unbuckled from the harness, leaped off Daemon's back, and sprinted after Skull-crusher.

Daemon sped around and landed in front of Skullcrusher. The ryuu scowled as Daemon advanced, teeth bared.

"I'm not scared of an animal," Skullcrusher said, although he took several steps back.

"That's fine," Daemon said. "I'm not insulted. Because there's something else you should be more scared of."

Skullcrusher shivered but shook his head defiantly. "What?"

"You should be scared of me." Sora materialized behind him, neutralized him with a choke hold, and jammed a knife into his rib cage through his heart.

The ryuu gasped as blood bloomed from his chest. "Trai-tor," he whispered.

"I don't think you quite understand the meaning of the word," Sora said, dropping him to the ground. "You and the Dragon Prince are the traitors, not me."

Skullcrusher glowered at her, but when he opened his mouth, nothing came out except his last breath. She was sure he didn't have anything worthwhile to say anyway.

Fairy ran over to rejoin her and Daemon. Sora looked around at the ruined skeletons on the ground. The navy was still active—probably controlled by Skullcrusher's brother—but from the sounds coming from the sea, Broomstick was blowing up a fair portion of them. Sora allowed herself a moment to feel triumphant anyway.

"Phase one complete," she said.

"That was so much fun!" Fairy said. "Wolf, you were incredible."

Daemon smiled, and even though his teeth were frightening, the effect was somehow still bashful. "Thanks. You were really impressive, too."

Sora kept her own smile buttoned up, but this was definitely progress between the two.

"Want to bet Empress Aki is inside Dera Falls where Skullcrusher was headed? Let's go."

"On the contrary," a man behind them said. "No one is going anywhere."

Chills ran up Sora's spine, and the soul pearl in her collar rolled insistently—almost maniacally—against the fabric, as if yearning to be reunited with the body it belonged to. She knew that poison-laced voice.

She hoped he wouldn't notice the pearl trying to escape her pocket.

Sora turned slowly. But the Dragon Prince wasn't the only one standing there. Sora let out a cry.

Prince Gin floated in a green orb at the top of Dera Falls. Tidepool was with him, and there were two people kneeling in front of them, their faces portraits of terror.

Mama and Papa.

No . . .

Then someone appeared a few feet behind them, visible

only to Sora because they shared the same kind of magic: Hana, wide eyed as if she was a lost little girl instead of the Dragon Prince's second-in-command.

Sora's gaze met her sister's for an instant.

But then Prince Gin pulled out his knives.

CHAPTER FORTY-SEVEN

Hana trembled as she watched Emperor Gin push the blades against her parents' throats. She hadn't seen them since she was six—something inside her had resisted visiting them before this moment, as if she was afraid of what they'd say when they found out she was no longer a taiga, even though she had good reason for helping the ryuu pursue the Evermore. But now her parents were here, and they could die any minute, and she'd never had a chance to say hello to them before she had to say goodbye.

"Let them go," Sora said to Emperor Gin, her voice shaking.

It was more than Hana could do. She'd never been more petrified since the Blood Rift raid on the tenderfoot nursery—not in the middle of battle, not when she was fighting her sister, not when she found out that her own soul was damned. All those things were terrifying, but Hana was a warrior; she was supposed to be in the path of danger.

But Mama and Papa weren't. They were innocents.

Hana should have thought to protect them. She should have taken them away from Samara Mountain and hidden them somewhere safe.

The emperor's orb transported Mama and Papa to the rocks beside the waterfall, and the sphere vanished. He pressed the blades harder against their throats as he sneered at Sora. "You've dismantled more than half my skeleton army, Spirit. I'm very unhappy about that and think I should be recompensed."

"You don't need my parents," Sora said, shaking even harder than before. "Please, I'm begging you. Let them go. We'll do whatever you want."

"You coward," Mama sneered at Sora. "Grow a backbone." Hana knew it was Zomuri's influence tainting her words, yet it still made her flinch. But she understood that her mother wanted Sora to stand up to Prince Gin.

How could her sister do that, though? She wouldn't risk her parents' lives.

Emperor Gin's lip curled at Daemon. "Spirit, tell your pet to release his electric shield around you and your fairy friend."

Daemon snarled. "I'm not a pet."

"No . . . ," the emperor said thoughtfully. "You're something more, aren't you? If you join me, you could go down in history. Imagine it—the Dragon Emperor riding a magical flying wolf to victory as they bring the Evermore to earth. There will be songs sung in your name and myths passed on for centuries. We would be glorified for eternity."

"I'd rather die now than be associated with you for even a day, let alone an eternity."

Hana didn't know what to do. Daemon and Sora were

standing up for their principles. But what did Hana believe in? She'd thought she'd known, but now, with her parents at Emperor Gin's mercy, all her previous doubts weighed more heavily than before.

"Don't give in," Daemon said to Sora.

But wasn't a huge part of saving the kingdom about protecting the ones they loved?

Sora leaned close to Daemon's ear and whispered something.

Then she jumped off his back.

"Spirit." Fairy gasped. Hana almost did, too, but she managed to restrain herself, to stay invisible as she tried to understand what she was supposed to do.

Sora bowed to Emperor Gin, and there was no deception in her movement. "I surrender. Just don't hurt Mama and Papa."

He laughed. "I suspected you'd give in. Your heart is too soft. Glass Lady didn't train the sentimentality out of you well enough."

Shackles made of ryuu particles clamped around Sora's wrists and hands, connected by glowing green chains. Whatever spell the emperor had used to make them, it was stronger than Sora knew how to fight. It didn't matter, though. Hana could see that Sora had meant it when she made the bargain to surrender, and it pained her to see her sister so beaten. Sora had always been full of fight. But now she was just . . . deflated.

But Sora still shouted at Daemon, "Go!"

It was too late, though. Chains bound him, and Fairy, too. They rattled as Daemon tried to shake them off, to no avail.

Why wasn't Emperor Gin controlling their minds, though?

"You can keep your shield against my powers of persuasion . . . for now," the emperor said, shrugging. "You'll tire eventually, and then I'll have you."

That blue glow around Daemon must be protecting them, even if it didn't know how to break through Emperor Gin's shackles.

"Weren't there more of you?" the emperor asked. "Where is the fourth?"

Hana looked around. Where was Broomstick?

Fairy gave Sora a pointed look that the emperor didn't catch, but Hana did. Fairy must have already alerted Broomstick through their bond. Hana exhaled in relief, and in that instant, she knew for sure which side she was on.

"My gemina is dead," Fairy said to Emperor Gin, managing to bring false tears to her eyes. "Your barbaric skeletons murdered him."

"At least they did something right," the emperor said to Tidepool.

He pressed the blades against Mama and Papa's skin again, and this time, he drew blood.

"What are you doing?" Sora said. "We surrendered. You have to let my parents go."

Emperor Gin clucked his tongue. "The Society raised you naive, too. Glass Lady really was a weak commander."

All the blood drained from Hana's face. She materialized and stretched her hand toward him. "Your Majesty, stop!"

But the emperor was already slashing his knife across Mama's throat.

"No!" Hana fell to her knees.

Mama's eyes went still with the shock. Blood gushed from her neck.

Sora lunged for her, but the chains jerked her violently back into place.

"I love you . . . ," Mama choked out, sounding like herself again, as if the blow of the knife had sliced away Zomuri's influence.

Then her gaze turned desperate, searching for something important in the mere seconds she knew she had left.

Her eyes settled on Hana.

"My daughter," she whispered, blood gurgling over the words. "My lost love."

It was the last thing Mama said. Her body stilled, soaked in its own blood.

Hana's hands flew to her mouth. "Oh gods. Mama . . ."

"Mina!" Papa cried. Whether it was irrationality caused by Zomuri's influence or Papa's own state of shock, he grabbed the blade at his throat with his bare hands and wrenched himself free. Emperor Gin merely laughed. Papa fell over Mama's body, oblivious to his bloodied hands. He cradled her in his arms and wept hysterically. "My darling, my darling, my darling . . ."

Sora crumpled, and this time, the chains allowed it. She fell in a heap on the ground.

Daemon let out a plaintive howl. Fairy clutched his fur, real tears brimming over now.

"I didn't know you were here," the emperor said to Hana. "I'm sorry you had to see this. But you understand, don't you?"

Hana didn't respond. She teetered where she stood.

"Virtuoso!"

Her head snapped up.

"Did you hear me, or do I need to compel you?" Emperor Gin asked. "I'm sorry you had to see this, but I need you to look me in the eye and let me know you're still with me. This storyteller was your mother by blood only, but *I* raised you and made you who you are."

Hana trembled, unable to tear her eyes away from Mama's lifeless body.

The emperor grabbed Hana by the collar of her tunic. "This woman was only one person, and one person is nothing compared to the greatness we are going to achieve for the kingdom. Do you understand? Are you with me?"

She looked at him with blank eyes. Yes, she understood. She knew now that his goals of bringing the Evermore to Kichona had always been driven by greed, by his need for glory, rather than wanting what was truly best for the people. Because if he had cared about his subjects, he wouldn't have been willing to throw their lives away so wantonly.

Hana was guilty, too. She had deceived herself as much as he had deceived her.

But she could still try to fix it. She could fight back, in the way her sister had taught her—with all her spirit and stealth. From the inside.

And so Hana nodded. She would pretend she was his loyal soldier, but she would destroy him from within his own ranks. "Yes, Your Majesty. I—I'm with you."

"That's what I like to hear. Tidepool, take care of this body. Virtuoso, show the rest of them to their new prison."

"Why don't you just kill us now?" Sora said through a sob.

Does Sora not care about her soul being damned? Hana wondered. Mama's death must have been the final straw.

I'll care enough for both of us, Hana thought.

Emperor Gin looked at Sora with disdain. "Because even though you're a piteous mess of snot, you are more valuable to me alive than dead. I could always use more ryuu, especially one with the power of invisibility, as well as whatever magic your pet has. And at some point, your wolf will give up and drop that shield. Then I'll have you." He turned to Hana. "Virtuoso?"

Whatever emotion she'd felt at Mama's execution, Hana had smothered it, at least on the surface. She smiled with steely coldness again. "I'll take care of everything, Your Majesty."

"Good girl. I have an appointment with the tsarina of Thoma."

"I hate you," Sora spat at Hana.

It was like a spear through Hana's heart. But she deserved it. She had to earn back Sora's love and trust, and she would have to take the abuse for now, until she could prove herself.

Daemon glared at Emperor Gin. "You won't defeat the Thomasians easily."

"Oh, but I already have," the prince said. "Did you think poking some holes in my ships would stop the ryuu for long? The tsarina is a prisoner aboard my ship. Now that I have dealt with you pests, I'm taking her back to my castle, where I'll summon Zomuri and offer him her heart. One monarch down, only six to go."

"No . . . ," Daemon whispered.

With that, Emperor Gin strode off to the other side of the island, where his ship awaited.

But Sora didn't seem to care about the emperor or the tsarina right now. She cared only for what was right in front of her, and she glared through her tears at Hana. "How could you?"

Hana couldn't look at her, couldn't face her disappointment. She stared instead at Mama's bloody, lifeless body on the rocks, and Papa bent over her, rocking and wailing.

"Tidepool, go take stock of the situation on the rest of the island," Hana said.

"But His Majesty tasked me with getting rid of that body."

"I said, take stock of our positions!"

The ryuu bristled but saluted and marched off to follow orders.

Then Hana summoned ryuu particles to surround Sora, Fairy, and Daemon in orbs and floated them down into the waterfall. They would be safer in there as prisoners, for now, and then she'd get them out when she secured the situation out here on the island.

But first . . . Mama and Papa.

CHAPTER FORTY-EIGHT

With her sister and friends gone, Hana walked over to Papa. She crouched beside him and touched his shoulder.

"I'm sorry," she said softly.

He turned on her, face red with rage, and grabbed both her shoulders. "Where have you been all these years? We thought you were dead. We mourned you. And then you reappear but on the side of that murderer, and you let him kill your mother. What is wrong with you? Why did you ever come back?" He shook Hana as if she were a rag doll.

"I'm sorry! I didn't mean for any of this to happen!"

Papa sobbed and kept shaking her, although his effort grew weaker. "The Dragon Prince tore our kingdom apart once already and killed so many of your own taigas. How could you side with him?"

"I . . . I didn't know any better. He was my family."

"*We* are your family!" Papa collapsed against Hana and held her tightly.

Tears spilled over Hana's cheeks. She'd been so young when she was abducted from the Citadel, but she still remembered some pieces of her childhood.

Whenever they had a school break like the Autumn Festival, she would ride together with Sora on a horse and Daemon would ride on a separate one, and they'd make the journey up the winding switchbacks of Samara Mountain together. Mama and Papa would rush out to greet them, Mama with tea and cake and Papa with a new ceramic trinket for Hana to take back to the Citadel.

They would spend the whole holiday together, packed into that tiny house, occasionally descending the mountain to the village for music and dancing and sweets. If it were All Spirits' Eve, Mama would make paper-lantern kites for them to light and fly into the sky. And every evening, they'd retire to the living room and cozy up by the fire, while Mama told them one of her new stories. It was Hana's favorite way to fall asleep.

She now looked over at Mama slumped and covered in blood. A new burst of tears wracked Hana's body.

"I'm not worthy of being her daughter," she said between gasps for air.

Papa tightened his embrace on Hana, as if wanting to strangle her and hug her forever at the same time. She buried her face into his shoulder.

"We have to give Mama a proper burial," Hana said. Her tears slowed with the prospect of being able to atone, even if just a little.

"Mina loved the sea," Papa said.

Hana nodded. Her parents' home overlooked the ocean, and Mama ate every meal out on that deck except when it rained or snowed. Sometimes even then. She could never be close enough to the water.

"Then we'll cremate her and scatter her ashes into the sea," Hana said. There was no way she was going to just dump her mother's body like Emperor Gin intended.

"You would do that?" Papa asked, looking up with red eyes.

"I've been wrong for too long," Hana said. "Now I need to do what's right."

CHAPTER FORTY-NINE

The chains shackling Fairy disappeared as her orb descended the waterfall. She rubbed at her ankles and wrists, watching her surroundings warily. Had Hana released them from Prince Gin's chains? But why? Fairy prepared herself for another awful surprise to come.

The waterfall ended, but her orb kept plummeting deeper. She couldn't see Wolf or Spirit through the churn of the water. Maybe she'd be imprisoned in this sphere beneath the surface forever.

Slowly, however, the orb began to rise. It arrived in a grotto, hidden from the outside by the waterfall, and the sphere floated to shore, where it opened.

Fairy stepped out.

A greasy voice welcomed her. "Hello there."

She spun with a pair of stiletto blades out.

A ryuu stepped into the dim light. He was flanked by two skeletons and a corpse.

It had to be Skullcrusher's brother, Skeleton.

Fairy had to disable his Sight.

Skeleton looked at her knives and chuckled. "Very amusing."

His magic knocked the blades away, and he advanced, grabbing her waist and drawing her up against his body.

But Fairy had slipped another dagger out of her sleeve, and she rammed it into his right eye.

He screamed.

"That's what you get for underestimating me," she said. "What kind of idiot thinks a girl carries only two knives?"

Skeleton held his hand over the gushing blood. "You'll pay for that."

He sent the corpse woman at Fairy. It wore an Imperial Guard uniform and lurched forward, circling its rotting hands around Fairy's throat.

Fairy tried desperately to breathe. The corpse's grip was too strong. Fairy tried swiping with yet another knife, but even though she plunged it into the body, it had no effect, because the dead couldn't feel any pain.

"You had to make this difficult, didn't you?" Skeleton said. "But you're pretty. I might lighten your punishment if you give me a kiss."

Good, Fairy thought. *Come closer. Because I have one more trick up my sleeve.* She pried at one of the corpse's fingers that was mostly bone, not flesh, and snapped it off.

Skeleton stalked over to Fairy and bent down, face close to hers. He wasn't worried about her fighting back this time. The corpse had her prisoner.

Fairy used her last bits of energy and breath to stab him with the corpse's finger bone in his uninjured eye.

Skeleton howled in pain. "You bitch!"

Without vision, his command on ryuu magic vanished. The corpse released Fairy, and they both tumbled to the ground. The two skeleton warriors collapsed into piles of bones.

Fairy wheezed and swallowed air, doubling over until her vision cleared.

But Skeleton wouldn't give up that easily. He drew a sword. He'd still be able to fight. Like Fairy, he was trained for hand-to-hand combat in the dark, where vision wasn't required.

"No, you don't." Fairy drew a stout knife from her pants leg and threw it into the artery in his throat. Skeleton cursed but kept advancing.

She scuttled to where he'd confiscated her stilettos and threw each of those into other major arteries.

Skeleton staggered forward.

Then he stilled and toppled to the ground, right on top of his corpse warrior.

Fairy fell to her knees, overcome with relief.

Daemon's orb surfaced from the grotto pool. His eyes were wide as his sphere opened.

"Did you do that?" he asked.

Fairy blinked at Skeleton, the corpse, and the piles of bones. Then she nodded.

"He tried to kiss me," Fairy said. "But this is what happens when you go around touching girls without their permission."

CHAPTER FIFTY

Sora was curled into a ball in the bottom of her orb, sobbing so hard she threw herself into coughing fits that left her gasping. Tears and snot dripped down her face, and she didn't care that her orb was passing through a waterfall. She didn't notice that their spheres carried them through a deep pool. She didn't try to get up when the orb opened onto the shore of a damp grotto.

Mama was dead, and Hana had Papa as a prisoner.

Strong arms slipped beneath Sora and lifted her. She couldn't uncurl her body to see who it was. The only thing holding her together was the ferocity with which she tucked into herself.

"I'm here," Daemon said, cradling Sora to his chest as he carried her out of the orb. "Whatever you need, I'm here."

Sora cried even harder.

He held her closer and didn't let go.

CHAPTER FIFTY-ONE

Tink, tink, tink.

Aki hit her metal spoon against the rock wall at the end of her tunnel.

Clank, clank, clank, something—or someone—answered in return.

She held her breath. It was possible she was imagining things. Or that there really was someone outside, perhaps another ryuu or skeleton, and this was a trap.

Still, she had to try again, because she didn't know when she'd have another chance. Gin had paid her a visit not long ago to remind her that he had every intention of keeping her alive and suffering in this prison. But then there'd been a commotion as Gin and the two non-ryuu he'd brought—were they ordinary Kichonans? What was their significance?—hurried out of the waterfall and up to the surface. Aki had used the excuse of being emotionally overwhelmed and needing a nap to retire to her little cell in the grotto walls. Her skeleton captors had been all too willing to believe her fragility in the face of their mighty emperor.

But instead of resting, Aki crawled down her tunnel. She hadn't known what she could do, since the solid rock still blocked her escape, but maybe she could dig in a different direction. She started scraping at the clay with her spoon, but each time, the metal had hit the wall. Until she'd gotten that clanking response.

Was it someone come to rescue her? Is that why Gin had left in such a hurry?

Aki was about to try again when a keening like an injured animal pierced the air. She jumped. The sound had come from the far end of the tunnel. What was happening out there? Aki had to hide the entrance to this route before the ryuu barged into her cell and she was discovered.

She hit her spoon against the rock wall rapidly, like an alarm, in case whoever was on the other side was here to help, and then she scurried down the tunnel back to her cell.

Aki exhaled in relief as she climbed out from beneath her mattress pallet and found no one in her room. She squeezed herself through the narrow passageway that led to the grotto opening, cautiously sticking out her head to see what had made the painful animal wail.

The awful ryuu Skeleton and his minions lay dead—truly dead—on the ground. Aki's heart skipped as she saw Fairy standing over the bodies.

But then she saw another taiga apprentice—Wolf, she recalled from her time at the Citadel—holding a hysterical girl in his arms. This was the source of the cry Aki had heard.

She pushed out of the passageway and ran to their sides. Oh gods, the girl was Spirit. "What happened?" Aki cried.

"Your brother murdered her mother," Fairy said, coming up behind her.

Aki took in a sharp breath. That's who that couple was. Gin had been using them as bait. Or vengeance.

Spirit let out a desperate sob. "And Papa . . ."

"What happened to her father?" Aki asked, not wanting to hear the answer.

"Hana—Virtuoso—has him," Wolf said with a snarl.

Aki shook her head. She had hoped she could still find some strand of goodness in her brother somewhere, but after the Ceremony of Two Hundred Hearts, the acid torture he'd intended for her, and now this, it was clear that there was no trace of the boy she used to consider her best friend. Perhaps because he was literally soulless, or perhaps he'd lost his conscience long before that. Either way, her twin brother was gone.

She looked at Spirit, the once fearless leader of this mischievous crew, crumpled like a wet handkerchief. "Mama . . . Papa . . . We have to save him . . . ," Spirit whispered between sobs.

"You're prisoners, too," Aki said, understanding.

Wolf's eyes flashed as he saw her face. "Your Majesty! What happened?"

A bitter sadness prickled Aki as she touched the remnants of the acid blisters on her cheek. "My brother."

"I'm so sorry." Wolf cast his eyes downward. "You've been imprisoned and tortured. Kichona has fallen. And Prince Gin has apparently already taken Thoma and their tsarina. We let you down, Your Majesty, in every way possible."

The confession hung in the humid air of the grotto.

322

But Aki shook it off. "Don't you dare say that." Even though she was filthy from being in this waterfall prison, she was imposing, too. She was born to lead, and that's exactly what she was going to do.

"The three of you have done more than any three taigas in our kingdom's history," Aki said. "You should be proud of that. I know you're feeling hopeless, and you should take whatever time you need to grieve."

Spirit looked up, the usual light in her eyes now dim.

Aki gave her a sad smile. "But when you're ready," she said kindly, "let's be angry—for your parents, for the Society, for our kingdom under my brother's rule. You are my League of Rogues, and you don't quit. Defeat only makes you fight harder, and we have a great deal to fight for. We'll make my brother pay for what he's done."

CHAPTER FIFTY-TWO

Daemon was angry all right.

No, not just angry. Pissed.

They were once part of a glorious society of warriors, living in a beautiful, peaceful kingdom. And now they were reduced to this—an empress and three apprentice warriors, imprisoned in an underground waterfall.

But worst of all was Sora shivering in Daemon's arms, sobbing. The devastation over her mother's death and the worry over her father had smothered his bold, fearless gemina's will to fight back.

He wiped away a stream of Sora's tears with his sleeve.

"I failed everybody," she said.

"You did not," Daemon said. "If it weren't for you, we'd all already be dead."

At the sound of the word "dead," Sora fell into another bout of sobs. "I'm useless! I couldn't even protect Mama and Papa. They had nothing to do with this war. But it's because of me that they got dragged into it, and now Hana has Papa,

324

and Mama is . . ." She couldn't finish.

"Shh." Daemon rocked Sora against him. "Don't for a second think this is your fault. It's the Dragon Prince's. We'll get out of here somehow and save your father. And you're not useless. I mean, look what you managed to do." He slipped his fingers into the hidden pocket in her collar and retrieved the silk drawstring pouch where she kept Prince Gin's soul.

"What is that?" Empress Aki asked.

"I'm not sure you'd believe us if we told you," Daemon said.

"I think I've seen quite enough in recent days that I'd believe anything now." She let out a mirthless laugh.

It was a fair point. "All right." He opened the pouch but left the pearl inside. It was rolling a bit, as if trying to get out. The grotto must have been enchanted with the prince's magic. "This is your brother's soul."

The empress startled. "What? He said he'd given it to Zomuri."

"You knew he'd made a bargain?" Fairy asked.

"Yes," Empress Aki said. "He gloated about it. But I thought that meant Zomuri had taken Gin's soul."

Daemon tugged the pouch's drawstrings closed. "Spirit and Broomstick found Zomuri's vault, broke in, and stole the soul pearl."

"You did what?" Empress Aki blinked at them. "And this all happened while I was locked up here?"

"We're sorry we didn't get to you sooner. We should have done a better job and protected you from Prince Gin's torture."

The empress began laughing. Sora's head snapped up.

"A better job?" Empress Aki shook her head as if in disbelief. "How many times do I have to tell you? No one could even dream of accomplishing what you've done. My brother came back with overwhelming magic, took possession of the minds of almost every taiga, and struck a deal with a bloodthirsty god to make himself unstoppable. In any other scenario, that should be the end of Kichona as we know it.

"But somehow, you're still here, and not only that but you're thwarting Gin against all odds. You broke into a *god's* lair and stole one of his most valuable possessions. So don't apologize for not doing 'a better job.'"

"See?" Daemon whispered to Sora. "You're not useless at all."

Sora mumbled a protest, but she sat up and wiped her eyes.

Suddenly, an explosion sounded. The entire grotto was rocked by the force of the blast, and everyone fell as dirt and rocks showered down on them from the ceiling. Water splashed from the falls.

"Get away from the waterfall and the pool!" Empress Aki shouted. "That's acid in there."

Daemon just managed to get himself and Sora away as another explosion shook the cave.

"What's happening?" Sora asked.

"I don't know!" Daemon crammed the pouch with the soul pearl into his tunic. "Just—whatever happens next—protect the empress!"

"I don't think you have to worry," Fairy said calmly. "At least not because of the blasts."

"Are you insane?" Sora said. The explosion seemed to have jolted her out of her grief, at least for the moment.

Fairy only smiled. "Haven't you guys wondered where Broomstick's been all this time?"

Daemon realized that the soul pearl wasn't reacting to the explosion; it wasn't ryuu coming to get them. Hope rose like a phoenix in Daemon's chest. "Are you saying—?"

Broomstick's voice echoed from inside the grotto walls. "Hey-o, Your Majesty, are you in there?"

CHAPTER FIFTY-THREE

W e're here!" a woman shouted from far away.

"Your Majesty, is that you?" Broomstick called. "I'm a taiga, come to rescue you, although it seems like you almost didn't need my help." The tunnel she'd dug was truly impressive. The Dragon Prince wouldn't have left her with a shovel, which meant she must have scraped her way through the clay with a stone. Wow.

"You were the one signaling me from the other side of the rock, weren't you?" the empress called from the other end of the tunnel. "I have all three of your friends with me. We'll come your way."

Broomstick heaved a sigh of relief that Fairy, Wolf, and Spirit were safe. He kept one ear on their approach and another on what was happening outside the hole he'd blown. The explosion hadn't exactly been quiet. They probably had company coming soon.

Fairy appeared first, mud smeared all over her face but grinning. "What took you so long?" she asked.

"It's good to see you, too," Broomstick said. "Everyone all right back there?"

"Yeah," Wolf said from farther down the tunnel, "except your massive backside is blocking the light, and I can't see where I'm going."

Broomstick laughed.

"Thanks for getting us out of here," Fairy said.

Empress Aki poked her head around Fairy and greeted him. "Ah, our savior. Thank you. Most would not risk their own lives to save those already doomed."

"Your Majesty, I didn't think twice about it."

"That's because you're cast from pure honor."

Broomstick blushed as he bowed. Or he attempted to bow in the cramped tunnel.

He could still feel the doubt from the Lake of Nightmares inside him, but Broomstick was also beginning to suspect that there wasn't water in his lungs. It was possible his friends and the empress were right. Maybe everyone had the potential for evil, but it was a choice whether to succumb or to fight it.

Fairy nudged him. "We should get out of here. If the ryuu aren't already waiting for us outside, they'll be there soon."

"Right, let's go," Broomstick said, turning and crawling toward the exit.

As they got closer to the part of the tunnel that Broomstick had blown apart, they had to watch for shrapnel from the rocks. By the time they got to the exit, he had several shards embedded in his palms.

Broomstick poked his head out of the opening to check for ryuu.

"Coast is clear," he said, waving them on. He climbed out first, then offered his hand to help the others.

Fairy and Empress Aki came out and clung to the steep, rocky ledge. Below, the ocean roared and spit at them. The clouds had covered up the moon again, and thick mist shrouded the night.

Then came Spirit, who looked like a phantom version of herself. Stars, what had Broomstick missed? He'd never seen Spirit this defeated. Even when the world was against them, she was their fearless leader.

Finally, Wolf emerged in boy form.

"What happened to Spirit?" Broomstick asked quietly as he pulled Wolf out of the tunnel.

"Prince Gin killed her mother in front of her, and now Hana has their father captive."

"Good gods."

"Yeah."

Empress Aki interrupted them, pointing into the fog. "Is that a ship over there?"

"Nines," Wolf said. "We killed Skullcrusher and Skeleton, so how are their navies still working?"

"They shouldn't be," Fairy said. "But Tidepool is here, too. Maybe she's behind this ship."

It sailed quickly toward them, no doubt investigating the source of the explosions.

"Gods dammit." Broomstick had led his friends and the empress here, to perch precariously on a ledge with nowhere to go but back into their prison or up over the top of the rock, which was a good ten-foot climb.

They were sitting ducks.

CHAPTER FIFTY-FOUR

Sora stared at the ship cutting through the fog.

Daemon touched her shoulder. "Sora? We need you."

"I . . ."

"You've been through something terrible. And I know you need time, but . . . I'm sorry. We can't do this without you. You have to make us all invisible."

Sora shook her head. "I—I don't know if I can concentrate enough to command the ryuu particles. All I can think of is Papa and Mama."

Daemon's entire face softened, and he smiled kindly. "Then think about them. Remember what your mother said to you during the Autumn Festival when we were visiting? What did she tell you to be?"

Sora almost broke down again. She would have tumbled off the rock face, but he held her fast. "'Be more.' That's what your mother said, and you rose to the challenge then. Honor her memory by doing it again. Save the empress. Kill Prince Gin. That's what we have to do."

Sora wanted to crawl back into the tunnel.

But she didn't. What Daemon said hit a nerve.

Mama and Papa had known what Sora was capable of. And Mama's entreaty had been about not only Sora's potential but also her duty to be the best person she could be.

That included pushing through sadness to save Papa, her friends, and her empress. To protect the kingdom.

So she did her best to stow away her grief. Sora knew it would come raging back again, but she needed to try to control it as much as possible right now, to let it out in smaller doses. Grief was a beast that didn't react well to being caged, but this had to be done.

"Everyone, huddle together. I'll try to make us invisible." Her voice cracked. She didn't know if her magic was strong enough to do this. But Daemon nodded at her, encouraging.

The ship breached the mist. Daemon and Broomstick pressed against Sora on her left, while Fairy and the empress pushed up on her right, all while holding on to the slippery crevices to avoid plummeting into the sea.

When they were packed together like sardines, Sora called on the emerald dust. The particles dove into her, taking away the cold of the ocean spray and infusing her instead with the heady warmth of ryuu magic. And then the magic spread to her friends on either side of her like ink traveling through water.

Just in time, too, because the ship sailed closer to inspect the rocks. Sora dared to look over her shoulder to watch the ship approach.

The collapsed remains of skeletons and corpses littered the deck. But it didn't matter; this ship didn't need an entire crew to sail it. Tidepool stood at the helm, directing the sea to guide her where she wanted to go.

Please hold, Sora thought to her ryuu particles as the ship lurched closer.

Tidepool leaned over the starboard side to examine the coastline. She noticed the hole in the cliff and stared at it for a while. Sora held her breath.

After what seemed like much too long, the ship swung away abruptly.

Sora exhaled. Tidepool was probably going to sound the alarm that they'd escaped, but at least Sora had managed to save everyone this time. She held on to the invisibility spell until the ship disappeared again into the mist.

"Bravo, Spirit," Empress Aki said.

"We're not safe yet, Your Majesty, but thank you."

"Now what?" Fairy asked.

"We find some place flat where Daemon can stand," Sora said, feeling a bit more in command now. "He'll transform into a wolf, we'll find Papa, and then we'll fly the hells out of here. Can you hang on a little longer while I go scope things out first? I can float everyone up individually once I make sure it's safe."

"Just be quick, please," Empress Aki said. "I'm rather weak."

Sora cast a spider spell and skittered up the rock face. At the top, she peered over the edge. There was a short cluster of bushes, which would suffice for cover as long as they didn't stay here long.

She pulled herself up, then leaned back over to get a view of everyone below. *Get the empress*, she commanded the ryuu particles.

They created a platform and, within seconds, lifted

Empress Aki to the top of the cliff. She crouched beside Sora, concealed from the rest of the island by the bushes.

Sora brought Fairy and Broomstick up, too, while Daemon transformed into a wolf and flew to them. They clambered onto his back.

Before Daemon could take off, though, a voice called from a short distance away. "Your Honor, wait!"

Papa!

Sora took off running. Papa crashed through the bushes and hurled his arms around her, his eyes and nose red from crying.

Sora's own tears began again as she embraced him. "You're alive!"

"Y-your sister . . ." He tried to say something, but he was too choked up.

"Is to blame for Mama's death," Sora finished for him. "Let's get out of here before Hana finds you again."

"I can't leave her," he cried.

"This isn't the Hana you knew," Sora said as kindly as she could through her own anger. "She could have stopped Prince Gin from killing Mama, but she didn't. You have to accept that Hana has changed. She's a terrible person."

Papa held Sora more tightly. "That's not true."

"No, she's right," Hana said, emerging from the bushes. She must have been following Papa. "I *am* a terrible person."

Sora pushed Papa behind herself to protect him. Broomstick and Fairy jumped off Daemon's back and brandished their weapons. Daemon stepped back to move Empress Aki farther away from the fight that was about to break out.

He had returned the soul pearl to Sora after they left

Dera Falls. It strained inside her collar, attracted to such a strong source of the prince's magic.

But Hana didn't look like the Dragon Prince's scathing Virtuoso anymore. She had more in common with a willow sapling beaten and bent by too many storms.

Hana held up both hands as if in surrender. "I'm so sorry for what I've done," she said, her voice subdued.

"I can't even look at you," Sora said, turning her attention to Papa instead. He sobbed softly against her.

Hana kept talking. "We gave Mama a proper burial. We cremated her and—"

Sora's head snapped up. "*You* buried her? What gives you the right? I should have been the one to lay her to rest."

"Your Honor," Papa whispered. "Please listen to your sister. She's trying to repent."

"How can you believe that?" Sora asked, horrified. "She let Prince Gin murder Mama."

Tears ran down Hana's face. "And I'll live the rest of my life making up for it."

"You can't," Sora said. "There's nothing you can do to atone."

"Spirit." Empress Aki had slid off Daemon's back and now stepped forward. She laid her hands on both Sora and Hana. "It's true that your sister can never bring your mother back. But I've watched you, and I know you have faith that there is good in the world. That's why you keep fighting. And if you believe that, then you also must have faith that people can change. Give your sister a chance. Let her leave Gin and Zomuri behind to step into Sola's magnanimous light."

"And what if it's another lie?" Sora asked.

Hana lowered herself to the ground into something like a bow. "I have no incentive to lie. If I still believed in what Emperor Gin—*Prince* Gin—wanted to do, I could have alerted the other ryuu to recapture you. But I can't support him anymore. He damned us all, and I just . . . I'll do whatever you need." She glanced up at Papa. "I promised him, and I promise you."

Papa broke away from Sora and crouched to hug Hana. She threw herself into him as if she was six years old again. "It will be all right, my little one," he said, stroking her hair. "I have you now. Everything will be all right."

Seeing them together like that toppled Sora's defenses. Ever since the Blood Rift Rebellion, all Sora had wished for was to go back in time, to have her sister with her again. That dream had almost seemed possible when Prince Gin returned to Kichona with Hana by his side. Sora had tried to persuade her sister to come back, to rejoin their family, to become a taiga again. Was Sora really going to give up on all those hopes so easily now, out of spite?

She knelt beside Hana and Papa. "We always talked about being a team, fighting side by side. We'd be the best taigas Kichona has ever seen—running faster, hitting harder, casting magic better than anyone in history. I'd still be interested in that, if you are. But you have to prove it's not a lie."

Hana let out a messy sob and nodded furiously. She looked up at Sora, and it was the same doe-eyed expression of admiration and love from when she was a tenderfoot watching her big sister's every move.

Papa reached his arm around to draw Sora into their embrace. Grief and joy mixed in her chest: sadness that

Mama was gone but happiness that Hana might finally be back.

"You have to be all in," Sora said. "One false move, one indication that you're still loyal to Prince Gin, and I won't hesitate to act against you. We serve Sola and Luna, Kichona, and Empress Aki. That much must be clear. There are a lot of good people's souls at stake, including yours and mine."

"I swear to you," Hana said.

"That's all fine and good, but I need proof, too," Sora said. "I have an idea for a good first step."

Hana looked at her expectantly.

Sora gestured at their small group. "There are only four of us that can fight. Five, if we can depend on you. But that's not enough. We need to build our army."

"Just tell me what you need and I'll get it," Hana said.

"I want Tidepool as our prisoner."

"Why?"

"No questions. Can you do it or not?"

Hana bit her lip. But then her uncertainty gave way to the commander she'd become, and she set her jaw and nodded curtly. "Give me ten minutes."

She ran away.

"I don't know," Daemon said. "What if she's going to get reinforcements? Now's our chance. I can manage flying everyone out of here. We can still get Empress Aki out of harm's way and come up with a final plan to stop the Dragon Prince."

Sora hesitated. But then she said, "Take the empress, Papa, Fairy, and Broomstick and fly high, out of reach."

"What about you?"

She looked at the empress, who nodded. "I'm going to

337

give my sister a chance," Sora said. "Ten minutes, and if she comes back fighting us, get everyone else to safety."

"I won't leave you."

"You're not. You'll be right above me. Swoop down and someone will pull me up if it comes to that."

Daemon grumbled about it, but he stooped to allow Empress Aki, Papa, Fairy, and Broomstick to climb onto his back. He flew them up into the air.

Sora's stomach tied itself into knots as she counted down the minutes.

Ten, nine, eight, seven, six, five, four, . . .

Three, two, one . . .

Zero.

Just a little longer. It wasn't an easy task she'd given Hana.

Sora decided to allow two more minutes.

But that time also passed.

Disappointed, Sora raised her arm to signal Daemon to come back. They had to get out of here if her sister had double-crossed her and was preparing again to attack.

But then Hana reappeared through the bushes with Tidepool, a dagger against Tidepool's throat.

"A ryuu who controls the sea," Hana said. "As requested."

A wry smile blazed across Sora's face. "It's the perfect reunion gift, Hana. Thank you."

CHAPTER FIFTY-FIVE

With the skeleton troops destroyed and Tidepool captured, Sora and the others were able to make quick work of the remaining ryuu stationed near Dera Falls. There hadn't been many, as Prince Gin had assumed that stationing his most powerful ryuu—Hana, Tidepool, Skullcrusher, and Skeleton—along with a navy of corpses would be enough.

But making assumptions about the League of Rogues was a grave mistake.

Still, Sora decided to move, and once they were on another of the islands in the tiger's paw, they hunkered down in the hollow of an enormous tree that must have been thousands of years old. It was broad enough to fit them all, and on top of that, Hana kept everyone invisible. Her ability to do so, like Sora's, was limited to proximity, but she'd been using ryuu magic for longer and could hide people even if they weren't right next to her. It would come in handy when they snuck back into the Imperial City.

"Congratulations," Sora said, once everyone was settled.

"We rescued Empress Aki, and we have Prince Gin's soul."

Daemon, Fairy, and Broomstick cheered. Hana and Papa looked a little confused. Empress Aki smiled serenely. Tidepool probably would have glared, but Fairy had drugged her, so the ryuu lay asleep against the roots of the tree.

"But we're not done yet," Sora said. "Hana and I are still damned, as well as every taiga and ryuu. And our family, friends, and the whole kingdom remain in danger. Prince Gin will continue to pursue the Evermore and bring death and destruction to Kichona. So we have a few things we need to accomplish. One, we have to get to the gods to beg them for the purification ritual. Two, we need reinforcements, because after those skeletons, it's painfully obvious to me that I underestimated his ryuu's abilities, and we can't fight them on our own. And three, we have to . . ."

Sora trailed off. She'd just seen her own mother killed and couldn't bring herself to talk in front of Prince Gin's sister about assassinating him. But she did touch her collar, where the soul pearl was safely stashed again.

Empress Aki sighed. "It's all right. I know it has to be done. We let my brother go after the Blood Rift, and look where that got us. I wish I had the opportunity like you did to see your sister return to our side, but I don't. Gin has to be killed, for Kichona's sake."

Papa bowed his head. "Your Majesty, what if he repented as Hana did?"

"Then I would give him a chance. But I don't think he will." She looked to Sora. "Please continue with your plans."

"Thank you, Your Majesty. I was actually wondering if you knew anything about Gin that could help us get close enough to reunite him with his soul? I can handle infiltrating the castle, but he's so well protected. . . ."

Empress Aki shook her head. "I'm sorry. It's been a decade since we've lived together. I don't know what his daily routines are, whether he's exposed at meal times, or when he's getting dressed in the morning or anything like that."

"Oh," Sora said, trying to hide her disappointment. It had been a long shot, but ideas were few and far between right now, and it would have been nice if something was easy for once. "That's all right. I'll think of something." She gave the empress what she hoped looked like a confident smile. "Let's start with the other part of the plan that requires your help. You have good diplomatic relationships with the mainland kingdoms, right?"

The empress nodded. "Most of them, some better than others."

"Do you think they'd respond to our call for help?"

"Well, not Thoma because . . ." Empress Aki's eyes watered.

Sora nodded grimly at the reminder that Tsarina Austine was Prince Gin's prisoner.

The empress wiped away a tear and shook her head as if to clear it. "I have no doubt that Ria Kayla and Emperor Geoffrey would offer their navies and marines," she said, refocusing on Sora's question. "Queen Meredith is a possibility if I asked her in person. I'm less sure about Queen Everleigh and Empress Viviana, because they don't have as much military might. And I'd ask High King Erickson last. He's mercurial and hard to predict."

"That's all good to know," Sora said. "I say we focus on just the first three kingdoms, then."

"But even if we could get distress messages to Kayla, Geoffrey, and Meredith," Empress Aki said, "it would take weeks for their troops to arrive. We don't have that kind of time."

Sora glanced in the direction of the sea. "Under normal travel conditions, that would be true. But we have a way to move across the ocean even faster than a sailfish: Tidepool."

Everyone turned to look at the unconscious ryuu. She was an intimidating brute of a warrior who wore a scowl even in sleep.

A slow smile crept onto Empress Aki's face. "You're going to have her propel me on a ship to each of the mainland kingdoms and then bring their navies back."

Sora grinned.

"It's a good idea," Broomstick said slowly, "but how, exactly, are we planning to control her? The only reason she hasn't drowned us yet is because we knocked her out."

On the way from Dera Falls, Sora had talked intently with Hana about Tidepool, learning everything her sister knew about the ryuu. From that discussion, Sora had concluded two very important things: Tidepool was more practical than emotional, and she loved herself immensely. This meant she was definitely not a martyr. While Tidepool believed in the Dragon Prince's pursuit of the Evermore, she wasn't going to fall on her sword just in the name of honor.

"This is where Fairy comes in," Sora said, pointing to her roommate, whose eyes lit up with anticipation. "I want you to poison Tidepool with something that would kill her if left unchecked but that could be held at bay if we gave her small doses of an antidote every few hours. Tidepool loves herself too much to let the poison simply take hold. I believe she'll do our bidding if it means she can stay alive. Do you have something in your botanicals that can do this?"

Fairy was already unlatching the satchel at her belt. She grinned as she pulled out a small glass jar that clinked with what looked like tiny black, star-shaped candies inside. "This is abrinori. If left unchecked, it dissolves internal organs, beginning with the stomach, then working its way through the bloodstream to the intestines, the kidneys, and the heart. And this"—she held up a slender vial full of a viscous, bright yellow liquid—"is the antidote. One drop every two hours will counteract the abrinori. And I can concoct a permanent antidote if we wanted to cure Tidepool after we successfully get to all the kingdoms and return with their navies."

"Perfect," Sora said. "The team for the mainland journey will be you for coercion, Broomstick for force, and Empress Aki for diplomacy. You'll have five days, which, with Tidepool's powers, ought to give you enough time to cross the ocean, spend a day each in Brin, Caldan, and Fale Po Tair, and return to Kichona. Everyone on board?"

The three of them pounded fists over hearts.

Papa snarled. It caught everyone off guard, and they jumped back from him. But a moment later, Papa rubbed his eyes as if trying to wake from a strange dream. "I'm sorry about that. I don't know what's come over me."

Daemon spoke up. "This is what's happening to Kichona's people with Zomuri's gloom influencing them. Even the kindest men lash out. That's another reason we have to kill Prince Gin soon and get Empress Aki back on the throne, so she can reinstate Sola as our patron god."

Papa looked horrified. Hana hugged him and said,

"Don't worry. You'll be yourself again soon. We'll make sure of it." He relaxed a little. Her word—even just her closeness—seemed to mean so much to him. Sora felt better about allowing Hana to join them.

"Our number one goal is to kill Prince Gin and restore our kingdom and our people to their peaceful ways," Sora said. "Carrying out the assassination will be a mission for me and Hana." She looked over at her sister.

Hana gave her a solemn nod.

"We'll wait five days to give Empress Aki, Fairy, and Broomstick time to return with our allies. In the meantime, Hana and I will head to the Imperial City to make sure we understand the lay of the land. You'll send me one of my dragonflies when you're on your way, so that we can time our attacks to coincide with each other. Papa will stay hidden here, where it's safe."

"And then what?" Papa asked.

Sora fidgeted with her necklace. She didn't know.

"I have an idea," Hana said.

Everyone stared at her.

"Prince Gin doesn't know I've turned," she said. "As far as he's concerned, I'm still Virtuoso, his second-in-command. We have to find a way to get the soul back into his body so that he'll no longer be invincible—I'm the only one who can get close enough to him to do it."

Sora mulled it over. She'd have to trust her sister completely for it to work.

"Believe in me," Hana said softly.

Sora stopped playing with the necklace.

This is what Mama would have wanted, for Sora to stretch beyond what a normal person would, to tap into the well of kindness inside her and believe that Hana could change.

Could she do it?

But she already had, hadn't she? She'd accepted Hana's capture of Tidepool as proof of her loyalty, and she had welcomed Hana into the planning.

"All right," Sora said. "We have a few days to plot out the details of how you'll get to the prince, but we'll figure it out."

Papa beamed at his two girls working together. Sora wasn't quite that enthusiastic—she was still working herself up to fully believing that Hana was on her side—but she still gave Papa a smile.

Then Sora turned to Daemon, who was guarding Tidepool by the roots of the tree. "And that brings us to the last thing we need to do—learning about the purification ritual. But I have to admit, I'm at a loss here. We could try to contact Liga again, but he's not that helpful—"

"I'll go to Celestae," Daemon said.

"You'll what?"

"Fly to Celestae. Pound on the gates or shout at the fortress walls or whatever it is that's supposed to keep me out. And then I'll find Luna and persuade her to tell me about the purification process. She's my grandmother and the taigas' patron god. She has to help."

"That's . . . crazy," Sora said. Not only the part about him trying to get into Celestae and convince Luna but also the possibility that he'd see his father, Vespre. She remembered how conflicted Daemon had been back in Jade Forest, when she'd originally come up with the idea of reaching out to his father. It had been almost a relief when they'd gotten Liga instead.

Now, though, Daemon crossed his arms. "And since when has the ever-mischievous Spirit been against crazy ideas?"

Fairy laughed. "He has a good point."

Everyone else nodded.

"Besides," Daemon said, "I promised to do everything I could to save you from an eternity in the hells, and I meant it."

Sora bit her lip.

"All right, then," she said. "I guess we have a plan."

"Yes, we do," Daemon said, "but could I talk to you privately?"

She frowned. "Uh, sure." She turned to the rest of the group. "Why don't you all get a little rest? Hana, watch over Tidepool. Daemon and I will be right back."

CHAPTER FIFTY-SIX

They walked a short way to a thicket of banyans—trees that grew one on top of another, their seeds landing on a branch of one tree and casting down roots, such that dozens of trees could fuse together, their long roots draping over one another and hardening into a forest of interwoven trunks.

"What's going on?" Sora asked.

Daemon spun and faced her. "I actually hate the idea of splitting up again."

"Sorry," she said, confused. "But didn't your part of the plan—going to Celestae—also involve dividing up? It makes sense, and we've been doing it this whole time."

"Yes, but I don't want . . . Ugh, I don't know how to explain it without . . ." Daemon closed his eyes as if it was suddenly all too overwhelming, and he rested his head against a banyan tree without finishing what he was saying.

She went over and touched his shoulder. "What don't you want?"

He mumbled something, but it disappeared into the tree.

"I'm sorry. . . . I couldn't hear you," Sora said.

Daemon paused, then pulled himself away from the branches. "I don't want to lose you," he said.

At first she thought he meant he was afraid she would die damned. But when Daemon turned back around, his eyes met Sora's, and their gemina bond buzzed as loudly as if his electricity was at its fullest. Sora gasped as her entire body vibrated with the charge between them.

"I don't want to lose you," he repeated, except this time, their bond also filled with rose—both the color and the sensation of blooms unfurling.

Sora's mouth parted. Did this mean . . . ?

Almost immediately, though, he raised his mental ramparts and cut her off. "I shouldn't have . . . You know what? Don't say anything. You're my gemina. I've probably ruined everything—"

She stepped closer, so there were only inches between them. She put her finger on his lips, and the warmth of his breath on that little sliver of her skin was enough to make her light-headed.

"You like me?" she dared to ask. "I mean, as more than just a gemina?"

Daemon cast his gaze downward but nodded, almost guiltily. "I know I'm not supposed to. I tried to fight it, but Fairy was right. I just can't. . . . I'm sorry."

Sora laughed softly to herself. "Don't be sorry." She traced the curve of his mouth with her finger.

His Adam's apple bobbed as he swallowed, and he looked at her again, his gaze intense, waiting, hoping. Actual sparks flickered off his skin.

Sora could barely breathe.

And yet she held back. There was a reason the Society forbade geminas from getting involved. If it didn't work out, you were still stuck with them as your partner for life. You'd have to see them with someone else and feel their love for that other person. There was no escape. She pulled her finger away from his mouth.

"You're scared," Daemon said.

"What if we mess everything up?" she asked. "You're my best friend. You're my favorite person in the entire world."

"And what if we don't try?" he said. "What if we miss out on the most amazing experience of our lives?"

Sora thought of Mama then. About how unpredictable life could be. How you never knew when it would end. And she also remembered Mama's entreaty for Sora to *be more*.

It wasn't only about being the best taiga or the best friend or the best sister. Mama meant it in every respect.

Be more than what ordinary expects.

Sora had taken plenty of risks while in school, pulling off pranks and pushing the boundaries on the rules. She'd put her life on the line to save Kichona. Surely she could take a risk on her heart, too?

She reached up and traced the scar on Daemon's face, where his wolf cub brother or sister had slashed him when they were young. He was wild and beautiful, the boy she'd fallen for so naturally over their years together that she hadn't even realized it until she was irretrievably in love.

Daemon took in a breath of surprise at her touch. But then he leaned in.

Sora closed her eyes.

His lips skimmed hers, soft, gentle. Despite the electric

charge between them, Daemon moved slowly, as if she were the most precious thing in the world. He released his mental ramparts, and the feeling of roses blooming filled Sora all over again. Sweet, floral perfume wafted through their gemina bond.

Daemon kissed her cheek. Her temple. Both closed eyelids. Each touch was a caress, as light as dragonfly wings.

Sora opened her eyes and ran her thumb across his wolf-claw scar again.

He stilled.

She didn't need him to complete her. She was already whole. But having Daemon like this—knowing she had someone by her side who would always be the mountain supporting her—amplified what Sora could be on her own.

Together, they could do anything.

He smiled, and then he kissed her again, his mouth like water in a brook. Sparks crackled all around them, lighting them with a blue glow. With every touch of his lips, Sora shined brighter on the inside and the outside.

"I don't ever want to lose this," she said.

Daemon pulled her in tightly against him, both arms wrapped around like he never wanted to let go. "I am yours, and you are mine. No matter what happens, that'll always be true. I promise you."

CHAPTER FIFTY-SEVEN

Hana watched Sora and Wolf come back from wherever they'd gone. They were the same, inseparable, yet there was something different between them. She couldn't put her finger on what it was.

Broomstick smirked. "You two finally figured out that you like each other, huh?"

Wolf shot him a dangerous look.

Sora, on the other hand, blushed. Hana made a face. It was bizarre seeing her tough sister embarrassed about a boy. But then she saw how Sora avoided Fairy's gaze, and she understood that there was more to this story than just Sora and Wolf.

"It's all right," Fairy said, smiling. "I'm happy for you guys."

"Really?" Sora asked, daring to look at her.

"Really," Fairy said.

Sora exhaled, and Hana found that she did, too.

"Thank you," Wolf said to Broomstick and Fairy. "I'm lucky to have friends like you."

"Yes, you are," Fairy said, winking. "Now get going. You have a heavenly island to break into and a god to persuade."

"Oh, um, right. I'll be as quick as I can," Wolf said. "I intend to get back to fight Prince Gin and the ryuu with you."

"Hold on," Hana said. She'd grown up in a camp full of people plotting surreptitiously; it had made Hana pretty sharp at seeing when someone was planning something different than his words conveyed. "What are you not telling us?"

"Nothing," he said, a little too quickly.

Sora frowned. "Daemon?"

He smiled and tucked her hair behind her ear. "Do you believe in me?"

"Of course."

"Then will you let me keep this secret if I promise to tell you later? I just need it to be mine for now."

She bit her lip but nodded.

Hana sighed. Love could really muck up your brain. Nevertheless, she trusted Sora, and Sora trusted Wolf, so Hana let it go. Besides, Hana wasn't the one in charge anymore. She was a taiga now, not a ryuu.

Before he left, Wolf conjured enough food and water for everyone. Then he shifted forms and nuzzled against Sora's face. It was probably the lupine version of a kiss, but it was a bit too sweet for the rest of them, and Hana, Fairy, and Broomstick groaned and turned away. Wolf laughed, said goodbye again, then took off into the sky.

Broomstick opened his mouth, about to say something.

Sora held up a finger. "Not a word. You tease me, and I will make you sorry."

He pinched his lips together, pretending to zip them while obviously trying not to grin.

Hana watched them with longing. This is how her sister and her friends had always been, a tight-knit group supremely comfortable with each other. Hana had always wanted to be a part of it.

But now I have a chance, she realized.

Fairy administered the poison to Tidepool, then woke her with salts that were part ammonia, part something even more noxious.

Tidepool opened her eyes groggily but snapped into a fighting stance when she saw her captors.

"I wouldn't do that if I were you," Hana said. "You've been given a poison that will dissolve all your internal organs unless we give you an antidote every two hours. If you want to live, you'll do as we say."

"You bitch," she said as she held her hands up in surrender. "I always knew the emperor should have made *me* his second-in-command."

Hana flinched. For most of her life, Prince Gin's esteem had been the measuring stick for her worth.

But now she'd have to find that elsewhere. Or in herself.

She quickly went over what they wanted Tidepool to do—bring over one of the ships from Dera Falls, use the ocean to sail Empress Aki, Fairy, and Broomstick to Caldan, Brin, and Fale Po Tair, and hopefully lead their navies back to Kichona to stop Prince Gin before his war bled past Thoma and into the rest of the world. Tidepool kept trying to get in snide remarks, but after a while, Broomstick started pantomiming painful deaths caused by the dissolution of his insides, and Tidepool shut up.

"Do as Empress Aki tells you," Hana said, "and when you've returned with our allies, Fairy will give you the permanent antidote to the poison. Agreed?"

Tidepool let out a violent string of Shinowanan curses but finally nodded.

"Good, then. Get started."

Half an hour later, the fiercest of the warships that had been guarding Dera Falls arrived onshore. Hana and Sora joined Empress Aki, Fairy, Broomstick, and Tidepool on the beach to see them off.

"Here are some messengers," Sora said, giving Broomstick a lantern full of glittering green eagle rays. "Send us updates at every kingdom."

Broomstick took the lantern. "I can't believe I'm voluntarily going to the kingdoms where the Lake of Nightmares said I'd cause so much death."

"I can believe it," Empress Aki said. "Self-doubt is a ghost that feeds on fear. Starve it with bravery, and you'll prevail." She patted him on the back. "As you have."

"Good luck, Your Majesty," Hana said, bowing.

The empress thanked both Hana and Sora, then boarded the ship. Fairy and Broomstick said their goodbyes and took Tidepool on board with them.

And then they were gone.

The space between Hana and Sora suddenly seemed both empty—without Fairy's constant chatter and Broomstick's laughs—and too full. There was so much Hana needed to say, but she wasn't ready to yet.

Sora seemed to feel it, too, because she kept looking straight out onto the ocean, even after the ship was far enough away that it looked like a toy in the distance.

Finally, she turned inland, and dread filled Hana at the questions and accusations that were sure to tumble forth.

Instead, Sora smiled kindly and said, "Want to make some dinner for Papa while you tell me what you know about the bloodstone castle?"

It was as if she knew that Hana couldn't say all her apologies, couldn't handle all the regrets and tears right now. And instead, she gave her this gift—just to be with her family for a little while, and to work together, as she'd always dreamed.

The next day, Hana and Sora left Papa safely hidden in the hollowed-out tree, then swam across the channel, back to the main island of Kichona. As dawn broke, they decided to make camp outside of Shima, since it would be wiser to rest during sunlight hours and travel at night. They'd easily be able to make it to Jade Forest and the Imperial City tomorrow to begin scouting and to wait for the empress to return, hopefully with reinforcements from the mainland.

Once Hana and Sora had settled into a cave in the hills just beyond Shima, Hana summoned her magic and conjured a three-dimensional, glowing, green model of Prince Gin's palace. Small figures paced around the perimeter and stood watch on the pointed towers. "I know every passageway, where the ryuu are stationed, their alarm and guard protocols . . . everything," she said.

Sora studied it. "It's less daunting than the actual castle. Still a challenge, though."

"Yeah," Hana said. "And even though we'll be invisible, we need to know where the ryuu are positioned because we don't want to run into them. They know you can make yourself unseen, so they'll be on guard for unexplained movement. Even if you brush one of their uniforms or dart out of sight but stir the air around them, they might notice.

"Emperor Gin . . ." Hana noticed Sora frown, and she quickly corrected herself. "*Prince* Gin isn't easy to pin down. Sometimes he's in his study mapping out attacks, sometimes he's at the Citadel inspecting and coaching the new ryuu, and sometimes he just sits on his throne, staring at the mural on the ceiling."

"He stares at the ceiling?" Sora asked. "That doesn't sound like him."

"The mural is of the moment he stole ryuu magic from the afterlife and came back from the dead," Hana explained. "He thinks it was a message from the gods that he was given a second chance at life—with even greater magic—in order to shepherd his people and his country to the future they deserved."

Sora grew painfully silent. Hana stopped, too, when she realized what else that mural represented—the moment Prince Gin had damned their souls.

A ship sank in Hana's gut. She had grown up thinking he was a visionary. He was wrong, but it would still take her time to fully process that he wasn't the gods-blessed leader she'd been told he was since she was six years old. She couldn't say this out loud, though. It would seem like lingering loyalty, and that wasn't it at all.

They had to cram that soul pearl back into his body and kill him. He was too powerful, too much of a threat, to be allowed to survive.

"When this is all over," Sora said quietly, "we'll blow up that mural."

"I'll help," Hana said.

After a moment, Sora pointed back at Hana's 3-D model of the castle, getting back to business. "Given how hard Prince Gin is to find, we'll have to be flexible in our approach. But maybe the soul pearl can act as a guide. It seems to be attracted to his magic, and it went crazy in my pocket when he was actually right in front of us at Dera Falls. Good thing it's small, or he might have seen it moving."

"It would be really good if the soul pearl can help lead us. So"—Hana pointed to one of the towers—"if Wolf is back in time, he'll drop us off up here, and we'll either follow the pearl or make our way through to the most likely places in the castle." She shifted the model to highlight where the ryuu were stationed—there were more guards now since Wolf and Fairy sabotaged the shipyard and broke into the prince's study.

Sora studied the map. "And you know the patrol schedules, you said?"

"Yes. I came up with them."

"Good. Depending on what time it is and how long it's taking us to track down Prince Gin, we can change our path inside to avoid the ryuu with the most difficult powers."

They spent a few more hours poring over the map, plotting the best paths, making contingency plans.

When they were finished, Sora rubbed her fist into Hana's hair, like she used to do when they were kids. "Nice work, stinkbug."

Hana lit up. It wasn't as intimidating as "Virtuoso," but it was suddenly clear that that wasn't what she needed anymore.

All she wanted was this.

CHAPTER FIFTY-EIGHT

It shouldn't have taken long for Daemon to get anywhere when he flew at the speed of light. But he didn't know where exactly Celestae was located. He'd figured that it would be obvious when he saw it. Who could miss an entire floating island in the sky?

Apparently, Daemon could. He'd been flying for several days now—stopping only when he needed to eat or take a quick nap on a cloud—and exhaustion strained his muscles.

"Liga! My lady, Luna!" he shouted, his voice hoarse from the endless yelling. "Can you hear me? It's Wolf. I need your help!"

As before, there was no response, as if the vast emptiness of the sky was just absorbing Daemon's entreaties. Where was everyone? There were hundreds of gods if you counted both the major and minor ones, plus who knew how many demigods like Liga there were. In order to give all those enormous personalities enough space, Celestae must be bigger than the entire Kichonan archipelago. And yet it was nowhere to be seen.

"I should have asked Fairy to gather some night-blooming flowers for me to bring," Daemon grumbled. "Maybe then I could get Liga to respond." His brother could probably get hold of Luna.

Daemon's sparks sputtered through his fatigue, and he decided to give in to it, just for a moment. He landed on a cloud and collapsed into the cushions of mist. In his wolf form, he was paradoxically sturdy and strong while also weighing very little, since he was composed of stardust and god magic; therefore, the clouds could hold him. It was still hard for Daemon to grasp how this was possible, but that was likely because he was trying to understand it from a human point of view.

"Liga," he called half-heartedly. "Where are you?"

A small flock of birds flew past Daemon's cloud. He followed them with his gaze until they'd vanished from sight.

His mind began to wander to what Sora was doing. She was probably laying out a detailed plot for how to assassinate Prince Gin. He hoped she was reconnecting with her sister, too, like he'd gotten to do with Liga. Maybe Sora and Hana were even training together, with Hana teaching Sora how to better use her invisibility.

Invisibility! Daemon bolted upright in his cloud. What if his banishment from Celestae wasn't as simple as the gods not letting him through the gates when he showed up? What if Vespre had made it so that Daemon couldn't see the gods' home at all?

"Nines," he swore. If that were true, he'd better get back to work at yelling for someone to come get him, because he wasn't ever going to find Celestae on his own.

Daemon rose from the cloud and shook off the tendrils of mist that clung to his fur. His sparks were bright again; the self-healing properties of demigods also meant his energy could be restored relatively quickly, even though his rest had been short. He leaped back into the sky and flew straight up, to where the atmosphere thinned and breathing would have been difficult if he weren't a demigod.

He began to cycle through a series of entreaties, shouting each at the top of his lungs.

"Liga, it's Wolf! I need your help!"

"Luna, this is your grandson. The taigas need you!"

And finally . . . reluctantly . . .

"Vespre, it's your profligate son! I've come home to apologize."

On the hundredth time of calling his father's name, the air suddenly began to blur in the distance. Daemon stopped yelling and held his position in the sky.

In what had once been empty space, a long stairway appeared. Hundreds of enormous silver torii arches lined it, each heavy-beamed gateway leading straight to the next, creating the sensation of a tunnel leading to the heavens.

Behind the torii-covered stairway, golden pagodas and archways and bridges materialized, like a Kichonan city built from crystallized honey, glimmering in the air. Every god had a towering castle, each tier elegant with curved eaves, broad balconies, and intricately carved gargoyles with fur that swirled like clouds. Around each castle was a sprawling estate, and as Daemon flew through the torii arches and drew closer to Celestae, he could make out some of the lush foliage in the nearest gardens.

Purple wisteria draped and swung in a subtle spring

breeze, perfuming the air with a scent of grape candy. Maple trees boasted autumn reds and oranges. And tall, snow-dusted fir trees presided over parts of the floating heavens. Daemon took it all in with wonder. Time didn't exist in Celestae, and neither, apparently, did distinct seasons. The gods could create and do whatever they wanted.

The rush of brooks, like giggling children, and the melody of crickets creating music that sounded a lot like Kichonan songs to the gods stirred something in Daemon's memory. He didn't remember anything specific, and yet he could feel that he'd been here before, that this place lived inside him, even when he was gone. He sped up, bursting out of the last of the torii arches and eager to see what else his first home would trigger.

A voice like thunder boomed across the sky and stopped Daemon short.

"My wayward son. How dare you return?"

CHAPTER FIFTY-NINE

Two days after Fairy, Broomstick, and Empress Aki left, Sora received a simple message via glittering eagle ray: *Emperor Geoffrey has committed the Imperial Caldanian Navy to help us fight.*

The next day, she received this message: *Ria Kayla has agreed to send the Royal Navy and Marines of Brin.*

And on the fourth night after they'd left, the last eagle ray flew into her hideout and landed on Sora's pillow: *Fale Po Tair will fight. Queen Meredith is leading the Faleese Navy herself. We are on our way.*

Goose bumps prickled Sora's skin. Things were falling into place. The only piece missing was Daemon.

Hopefully, he'd return soon.

CHAPTER SIXTY

It was time. A day after the last of the eagle rays arrived, Sora and Hana stood at the edge of the Field of Illusions, outside the Citadel's western fortress walls. The troops from Caldan, Brin, and Fale Po Tair were hidden just outside the Imperial City, ready to fight. Soon, they would try to overwhelm the ryuu by sheer numbers, while Sora and Hana slipped into the castle, reunited the soul pearl with Prince Gin, and killed him.

And then there was the question about Sora's soul and whether it could be purified . . .

Daemon, where are you?

Sora and Hana needed to get into Prince Gin's castle, but their original plan to fly in would no longer work without Daemon. The quietest way in, then, would be down through the secret passageway that Empress Aki had shown Sora.

"You're sure the tunnels are still there?" Sora asked as they approached the spiraling swirl of black-and-white sands that hid the entrance.

"Yes," Hana said. "Prince Gin built his castle on the foundation of Rose Palace and left the escape routes that had been dug into the mountain."

"All right, then the center of that spinning illusion marks the entrance. It's a short fall. I'll go first."

Sora checked to make sure patrol on the Citadel wall hadn't returned yet, then stepped into the middle of the swirling sand. It sucked her in like a whirlpool and spit her out eight feet below. She landed on the ground of the tunnel and rolled out of the way so Hana could join her.

A few seconds later, Hana fell through, touched down, and rolled effortlessly to her feet. She coughed in the sand dust, though.

"How is that supposed to be an escape route?" she asked when she'd finally finished coughing.

Sora glanced up at the ceiling, which gave the illusion of being solid, albeit in a moving pattern of black and white. Then she saw a ladder propped against the tunnel wall. "I suppose they move that over and climb up and out."

"Oh, that makes sense." Hana coughed again. "Let's get out of this dust."

The soul pearl tugged in Sora's collar desperately, sensing that its owner was near.

Lead us to the Dragon Prince.

Sora set off through the tunnels, trying to interpret the minuscule movements of the pearl. The red streaks in the black stone seemed to glow more ominously than ever as they wound their way through the storage rooms.

In the distance, explosions sounded.

"Broomstick, Fairy, and the empress have begun their assault," Sora said.

"That means the ryuu here in the castle will be on high alert," Hana said. "Why didn't we have them wait until *after* we'd tried to kill Prince Gin?"

"Because this way, the ryuu will be focused on the attack, not on us," Sora said. "The castle will be mostly empty, because the warriors will all go outside to deal with the assault. And don't forget we're invisible. If we play it right, they won't know we're here until it's too late. You just have to get close enough to Prince Gin to get the pearl back down his throat."

"You never did like doing things the easy way."

Sora cocked her head. "No, I suppose not."

They slipped out of the storage rooms, up a dark staircase, and into a corridor on the first floor.

The pearl rolled to the left of Sora's pocket. "That way, I think." She pointed.

"That's the direction of the throne room," Hana said. She took off, and Sora followed.

A half dozen ryuu turned a corner ahead of them, hurrying into the hallway. Sora smashed herself against the wall, hoping they wouldn't hit her as they ran past.

Hana shook her head furiously, as if to say, *Are you kidding me?* She pointed to the ceiling and leaped, adhering her hands and feet to it.

Gods, why hadn't Sora thought of that? She jumped up and crouched against the ceiling next to Hana.

The ryuu ran beneath them only seconds later. The warriors jostled one another in their rush. One of them stumbled and brushed the wall where Sora had stood.

Hana mouthed, *I told you so.*

Apparently, the ryuu hadn't taught her that saying that

was incredibly annoying. But Sora ignored it. Some things didn't matter anymore when you were dealing with life and death.

Sora and Hana decided to stay on the ceiling. It would lower the chances of running into more ryuu. They crawled onward—the only downside of being up here was they had to move slower—and peered into every room they passed.

The dining hall was empty, chairs probably knocked over from the ryuu hurrying to their posts once Broomstick's explosions began.

Likewise, there was no one in the ballroom, the receiving hall, and the other common rooms. But that was no surprise, and Sora and Hana climbed higher into the castle.

Hana steered them into a familiar dark corridor made to look like the maw of a dragon. Inside lay Prince Gin's throne room.

Still on the ceiling, they snuck up to the heavy wooden double doors. Sora pressed her ear against one of them.

Instead of the Dragon Prince's deep voice, though, there was only a reedy whimper.

Hana had crawled down onto the other door and was looking through one of the keyholes. "Prince Gin's not there."

Sora touched her collar. Had the pearl led them astray?

"If Prince Gin's not in there, then who is?"

Hana pushed her eye harder against the keyhole. "I think it's Tsarina Austine of Thoma."

Sora dropped to the ground and looked into the other keyhole. "He captured her days ago. Why would he wait to give her heart to Zomuri?"

"I doubt he did. But gods don't always come right away when summoned, or sometimes at all."

Is that why Daemon wasn't back yet? Was he having trouble getting the gods in Celestae to pay attention to him?

As for Zomuri, Sora didn't think that god would fail to show up for one of the mainland monarchs' hearts. It was only a matter of time. She reached for the door, her fingers wrapping around the dragons carved into the wood.

"What are you doing?" Hana hissed.

"We have to save the tsarina."

"No, we have a plan, and our job is to kill Prince Gin. It's Fairy's task to get Tsarina Austine."

"But—"

"You're the one who said it's safer for the tsarina to wait for Fairy than to wander around with us in the middle of a battle," Hana said. "Tsarina Austine will be safe as long as Zomuri doesn't come. We have no control over that, and we're no match for a god, but we can try to get to Prince Gin. That's how we save her and our own kingdom."

Sora held on to the door handle, having a hard time letting go when there was someone in need on the other side. But Hana was right. They had to stay on task.

"Be safe," Sora whispered to the tsarina through the door. She released her grip on the handle.

"Crawling on the ceiling is too slow," Sora said. "We have to risk moving on the floor."

Hana agreed, and they dove back into the castle, following the movement of the soul pearl in Sora's collar.

On the next floor, two more contingents of ryuu nearly ran into them. Sora and Hana managed to leap to the ceiling with only a hairbreadth of space to spare.

Eventually, they reached Prince Gin's study. The soul pearl didn't react much to the location, but a pair of ryuu stood guard in front of it, firmly planted at the door. Maybe Sora was wrong about using the pearl as a compass. Maybe the Dragon Prince was inside.

"Gods dammit," Hana said. "How are we going to get in?"

"Remember the plan," Sora said. "They're predisposed to trust you, because you've been the most loyal ryuu out of everyone for ten years. Make yourself visible. Tell them you and Tidepool were overpowered at Dera Falls and you've just returned to the castle. Act normal."

"Right." Hana took several deep breaths.

"Stinkbug?"

"Yeah?"

"You can do this."

Hana breathed in deeply again, then nodded. "Okay."

She backed down the adjacent hall, materialized, then turned the corner as if she were just walking to the study. Sora, still invisible, stayed a safe distance away but close enough in case Hana needed help.

"I have a report for His Majesty," Hana said in the caustic tone she had used as Virtuoso.

"Where have you been?" one of the ryuu asked. "We got word the prisoners broke free from Dera Falls days ago."

"You're not important enough to know," Hana snapped.

The ryuu bristled. But he couldn't argue against it. After all, Hana was the Dragon Prince's second-in-command. He cleared his throat, then said, "His Majesty isn't here."

"Where is he?"

Smart, Sora thought.

"Don't you know we're under attack?" the other ryuu said.

He received a glare from Hana, and it chastened him like the blunt end of a sword to the head.

The first ryuu said, more respectfully, "His Majesty went up to the highest spire. He needed a better vantage point for what was happening out there."

Hana nodded curtly. "If I somehow miss him and His Majesty comes back here, tell him I'm looking for him." She spun on her heel as if she couldn't bother to wait for a response.

Sora hurried after her as Hana marched down the hallway.

When they were out of earshot, Hana stopped. "Did you hear all that?"

"Yes, you did great. Now let's get to the highest spire."

Since the ryuu knew Hana was back now, she continued without making herself invisible. Sora jogged next to her but kept herself unseen. They didn't encounter any ryuu as they wound up the narrow spiral staircase of the tower—the warriors were mostly stationed at defense posts on the outside of the castle—but the eeriness of the quiet only heightened Sora's nerves.

The door into the tower was a slender piece of oak on iron hinges. Hana knocked. "Your Majesty, it's Virtuoso."

He didn't answer, but the door flung open as if of its own accord. The soul pearl practically leaped against the fabric of Sora's collar, yearning to be reunited with its owner.

Soon, Sora hoped.

The room was small and cylindrical, with a bare stone floor. A lantern flickered, casting dancing shadows on the walls. Prince Gin stood outside on the balcony, his back to the door.

"Virtuoso," he said, his arms crossed calmly behind his back. "What have you done?"

Hana stepped tentatively into the room. Although invisible, Sora crept closer to the shadowed walls. Hana proceeded to the balcony. "What do you mean, Your Majesty?" she asked.

"I mean," Prince Gin said, "why am I being attacked?"

Sora shivered from where she stood, unseen. The eerie evenness of his voice belied something much worse than the anger she'd expected.

"I had nothing to do with the Faleese, Brin, and Caldanian navies," Hana answered him.

He sighed, as if annoyed by a mosquito. "Never mind them. The ryuu will finish them shortly." He gestured to the smoke and chaos coming from the Citadel and the road leading up to the castle. From what Sora could see, the reinforcements from Ria Kayla, Emperor Geoffrey, and Queen Meredith scrambled to stay in formation in the face of the ryuu defense. They may have had numbers on their side, but it still wasn't looking good. Why had Sora thought this would work?

Prince Gin kept talking to Hana. The lantern light accentuated the scarred ridges of his face, and his skin really did look like dragon hide. "How did my prisoners escape from Dera Falls? Or . . ."

"Or what, Your Majesty?" A quiver found its way into Hana's voice.

"Or did you let them go on purpose?"

"I would never."

"Then why is your sister lurking behind you?"

Hana blanched. "You can see her?"

371

Prince Gin scoffed. "No, but I called your bluff, and now I know you've betrayed me."

Sora let go of her spell and stepped out onto the balcony to join them.

"It's rather foolhardy of you to come without your wolf," Prince Gin said, his tone hardening now that he'd revealed them. "I can control your mind if I want to."

"Daemon protects me through our bond," Sora said.

Where is *he?* She could really use him here right now.

"But your gemina doesn't protect your sister." Prince Gin seized Hana.

Sora panicked for a second. Then she remembered she and Hana had a plan. It hadn't involved the Dragon Prince threatening her life, but it did rely on Hana being close to him. Sora just had to keep him distracted.

"You're going to die before you kill me." Hana produced a gold pearl from the hidden pocket in her sleeve and held it up so he could see. "Because I have your soul, and I'm going to destroy it."

Prince Gin laughed. "I don't know how you got that, but you can't destroy it. My soul is protected by god magic, and I'm invincible."

"Not if I reunite the soul with your body." Hana wrenched free from his grasp and stuffed the pearl into his mouth. She held him in a choke hold and tried to cover his nose and mouth with her free hand to force him to swallow.

"Stand clear!" Sora said to Hana as she hurled two throwing stars at Prince Gin's eyes.

Thwack, thwack.

He tried to scream, but Hana kept her hand over his nose and mouth.

Even without oxygen or Sight, though, Prince Gin swiped at her. Hana held on as tightly as she could while shifting onto his back at an awkward angle for him to reach.

Hana gasped. "He's healing." Zomuri's gift of invincibility worked quickly; the skin around Prince Gin's eyes began to mend itself. The eye sockets spit out Sora's throwing stars, which fell to the balcony floor with a clatter. The whites of his eyeballs swirled like clouds, stitching themselves back into spheres. "He'll be able to see again any second!"

Sora advanced with her sword out. "This is for Mama."

She plunged the blade into Prince Gin's belly.

"Aghhh!" His shriek of pain broke through the seal Hana had on his mouth. The gold pearl flew out.

At the same time, his eyes reabsorbed the blood. Prince Gin's pupils shone black, clear, and newly refocused.

He roared in fury.

"Now I've got you." His ryuu magic snatched Hana off his back. He grabbed her by the throat and yanked Sora's sword from his belly.

Prince Gin sneered at Sora. "I'm the greatest ruler Kichona will ever know. You really thought you could defeat me by making me *swallow* the pearl?"

The wound in his stomach closed. Other than the tear in his tunic, there was no evidence he'd been harmed.

"No, I didn't," Sora said.

He looked quickly around the balcony, trying to figure out what he'd missed. But then he moved his boot. Beneath the sole was the gold pearl Hana had tried to force upon him. His ryuu particles encircled it, and he laughed derisively. "Whatever trick you thought you pulled, you didn't."

Hana tried to pry his fingers off her neck. "It's called

373

sleight of hand, and we *did* pull it off."

Sora looked pointedly at his stomach, while she touched the necklace around her throat. The pearl pendant was missing.

Prince Gin followed her gaze. "No . . ."

"Yes," Sora said. "The pearl beneath your boot—the one that was in your mouth—was a decoy. I crammed the real pearl into your belly after I sliced you open. But now that wound is healed, and your soul is inside you again."

He stared horrified at the tear in his tunic and the perfectly smooth skin beneath it.

But when he looked up again, his dragon scars pulled taut, and he said, "It doesn't matter. I still have an army stronger than any that's ever existed, and we will achieve the Evermore."

Prince Gin lifted Hana off her feet and squeezed her throat. Her face purpled.

"Stop!" Sora screamed, but if she moved any closer, he might kill her sister, and Hana would be sentenced to eternal torture in the hells.

He ignored Sora. His voice took on a lullaby softness. "Virtuoso, you are my most loyal warrior, are you not?"

Despite being choked, Hana's body relaxed in his grip. She nodded.

"Hana, don't let him brainwash you."

Prince Gin bared his teeth in a vicious smile. "Virtuoso, you are also honorable. And you know what honorable warriors do when they make the mistake of crossing their sovereigns, don't you?"

"I do," Hana said.

"Good." His ryuu particles whisked Sora's sword off the

floor and floated it into Hana's hand. "Then you will die by suicide, disemboweling yourself. Hara-kiri is the way of death for traitors."

"Hana, don't!" Sora dove toward her sister.

But Prince Gin's magic hurled Sora backward and pinned her to the wall inside the tower. Hana pointed the sword tip to her own belly, her free will a mere plaything for the Dragon Prince.

Tears streamed down Sora's face. She'd just lost Mama. She couldn't lose someone else, not now, not ever again. And especially not when she knew Hana's soul would be damned.

Sora looked at the sun setting outside and shrieked at the gods. "What are you doing up there? We're not just ants. If you ever loved Kichona, come help us now! Do you hear me? Don't let this happen!"

As if on cue, the sky burst in a blaze of blue lightning. It was blinding, and for a moment, Sora had to avert her eyes.

But when she looked back, she saw what was at its center.

A flying wolf, glowing like a beacon.

CHAPTER SIXTY-ONE

Daemon flew through the break in the clouds. The sky lit up with his arrival, and whatever insecurities he used to have, they were blasted away by his thunder and lightning. He was a demigod who could harness electricity and gravity. He had gone back to Celestae and wrangled a deal out of Vespre, who had been recalcitrant but, in the end, outnegotiated by Daemon. There was no room anymore for doubt about his identity or ability.

He glanced over his shoulder. Liga, in constellation alligator form, glided behind him.

Daemon's eyes narrowed as he flew closer to the Imperial City. He spotted Empress Aki and Broomstick leading some troops up the road, nearly obscured by the smoke of explosions. They saw Daemon and waved for help.

He and Liga swooped down.

"Boy, are we glad to see you two," Broomstick said.

"Where's Sora?" Daemon asked.

"She and Hana are supposed to be in the castle," Empress

Aki said. "Fairy, too, but she snuck in a different way."

A hurricane blasted toward them. The soldiers shouted and held up their shields to try to block it.

"Liga," Daemon shouted over the noise of the wind, "stay down here and help the empress and Broomstick."

"What will you do?" Liga asked.

Daemon pointed his nose at the highest tower. It was shadowed, but he could make out figures on the balcony. His gemina bond was taut with tension, as if trying to reel him closer, and he knew. "Sora needs me."

Liga nodded. "Gods-speed."

In the past, that expression had just been a phrase said to someone going on a mission. But now, it suddenly meant so much more to Daemon, and his sparks flashed brighter. "Gods-speed, brother."

Empress Aki ran up to Daemon. "Take me with you."

He hesitated for a moment to bring her to the crux of the fight. But then he scooped her up onto his back. The empress was in as much danger down here as she would be up in the castle. Besides, if this was truly the end of Prince Gin, she deserved to see her brother one last time. "Hold on tight," he growled, then leaped straight up into the sky.

The ryuu at both the castle and the Citadel continued their attacks. Flames shot out like fiery claws. Metal shrapnel hurled itself into the air, slicing and impaling flesh. Blood literally boiled when one of the ryuu got too close.

Screams filled the air.

Below, Broomstick detonated more bombs.

Then Liga roared as he dove into battle. His thunder shook the entire Imperial City, and chunks of bloodstone broke loose and fell from the castle.

"Are you ready to face your brother?" Daemon shouted to Empress Aki through the chaos.

"No," she said. "But I'm ready to take my kingdom back."

Urgency lanced through his gemina bond. *Sora!* There was no more time to lose.

Daemon aimed at the tower and dove.

CHAPTER SIXTY-TWO

Prince Gin stared aghast at the arrival of Daemon and Liga. Sora didn't waste the opportunity. She ripped herself free of his ryuu particles holding her to the wall and lunged back onto the balcony. Just as the tip grazed Hana's stomach, Sora grabbed the sword out of Hana's hand. It sliced through Hana's clothes and broke the skin. Blood welled, but Hana, still under the prince's control, didn't even react.

It was enough to snap Prince Gin out of his shock, though. He tightened his grip on Hana. "Not one step closer," he said to Sora.

Daemon burst upon them at full speed and plowed into the Dragon Prince. Sora, Hana, and Prince Gin flew apart like bowling pins, each hitting a different part of the tower inside. Empress Aki jumped off Daemon's back.

Hana scrambled for the sword Sora had dislodged from her. "I have to die honorably," she muttered.

"No!" Sora sent a wave of ryuu particles at the sword, knocking it out of Hana's reach.

Empress Aki grabbed Hana by the back of her tunic.

But Hana shook her off easily.

Daemon's blue glow buzzed and filled the room. Sora was already protected through their gemina bond, but now his shield enveloped Hana and Empress Aki, too.

The anger fell away from Hana's face as the Dragon Prince's spell lost control of her. She looked at her stomach and rubbed the cut. "What did I almost do?"

Prince Gin staggered away, his back against the tower wall.

Sora wanted to run to Hana and hug her, but they needed to deal with Prince Gin first. "You're outnumbered," she said.

He didn't look at her, though. Instead, he turned to his sister. "Go ahead and kill me. It's what you've wanted from the start."

Empress Aki took a step forward. "No, it isn't," she said. "I wanted Kichona at peace, and I wanted my brother with me, helping me to rule."

"You never would have shared power."

"I offered it to you when Father died; your memory is selective. I would have been happy to lead our kingdom together. It's the Cult of the Evermore and your pursuit of empire that I would never subscribe to."

Prince Gin looked around the tower, as if assessing whether he had any chance of escape. But Daemon put a quick end to that speculation by taking away gravity's hold on the prince, and the Dragon Prince floated up until he was pinned against the ceiling.

"Put me down!" he said, thrashing.

"It's over," Sora said.

"My ryuu will be here any minute."

"No, they won't," Daemon said. "There is more than one demigod like me, and they're out there now, capturing your army."

Sora wasn't sure if he was bluffing. She thought she'd seen only him and Liga. Were there really more of his brothers and sisters out there?

"Demigod . . . That's what you are?" Prince Gin's entire body slumped, his arms and legs dangling uselessly in the air.

"Yes, and my father will see to it that all the souls you damned will be redeemed."

"Vespre conducted the purification ritual?" Sora cried. Joy and relief rose tentatively in her chest. "You convinced him?"

"I struck a deal," Daemon said, suddenly refusing to look at her.

Hana let out a small gasp of understanding. "That was the secret you hid from us before you left."

The relief Sora had momentarily felt now vanished. "Daemon . . . what did you do?"

"What I had to. He tried to cast me away as soon as I showed up, but I made him listen by offering the only thing he truly wanted of me. I promised to live in Celestae—"

"No . . ." Sora stumbled. It seemed that all the air had been sucked from the tower. She and Daemon had just begun their new journey together as more than geminas, and now it was being dashed to pieces.

She whirled on Prince Gin. "This is all your fault! You claim to love your kingdom and its people, but all you've caused is misery."

"Sora." Daemon sent her a cascade of tenderness, like a bolt of rich velvet unfurling in their gemina bond. "You didn't let me finish. I compromised with Vespre. I'll spend fall and winter in Celestae, and spring and summer here with you."

"But that's only half your time . . ."

His voice went soft and quiet. "Believe me, I wish I hadn't had to promise that to him. But it was the only way. During life, souls are marked as pure, tainted, or uncertain. Your soul—and all the taigas' and other ryuu's—were tainted, destined for an eternity of torture. Vespre was able to change the mark on your souls to 'uncertain,' giving them a chance to go either way when you die.

"The bargain with my father was worth it, Sora," Daemon said. "And it won't be that bad. I'm a demigod now; I'll find a way for us to communicate even if I can't be with you. Maybe I could use our gemina bond to visit your dreams."

"Without genka?"

He laughed. "Without genka." But then his smile faded. "The deal with Vespre only stands, though, if we survive this war. My father did his part of the purification ritual, but we still have to do ours."

"Tell us what to do," Hana said, stepping up so her sister could recover.

Sora was overwhelmed. But everyone had made sacrifices, and she wouldn't let them do it alone. That was the taiga way.

She nodded at Daemon. "How do we finish the purification ritual?"

Strength like steel surged through their bond, and Sora no longer had any doubt that she and Daemon would be together through everything, even if they had to be apart. They would figure out the little details, but the big things were easy because they already knew how to be partners, and now they were more committed to each other than they'd ever been before.

"Vespre removed the shackle that was on all ryuu and taiga souls," he said. "Even so, as long as the original thief is alive, no one who used Sight will be allowed in the afterlife." Daemon turned to look at the Dragon Prince. "The originator of the curse has to die in order for the curse itself to die, too."

Sora also looked at Prince Gin. All it would take is a knife. . . .

"I truly only wanted what was best for Kichona, Aki," the Dragon Prince said, the fight in his voice gone.

"He's trying to make you pity him, Your Majesty," Sora said. "Don't fall for it."

Empress Aki looked at her brother on the ceiling, her eyes rimmed red with tears. "Despite everything, I love you, Gin. I would spare your life if you'd repent for all that you did."

"Your Majesty—" Daemon began.

But Sora sent him the feeling she'd experienced upon being reunited with Hana, a dizzying sense of glee and relief that transcended any past misdeeds. She worried about Empress Aki forgiving Prince Gin, but Sora understood it, too. There was something about family that allowed you to forgive them even the most atrocious wrongs. It was the most incomprehensible yet noble gift. Daemon stopped his protest.

Prince Gin, however, shook his head. "I could no more

repent what I've done in the name of Kichona than you could repent what you've done for the kingdom."

Empress Aki furrowed her brow. "But I've built schools, encouraged Kichona's rich traditions by paying for festivals and celebrations, and opened up our borders to bring more prosperity than our kingdom has ever seen."

"And you believe this is right and what is good for Kichona."

"Without a doubt."

"Then you understand how I feel," Prince Gin said.

Empress Aki let out a mournful sigh, and Sora, Daemon, and Hana all looked away. They knew what the conclusion was. There was no compromise that could guarantee Kichona would be safe. Prince Gin had to die.

A wave of sadness washed over Sora, not because she thought he didn't deserve the sentence, but because she knew how much it would pain the empress to give it. Sora couldn't imagine being the one to end Hana's life.

"Lower me to the ground," Prince Gin said to Daemon.

Gravity regained its hold on the Dragon Prince, and it pulled him to the floor. For good measure, Daemon applied extra gravity to prevent Prince Gin from trying to run. But it was unnecessary, because he stayed where he landed.

"Do it, Aki," Prince Gin said. "Tell one of your warriors to kill me now."

"I won't make them commit regicide," she said, her voice trembling. "I'll do it myself." The empress unsheathed a blade from her own belt.

She approached him slowly, as if hoping, with each step, that everything could be undone. Her grip around her knife tightened.

But when she was right next to her brother, she threw her arms around him, embracing him tightly instead of stabbing him.

"You used to be my best friend. What happened to you?" Her body shook with the tears she tried to keep bottled up inside.

Sora glanced at Empress Aki's knife. Prince Gin could snatch it from her. Sora was just about to do something about it when green smoke filled the balcony outside.

A bearded giant stepped out from the cloud.

CHAPTER SIXTY-THREE

Sora's mind raced as she watched Zomuri approach.

The god smirked at her. "You broke into my vault and stole from me. I thank you for providing me with such entertainment. However, I have allowed you to remain free for long enough. You must be punished for your transgressions."

"I . . ." Sora had nothing to say. She'd known this would catch up to her. How could you steal from a god and expect to get away with it?

Daemon growled and moved in front of her, blue electricity blazing, baring his teeth at the god.

Zomuri chuckled. "As if a mere demigod has a chance against me. But I'll deal with you children later. First . . ." He looked down upon Prince Gin and Empress Aki. "You summoned me and promised me the heart of a monarch."

"Yes, my lord," Prince Gin said eagerly, as if realizing he still had a chance to live. "Tsarina Austine of Thoma is waiting for you in my throne room."

"Deception!" Zomuri's spittle landed on the prince's

face. "There is no one there."

"No . . . ," the Dragon Prince said at the same time Sora heaved a sigh of relief. If the tsarina was gone, Sora hoped that meant Fairy had succeeded in saving her.

"I do not like being summoned for no reason," Zomuri said to Prince Gin. "You owe me a royal heart, and I want it now."

"Take my sister's," Prince Gin said.

"What?" Empress Aki jumped back.

"You should have killed me when you had the chance," he said.

Zomuri snatched Aki off the floor.

"Spirit, help me!" she cried.

The god's long sharp fingernail traced her chest, drawing a circle to scoop out her heart.

"You're making a mistake!" Sora screamed, and somehow, that was enough to make Zomuri pause. She glared at both the god and the Dragon Prince. "All this death and destruction is happening based on a fable. But do you even know if the Legend of the Evermore is true?"

The prince scoffed. "Of course it is. Do you doubt the greatness of the god before you?"

She looked again at Zomuri. He filled the small tower, not only with his size but also with the iron stink of blood. And then there was the matter of him holding Empress Aki captive. Sora needed to approach this carefully.

"I don't doubt his power," she said. "But I know that myths are stories spun from a combination of reality and fiction. And I also know mischief rather well. This scene reeks of it. Isn't that right, Zomuri? You never expected Prince Gin to be able to overthrow all the mainland monarchs. The

Evermore was never a prize he could achieve."

The god snorted, and the room filled with his rank breath smelling of rotten eggs. "Do you think the other gods would allow me to simply give away the equivalent of Celestae? There is no Evermore. But humans will forever want more than what they have. Even if you did have paradise on earth, you'd sell your soul for something else. But I pit you against each other, and I receive quite a show, as well as the occasional heart. Royal blood is delightful." He salivated again, eyeing Aki.

"How dare you play with our lives as if they mean nothing!" Empress Aki said, wriggling in his grasp.

Prince Gin bowed his head. "But my lord, even if the Evermore itself doesn't exist, there must be something you can grant to me and my people. I *can* prevail against the mainland monarchs, all seven of them. I promised you an empire to worship you, and I can still deliver."

"No, you can't," Sora said. "And Kichona doesn't want you at its helm."

"What are you—?"

She gave Daemon a quick nod.

Daemon unleashed a stream of blue sparks and brought Prince Gin to his knees. Sora called on the ryuu particles around her and sent them charging into the Dragon Prince's chest. They rammed straight through his breastbone and cut a hole in it.

Prince Gin's eyes bulged as he looked down in horror. "You fool."

"It had to be done," Sora said.

Then the Dragon Prince toppled. His heart flew forward. Sora lunged and caught it.

CHAPTER SIXTY-FOUR

Prince Gin's body crumpled onto the floor of the tower. Blood spilled over Sora's boots, and his heart pulsed hot and strong in her hand. Zomuri lunged toward the heart, dropping Empress Aki in the process, and she raced to safety behind Daemon and Hana.

Sora's entire body felt strangely warm. It was more than the familiar swell of ryuu magic filling her to brimming, and suddenly, the heat began to drain away, as if someone had opened the bathtub stopper. She gasped as she literally saw the emerald dust streaming out of her and into the Dragon Prince's heart in her hands.

On the other side of the room, the same thing happened to Hana, whose mouth hung open.

A rivulet of green glitter trickled in through the balcony, also drawn to the beating heart. Then more and more magic came, until the rivers became a flood.

The Dragon Prince's heart absorbed it all.

Sora gasped. "What's happening?"

Daemon circled the heart. "The last part of the purification ritual. Vespre began it, but the taint wouldn't come off your souls until the originator of the curse was dead and you were free of the stolen magic."

She stared at the throbbing heart before her. "You're saying the curse is leaving me, Hana, and all the other taigas and ryuu by returning the magic to Prince Gin's heart?"

"Yes, that is what he means," Zomuri growled. "Now give it to me!"

Sora cocked her head. Why was the god asking her for the heart rather than just taking it? Surely he could use his magic to seize it.

Maybe it actually had to be *given*, like in the Ceremony of Two Hundred Hearts or how Prince Gin had offered up Tsarina Austine's heart. Whatever the reason was, though, Sora wasn't going to lose this opportunity.

She cradled the heart to her body. An idea was forming, but it required defying Zomuri—again—and she had to brace herself before she spoke. "I—I'm not giving up the heart yet."

"What do you mean?" The god's voice echoed throughout the whole castle.

She stood tall, shoulders proud, trying to channel the confidence she'd seen in Empress Aki. "I mean, you have to agree to my terms first," Sora said.

"You impudent child! The deal has been struck. Gin owed me a royal heart, so it's supposed to be mine." The torrent of ryuu magic had lessened to barely a trickle. The heart was almost done collecting stolen magic from the taigas and ryuu, and the pulse had visibly weakened, barely thumping anymore. "Give it to me now," Zomuri said, "while the heart still beats! It loses flavor with every pulse."

Sora smiled smugly. She definitely had leverage now. "I agree that you and Prince Gin had a deal, but that doesn't involve me. Now *I* have the heart, and if you want it before it dies, you'll agree not to punish me or my friends for breaking into your vault and stealing the soul pearl. It will be as if that never happened."

"But it did!"

"I know. But you'll agree to treat it like it didn't. My friends and I are completely innocent." She pointed a dagger at the heart. She could stop the beating with a single plunge.

Zomuri's eyes narrowed, but he held out his hand. "All right, all right. You're innocent and free to go. Just give me the heart before you ruin it!"

Sora dropped the knife and tossed Prince Gin's heart into the air. Zomuri snatched it, stuffed it into his mouth, and disappeared in a puff of green smoke.

Holy heavens.

The Dragon Prince was dead. Empress Aki was the ruler of the kingdom again. And Zomuri would no longer be the patron god of Kichona.

Sora wouldn't allow herself to exhale yet, though. There was still a battle raging outside, and she didn't know if Fairy and Broomstick were alive.

But then the explosions outside came to an abrupt halt. A minute later, a cheer erupted.

Daemon rushed out to the balcony. Sora and Hana followed on his heels.

Liga flew toward them, with Fairy and Broomstick on his back. Their faces were smudged with ash and their clothes torn and bloody, but they smiled and waved. When Liga landed on the balcony, they jumped off and ran to hug Sora and Daemon.

"You did it!" Liga said. "With the Dragon Prince's spell gone, the taigas became themselves again!"

"And they're rounding up those who were loyal to the prince," Broomstick said. "Their Sight is gone, and with it, the ability to cast ryuu spells."

"Tsarina Austine is also safe, under the protection of Queen Meredith," Fairy said. "So tell us everything. What happened? How did you kill Prince Gin? How did Wolf convince the gods to carry out the purification ritual? Was that Zomuri we saw up here?"

Sora glanced over her shoulder. Empress Aki had gone to Prince Gin's body, where she cried softly. Even though he'd never repented for what he did, he was still her brother.

This ending had been less celebratory than Sora had envisioned, yet that was life—unpredictable. But she and her friends had done what was right, and time would hopefully heal their wounds.

"I think we all have a lot to tell each other," Sora said. "Let's not do it here, though. Her Majesty needs some privacy."

They went outside to the far end of the balcony. Sora took in the smoke and destruction below. But rising from them was a happy sound: the chattering of their taiga classmates and teachers, fully in control of their minds again. And they were no longer damned.

"Where to?" Daemon asked, bending down so Sora and Hana could climb onto his back. Fairy and Broomstick got onto Liga.

"To the best place I can imagine being with friends," Sora said. "On the dormitory rooftop under the open sky. With lots and lots of cake."

EPILOGUE

A week later, Sora, Daemon, and Broomstick stood backstage in the Citadel's amphitheater.

"I can't believe we're being promoted to full-fledged warriors," Sora said.

The week since the fall of the Dragon Prince had been a blur of activity. Empress Aki had buried her brother, then resumed her duties immediately, meeting with Tsarina Austine and Queen Meredith and negotiating new peace treaties and trade pacts with them. Prince Gin's loyal ryuu were imprisoned while they awaited trial.

Now, the sound of wine-barrel drums filled the amphitheater, announcing the start of the Warrior Initiation Ceremony. Fairy led the performance on the black stone stage, yelling commands, clacking her sticks in time with the other members of the troupe, pounding her drum to the rhythm that throbbed from the stage to the arced benches carved into the grassy knoll. The audience of taigas sat rapt.

Sora could see Hana and Papa in the front row. Samara Mountain beckoned Papa home, but he wasn't ready to go yet without Mama there, so for now, he stayed at the Citadel to be close to his daughters.

Liga was sitting in the front row, too. He had gotten permission to spend some time on earth to look for his mother, but he certainly wasn't going to miss his brother's big day.

The performance finished with a resounding boom as all ten drummers hammered their drums at once. The amphitheater vibrated. The audience broke out into whistles and cheers.

Fairy and the rest of the drum corps bowed. Then, as the applause died down, they cleared away the enormous drums and their stands, and Fairy jogged offstage to her place next to Broomstick. Sweat soaked the black handkerchief she'd wrapped around her head.

"Beautiful performance," Sora said.

"It was brilliant, as usual," Daemon said.

Broomstick just beamed at her proudly.

Empress Aki walked over. "Are you four ready?"

"Yes, Your Majesty," they said in a mottled sort of unison.

She climbed the steps to the black stage. The Councilmembers already waited on the far end, each holding a black wooden chest. The boxes contained the pendants that would mark Sora, Daemon, Fairy, and Broomstick as warriors: silver chains each with a round black medallion at its end, engraved with Luna's triplicate whorls.

"We are here today to honor four of our taiga apprentices," Empress Aki announced to the amphitheater. "They have fought bravely, thought shrewdly, and above all, they have done the ultimate duty—they have saved Kichona and its people."

Any remaining conversation in the audience hushed like a campfire suddenly doused by a tsunami. Despite everything Sora had been through, her nerves still jangled as she waited to be welcomed on stage.

"Spirit, Wolf, Fairy, and Broomstick, please join me," the empress said.

Sora led the way up the short flight of steps onto the stage. She and the others lay prostrate on the gleaming black floor at Empress Aki's feet. Then they rose and bowed together, deeply, to each of the Councilmembers.

"It is with great pride that we have watched you grow," Bullfrog, the most senior member of the Council, said. "From the day each of you arrived as a tenderfoot, through your classes, your exams, your missions, all the way to this day when you stand before us, ready to take your place among the ranks of the warriors. You have humbled us with your prowess. You have honored us with your dedication."

He opened the lid of one of the black chests. "Fairy, step forward, please."

Empress Aki picked up the pendant. "By my right as ruler of Kichona, I hereby declare you a taiga warrior."

Fairy bowed to an almost ninety-degree angle. The empress draped the pendant around her neck.

"I am also going to make an unorthodox request of you," Empress Aki said. "This war with the ryuu has taught me something very important. While we have much to learn from the old ways, fresh perspective is also invaluable. As such, I would like to ask if you, Fairy, would like to serve as one of my Imperial Taigas."

Fairy gasped. Sora did, too. Becoming an Imperial Taiga was only for the best of the best, and it took a decade or more to even have a chance to be one of Empress Aki's elite guards. But she was offering to let Fairy skip all that. Would she make the same offer to the rest of them? Sora could hardly believe it.

"I—I . . ." Fairy couldn't get any words out, which further underscored what a shock this was. She usually had an answer for everything.

Empress Aki smiled kindly. "You can just nod to accept."

Fairy nodded furiously, stars still in her eyes. She stood there, unmoving.

Bullfrog led her back to the line. Sora mouthed, *Good gods!* and Fairy clamped her hands over her mouth as though she was using everything she had not to squeal on stage in front of the entire Society.

"Please step forward, Broomstick," Empress Aki said as Renegade, another Councilmember, brought forth a new black chest.

Broomstick lunged forward, more like an eager little boy in a sweets shop than an enormously grown one on the brink of official warriorhood. Some of the apprentices in the audience laughed. Broomstick either didn't hear or didn't care. He bounced on his toes while he bowed to receive his pendant and accepted a position as an Imperial Taiga.

Daemon was next. He was cool and collected as he received his warrior pendant, carrying himself with the dignity of a demigod.

"Wolf," Empress Aki said, "I know you recently reunited with your celestial brethren and have obligations in Celestae in the autumn and winter. I would like to offer you a position in my Imperial Taigas during your months on earth, but I understand if you prefer not to spend your time in my service—"

"Your Majesty," Daemon interrupted, and Sora was taken aback because he'd never been this bold before. She liked this new side of him. "I would be honored to serve as an Imperial Taiga," he finished.

Empress Aki's elegant composure faltered for a moment as she pursed her lips, not quite able to contain the excitement of having a demigod in her guards. "It is *my* honor to have you."

Daemon smiled, then bowed again and returned to his place in line between Sora and Fairy.

It was almost Sora's turn. Her heartbeat fluttered in her chest, like a dream knowing it was about to be released from its cage.

"And last, but certainly not least," Empress Aki said, lifting the last pendant, "Spirit."

Sora stepped forward. Her heart tried to burst through her ribs.

"By my right as ruler of Kichona, I hereby declare you a warrior."

The empress placed the pendant softly around Sora's neck.

Luna's mark on the small of her back warmed, just a little. Sora smiled broadly, as Aki's gesture meant more than just being inducted into the warrior ranks. It also meant that Kichona and the Society still existed, that Sora had succeeded in saving what she loved.

"Now I have a question for you," Empress Aki said. "It isn't what you expect."

Sora looked blankly at the empress, then at Daemon, Fairy, and Broomstick. They all shrugged, just as clueless as Sora was.

Empress Aki faced the audience. "War has changed all of us, and what we've learned is that bravery is not measured in age or experience but in the spirit of the heart. It is a new era for Kichona and for the Society of Taigas. Which means it's a new era for the Council as well."

She turned to address Sora directly. "The Councilmembers and I agree that we want new ideas and new ways of thinking. And what we need now, more than ever, is formidable leaders. Therefore, it is my great honor to ask—will you, Spirit, be the fifth—and newest—member of the Council of the Society of Taigas?"

"What?" Sora's jaw dropped in what was probably the most inelegant induction of a Councilmember in the history of Kichona. She stood on stage, unable to fully comprehend what the empress had said. For her friends to be invited to become Imperial Taigas was already unprecedented but this . . .

"M-me?" Sora asked. "On the Council?"

Empress Aki nodded. "If you say yes."

"Yes! Yes yes yes! Thank you. I can't believe . . . I'll do you proud, I promise," she said to the empress, the four Councilmembers, and, really, to the entire Society sitting in the amphitheater.

"I know you will," Empress Aki said. "Hence, by my right as ruler of Kichona, I hereby declare you a member of the Council of the Society of Taigas."

Sora's breath caught in her throat. But her fellow Councilmembers—*fellow* Councilmembers!—began to clap. Fairy shrieked in delight, Broomstick pumped his fists and cheered, and Papa and Hana stood on their benches, whistling.

Daemon stood back, just watching Sora and smiling.

Is it real? She mouthed the words and sent the disbelief through their gemina bond, the same shock wave of emotion as the first time she saw him shift into a wolf.

He strode over, put his hands on either side of her face, and said, "Yes, Sora. All of this is real."

Then he kissed her, right there on stage, and even though the amphitheater went wild with cheering, and even though they'd have to deal with his promise to live with the gods for half of each year, for that moment, it was only Sora and Daemon in the world.

Best friends.

Geminas.

A demigod and a girl who saved a kingdom when no one else believed there was danger.

Liga flew overhead, and the air above Sora and Daemon lit up with a thousand shooting stars, the celestial project he'd been working on.

And everything was exactly as it should be.

ACKNOWLEDGMENTS

This book would not be what it is without an incredible team behind it. Special thanks to my editor, Kristin Rens, and everyone at HarperCollins, especially Caitlin Johnson, Alice Wang, Alison Donalty, Jon Howard, Sabrina Abballe, Kristopher Kam, Rosanne Romanello, Kelsey Murphy, and the EpicReads crew. Thank you also to Ronan LeFur for another beautiful cover.

It's a special thing to have an agent who not only loves your work but also gets you as a person. Thank you to Brianne Johnson at Writers House and Alexandra Levick and the whole foreign rights team for always believing in me.

A huge thank-you to the Skye Guard—the most enthusiastic fan club ever—with an extra loud shout-out to my Major General, Brittany Press, and superstar supporters Freya Austine, Adriana & Ryan Erickson, Camille Simkin, Kayla Bauck, Geoffrey Stafford, Lee-ann aka @Grumplstiltskin, Meredith aka @Gryphongirl2007, and Elsa Viviana Munoz.

Thank you to all the librarians, teachers, readers, book-stagrammers, BookTubers, bloggers, and everyone else who has picked up one of my books or told someone about them—you make it possible for me to live my dream.

I'd be very lonely without my bookish besties—Angela Mann, Elizabeth Fama, Dana Elmendorf, Karen Grunberg, Stacey Lee, Anna Shinoda, Sara Raasch, C. J. Redwine, and the wonderful Fantasy on Friday ladies.

A giant thank-you to my incredible family. Mom & Dad, thanks for buying every version of my books (even the compact disc!) and for schlepping them around the world to give to family and friends. To Ryan Stripling, for telling your brother he'd better marry me because authors are keepers and for passing along the love of literature to future generations. Thank you to Barbara Stripling for talking up my books to librarians everywhere. To Jeff Stripling, Doris Patneau, and all the other Striplings and Patneaus and this beautiful, massive extended family—thank you for reading my stories.

And last, but actually, always first—Reese and Tom, I literally don't know what I'd do without you. Every word of every book is only possible because of your love and unerring support. I love you, I love you, I love you.